Miss Georgiana Darcy of Pemberley

Sequel to *Pride and Prejudice* and companion of *The Darcys of Pemberley*

Shannon Winslow

A Heather Ridge Arts Publication

Copyright 2015 by Shannon Winslow
www.shannonwinslow.com

All Rights Reserved
No part of this book may be reproduced or distributed in any manner whatsoever without the written permission of the author.

The characters and events in this book are fictitious or used fictitiously. Any similarity to real people, living or dead, is coincidental and not intended by the author.

Cover design by Micah D. Hansen

This book is dedicated to

Sharon Peters

It has been my honor to be her daughter-in-law these many years and my pleasure to be her friend.

Soli Deo Gloria

Author's Foreword

This work is intended as a companion of sorts to my previously published novel *The Darcys of Pemberley* (sequel to *Pride and Prejudice*). That story was told primarily through Elizabeth's eyes and focused more than anything else on her relationship with her husband, Fitzwilliam Darcy, during their early married life. But there was a third Darcy represented in the title: Miss Georgiana Darcy. Her part provided the courtship story we Jane Austen fans would not be satisfied without. Georgiana's role was decidedly secondary, however, and I sometimes have worried that I shortchanged her by making it so.

I suppose, when I first wrote the book, I could have switched back and forth between the two Darcy ladies' points of view, to give Georgiana more space on the page. Many modern authors skillfully do that kind of thing. But Jane Austen never did, and her example was my model for *The Darcys of Pemberley*.

Four years and thousands of readers later, I was still thinking there might be more to Georgiana's side of the story that deserved to be told, and still wondering what I should do about it. Then I remembered a pair of novels by Julia Quinn that I read a few years ago: *The Lost Duke of Wyndham* and *Mr. Cavendish, I Presume*. It was essentially the same story in both books, just told from the widely divergent viewpoints of the two gentleman involved. And what's more, it worked beautifully! Each novel stood well on its own merit, but together they made a fuller, more complete story.

So that's what I decided to do. Rather than going back to amend the original into a longer second edition, I wrote this new novel to augment *The Darcys of Pemberley*, to tell the tale from Georgiana's perspective this time. But don't worry; there's plenty of "Darcy and Elizabeth" and even some "missing scenes" from *Pride and Prejudice*.

Read this novel before, after, or side by side with its companion. The two go hand in hand, with parallel timelines and chapter numbers that closely correspond.

This is, for the most part, new material. Although some overlap was obviously unavoidable, it is kept to a bare minimum. One book simply fills in the "off-camera" scenes of the other and the thoughts hidden from view. Although each is complete in itself, I trust that together they supply an even richer reading experience.

I thoroughly enjoyed getting to know Georgiana Darcy better – learning how events of her early life shaped her character and discovering what she was up to all the time she was out of Lizzy's sight. I hope you will too.

Prologue

It is a truth universally acknowledged – at least by the male portion of the population – that a young lady in love is invariably a mysterious and nonsensical creature. Her heart goes before her head, making her more than generally prone to mistakes of judgment, which are then frequently followed by bouts of self-recrimination and unproductive melancholy. This is the indisputable wisdom derived from countless documented cases.

Miss Georgiana Darcy of Pemberley in Derbyshire, for all her wealth and beauty, is no exception. When it comes to romance, it seems her good sense, considerable charm, celebrated accomplishments, and known sweet temper cannot prevent her tumbling headlong into one scrape or another. Unfortunately, neither can her illustrious brother, try though he might.

Still waters run deep, it is said.

Past events have forced Mr. Fitzwilliam Darcy to accept that this disquieting idea is just as true in the case of his young sister and ward as it is in his own. Once Georgiana entered the uncharted territory of adolescence, she stopped confiding in him. Now, her ways are entirely inscrutable, her thoughts unreadable. Even a year of marriage, gratifying as it has been for Mr. Darcy, has proved insufficient education to acquaint him with the intricacies of the female mind – not his wife's, and still less so his sister's. However, a *man's* mind and a *man's* motives he has no difficulty developing. And, when it comes to Georgiana's safety, that is what worries him most of all.

- 1 -

Georgiana Begins

I have fallen victim to love twice in my life, and the outcome has been only heartache. Neither man involved, for vastly dissimilar reasons, proved a wise choice. Not that one has much conscious power of decision in these matters; the heart, perversely, attaches where it will. Yet I am determined to be more circumspect in future. Every day I feel the embarrassment of my first attachment and the cruel disappointment of my second. I doubt I could bear a third failure. But, lest I fall into overly gloomy reflections at the very outset of my story, I shall begin with a different man entirely. The others will come along in due course.

It was last autumn when word arrived at Pemberley that Mr. Collins had died. And while I was sorry for it, especially for the pain it unquestionably occasioned his family, I could not feel it deeply myself. I had only met the man once, after all – that being a year earlier and very briefly at the wedding breakfast for my brother and his new wife, Elizabeth. Even she, to whom Mr. Collins was some relation, seemed not too deeply wounded when the news came by post from her family at Longbourn.

"Mr. Collins is dead!" Elizabeth had read out in surprise almost immediately upon opening the letter.

"Dead?" my brother, sitting across from her, repeated, appearing likewise incredulous. "How can that be?"

I interrupted. "Pray, who is – or I suppose I should say 'was' – this Mr. Collins of whom you speak?"

"He is a cousin of mine," Elizabeth explained, looking up, "and married to my dear friend Charlotte. You will remember him as the rector of Hunsford. It seems he choked on a mouthful of mutton! Can you believe it, Darcy? Mama says here that she had the story straight from Lady Lucas." Returning her attention to the page, she scanned further down. "Oh, poor Charlotte! It happened right in front of her, apparently, without her being able to do anything about it. Imagine!"

Upon hearing these revelations, I could not help but shudder and do just that.

"What else does your mama have to say?" asked my brother more calmly.

"Oh, she goes on to praise Mr. Collins as if he had been some kind of saint. I understand that one does not like to speak ill of the dead, but why is it that people always feel compelled to improve upon the disposition of even the most ignoble person once he is gone? Mark my words, Darcy. Before many days have elapsed, Mr. Collins's character will have been wholly remade – his faults will sink into insignificance and his virtues will soar to unprecedented heights. He will be quite unrecognizable, I daresay, described as the kindest person and the finest clergyman who ever lived."

"Now, really, Lizzy," my brother scolded mildly, but I thought I saw him stifle a laugh at the same time.

In some confusion, I asked, "And you mean that such a testimony would be completely false?"

My brother exchanged a speaking glance with his wife before answering. "You did not know the man, Georgiana, clearly. And Elizabeth is right that one does not like to speak ill of the dead. Let us just say that such a positive endorsement of Mr. Collins's character would be a very generous exaggeration of the truth."

"Very generous, indeed!" agreed Elizabeth. "Nevertheless, I do genuinely sympathize with Charlotte. I wonder how she is bearing the shock of the thing and what will become of her now. I doubt Mr. Collins has left her very comfortably provided for, and I cannot suppose Lady Catherine will allow her to stay on at the parsonage indefinitely. Her entire life will be in upheaval." Looking at her husband, she appealed, "My love, I think we must go to her and give what comfort we can."

"Of course. We shall deliver our sincere condolences to Hunsford in person and make certain Mrs. Collins knows she can call on us for anything she may need. We should begin preparations for our departure without delay. There is much to be done." He stood and extended his hand.

As Elizabeth took it and rose to his side, her eyes shone with love and gratitude.

"Shall I go as well, do you think?" I asked, rather hoping to be included in the expedition. "Although I did not really know Mr. Collins, I would be gratified to be of service to you, Elizabeth, in this time of sorrow."

Elizabeth smiled and squeezed my hand, saying, "Thank you, my dear. You are very kind. Although I much appreciate your offering, it is quite unnecessary, I assure you. I am in no danger of being overcome by grief on the occasion. And as for attending the funeral yourself, you mustn't think of it. No one will expect it of you. Women are still largely excused, and besides, as you say, you barely knew the man."

"I doubt there will be any social calls of interest on this trip," added my brother, "and we will not be long away. You had much better stay here at Pemberley and be comfortable."

"Is there anything I can get for you in town?" Elizabeth asked me. "Books? Music? Something from the draper's or milliner's perhaps?"

I went through a mental checklist. "The only thing I desire is some new music, if you would be so kind. I shall write down for you the names of the pieces I have in mind. Are you sure it will not be too much trouble?"

"Trouble? Heavens, no!" exclaimed Elizabeth. "When we treat you to new music, we treat ourselves, for we are the clear beneficiaries when you play it."

So the plan was made. Mr. and Mrs. Fitzwilliam Darcy were to travel south for Mr. Collins's services without me. Inwardly, I repined. Outwardly, I submitted to my brother's decision without protest, even though I knew that when he and Elizabeth quit Pemberley the next morning, a precious portion of the life of the place would escape out the doors with them, as if the house itself had emitted a deep sigh from which it would not soon recover. The time would pass more slowly for me until they returned, and with less variety. I would miss my brother, yes, but Elizabeth probably more. And Mrs. Reynolds, dear though she was to me, could never be expected to supply what I would thereby lose in the way of close companionship and conversation – generous luxuries I had grown accustomed to over the previous year.

Marrying Elizabeth Bennet was the best thing my brother had ever done, for himself *and* for me. In Elizabeth, we acquired a treasure, one for which I expect our family will be forever the richer.

Fitzwilliam (or William, as I more commonly call him) is happy, as is Elizabeth. No one who sees them together can doubt it or that they are still, all these months later, deeply in love. It is an union that has operated to the advantage of both. Most would undoubtedly presume the former Miss Bennet, a girl of little fortune or status, to have been the winner in the case. While it is true that her new husband's experience, resources, and place in the world brought her benefits incalculable, *he* has profited by the match as well, perhaps more so, only in less tangible ways. Elizabeth's ease and liveliness have softened his rough edges and improved his disposition. In general, he is less dogmatic in his opinions now, less rigid in manner, and consequently far less likely to cause offence where he means not to give it.

As for myself, I acquired a longed-for sister when they married – one young enough to enter into my concerns and yet enough older to help and advise. Accordingly, I found in Elizabeth something of a replacement mother as well, to fit alongside the paternal position my brother had been forced to adopt by the loss of our true father a few years before.

Together the two of them soon formed the better, brighter part of my limited world. Together they also live out before me the example of what wedded life should look like. It is not the settled, sedate variety of marriage I have so often observed. They are comfortable with each other, it is true, but there is also a spark continually smoldering between them, ready to burst into flames at any time. Although they secrete it well from others, I occasionally catch a glimpse.

It is that mutual passion I envy.

The same fires burn within me, I believe, although as yet without any return, the same capacity to give myself without reservation. There is danger in it, however. Having been led astray once before by my amorous feelings, I now endeavour (with only limited success) to keep them under strict control. Perhaps my shyness was given me as some protection; in most cases, it effectively holds me back.

I often wonder if my parents enjoyed, albeit much too briefly, the same kind of connubial felicity as William and Elizabeth. I was far too young when my mother died to have made such observations myself, but I have sometimes been able to persuade Mrs. Reynolds, who has served this family for thirty years, to share her stories with me. She speaks of her former master and mistress in tender terms that seem to imply it was a good marriage. I like to think so.

Although I am eager to carry on that heritage, I fear it may never be, that perhaps I am not destined for that sort of contentment. Early indications certainly are not promising. They tend to support the idea that loving without return may be my lot in life instead – a most distressing prospect. It is bad enough to discover one has bestowed one's affections where they were undeserved. But to bestow them on a person eminently worthy and yet unable to reciprocate is more painful still, I find. How shall I endure it? I feel myself quite unequal to the task.

Yet, apparently, endure it I must. And therefore I will.

I am a Darcy, as my brother is fond of reminding me, by which he means not only that I have an obligation to comport myself with decorum and modest restraint, even in the face of the most difficult circumstances, but also that I inherently possess the fortitude to do so. I may doubt the latter part, having on at least one prior occasion failed to uphold this high expectation. But I cannot argue with him, for I know he has felt the same kind of pain I experience, coming through it with dignity. And to a brilliant result besides! Who would have guessed from the miserable way he and Elizabeth began that a bright future lay before them? God grant me the same strength and courage to persevere... and, if it pleases Him, to find a similar reward in the end.

- 2 -

Darcy and Elizabeth

In those days, my mind very naturally tended toward romance, and all the more so for seeing my own revered brother fall under love's spell. Having risen to somewhat of an unassailable father figure in my sight, I suppose I had before that point unconsciously considered him immune to such things. But then the first chink in his armor appeared. I noticed it when he returned from visiting our Aunt de Bourgh at Rosings that year.

His mood was as dark as ever I had seen it, at least since the gloomy period when our father died. He was kind as always to me and to his servants – perhaps more so than usual – yet he punished himself without mercy. My brother was never one to shrink from the duties entailed in managing all the Pemberley estate, but now I noticed he pushed himself even harder, as if by diligent work he could drive off the unnamed demons haunting the corners of his mind. In whatever time remained, he doggedly pursued some physical diversion, such as riding or swordplay, to keep himself occupied – anything to avoid idleness. At least that is the way it seemed to me.

Although now I know that an unprosperous love was to blame, I was very far from suspecting it at the time. I only knew my brother was mightily unhappy. And it went on for months without relief.

William had told me before about some people he met while staying with Mr. Bingley at Netherfield Park, just in a casual way. But the name of Bennet was not mentioned then with any particular admiration. It was only much later, shortly before he introduced Elizabeth to me at Lambton that I began to comprehend the truth.

"I have an acquaintance staying nearby whom I wish you to meet," he told me privately that day as we sat together in the south drawing room.

I had only just arrived home to Pemberley with a party from town that same morning and, after taking some refreshment, I looked forward to spending a quiet afternoon resting from the long journey.

"It is one of the Miss Bennets from Hertfordshire, of whom I told you," he continued. "Miss Elizabeth Bennet, who is traveling with the Gardiners, her aunt and uncle. They visited here yesterday, and I promised to return the call after you arrived. We had engaged for tomorrow, but no doubt today will do as well or better. Would you mind terribly, Georgiana, spending another hour in a carriage going with me to Lambton and back?"

Although he had affected an air of nonchalance, I thought I perceived an unusual undercurrent of excitement in his voice... and in his impatience to return the call.

"Do you think it wise," I asked with some hesitation, "coming in on people before they expect? They may not thank you for it. And neither may your guests here, for deserting them nearly as soon as they arrive."

"Look about you, my dear sister. The entire company, with the possible exception of Mr. Bingley, appears intent on sleeping the afternoon away. If we were to slip out and back quietly, I daresay not one of them will know we have ever been gone."

It was true enough. Mr. Hurst was already snoring loudly, and the women, though their eyes were open, seemed barely more conscious of their surroundings. Since it was also true that my curiosity had been decidedly aroused to see the lady who had the power to command my brother's earliest possible attendance, I consented to the plan. With an eager Mr. Bingley joining us, off to the inn at Lambton we drove.

"Can you tell me something about this Miss Bennet, so that I may know what I am to expect?" I asked my brother along the way, nervous as I always was to meet someone new.

He did not answer immediately but looked off into the distance. His visage took on a softened appearance while he, according to my interpretation, pictured the lady's countenance in his mind's eye rather than the familiar pastoral scene before him. Then he seemed to remember himself and said, almost brusquely, "She is not particularly high born, but she is a gentleman's daughter and therefore a perfectly respectable person for you to have amongst your acquaintance."

"I do not doubt it. Indeed, it never occurred to me she could be otherwise. But how well do you know her?"

My brother looked to Mr. Bingley, who quickly came to his aid.

"We were very often thrown together with the Bennet family while we were staying in Hertfordshire," Bingley informed me. "Meryton is a small community, so we saw them at nearly every assembly – public and private. And then, of course, Miss Elizabeth Bennet was several days at Netherfield, nursing her sister who had become ill while visiting us there."

"Several days?" I repeated, lifting my eyebrows in question. "You must have formed some opinion of the lady in that time, Brother. Did you not?"

He gave a very unsatisfactory reply. "I suppose I did, yes."

"And what *was* that opinion?" I gently prodded when he volunteered nothing further.

"I concluded that she was a person I should not object to knowing better, and one who I hoped someday to introduce to my sister's notice. Really, Georgiana, I think that will do. You shall judge for yourself in a few minutes when you meet the lady."

"Only one question more. Is this Miss Bennet musical?"

William gave a tranquil smile. "You will find her very modest of her own claims, but I certainly found nothing wanting in her performance. In fact, I have rarely heard any thing that gave me more pleasure."

We covered the remaining mile in near silence. I fancy that my brother was thinking of Elizabeth Bennet, as, indeed, was I. And even Mr. Bingley seemed more contemplative than usual.

Mr. and Mrs. Gardiner received us when we arrived at the inn – surprised but cordial – after which my brother turned his full attention to their niece.

"Miss Bennet, may I present my sister, Miss Georgiana Darcy? Georgiana, *this* is Miss Elizabeth Bennet."

His countenance fairly glowed when he said it. If this had not been enough to give his feelings away, the alteration in his manner surely would have. I had never seen him more desirous to please, and this in a case where there could be no extraordinary advantage to doing so. The Gardiners, though highly gracious and respectable people, were not of great consequence, and neither could the Bennets be. No, I quickly confirmed it must be Elizabeth herself who was of special interest to my brother. *She* was the one to whom he wished to make himself agreeable. Therefore it was to her I must make myself agreeable as well, for his sake.

My being thus predisposed in her favor, and having every high expectation soon verified by my own observations, should have cleared away every obstacle. But alas, my shyness, made more profound by the apparent import of the occasion, once again arose to sink my every confidence and confound my speech.

I blushed and stammered. "I… I am very happy… happy to meet you, that is, Miss Bennet."

"As am I to meet you, Miss Darcy," she said, looking a little embarrassed herself and likewise anxious to please.

It was my turn to say something, and I could feel my brother, who stood at my elbow, silently urging me to do so. "I hope… I hope you have had a pleasant journey here," I finally produced.

More standard pleasantries followed, as did Mr. Bingley's entrance to facilitate the conversation for another half of an hour. I spoke very little, but before we took our leave, I was called on to join my brother in extending the invitation for Miss Bennet and her party to dine with us at Pemberley before they should quit the country.

This I did very willingly if not very fluently. I was already charmed by Miss Bennet – for myself, but more particularly for my brother. She was not his usual sort of fawning female admirer, something which I can only imagine he found refreshing. He clearly esteemed her very much indeed, and I was ready to do my best to promote his happiness, wherever it might be found.

My only concern was for how Miss Bennet and the Gardiners might be received by our other guests at Pemberley, some of whom indulged themselves in airs of superiority, and one who (if she were the least bit perceptive) had an even more personal reason to disapprove. Miss Bingley, I was certain, would demonstrate a fundamental dislike for the lady who so obviously threatened her long-suffering aspirations in regard to my brother. And so it proved to be.

I was very much gratified by the kind attention Miss Bennet and her aunt showed by waiting upon me the following day at Pemberley. They were ushered into the saloon when they arrived, where I had been sitting with Miss Bingley, Mrs. Hurst, and my companion, Mrs. Annesley. Once again, although I was eager to please, my crippling shyness prevented me from receiving my guests as graciously as my conscience told me I should have. Miss Bingley and Mrs. Hurst, being barely civil, were no help at all in filling the awkward silence that followed. Thank heaven for Mrs. Annesley, who by true cordiality proved her merit. She introduced some suitable topic of discourse, in which she was immediately joined by Mrs. Gardiner.

I am afraid I contributed very little. Elizabeth was not seated near enough for me to make myself easily heard by her. And every attempt I did make at distinguishing her by venturing a comment in her direction seemed to make the situation more uncomfortable by drawing some expression of scorn from Miss Bingley.

Relief arrived in the form of new employment for the whole party when the servants brought in a variety of refreshments for us – cold meat, cake, and a beautiful pyramid of the finest fruits. As hostess, I then had a clear duty to perform, and the others did as well. Though it seemed we were not all able to talk, we were all able and willing to eat.

While we were thus occupied, the gentlemen (including Mr. Gardiner and my brother) entered the room, whereupon I exerted myself to ask, "Had you good fishing, Mr. Gardiner?"

"We had! Thank you, Miss Darcy," he replied, giving me a friendly smile and little bow.

"It is true," agreed my brother, directing his address very particularly to Elizabeth. "Miss Bennet, your uncle's presence at the stream seems to have brought us all luck. I hope you have been getting on just as well here."

Upon this marked attention, all eyes turned to Elizabeth in a way *I* should have found very distressing. But she, after only a moment's pause to collect herself, responded with an air of apparent ease. "Very well indeed, sir. As you see," she continued, gesturing to the elegantly laid table and the airy saloon as a whole. "Miss Darcy has received us in this delightful room and provided for our every comfort. I could not be more pleased."

"Excellent," he said, returning her contented smile and unwavering gaze.

While the two of them seemed hardly aware of anything beyond themselves, I felt most acutely the passing of every second of silence. Before I could contrive anything to say, however, Miss Bingley jumped in to fill the void.

"Yes, Mr. Darcy," she said, interposing herself between them with a swish of skirts and a flutter of eyelashes. "But then your sister is always such a gracious hostess, no matter *who* comes calling. She does everything the best in the world, and I am forever boasting over her. 'Miss Darcy is by far the most accomplished young lady of my acquaintance,' I always say. I care not if my friends grow weary of hearing it."

Though far from genuinely gratified by Caroline's pretty speech, I felt compelled to make *some* response. "You flatter me, Miss Bingley, but this is much more credit than I deserve."

"No, no," she said resolutely. "I will not be talked out of my opinion on the subject. I am quite immovable, you see."

My brother, whose attention had thus been demanded against his will, glared at Miss Bingley and said, "Yes, I do see. But you have been much at Pemberley before, Miss Bingley, and have become accustomed to treating it as your own. I do not, therefore, fear for your comfort. It is for Miss Bennet and her friends, who are new amongst us, that we must endeavor to make an effort."

"It is just as you say, Mr. Darcy. And they being so far from home too!" Facing about, she continued, "Miss Bennet, you must be missing Hertfordshire dreadfully by now and anxious to return to your family."

"Not at all, Miss Bingley," Elizabeth answered with a decided glint in her eye. "I find the glories of Derbyshire quite surpass my expectations, and I should not object to remaining here a good deal longer. I certainly could not hope to be half so well entertained at home."

"Poor Miss Eliza. I see what you are feeling, and I daresay it is true." In a sneering civility, Miss Bingley asked, "Are not the regiment of militia now removed from Meryton? That must be a great loss to *your* family."

Elizabeth looked momentarily distressed, and I was overcome with confusion. Though I did not fully comprehend Miss Bingley's meaning at the time, I could not hear any reference to the militia without thinking of Mr. Wickham (for I had learnt that was now his profession) and all the alarming recollections necessarily attached to him. My brother's heightened complexion seemed to confirm that he had the same idea in mind.

Elizabeth recovered quickly, however, and answered the ill-natured attack with composure. "As to the removal of the militia, your information is correct, Miss Bingley. But I consider it no loss at all. We shall go on very quietly and very happily without them, I assure you."

I could not help but admire Elizabeth's collected behavior, and I read approbation in my brother's countenance as well. Miss Bingley, who apparently had no smart rejoinder at the ready, looked vexed and retired to another part of the room.

After the visitors shortly departed, Miss Bingley resumed her attacks on the now-absent Miss Bennet forthwith, criticizing nearly every feature of her face for want of character and beauty, and her air for an intolerable want of fashion. In this opinion she was joined only by her loyal sister, Mrs. Hurst. The rest of us observed a diplomatic silence.

Unsatisfied, and driven on by jealousy, Caroline pressed blindly ahead, piling high her disparaging words in her case against Elizabeth. "I remember, when we first knew her in Hertfordshire, how amazed we *all* were to find that she was a reputed beauty! And you yourself, Mr. Darcy, made a very droll and cutting remark to that effect, I recollect. But later she seemed to improve on you, and I believe you even thought her rather pretty at one time."

I saw my brother's eyes flash as he was finally moved to retaliate on Elizabeth's behalf.

"Yes," he replied, "but that was only when I first knew her. For it is many months since I have considered her as one of the handsomest women of my acquaintance."

So saying, he left the room and left Miss Bingley to consider what her failed strategy had cost her. She had by her relentless provocation forced my brother into declaring what could injure no one so much as herself. Whatever hopes she had cherished with regards to him were surely put to a final death that day. I can now sympathize with her to some degree, having been made familiar with the pain of that kind of disappointment. Otherwise, I am delighted – delighted that my brother chose far better than Miss Bingley for himself, and that I had been given these small glimpses into his courtship of Elizabeth.

I wish I could report that it was smooth sailing for the couple from that time on. As I now know, they had already overcome many obstacles, but there was one more challenge ahead before their happiness could be finally secured. Miss Bingley's interference was a mere trifle compared to the trouble Mr. Wickham created for them – past, present, and future to this time.

Some say it is best to leave the past behind, to never think of it except as it gives us comfort. However, I cannot agree. Even if it were possible to forget at will, it is my belief that such a practice would be unwise. One cannot deny that past events have shaped the present – the person each of us is now and our current situations. They also stand as a guide for how one must proceed into the future.

And so I remember. When circumstance or Providence brings something of the past to my mind, I take a moment to ponder if there might be a lesson in it – some encouragement or warning that has bearing on my present state. One would be foolish indeed to disregard the sagacious counsel of past experience. I think this is particularly true where Mr. Wickham is concerned.

- 3 -

The Matter of Mr. Wickham

My brother and his wife had been away for about a week when I received this missive from Elizabeth:

Dearest Georgiana,

I trust you are well and are not missing our company so very dreadfully. We have been to Hunsford to see Mr. Collins buried and to comfort his unfortunate widow in her distress. Dear Charlotte bears her loss bravely, I am proud to say, although there is still much uncertainty for her future.

We did not see anything of your cousin Anne, but Lady Catherine condescended to attend the memorial – a beneficence for which I daresay Mr. Collins would have been duly grateful. She certainly accorded him more regard than she did us, since she distinguished us with neither look nor word. This suited your brother very well; he declared he would not have tolerated it to be otherwise. Although months have passed since the breach between them, there seems as yet no sign of a softening on either side.

Following the services, we returned to town, where we enjoyed the quiet convenience of our house to ourselves. The Bingleys went to the Hursts in Grosvenor Street. Mercifully, my own family was invited to stay with the Gardiners, who were better prepared to bear with whatever noise and questionable conduct the visit may have entailed. I am pleased to spare your brother that kind of thing whenever possible. In any case, we will all reconvene soon enough in Hertfordshire, where we go tomorrow for a stay of two days. I shall be glad to see Netherfield and Longbourn again, but even more happy to retire to the north afterwards. Pemberley has thoroughly spoilt me for any other place on earth, I find.

In the meantime, we bear you greetings from all your friends – Jane and Mr. Bingley, of course, and also the Applewhites and the Heywoods, with whom we shared a dinner on Wednesday. Young Henry Heywood asked after you most particularly. He seemed quite disappointed that you had not accompanied us on this trip. And indeed, so am I. Another time, I will not part with your companionship so easily, my dear sister.

Until we meet again, then, we send our love, etc.

Elizabeth

This was good news; my family would be returning soon, following two or three days behind the letter, if my calculations were correct.

I read the prized correspondence again, this time more specifically noticing Elizabeth's allusion to the indecorous behavior to be expected of some of her family members, from which she had been glad to shield my brother on this occasion. I had enough exposure to the Bennets to know her fears were well founded. Yet, despite her very commendable scruples, it occurred to me that she should not have worried over the possibility of offending one of our family by the behavior of hers, for it had at times been the other way round. I could not acquit my own relations (or even myself) of all crimes of impropriety.

Elizabeth's missive unintentionally hinted at this too, and she herself has been a sufferer by it. Had not my own aunt – my mother's sister, Lady Catherine de Bourgh – sorely abused Elizabeth, first to her face and then in a scathing letter, for the unpardonable crime of daring to marry my brother? And then there was the matter of Mr. Wickham. While he is not strictly speaking any true relation, he is still a son of Pemberley in a way. Therefore I cannot help feeling that the Darcy family bears some responsibility for him and for the harm he has done to others. It seems we shall never succeed in shaking free of him now, since he has married one of Elizabeth's sisters. By so doing, I fear he has made himself a permanent plague upon the Bennet family as well.

~~*~~

As son of the estate's steward, George Wickham grew up at Pemberley. And although he was treated much like another of my father's children, I learnt to regard him in a very different light. He was no brother to me; he was my first love.

It is true, and this is how it happened.

I was fifteen and had been away at school in Staffordshire. Although I had first desired to go there, the place turned out not at all to my liking, its strict mistress and rustic isolation being the two chief failings in my eyes. I became convinced that I would only be content in town, where I could hope to enjoy the cultural advantages and see my friends more often. The melancholy letters I wrote to my brother on the subject soon did their work. He sought out a new situation for me, settling on an establishment in London managed by a Mrs. Younge. She had come recommended through a trusted friend, who had sometime earlier placed his own daughter in the same lady's care.

I was overjoyed at the change, and I profusely thanked my brother for his kindness in arranging it.

Mrs. Younge and her small school suited me well. She allowed her charges considerable freedom to pursue their own interests, which for me translated into more hours spent at the pianoforte and fewer with my academic studies. She also fulfilled my dearest wish by personally escorting me, at my brother's expense, to the debut of every new concert and opera. By this and by dint of other similar attentions, I soon supposed myself her favorite amongst the girls. And so it was no great wonder when she very particularly invited me to accompany her on her holiday to the seaside that summer.

Ramsgate. That is where I met Mr. Wickham again.

I saw him at once when he entered the dining parlor at our inn that first evening. He looked about himself, and then his eyes settled on my chaperone. With an expression of happy recognition, he approached our table, saying, "Why, Mrs. Younge, what a delightful surprise!"

She lifted her eyes and immediately offered him her hand. "Mr. Wickham! Well, I declare, this is a happy coincidence, running across you so unexpectedly in such an out-of-the-way corner of the kingdom. Allow me to introduce my friend. Mr. Wickham, may I present Miss Darcy from Derbyshire?"

Mr. Wickham turned and for the first time seemed to register my presence. "Pleased to meet you," he said smoothly. Then he scrutinized me more closely and continued. "Can it be? No, surely not. Mrs. Younge, your fair companion cannot possibly be Miss Georgiana Darcy of Pemberley."

"The very same, Mr. Wickham. Why? Do you know the lady?"

"I do," he answered, never taking his eyes off me. "Perhaps I had no occasion to mention it to you before, but I grew up there. Yes, I knew *that* Miss Darcy very well, but as a mere child. You have presented me the woman, and a mature beauty at that."

"Well, then, it is high time you two were reacquainted. Do sit down and join us, Mr. Wickham."

And so it began.

If I am still painfully shy, I was more so then. Indeed, I doubt if I spoke in excess of two dozen words to George Wickham that evening. But my reluctance was soon overcome with the attentiveness of his repeated visits.

Although Mr. Wickham had spent all his youth at Pemberley, he was enough older that he was away at school and then at Cambridge during my own adolescence. At first, he had occasionally still visited between terms, and then, after my father's death, he stopped coming to the house altogether. Thus, I had seen nothing of him in years. I still retained a strong impression of his kindness to me from those earlier days, however. This, added to the knowledge of my father's past partiality towards him and Mrs. Younge's obvious approbation, supported the aptness of rekindling our friendship.

As friendship it began, but it did not remain so for long. Dashing and gallant as he was, Mr. Wickham rapidly became the natural object of all my girlish ideas of romance. He was tall, mightily good looking, smartly dressed, and so well spoken. The extent of his charm and the superiority of his address were things I had never encountered before. And that such a man should be interested in me… Well, that was flattering beyond my imagination.

Therefore, winning my love on top of my already-ceded admiration presented no very difficult challenge to a skilled operator like Mr. Wickham. By the second day of our renewed acquaintance, I was utterly besotted. The gentleman gave the most positive proof of his feeling the same for me by proposing marriage less than a week later.

I was in a state of pure rapture. "Oh, Mr. Wickham, I am so happy," I began as we strolled along the beach together, moments after coming to our mutual understanding.

He interrupted. "Wait. Now we are engaged, you must call me George whenever we are alone."

I smiled shyly up at him. "If you wish it, *George*," I said, delighted to try his name on my tongue for the first time.

"That sounds very well, indeed. Now, what were you saying, my dear?"

"I meant to say that I must write to my brother of our good news at once. Think how happy this will make him – to learn of an attachment between his sister and someone he knows so well."

Wickham patted my hand, which rested on his coat sleeve, and sighed deeply. "Yes, I pray Darcy will learn to acknowledge it as good news, at least in time, but I cannot share your optimism for his immediate consent."

Detecting the first threat to my high spirits, I paused our walk and turned my face sharply upward to view Wickham's handsome countenance clearly, hoping to find there the reassurance I sought. "Surely my brother can have no reason to disapprove," I said, for I had never heard him utter anything that would have caused me to suspect a prejudice against his old childhood friend.

"No *valid* reason, Georgiana, but that is not quite the same thing, is it? *I* know you are a grown woman, able to make intelligent decisions for yourself, and yet I doubt your brother will agree with me on that score. I would wager he still thinks of you as little more than a helpless infant – someone needing to be protected and controlled."

I considered this. "There may be some truth in what you say, but William never can deny me anything for long. When he understands how happy you have made me, he is sure to give his blessing to our plans in a moment."

"Are you so certain that you are willing to bet our future on it?"

"What do you mean?"

"Just this. He is your guardian, and you know we cannot marry – not in the customary way, at least – without his consent. If you tell Darcy of our engagement and he, on some whim or another, should disapprove, he could refuse to allow us to marry or even to see each other until you come of age."

"Separated and kept waiting for years? How should we endure it?"

He shook his head. "And it may be worse than that. Before then, your brother may have married you off to someone more in keeping with his high-flown ideas – probably someone with a title who is old enough to be your father… or even your grandfather." He shrugged. "But perhaps you should like such a man as well as any other."

"No!" I protested, close to tears by this time. "How can you say such a thing? Dear Wickham, I could never love any man but you."

Wickham smiled wistfully at me and lifted my chin. "I'm afraid love has little to do with the matter in such cases, and I have seen the unhappy outcome time and again. Your brother will arrange the marriage as he sees fit, believing he is doing you a great kindness. And you? You, my angel, will have no way to oppose his plans until you reach your majority. Sadly, by then, it will almost certainly be too late for us. We will both have been disposed of against our wishes."

"This must never be!" I cried. "Is there not some other way, some way we can assure our being together now and forever?"

"It is true that you deserve a better fate, my dear. And so do I, for that matter. Perhaps…" He discontinued this thought and strode off down the beach, saying resolutely, "No, it would never do."

Hurrying after him, I demanded, "Tell me. You have an idea for how it can be managed, and I insist on knowing what it is!"

"No, my darling," he reiterated. "I could never allow you to make such a sacrifice for me."

"I can think of no sacrifice that would be too great, dear George. Now tell me what I must do. Please!"

Looking back, I can scarce believe that I, in effect, begged George Wickham for the privilege of running off with him, and that he so easily maneuvered me into thinking the elopement my own idea. For I now know it was all premeditated.

Meeting Wickham at Ramsgate was no accident. Mrs. Younge, whom I mistakenly believed my friend, had only her own interests in view when she arranged it. No doubt with the promise of a sizable reward, she promoted Mr. Wickham's visits and allowed his ardent wooing, their common goal being the clandestine marriage that would deliver my fortune into my new husband's hands.

I daily thank God that my brother turned up in time to disrupt the plan. I shudder to imagine what might have happened otherwise and where I might be now. In any event, his arrival was enough to awaken me from my foolish delusions. I perceived how wrong I was to have trusted a comparative stranger over my faithful guardian, over my own blood. And so I confessed the whole affair to William at once.

Forced to relinquish his claim, Mr. Wickham beat a hasty retreat from the fire of my brother's righteous wrath. None of that anger was allowed to touch me, however; I received only gentleness and compassion. No, I paid my penance in other ways – by the humiliating knowledge that I had been duped, by the pain of my unrequited love living on longer than it had any right to do, and by the private shame I have quietly carried ever since.

To this day I cannot satisfactorily explain my conduct in the case. I wonder how I could have been so foolishly blind. Although I was very young at the time, and although others before and since have been led astray by the same man, I still cannot conceive how I saw truth and beauty where there was only vanity and guile. The remembrance of such a lapse will, I hope, make me forever wiser, more prudent, and suitably humble. Put to proper use, a little mortification now and again can be good for the soul, I suppose.

I have never again laid eyes on George Wickham, from the day he left Ramsgate until this. Another far superior man has long since supplanted him in my affections. But, as I began by saying, it seems we shall never be entirely rid of Mr. Wickham. I sometimes still cannot help thinking he lurks just out of view, ready to step forward and remind me of my past folly or threaten some new trouble.

- 4 -

The Travelers Return

Time hung heavily on my hands as I waited for Elizabeth and my brother to return from their expedition to the south. The fact that my mind had strayed so far afield as to think of Mr. Wickham was proof that I desperately needed some useful occupation. Since Elizabeth was now firmly mistress of the estate – a role I happily surrendered to her when she arrived – I had almost no household duties. And, for once, I began to grow weary with my usual solitary diversions. I had already read three of my favorite novels over again. I had written letters to every one of my steady correspondents, and even a few of the more negligent ones. And I had reviewed, practiced, and filed (alphabetically, by composer and title) my entire library of sheet music.

At times like this, I could have wished Mrs. Annesley back again. Shortly after William and Elizabeth married, she left us to care for her ailing mother. Although I was sorry to see my dear companion go, there seemed no need to replace her with another since I had by then acquired a beloved sister. The void appeared all the larger now, though, for their both being gone. Finally, when I had been reduced to wandering the halls and galleries of the house, I decided to seek out our faithful housekeeper for some company.

"Good morning, Mrs. Reynolds," I said upon finding her in her offices.

She looked up from her work in surprise. "Oh, good morning, Miss. What brings you below stairs? If you were needing anything, you could have just rung the bell."

"I know. I was not, though, needing anything, that is. Nothing except occupation. I hoped you might supply me some task. Perhaps I could help you. What is it you have there?" I asked, peering over her shoulder at what seemed to be a very detailed chart. "It looks… intriguing."

"This? I shouldn't think so, child. It is only the linen record, after all. Not much to interest a young lady in that, now is there?"

"I hardly know," I answered with a sigh.

Mrs. Reynolds turned in her chair and gave me her full attention. "My goodness, you *are* at loose ends, aren't you, Miss Georgiana? I shouldn't wonder, rattling about in this big house all by yourself for eight or nine days together. Take heart, though. The master and mistress will be home any time now. That should cheer you up. In the meanwhile, you can help me inventory the store of preserves, if you like."

"I would be happy to, Mrs. Reynolds."

"Very good, dear. Come with me, then," she said as she bustled down the corridor ahead of me. "I do hope we made enough marmalade to see us through the winter," she added fretfully. "You know how your brother favors it most particularly…"

The job was quickly done, and I was again left to my own devices. When I retuned upstairs, however, I discovered the post had arrived, the letters neatly arranged on a silver tray, as always. I plucked the only item of interest from the pile to examine more closely. I felt a flush of excitement when I confirmed the handwriting on the direction as being Colonel Fitzwilliam's.

Colonel Fitzwilliam, I mused – friend, cousin, guardian, gentleman. Now there was a man truly worthy of occupying my thoughts and imagination. Unfortunately, I was left with those resources alone to divine the contents of his missive, since he had clearly addressed it to my brother and not to myself.

Nevertheless, seeing the letter had done me good. My lethargy fled. I felt suddenly energized. And what was more, I knew what to do about it.

Spotting the butler, I told him, "Henderson, please send word to the stables for me. I want my Ginger saddled at once."

~~*~~

An hour's hard ride, with the wind flying in my face, was the best tonic I could have imbibed. I cannot imagine why it took me so long to think of it. In any case, by the time I returned with my groom escort dutifully trailing behind me, I was thoroughly revived.

Later that afternoon, I began keeping a sharp eye to the gravel drive in hopes of receiving the earliest possible information of an approaching carriage. That was the time when the travelers could reasonably be expected to arrive, I had calculated, and I did not have long to wait.

With girlish excitement, I rushed out to meet them as they alighted from the carriage. I fairly flew into my brother's arms, embracing him and stretching to deposit a kiss on his rough cheek before turning to Elizabeth with the same enthusiasm.

"What's this?" she asked. "Tears in your eyes? Is anything the matter, my dear?"

"No, nothing," I assured her. "I am just so happy to see you both home, safe and sound. Did your journey go well?"

"As well as one could hope for under the circumstances," my brother replied. "It was hardly a pleasure scheme, though it did afford us the opportunity to visit the Bingleys and Elizabeth's family. Do you continue in good health, Georgiana?"

"Oh yes. I suffered nothing more substantial than boredom while you were away. But, now you are come back to amuse me, I feel on the verge of a full recovery."

"I think you give us too much credit for being entertaining," said Elizabeth. "I fear we will disappoint your high expectations."

"Good heavens, no!" I said, laughing. "You could not disappoint me because I require so very little. All I ask is a bit more liveliness of conversation than I can expect from dear Mrs. Reynolds. And also, I shall be glad to resume our musical collaborations, Lizzy. I have carried on alone in your absence, but it is not the same."

"Not the same perhaps, yet I daresay the quality of the performance did not suffer for want of *my* poor contribution. Your brother is the one to be pitied. For a week, he has been subjected to my playing in place of yours."

"You will allow me to be the judge of that, if you please," said he. "Georgiana may be more skilled at the pianoforte, but I have never heard a singing voice finer than yours. I must, therefore, side entirely with my sister; your individual talents display to best advantage when you perform together."

Elizabeth yielded. "Very well. I can hardly stand against you both. I did purchase the music you requested, Georgiana, along with a couple other pieces that looked interesting. Here," she said, handing a paper-wrapped package to me. "We have some practicing to do."

"Oh, thank you. How delightful!" I exclaimed, unable to resist the temptation to tear the parcel open right then and there. My eyes hungrily took in the black-and-white pattern of dots and lines dancing boldly across the foremost page. Already I could hear the notes singing in my head, and my fingers itched to give them a more substantive voice at the keyboard. While the travelers retreated to their private apartments to refresh themselves from their journey, I went straight to the music room for my first perusal of the new scores.

An hour later, when I had sated my immediate appetite with fresh sounds, I retreated to the saloon. It has always been one of my favorite rooms. The light and the air are incomparable because of the many windows, which open all the way to the floor.

My brother and his wife soon joined me there, both looking just as content as I felt at that moment. After strolling about the room and then settling next to her husband on the sofa, Elizabeth said, "Oh, Georgiana, I told you that your brother and I would provide little entertainment, but we do at least bring you some news from the Bingleys. And what excellent news it is too! Though it is a great secret, it can do no harm to tell you. Mr. Bingley and Jane are planning to move to this vicinity, to buy an estate and settle permanently near here."

This was excellent news indeed. I had always liked Mr. Bingley – for his cheerful manners, by which everybody who knew him benefited, and for his particular kindness to me over the years. That my brother had chosen him for a friend was a fair surprise, given their obvious differences in station and temperament. But I took it as a positive sign, as proof that William was not nearly so proud and conscious of class as some people liked to think. He was also enough aware of his own shortcomings to guard against his tendency toward graveness by surrounding himself with people of less serious bent. At least, that is my theory as to why their friendship endures.

As for Mrs. Bingley, I barely knew her. But my first impressions had been so encouraging that I was delighted to learn I would have the chance of furthering our acquaintance.

~~*~~

The travelers retired early, slept late the next morning, and then went straight to their work – Elizabeth addressing her correspondence and meeting with Mrs. Reynolds, and my brother shutting himself up in the library with his steward, Mr. Adams. I did not feel myself neglected or lonely, though. On the contrary, I was happy in the knowledge that things were once again as they should be – that the heart and soul of Pemberley had returned.

When I came down to dinner later, I found Lizzy hovering not far from the closed library doors.

Coming alongside her, I whispered, "Is he still in there?"

"Yes, and it's been hours," she answered with a frown furrowing her brow.

"Is there trouble?"

"Nothing out of the ordinary, as far as I know. But a week seems never to go by without one problem or another arising. I worry about the strain of it all, Georgiana. How can one man be expected to carry such a weight of responsibility? So many decisions, so many people depending on him for their protection and livelihood."

These were concerns I shared, but, wishing to allay her fears, I said, "He never complains."

Elizabeth gave me a knowing look and said sardonically, "No, he only storms and broods in silence. I find no comfort in that."

We were both quiet for a few moments, staring at the library doors and listening to the muffled hum of male voices behind them. Presently, I spoke what I had been thinking. "It would indeed be too much for an ordinary man, Elizabeth, for one who was unprepared. But you must remember that my brother was born to this position, trained up for it from an early age. I daresay he bears the responsibility entailed as well as any person could."

She smiled a little at this, took my hand, and squeezed it. "True, and we would not admire him so well as we do if he were not so exasperatingly conscientious about it, would we? Only sometimes I wish his strength were not always needing to be proved by testing."

"At least now he has you to stand with him and Mr. Adams to help."

"Yes, Mr. Adams is a very capable man, from what I have observed. As for me, I wonder what assistance I can be. I understand so little of business matters."

"Does a man generally look to his wife for help in business, Lizzy?"

A low laugh rumbled in her throat. "No. Quite right. A man looks to his wife for a very *different* kind of consideration, which I shall always do my best to supply. Now..." Shaking off her private reverie, she flashed me a winning smile. "...see how you have cheered me? Go on in to dinner, dear. Your brother and I will be along presently."

When they did come in to take their places at table, I saw no evidence of particular strain in my brother's countenance. All the same, I was glad for his acceptance of Elizabeth's suggestion that they go riding afterward. In view of how well that exercise had cleared away my melancholy the day before, I felt it must do them both good.

It was only after they had gone out that I remembered the letter from Colonel Fitzwilliam.

- 5 -

Colonel Fitzwilliam

That evening, I looked for the right opportunity to give my brother the letter I had so thoughtlessly withheld before. "I think it is from Colonel Fitzwilliam," I said, handing it over at last.

"It is indeed," he agreed upon examining the handwriting. "When did this arrive?"

"Yesterday."

He looked up at me quizzically. "Yesterday? Where has it been hiding all this time? It was not with the other letters, and it is not like Henderson to be so careless about the post."

I felt heat creeping up my neck and into my cheeks. "No, you mustn't blame Henderson. I'm afraid it is all my fault. I… I picked this one up to look at it, and then I suppose I simply forgot to put it back on the tray."

"Well, no matter. I doubt it could be anything urgent. Let us see what Fitzwilliam has to say, shall we?" He opened the letter and, as I had hoped, he read the short note aloud for me and for Elizabeth to hear.

My Dear Friend,

I find myself summoned once again by our aunt to Rosings. Since her disappointment over you, she has relied more and more upon me for company and entertainment. I know that I can be rather amusing at times, yet I can hardly imagine why she requires my presence there so often. Alas, duty calls, and, as you know, a military man cannot shirk his duty. I do at least propose myself the satisfaction of enjoying your hospitality for a few days on my way. According to my plans, I should be with you at Pemberley on Thursday next. You ought to feel an obligation to cheer and fortify me for the journey. After all, it is entirely your fault that I must now suffer these visits alone. Not that I blame you for marrying outside her ladyship's will. I would have done exactly the same in your position. You are a lucky man, Darcy. You have married the perfect wife, and, in so doing, you have cleverly exempted yourself from waiting upon our aunt.

Yours sincerely,
J. Fitzwilliam

"Poor Fitzwilliam. I do not envy him being Lady Catherine's new favorite," said Elizabeth. "At least his errand provides him a reason for visiting us; that is cause for celebration. And what a charming letter he writes. Do not you think so, my dear?"

"Yes, he pays you a fine compliment, and he accurately summarizes my happy situation. My only regret over losing Lady Catherine's society is that it has left Cousin Anne even more isolated than before. I am glad for her sake that Fitzwilliam is still prepared to go. No doubt he supplies Anne better company than I ever did."

"I really do feel sorry for Anne," I added. "It must be a severe trial having a sickly constitution. If anyone can cheer her, though, it is Fitzwilliam."

I could not attend to the rest of their conversation. All I could think of was the blissful news that Fitzwilliam was coming to Pemberley. This was not an unusual occurrence, but it was one to which I always looked forward with uncommon anticipation. And even more so now, now that I understood that I was deeply in love with the man.

Everybody loved Colonel Fitzwilliam, of course, including Lady Catherine, it seemed. Ladies and gentlemen alike found his affability, well-informed mind, and good humor engaging. He even had a gift for charming children, as he had begun with me more than a decade past. But, as I grew, I appreciated his other qualities more. He was much like my brother in essentials, I perceived. I may have been the only one to mark any resemblance between the two, however, since dissimilar outward manners would tend to overshadow like inner nature in the eye of the casual observer.

I was no casual observer, however. I was a serious student and had been for years. Now, studying Colonel Fitzwilliam in my mind's eye once again – his image invoked on this occasion by his charmingly worded letter – I still could find little fault with him. I saw a pure heart, pleasing manners, and character as sound as anyone might wish for. Even his person was everything I could desire. Oh, I know he is not generally thought handsome, but I cannot agree. Having once been taken in by a roguishly good-looking face, I hope I have learnt to see beyond such superficial attractions. Affection improved my perception by degrees until I came to truly regard Colonel Fitzwilliam as one of the handsomest gentlemen I had ever met. Alas, his one deficiency seemed to be that he did not return my love, at least not in the way I wished him to. I still had the hope that he would in time, however, and every meeting supplied a fresh opportunity for that miracle to occur.

"May I see the letter," I asked my brother. "I should like to read it through again."

"Certainly. Do as you like with it," he said, passing the single page across to me. "I have no more need of it."

"But perhaps I have, Darcy," said Elizabeth, teasingly. "It may come in handy to have documentation of the fact that you have married the 'perfect wife,' just in case you are inclined to doubt it at some… some *awkward* point in our future."

After a moment to consider, he answered. "You yourself have proved there is no need to retain the letter, Elizabeth. Having obviously committed the pertinent line to memory without delay, I feel certain you will kindly remind me of it as often as need arises – with or without the written words as evidence."

Elizabeth laughed in delight. "I will indeed, Mr. Darcy. You may depend on it!"

So engaged were husband and wife with each other that I felt quite sure they had entirely forgotten me… and the letter. So I quietly excused myself and carried off the treasured missive to my apartments for a private review.

Only when I had assured myself of plenty of light and settled comfortably into my favorite chair did I begin examining my prize again. I first shook my head in amusement at the scrawling, nearly illegible handwriting. Then, rather nonsensically, I brought the thing to my nose, hoping some trace scent of the man who had folded and sealed the paper might still be detectable. Nothing, unfortunately. No hint of the saddle soap I always associated with the colonel, who was an avid horseman, and not a whiff of the tobacco he occasionally smoked. My satisfaction must come from the content alone, I decided.

With a comprehensive second reading, I admired every clever turn of phrase, every carefully chosen word. As for the actual message conveyed, I wholeheartedly approved Fitzwilliam's admiring Elizabeth, and I fiercely envied my aunt's power to summon him according to her whim. But, most importantly, I would see him myself in a matter of days.

On the following Thursday, he came as expected and was welcomed in as one of the family. "My dear Georgiana," he said, "I think you grow taller and more beautiful each time I see you." This was his brief opening speech to me, and very gratified I was by the sentiment too, though a little embarrassed.

The pleasant conversation over dinner and afterward, to which I contributed my small share, encompassed nothing particularly remarkable. That did not signify in the least. Although I was interested to hear from Fitzwilliam that our cousin Anne's health was vastly improved of late, I would have been just as happy to hear him speak on the price of tea in China or any other topic. I drank in the sound of his voice on every word. Unrestrained listening was safe. But lest I give my feelings away, I had always to be on my guard against looking too long at him or with undue warmth. I could not bear the idea that anybody should discover my love for him until such time, if ever, as I could be secure of his for me.

My moment to shine came later when my brother and his wife retired for the night.

I would have followed suit, and I was already on the point of rising from my seat when Colonel Fitzwilliam asked, "Are you tired, Georgiana?"

"No," I claimed. "Not at all."

"Stay, then, will you?"

"If you like."

"I would very much. We can talk about whatever you wish, or perhaps you would consent to playing something more for me. Now that Elizabeth is gone, I need not fear of affronting her by admitting that I prefer your playing even to hers. In truth, I believe I prefer it to anybody's that I have ever heard. It never fails to lift my spirits."

I blushed and looked down. "Thank you, Colonel, but I do not merit such praise."

"You are too modest, Georgiana. You deserve that and more. But I have made you uncomfortable. I should have known better. Even as a child, you always did seem to have a particular horror of being singled out, whether for praise or for a bit teasing. Never could quite understand it myself, since I rather like it when all eyes are focused on me!" Here, he laughed. "Well, perhaps you will outgrow your shyness in time, or at least endeavor to put it to one side. When you are grown and take your rightful place in society – as the wife of some smart gentleman and the mistress of a great house of your own – you shall have to learn how to bear a little admiration, I daresay."

I could make no reply to this, especially since the "smart gentleman" conjured up by my mind wore the same face as the man who had imparted the suggestion.

Presently the colonel continued. "Very well. I can see I have only made things worse by carrying on in this foolish manner. I promise I will leave off at once. Will that be agreeable to you?"

I forced myself to speak at this, although a little breathlessly. "Yes, thank you, Colonel. I will play for you now, I think. Is there anything in particular you would like to hear?"

"Oh, nearly anything will do, but perhaps the Haydn you have delighted me with before. I find it so soothing – just the thing to prepare the mind and body for pleasant dreams."

"Then Haydn it shall be." I hastened to take my place behind the beautiful instrument my good brother had procured particularly for my use. After a deep breath to compose myself, I began. As the music poured out through my fingers, my embarrassment was quickly carried away. Even Colonel Fitzwilliam's presence receded a bit as I was thoroughly caught up in the character of the piece I was playing for him instead.

I know some find the act of performing at the pianoforte the most terrifying prospect of all. And yet for me it is quite the reverse. Although a large audience is a specter of considerable dread, I still had much rather play for than talk to them. Music is the language I speak most fluently, after all, and the seat behind the keys by far the most comfortable of any in the room. There I feel myself in my natural element; there I am clothed in the skin I was meant to inhabit – a protective and concealing cloak. It is then, not I, but the work of the brilliant composer on display; it is to him and to his God-given talent all compliments must be referred. I, like the pianoforte itself, am but the instrument by which the work of art is delivered. I truly could not ask for any greater privilege than that – to be useful to such a high purpose.

Glancing up at Colonel Fitzwilliam occasionally, I could see that the music was having its way with him. His countenance, which otherwise seems always on alert, had quieted into one of calm contentment.

"That was a job well done," he said languidly when I had finished, "and I thank you most sincerely for that excellent tonic. Now I think I am off to bed." He rose and helped me up from my seat behind the pianoforte, retaining my hand long enough to lightly brush it with a kiss. "Goodnight, my dear."

There was nothing inherently romantic in it. On the contrary, I understood he intended it as a gesture of mere friendship, of familial affection. And yet I could not help but, in my silliness, store it up as a kind of treasure in my heart.

~~*~~

It is difficult to say when I first fell in love with Colonel Fitzwilliam, for I have in some sense adored him as long as I can remember. He visited frequently and at length when I was a child, being my brother's closest friend as well as a great favorite with both of my parents. He must have considered Pemberley his second home for all the time he spent with us.

I have very fond memories of Colonel Fitzwilliam's attentions to me during those years (of course, we all just called him John or Jack back then). He spent more time amusing his younger cousin than one might expect, perhaps taking his cue for how to behave towards me from William. However, I particularly recall one time when he championed my interest even more strongly, willing to oppose my brother for my sake.

When I was seven or eight, Papa went so far as to procure a pony for my exclusive use, but then he could not be troubled to teach me to ride it – too busy with estate business, he said. The best I could do was to visit my pony in the stable block, carrying sweets to him, then sit in my empty saddle and pretend. William found me there one time and took pity, promising to teach me the next day if my father still could not. And he would no doubt have done so were it not for

Fitzwilliam's unexpectedly arriving first. More exciting plans were soon being made. What young man would not prefer the prospect of a rough and tumble ride over hill and dale with his comrade to the sedate pace required for a little sister just starting out?

But when Fitzwilliam learnt my brother intended to put me off, he spoke out against it.

"I won't hear of your breaking your promise, Will," he said. "Your sister's lesson must come first. Everybody should have the chance to experience the thrill of riding, and Georgiana has waited long enough. It can do us no harm to delay our plans a little for her sake."

So I got my lesson as originally promised, and Fitzwilliam became my hero.

Later, after he took a commission in the army, he was called the same by many others for distinguishing himself in battle. I do not know any of the details, but apparently one incident reported in the papers told how Colonel John Fitzwilliam risked his own life to rescue a wounded man under his command, and then went back a second time for another. "It was nothing," he always says when asked about it. "The papers tend to exaggerate these things."

His modesty only added to his other perfections in my eyes, especially when compared to the true, unmasked character of Mr. Wickham. With a little time and distance, I was able to distinguish which of the two was the superior man. And soon my girlish hero worship, my longstanding fondness for Fitzwilliam, my delight in all the facets of his amiable character, matured into love. I began to hope the feeling would one day be mutual. I began to dream of a future with him. And so I have ever since.

~~*~~

After three days with us at Pemberley, Colonel Fitzwilliam took his leave, promising to stop again on his return from Hunsford, where he planned to stay about a fortnight. In the interim, there was plenty of employment for those of us who remained behind. In addition to his usual occupations, my brother initiated some inquiries toward finding a suitable estate for the Bingleys, as he had offered to do. Elizabeth began making plans for my eighteenth birthday ball, set for January, closely consulting with me on some points and with Mrs. Reynolds on others.

Meanwhile, my thoughts were occupied with counting the days until Colonel Fitzwilliam should return. And, rather sooner than expected, he did come.

I was the only one immediately at hand to receive him when he arrived – a circumstance at first completely to my liking. But I noticed at once that he did not seem quite himself. There were dark circles beneath his eyes, and his greeting to me lacked his usual spark of humor. "Are you well, Colonel?" I asked him even before we had settled ourselves in the small sitting room at the back of the house. "Indeed, you look very ill to me, sir."

He smiled unconvincingly and tried to make a joke of it. "A fine thing! This is how you greet a man tired from travel? 'You look very ill to me, sir.' Do you know, I have half a mind to take offense."

"Oh, no. I pray you shall not. I think you understand it is out of true concern that I ask."

"I do understand it," he said more earnestly. He took my hand and squeezed it. "Dear Georgiana, you must forgive me. You are the last person I should ever suspect of cruelty or of sporting with a friend's feelings when he is down…"

I waited for him to go on, hoping for some explanation of his uncharacteristic demeanor and of his last remark.

"…You are kind to ask, but I assure you I am well. If you wish to account for my apparently haggard appearance, you must blame the devilishly deep ruts in the road or the sluggish pace of the horses. I am inclined to think they have conspired amongst themselves to make a lengthy journey even longer." Here he brightened, giving my hand another affectionate press before letting it go. "However, seeing *you*, my dear, I feel nearly revived, so you mustn't worry about me any more."

Although I was unconvinced, I appreciated his effort to allay my fears. In turn, I exerted myself more than usual to assist with the conversation over dinner. The others did their share as well, but Fitzwilliam would not be cajoled out of his low humour, which he persisted in attributing to the fatigues of travel. Then, after the meal, he disappeared into the library with my brother and sister-in-law for some sort of private conference, one to which I was not invited.

I hardly know which upset me more – that dear Colonel Fitzwilliam was suffering some kind of distress or that I was very deliberately excluded from what I could only presume was a discussion of the cause.

Whatever was taking place in the library behind closed doors, I could have no part in it. Did they think me disinterested? No, more likely I had been disqualified on the basis of my age. The colonel had said to me less than two weeks before, "When you are grown…" implying I was still a child. Now here was more evidence that I was not yet to be taken seriously. I was to be sheltered and set aside rather than being consulted on adult matters for a mature opinion. Not only did I find this personally vexing, it did not bode well for my chances with Colonel Fitzwilliam either.

- 6 -

The Bingleys

I saw nothing more of Colonel Fitzwilliam that night, and I heard in the morning that he intended to take leave directly after breakfast. I could plainly see that he was still not himself, and yet I was apparently expected to continue in total ignorance as to why. Or perhaps I was thought not perceptive enough to even have noticed the gloomy mood of my companions. In any case, no one offered me an explanation. All the help I was allowed to be was to contribute cheerful conversation over breakfast and to play once more for the colonel before he departed.

It was difficult to see him go, especially looking so glum, but there was nothing else I could do for him. My brother and Elizabeth, though presumably better informed on the subject, seemed equally at a loss as the colonel rode away.

We soon had other news to lift our spirits, however. Jane and Mr. Bingley were coming, and they would stay with us while they investigated the two available estates proposed as candidates for their new home. In another letter, Elizabeth received welcome information from her friend Charlotte Collins.

"Listen to this, Georgiana," she said, reading a portion of the letter out to me one afternoon in the saloon.

> *...As sorry as I will be to leave my home here at Hunsford parsonage, I am grateful to have been offered a very appealing substitute. Ruth has been given the use of a cottage on her brother-in-law's estate and, as we get on so well and I needed a place to stay, she has invited me to join her there. I would have agreed in any case, but when I heard that Reddclift was in Derbyshire, I could not have been more delighted. Perhaps*

we shall be neighbors again, dear Lizzy. Can you imagine my luck?...

"Who is Ruth again?" I asked.

"She was Mr. Collins's sister, also a widow, and she has been staying with Charlotte ever since the funeral. Now it seems her dead husband's brother is prepared to do her the great kindness of offering her, and by extension Charlotte, a comfortable home. How wonderful if it should turn out to be near here." Seeing her husband passing the doorway, Elizabeth called out to him. "Darcy, do step in a moment, if you please. I have a question for you. Are you by any chance acquainted with a man hereabouts named Sanditon or do you know of his estate called Reddclift?"

"Reddclift? Oh, yes, I have heard of it. It lies a few miles north of Kympton, I believe, but I am not at all acquainted with the family. You said Sanditon, though. Any relation to Ruth Sanditon?"

"Indeed. He is none other than Ruth's brother-in-law, according to this letter from Charlotte, and Reddclift Cottage is to be their new home."

"Extraordinary. I wonder if Mr. Thornton knows the man."

"That is a very good thought. As rector, I daresay he is somewhat acquainted with everybody in the parish and many beyond it. We can inquire of him on Sunday."

~~*~~

I had long looked forward to making the better acquaintance of Elizabeth's sister, who thus far struck me as the kindest and gentlest of ladies. So I was determined to make a particular effort toward that end during the Bingleys' stay at Pemberley. We all went in to dinner shortly after their arrival.

"Do sit here beside me, Mrs. Bingley," I invited her.

"Of course, Miss Darcy," she said mildly. "I would be delighted. But you must call me Jane. We are sisters, you know, after a fashion."

This sentiment pleased me very much. "I will, and you are to use my Christian name as well." After we five had seated ourselves at the near end of the long table, which had been prepared for our use, I continued. "I should like us to be good friends, especially now that we can all expect to see one another more often. How excited you must be to be searching for a new home."

"I cannot deny that part of me will be sorry to leave Netherfield, where we have been so happy. But it is time to make a change. We always hoped to be settled in a permanent home before any children came along, you see, and now we have no time to lose." She smiled demurely and dropped her gaze to where her hand rested on her belly. "Since we are to be such good friends, Georgiana, you may know what I have just confided to Elizabeth."

"You honor me, Jane. May I offer my sincere congratulations?"

"Thank you. God has been very good to us."

"It seems so, and now a new home as well. What sort of house do you hope to find?"

"Oh, I am not too particular. Mr. Bingley considers Pemberley his ideal, but we do not require anything so grand as this," she said, glancing about the expansive dining parlor. "Nor could we afford it. No, a more modest establishment will do very well. I can be happy anyplace, I believe, so long as I have my husband with me and family close at hand."

"There is sense in what you say, although it is difficult for me to imagine being really at home anywhere but Pemberley."

"You may feel quite differently some years hence, Georgiana. Who knows? Perhaps one day you will find yourself in my place, looking for a new home with your new husband."

Our attention was then captured by the animated conversation going forward between my brother and Mr. Bingley. Mr. Bingley was saying, "Now, Darcy, tell me about these two houses you have discovered for us. I have been desperately curious ever since we received your letter, and I cannot wait another minute."

"They are both good candidates," William began, "with houses on a similar scale to what you are become used to at Netherfield. But you must understand that I have never laid eyes on either of them myself. Still, what I do know I have on the best authority, so I think you can depend on the veracity of the information."

"Yes, yes," said Mr. Bingley impatiently. "I understand. Get on with it, man. I need facts."

"Very well, Charles, as you wish. The first is Northam Hall some twenty miles east of here – a brick house built about a hundred and fifty years ago, with some recent improvements. The estate is not large but it is highly productive, chiefly through the mining of slate, I am told."

"Marvelous! And the other?"

"The other property is Heatheridge in Staffordshire, about twenty-five miles to the southwest. The house is somewhat older, built of locally quarried stone, and nicely situated, from the way it was described to me. The estate itself is considerably larger and has most of its income from agriculture and timber."

"Excellent!" Bingley exclaimed. "This one sounds equally promising. It may be a challenge choosing between the two in the end. When do you suppose we could arrange to have a look at them, Darcy?"

"Whenever you say, I should think. With the distances involved, however, it would be far too much to attempt both places in one day."

Bingley turned to his wife, saying, "Jane must certainly have a day to rest from our journey before being expected to set forth again." She nodded in agreement. "And tomorrow is Sunday, in any case. Monday, then, by all means, and let us start with Northam Hall."

Accordingly, the two couples set off early Monday morning. Although there was no real reason I should have been included in the outing, I would have preferred being invited to join the party rather than not. I believe I should have found it an interesting and potentially useful exercise as well, having the chance to judge the comparative merits of the houses for myself, as if I were to be the mistress of one of them.

Jane's suggestion that I might at some point find myself in similar circumstances had set me to thinking. Perhaps she was right that I would willingly leave Pemberley behind when I married. And perhaps my husband and I would need to embark on the adventure of finding a new establishment of our own. If, like Colonel Fitzwilliam, the man were a second son who would not inherit the family estate, he would be obliged to acquire a place of his own, and I with him. Where might we light in the end? What sort of house might we be able to afford, and what other factors would most influence the choice? It was Jane and Mr. Bingley's turn to determine the answers to these questions, but it might one day be mine.

Since I was given no opportunity to evaluate the merits of Northam Hall myself, I settled for the next best thing. I solicited the reports of those who *had* seen it, when the party returned that evening.

"An altogether suitable house," declared Mr. Bingley. "Not nearly so grand as Pemberley, of course, but I declare it presents a very stately and dignified appearance. I believe even my sisters would be satisfied!"

My brother said, "More importantly, the place seems sound from a business point of view. And the steward appears to have a good head on his shoulders. I believe you could rely on him to steer the course, Charles, at least until you learned to manage things yourself."

"There is the sweetest little music room, Georgiana," said Elizabeth, "and the grounds are lovely. They flooded an old, retired slate pit – one within sight of the house – to form a lake. So instead of being a blight on the landscape, it becomes rather an embellishment."

"What did you think," I asked Jane, who had been very quiet to this point. "Did you like the place?"

"Oh, yes, and yet for me there was something indefinable left wanting. The rooms were large and nicely appointed, but still it did not feel like… like home. I suppose that is the best way to describe it. Perhaps it would in time, however. It is difficult to say."

"Well, there is no call for deciding anything just yet," said Mr. Bingley. "We have another place to see first, and we needn't buy that one either if you decide you do not like it, my dear."

A few days later, the report on Heatheridge was in as well, this one even more favorable than the first. While the estate measured up in all ordinary respects – appearance, rooms, grounds, financials – it was clearly preferred more for the intangibles .

"Oh, Georgiana, I wish you had seen the place," Jane enthused upon their return. She had come straight to me with eyes shining and taken my hands in hers.

"And you *shall* see it before long, if we have our way," added Mr. Bingley to me. "Jane and I have just been settling it between ourselves to lay claim to Heatheridge as soon as may be."

Jane went on. "It is simply delightful. I can think of no other word that suits the place so well. I knew almost from the first minute that it was to be our home. I could picture us there – our family – now and many years to come, and it was exactly right."

So the matter was decided. The Bingleys' purchase of Heatheridge went through without a hitch, and plans for their relocation commenced immediately. To avoid the strain of travel, Jane was to stay on with us whilst Mr. Bingley returned to Netherfield to make all the arrangements. The night prior to his departure was set aside to commemorate the shared anniversary of the two couples, who had wed exactly one year before. The Bingleys had two additional causes for celebration, of course – the new house and the anticipated birth of their first child.

I was included in the celebration out of politeness but, feeling very much the odd one out, I excused myself immediately after supper. As I made my way down the corridor, their festivities continued with the sounds of laughter and the clink of glassware echoing after me.

Naturally, I was pleased for them all – Jane and Mr. Bingley, my brother and Elizabeth – yet I admit to also feeling a small twinge of envy. Before I could go too far down that path, however, another thought occurred to me. If the Bingley sisters had got their way, I suppose *I* would have been the one married to Charles by now, carrying a Bingley child and celebrating the purchase of a Bingley estate!

That preposterous picture banished every tendency toward self-pity. I might envy Jane her happiness, but I did not envy Jane her husband. As fond as I was of Mr. Bingley, I had *never* thought of him in romantic terms. In fact, the idea would not even have occurred to me. It was Elizabeth who had told me, only a few months before, what Caroline and Louisa originally had in mind.

I cannot even recall how the subject came up, but when it did she said, "You know, of course, that they wanted their brother to marry you and not Jane."

I nearly gasped. "Really? No, I had not the least idea, I assure you."

"It is quite true."

"I suppose I should be flattered, then. I had no notion that they liked me so very much."

"Yes, well, you mustn't feel too obliged to them. I will not say that their regard is insincere, dear Georgiana, for even those ladies must appreciate your true merits. But, since Jane has the same sweetness of temper, I rather suspect they were won over to your side by the superiority of your other claims – rank and fortune – thinking how nicely these things would enhance the prestige of the Bingley name. And perhaps with one alliance between the two families secured…"

"…another would soon follow. I see. A sister and brother marry a brother and sister. It has happened before. All very neat and tidy."

"Oh, yes, very neat and tidy, keeping all that lovely money in the family!" Elizabeth shook her head and laughed. "Poor Miss Bingley – to be so cruelly disappointed twice in one fell swoop. For her, our double wedding was nothing short of a double disaster, at once crushing all her hopes for herself and for her brother as well."

- 7 -

Sisters and Friends

With Mr. Bingley away to supervise the move, Jane became Elizabeth's constant companion. I knew they had been the closest of sisters all their lives. And now, with these few weeks again under the same roof… Well, I could see it was a special treat for them both. I did not wish to interfere, so I was sure to make excuses for allowing them plenty of time to themselves. Practicing my music for an hour or two every day gave them that while providing me pleasant occupation as well.

I do not mean to say that my company was ever shunned by them. On the contrary, the sisters made me feel very welcome in their intimate society, and I am convinced they were entirely sincere in their desire to include me at these times. Perhaps they both missed the presence of their younger siblings and I thereby helped to fill a void for them. They certainly did for me. Elizabeth was already become the sister I never had, and in Jane I found another.

Since they were both older and had gone ahead of me in many of life's important steps, they were in the position to tell me much of interest – the sort of information my mother would undoubtedly have supplied me, had she lived. I wanted to know a woman's place in marriage. What were her duties, responsibilities, her pleasures and vexations? What was necessary to keep a husband happy and a home running smoothly? Jane and Elizabeth had experience in these matters whereas I had none.

However, between my shyness in asking straightforward questions and Jane's particular modesty in speaking on delicate topics, my progress toward discovering these secret mysteries was slow. Enlightenment came bit by bit, more by my diligently gleaning what was incidentally dropped than by a calculated harvest of information all at once.

So I accumulated knowledge over time, primarily just by keeping my ears and eyes open. But one day, when the three of us were sitting quietly together over our needlework, I did find courageous enough to ask Jane to tell me how she and Mr. Bingley fell in love.

"Oh, my," she said in answer, demurely laying a hand to the side of her face. "Can you really be interested?"

"Very much so, but perhaps you had rather not."

"No. Although I would not care to talk about it to just anybody, it *is* the kind of thing sisters share, is it not?"

Elizabeth nodded. "Exactly, and it is a story well worth telling, Jane, especially in light of the happy way it has turned out."

"As you wish, then," Jane agreed. "Yet, as for falling in love, it will be a very short story on my side, for I believe I was fairly smitten the first night I saw Mr. Bingley, at that ball in Meryton."

"It was the same for him, Jane, and you know it," Elizabeth added. Then she turned to me. "Mr. Bingley thought Jane the most beautiful, most angelic creature he had ever come across. He has told me so himself. And of course, I quite agree with him."

"Now, Lizzy, you mustn't say such things," returned Jane. "Sometimes I think you take delight in embarrassing me."

"I speak only the truth, but I will let you tell it your own way."

"Yes, please," I said to further encourage her.

"Very well, Georgiana. As I was saying, I liked Mr. Bingley at once. He was exactly my idea of what a young gentleman should be – not only handsome, but also very good, amiable, and well mannered. He sets everybody at their ease from the first moment. We danced four dances together that night, and he paid me the further compliment of introducing me to his sisters. Then, for as long as he remained at Netherfield, we saw each other frequently and spent as much time in each other's company as possible. Our familiarity naturally increased and, from his continued attentions, I began to hope – and other people began to expect – that he would soon make me an offer. Instead, he and all his party, which included your brother, went away to London. I was told he had no definite plan of ever returning to Hertfordshire.

"All seemed at an end, and although I endeavored to overcome my low spirits at the likelihood of never seeing Mr. Bingley again, I'm afraid I really was quite miserable. As it turns out, he was as well. Nevertheless, we were kept apart for months by…" Here Jane glanced at Lizzy. "Well, that hardly matters now. In any case, looking back, I see it as a time of testing. No matter how painful the separation, it served to prove the strength of our devotion. Neither of us could forget the other, you see. So, when we next met, there could no longer be any doubt of our mutual attachment. Mr. Bingley quickly came to the point, and we were married shortly thereafter. Now here we are as you see us these many months later."

I sighed. "Beautiful," I said, thoroughly captured by Jane's story and the embellishments added by my own imagination. "If I could but marry for love, as you did, and live always near Pemberley, I believe I should be truly happy."

"That sounds lovely, dear," said Elizabeth. "Do you have anyone in mind to play the role of your husband in this charming picture of connubial bliss? Your brother has taken great pains to see to it that you are introduced to suitable young men. Has one of them caught your fancy?"

"Oh, no! Well… not really," I stammered. None of the 'suitable young men' I had been introduced to interested me in the least. I had in mind a less suitable, somewhat older man instead when I continued. "That is to say, there *is* someone I admire very much, but it would be impossible."

"Do not despair, Georgiana. The most surprising things do occur," Jane encouraged. "Elizabeth and I are examples of that. You know our histories; what seemed out of the question once, ultimately came to pass."

"Yes, and in the meantime, try to keep open to other possibilities," Elizabeth advised, pressing my hand. "Your future happiness may not lie where you think."

It was sound counsel Elizabeth gave me that day, and her words often came back to my mind in the months that followed, when I began to consider that I might have been wrong to pin all my hopes on Colonel Fitzwilliam. Perhaps there was someone else, nearer at hand, who would be a better caretaker of my future happiness.

~~*~~

In early December, a communication from Charlotte Collins announced that she and Ruth Sanditon had arrived at Reddclift cottage, and that they proposed to call at Pemberley as soon as they were settled. We – Jane, Elizabeth, and I – received them a few days later.

Elizabeth, who was central to this group, led the way. She introduced me to her longstanding friend, Charlotte, whom I had met once before in passing, and her more recent acquaintance, Ruth. From these ladies we heard a description of their pleasant cottage and their good opinions of the rector, Mr. Thornton, who had already paid them a welcoming visit. The merits of Ruth's brother-in-law, Mr. Sanditon, – a widower with two very young daughters, it seems – were also canvassed at some length in their conversation. I found both these women well-spoken and obliging, and I was happy at the thought of them becoming a permanent part of our local social commonwealth.

A large number of visitors were expected at Pemberley for Christmas that year – the Bennets (Mr. and Mrs. along with daughters Kitty and Mary) and Elizabeth's Aunt and Uncle Gardiner with their four offspring – by which time Mr. Bingley would have returned from the south as well. One other person of particular interest to me had also been invited. But instead of Colonel Fitzwilliam arriving, his letter came as a poor substitute.

My brother, to whom it was addressed, read the lengthy missive first, frowned, and then passed it to his wife without comment. Elizabeth then perused it, also in silence, only sharing the pertinent information aloud after she had finished.

"How disappointing," she said. Then turning to me, she added, "Fitzwilliam will not be with us for Christmas after all. He is obliged to return to Rosings instead."

"But why?" I asked in disappointment. "He was just there so recently."

"True enough," Lizzy agreed, looking to her husband.

"Some unfinished business, I expect," he said cryptically. "Unavoidable, no doubt."

Before I could inquire as to what he meant, Elizabeth volunteered, "But there is good news as well, Georgiana. He promises to return in time for your birthday ball next month. '*I would not miss it for the world.*' Those are his very words. That is cause for celebration, is it not?"

"Yes, I suppose, if we can believe him."

"He is a man of his word," William reminded me. "And he has a very high regard for you."

"Yet he seems to be entirely at Lady Catherine's beck and call of late. I suppose we must hope she does not contrive some excuse for detaining him."

~~*~~

Despite the absence of Colonel Fitzwilliam, the halls of Pemberley soon rang with the cheerfulness of a large assembly in holiday spirit. It was a noisy but vastly congenial group, prepared to be merry and to fully partake of the seasonal delights laid out for their enjoyment. As for me, I took the most pleasure in the Gardiner children. Since I almost never had the opportunity to spend time in such youthful company, it was a real treat for me. I held the littlest ones, reading them stories, and I played games with their older siblings, all the while thinking how I should very much like to have children of my own one day. That thrilling possibility seemed a long way off, however. A nearer expectation was that I should have a niece or nephew to love before many more months had elapsed. Although Jane had taken the lead over her sister, could Elizabeth be very far behind? I hoped not.

The other interesting development over Christmas was that we finally met the enigmatic Mr. Sanditon, whom we by then understood to be somewhat of a recluse. He had been drawn out of seclusion by the ladies at the cottage just long enough to attend services in Kympton on the holy day. He might have later wished he had stayed at home, however, for, following the service, he had a fearsome ordeal to confront. Mr. Thornton introduced him to us, and then my brother in turn introduced him to all our party – the Bennets, the Bingleys, and the Gardeners.

Mr. Sanditon – a tall gentleman with a most pleasing aspect, not much beyond thirty years of age, I surmised – dutifully shook hands, bowed, or murmured appropriate greetings to every one of this multitude in turn. But it was painfully obvious how much it taxed him to do so – something I could well understand myself.

Feeling his discomfort as if it had been my own, my sympathies were at once stimulated on his behalf. Had the situation been different, I would have liked to engage him in conversation at least long enough to inquire after his children. As it was, however, I quickly concluded that the poor man deserved to escape the crowd as soon as he was able.

Still, I remember feeling intrigued by him that very first day and looking forward to the time when we might meet again under more favorable circumstances.

- 8 -

Preparations

Jane and Mr. Bingley quit Pemberley shortly after Christmas. So keenly did they anticipate installing themselves in their new home that, once their furniture and servants had arrived, nothing could detain them any longer. The Bennets remained a few days more before likewise setting off for Heatheridge. Lest we be bereft of all our company, we persuaded the Gardiners to twice forestall their departure. Ultimately, however, we were forced to give them up, and their children also.

For Elizabeth's sake, it was as well that they had all finally gone, for she was then able to turn her full attention to the upcoming ball. Preparations were well underway – the invitations sent, the menu planned, the food and wine ordered, and the musicians and extra servants hired – yet much remained to be done. And although I did not doubt her abilities for one moment, I could see Elizabeth was on edge at the daunting prospect of organizing such a major affair for the first time.

"I just want everything to be perfect for you, dearest," she told me more than once.

But I knew she was nervous for herself as well, and understandably so. For any of our society who had yet to make up their minds on the subject, this would be the deciding test of whether or not Elizabeth was a fit mistress for Pemberley. The fact that no one except my brother had the right to judge would not stop them.

There was one late addition to the guest list, and that was Mr. Sanditon. After meeting him Christmas day at church, my brother had taken it upon himself to ride over to Reddclift to pay a courtesy call, one gentleman to another. Apparently, the two got on rather well together. I gathered from what William said of the meeting that he found Mr. Sanditon much more relaxed in his own environment and more forthcoming with conversation in an intimately sized group, a phenomenon which I thoroughly understood and which I observed for myself when Mr. Sanditon returned the call a week later.

Elizabeth received him upon his arrival, sending servants to summon me and her husband to join them in the drawing room as soon as possible. I came within five minutes since I was only in the music room.

"Ah," said Elizabeth when I entered, "here she is. Mr. Sanditon, you may remember meeting Mr. Darcy's sister, Miss Georgiana Darcy."

He had risen and now offered me a neat bow, saying, "Yes, of course. How nice to see you again, Miss Darcy." When we were both seated again, he continued. "Was that you I heard playing a moment ago?"

"Yes, it was. Music is one of my chief delights, Mr. Sanditon."

"I can well believe it. Your playing is not just accomplished; there is spirit and brilliance in it as well, if I may be allowed my opinion. My late wife was not perhaps so skilled, but she also had the soul of a true musician. It is something I admire in others but cannot claim myself."

Noting the sadness in his expression when he spoke of his dead wife, I was compelled to say something encouraging. "One need not be able to play an instrument to claim the soul of a musician, Mr. Sanditon. The right appreciation of music requires a talent of its own, I think. Perhaps you have the ear for it."

"You are too kind, Miss Darcy, but it hardly takes a genius to recognize beauty in the music you play."

William entered at this moment and greeted our guest warmly. I had far less share in the conversation after that. I was content, for the most part, to be an observer. Mr. Sanditon interested me, especially as a friend to my brother. With his obvious reserve, he was so different from William's other closest male companions – Mr. Bingley and Colonel Fitzwilliam – and yet much more like himself. It struck me that this could be a very good thing. We each require at least one friend who shares our nature, and therefore more perfectly understands us. Perhaps Mr. Sanditon would turn out to be that kind of friend to my brother. At any rate, they were off to a good start.

While the two men were engaged in earnest conversation, Elizabeth slipped from the room, returning a few minutes later with what I recognized to be an invitation to the ball in her hand. She looked at me with raised eyebrows. I understood her unspoken question and quickly nodded in answer.

"Mr. Sanditon," she said at the first opening. "I know this is rather short notice, but I hope you will accept this invitation. It is for a ball here at Pemberley to celebrate Miss Darcy's eighteenth birthday."

"Yes, do come, Sanditon," William added, passing the invitation on to him.

"Thank you," Mr. Sanditon said solemnly, taking the engraved document and dropping his eyes to study it.

I thought I perceived some pain in his aspect. Or perhaps I only imagined it as I considered that attending such a populated event could hardly be a pleasant prospect for a man who generally preferred solitude. "You must feel no obligation, Mr. Sanditon," I hurried to say, hoping to ease his discomfort. "You certainly need not come if you do not like it. But you would be exceedingly welcome, I assure you."

He looked up then and smiled at me. "Just eighteen, Miss Darcy? What a remarkable age to be. The whole world is before you." He paused a moment longer in thought before adding, "I would be honored to celebrate the occasion with you and your family."

"Excellent!" said William. "Then it is all settled."

~~*~~

I was pleased Mr. Sanditon had decided to accept the invitation and flattered that he should be willing to do so when he could easily have begged off. Though I was equally uncomfortable in a crowd, I had not the luxury of declining. I never would have done so in any case. I viewed this ball as a necessary rite of passage, a course I must traverse in order to graduate into full womanhood. And, since I was desirous of being seen and treated as an adult, especially by those closest to me, I looked forward to the day it would finally be accomplished.

It was primarily the size of the event that frightened me, not any of the individual elements. I love dancing as much as other young ladies do, and I am always proud to see Pemberley at its finest, offering generous hospitality to friends and neighbors. The only other cause for discomfort in it was the knowledge that I would be looked at. The fact that the ball was given in my honor ensured that much. But then, for many, there would be the added intrigue of chancing to spy a courtship in progress. I could just imagine a pack of old ladies sitting about, months later, gossiping about my recent engagement and claiming to have been the first to discover the partiality that led to it.

"I was not surprised by it," one says. "Not in the least. For I watched her carefully in January, at her birthday ball. I could see then that she was ripe for the picking."

"Very true," says another. "But who would carry off the prize in the end? That is all I wondered at the time. Well, now we know."

"I perceived it the moment I saw them dancing together," claims a third. "Nothing much escapes *my* notice."

The first agrees and adds something more. "It was in the way she looked at him. When you are as careful an observer as I am, you are alert to the smallest detail – the expression of the eyes, a slight inclination of the head, a blush upon the cheek. These things are what I watched for in January, and my sharp attention to detail did not lead me astray."

I shuddered at the idea.

Although I certainly had no objection to being courted, provided it was by the right man, I abhorred the notion that it must take place in public, in full view of every person with a critical eye or a gossipy tongue wanting employment. Such thoughts had to be entirely banished if I was to go forward, however, and accordingly I adopted this strategy for the ball. I would give no opening for undue speculation by showing favoritism for anybody. I would dance once, and only once, with whoever asked me. I would speak politely but not overly warmly to all our guests alike. This would afford me some protection, if I could only carry it off.

My resolve was still holding firm when the night of the ball at last arrived. So it was with tolerable equanimity that I began my toilette. Instead of my one maid to help me, I had two to carry out the necessary tasks for the important event. Beginning hours beforehand, they bathed me and dusted my skin with scented powder. They expertly styled my hair, ornamenting it with individual pearls as a compliment to the strand I would be wearing wrapped round my neck – my mother's pearls. Lastly, they helped me on with my gown – a pale blue silk creation made especially for the occasion.

When I examined the resulting image in the large mirror of my dressing room, I was well satisfied. One thing was certain; I did not look like a child. Although the neckline of my gown was modest enough for my comfort, the figure and face were unmistakably those of a woman. Surely, even Colonel Fitzwilliam must see it. The first test would be my brother, however.

The knock at my door told me it was time to go down. My heart gave a great lurch of excitement. I took one final look in the glass and two deep breaths to calm myself before stepping out into the corridor to meet William and Elizabeth.

Their eyes were the first to examine me, and they apparently approved of what they saw.

"You look simply beautiful," said Elizabeth at once. "Your hair, your gown! I am so glad we decided on the blue. Everything is precisely as it should be. Your guests will be delighted with you, my dear. You have left them no other choice."

I thanked her and gave her a light embrace, so as not to spoil either of our gowns. Then I looked to my brother for his reaction, which was slower in coming.

"Perfection," he said at last in a faltering voice.

I could not have asked for anything more gratifying than that one word and his clear expression of approbation. Yet, when the other two turned to start downstairs, I froze in a kind of renewed panic at the thought of the many people who were already beginning to assemble below on my account. It took several minutes and many assurances from my kind brother and sister to rebuild my confidence enough to proceed.

Friendly faces met us upon our descending the stairs – Jane, Mr. Bingley, and Kitty Bennet, newly arrived from Heatheridge. We were greeting them when I noticed another person with them, a robust young lady whom I had never met before. A small suspicion of who it might be entered my brain. When I turned to Elizabeth for assistance, my inkling was confirmed by the look of discomfort on her face.

After an awkward pause, during which we all seemed to be staring at one another askance, Elizabeth addressed the duty of introductions. "Forgive me," she said. "Georgiana, do allow me to acquaint you with my youngest sister. This is Lydia. Lydia, this is Miss Darcy."

I understood at once that Elizabeth, being familiar with my history, was attempting to soften any blow to me by omitting the newcomer's last name. I knew what it was, of course, but it was some relief to avoid hearing it spoken aloud. I was not spared for long, however.

"So nice to meet you," I said. And though she had not been invited, I added, "I am so pleased you could come… uh…"

"It's Mrs. Wickham," Lydia contributed, looking quite amused. "My proper name is Mrs. Wickham. What a clumsy job Lizzy has made of our introduction! I believe the surprise of seeing me has caused her to forget her manners. I hope *you* do not mind my coming, though, Miss Darcy. I do so love a ball."

"Not at all," I answered as graciously as I could. "You are very welcome."

Although Elizabeth directed a look of silent apology at me, I really was not much shaken at meeting Mrs. Wickham. Seeing her husband would have been a different thing entirely, but I felt no resentment for this lady having married him, only pity. In fact, we shared something in common, having both been led astray by that man. The difference was that I now understood his true character, whereas I doubted his wife did, considering the unmistakable note of pride I had heard in her voice when she called herself *Mrs. Wickham*.

As for Mrs. Wickham herself, I was not given much immediate reason to think well of her other than my desire to do justice to any person Elizabeth should care for. Lydia's bursting in upon a private ball uninvited had to be considered discourteous if not downright boorish. And then I was obliged to hear her sportive comments to her sisters during the few minutes the men left us alone. When she made a tactless remark about Jane's delicate condition, I could hardly keep my countenance. But perhaps I am overly severe upon her; perhaps this type of behavior is not uncommon in a large family of sisters, three of whom are married women.

In any case, I was embarrassed to have been made an unwilling party to the conversation and glad when it was over.

The sound of horses and carriage wheels grating on the sweep called us – William, Elizabeth, and myself – to our stations in order to welcome the stream of guests who began flowing in, all elegantly dressed and coiffed. Soon the whole house reverberated with an agreeable hum of chatter, music, and laughter as everybody waited for the official commencement of the ball. Lydia Wickham was forgotten. If she had not been beforehand, then certainly the sight of Colonel Fitzwilliam coming through the door would have made it so.

- 9 -

The Ball

According to my resolution of showing no partiality to one man or another, I should by rights have betrayed no special interest in Colonel Fitzwilliam's arrival. But this was impossible for two reasons. The first was that he looked particularly handsome to me that night, arrayed in his evening clothes and returned to his usual, genial spirits. The second point of interest was that he had a pretty young woman on his arm.

I did not initially count *this* detail an advantage. Then, upon closer examination of the cheerfully smiling lady, I detected something familiar in her countenance. She was in fact my cousin, Miss Anne de Bourgh, I realized of a sudden. I had not recognized her immediately because of her dramatically altered appearance. Anne had always been a pale, thin creature due to her sickly constitution. Now she was entirely transformed. She was changed into the picture of well being, complete with glowing complexion and healthy figure. I could not have been happier for her.

Elizabeth, who seemed the first to recover from the surprise, said what we all were thinking. "Why, Anne, how wonderfully well you look, and how splendid, Colonel, that you persuaded her to accompany you. We are so pleased to have you both with us tonight."

My brother and I echoed these sentiments.

"Thank you for receiving me," said Anne. "Fitzwilliam said you would not mind."

"Mind?" said Elizabeth. "Why, we are delighted!"

The colonel added, "As you see, Anne is now strong enough to undertake such a journey, which is another cause for celebration, is it not?"

My brother agreed, although I thought I noticed something peculiar in his eye as he did so. Then he turned to Anne with a more open expression, saying, "Fitzwilliam told us you were much improved, but I must say this is even more than I had hoped for. Anne, you look quite recovered. I understand the credit for your newfound health belongs in part to a clever young physician."

Anne dropped her eyes and her voice. "I daresay I owe my recovery almost *entirely* to him. Dr. Essex is an uncommonly kind and learned man. I shall be forever in his debt."

"Then *I* am grateful to Dr. Essex as well," said I, "since it is apparently due to his care that we have the pleasure of your company now." I would have liked to continue this conversation with my cousins, but there were other guests requiring our attention. So, after this exchange, we were obliged to allow the pair to move on to the ballroom.

Seeing Anne – at Pemberley and looking so well – was a genuine delight. However, truth be told, this was not my primary cause for celebration at the time. Fitzwilliam had come; that was what mattered most. I had been so afraid he would be detained by Lady Catherine or otherwise prevented. But he had come, and now I would dance with him. He would see that I was no longer a child; I was a woman fully grown, who was to be taken into some account.

I was still thinking of these things when the Heywoods entered – my friend Andrea, her brother Henry, and their parents. As I have heard the story told, my father first become acquainted with the senior Mr. Heywood by doing business with his bank in London. But the association had long since developed into something far more of a social character, involving the families as well. We often saw them when we were in town, and the Heywoods had visited Pemberley at least twice in my lifetime. Whenever we were together, I got on very well with Andrea, who was of an age with me. Henry, who was four years older, was just as amiable, and I liked their parents too. So I was naturally very pleased to see them arrive to my ball.

While the two elder Heywoods stopped to speak with William and Elizabeth, the two younger came directly to me.

"Oh, dear Georgiana, how excited I am to be here!" said Andrea at once. "And how pretty you look! That gown, your jewels, your hair… Does not she look particularly well tonight, Henry?"

"I would not disagree with you, dear sister, but then Miss Darcy always looks very fine to me."

"You are too kind, sir." Then turning back to Andrea, I continued. "I am delighted you and your family could come. I hope you will enjoy the dancing."

"Oh, yes! As for myself, there can be no doubt of it. My brother has very different ideas, however."

"Is that so, Mr. Heywood?" I inquired.

"Not so different, Miss Darcy. My sister is always happy to dance, and it matters very little to her with whom. My enjoyment is more dependant upon my partner. I hope *you* will do me the honor of reserving a dance for me, Miss Darcy. May I ask for the last before the supper break?"

"As you wish, Mr. Heywood."

"Thank you." He bowed and they moved on.

It was soon time for the dance itself to begin. True to my plan, I accepted the invitation to dance once with every gentleman who asked me, but never a second time. I would have been sorely tempted to make an exception for Colonel Fitzwilliam had I been given the chance, but I was spared this test to my resolve.

Mr. Frank Osborn was one of my first and most pleasant partners. Not only was he an accomplished dancer, he knew how to keep a comfortable rate of conversation as well, talking to me just enough to be attentive without distracting from the enjoyment of the dance itself.

Mr. Sanditon, who succeeded him, spoke hardly a syllable. Afterward, he bowed, thanked me for the dance, and offered this in explanation.

"You must forgive my ill-mannered silence, Miss Darcy. I fear I am not equal to conversing and dancing both at the same time – out of practice at both, you see."

"Not at all, sir. You have no need to apologize, I assure you. Your dancing was very elegantly done. As to lack of conversation… Well, I would never presume to judge anybody for that."

My encouragement may have failed to sufficiently bolster his confidence, however, for I only observed him dancing once more that evening.

Colonel Fitzwilliam suffered no such reticence, I noticed. He looked very merry indeed and was never without a partner. He danced with Anne, of course, and Elizabeth, and even Miss Bingley. I could not help being a little jealous of each of them and all the others in turn. But I knew my chance would come; Fitzwilliam had bespoken the first dance with me after supper. Although I had wondered if he might join me earlier, during the intermission and not only afterward, he instead seemed very much occupied with amusing a group of ladies across the way.

Meanwhile, I had Mr. Henry Heywood to entertain me – a perfectly agreeable arrangement, since he was someone with whom I was already comfortably acquainted. He was a nice looking young man as well, and he had moved gracefully through the figures of our dance. Afterward, as traditionally belongs to one's last partner before the break, he claimed his place beside me at the supper table. And now he was behaving very solicitously.

"When do you come to London next, Miss Darcy?" he inquired of me.

"I really cannot say, Mr. Heywood, however, I imagine we will be in town for at least some portion of the social season."

"But that is still a long way off. I had hoped to see you again much sooner." Then he quickly added, "What I meant to say is that my family is very fond of you, and it would be a shame for you to miss all the diversions available in town. It must be unbearably tedious to be fixed here in the country for months at a time."

"If you knew me better, Mr. Heywood, you would appreciate that I generally prefer the quiet of the country. It is not dull to me, not so long as I have friends about me and my music to fill my time."

"Yes, yes, your music!" he said enthusiastically, as if delighted to have been reminded of the subject. "May I have the privilege of hearing you play, perhaps tomorrow before we leave, Miss Darcy? Nothing would give me more enjoyment, I assure you."

Just then, some sort of noisy disturbance erupted in the vicinity of the entry hall. Like everybody else, I turned to find out what it was. I could see nothing useful, however.

Mr. Heywood instantly rose to his feet, saying, "Be not alarmed, Miss Darcy. I will protect you, should the need arise."

I thought is was rather sweet. He must have imagined we were about to be overrun by a great horde of ruffians or another such calamity. But it turned out to be nothing so monumental, just a single hooligan instead, a man without an invitation, apparently drunk on wine and trying to force his way into the party. He never made it so far as the ballroom, however, and the unpleasantness was over in a matter of a few minutes. Then my brother gave a brief announcement of explanation to set the assembly at its ease again. It was only a minor interruption in what was otherwise a delightful party.

As the evening progressed, I found I was for the most part able to let go of my self-consciousness and of my apprehension of being placed under a magnifying glass for inspection. Everybody had been so kind to me. I began to think that if there were any sort of conspiracy afoot, it was not to ferret out my secret romance, but rather to be sure I felt secure and appreciated, and that I was having an especially fine time. Fitzwilliam played a crucial part in the scheme when he came at the conclusion of the break to collect me for our dance.

"Miss Georgiana," he said with an elegant bow. "I have been waiting all evening, and now at last it is my turn. Will you do me the honor?" He extended his gloved hand for mine and helped me rise. As we moved to our places on the floor, he continued. "Now that I finally have you to myself, my dear, I must tell you what I thought the moment I first saw you tonight – that you seem to have matured into a beautiful young woman since last we met. I never realized before… That is to say, I had not noticed… Well, never mind. It is time to begin."

I was glad it was one of the less hectic dances with less complex figures, for it afforded us better opportunity to look at and talk to one another. We seemed to do more of the former than the latter in this case, which was a little surprising. Although I am naturally reserved, Colonel Fitzwilliam is never at a loss for words. Still, it exactly suited me that we should refrain from inconsequential chatter, made simply for the sake of filling the air between us. Such artificial exertions were unnecessary for two people who had known each other as long as the colonel and I had. Besides, Fitzwilliam had already said what I wanted most to hear – that he now saw me as a grown woman, and a beauty at that. This was more than enough to carry me through.

We were not completely silent, however. Early on Fitzwilliam commented, "An excellent orchestra. Hired from London, are they?"

"Yes, William said nothing but the best would do, especially considering my fondness for fine music."

"Quite right. Worth every penny, but then your brother has never been miserly, especially where you are concerned."

Later, after we had passed by Elizabeth, who was dancing with Mr. Sanditon, my partner made a generous compliment to her talent as a hostess. This sentiment pleased me as well as the first. Together they showed an appreciation for precisely the same things I venerated most – music and my dear family. Then, toward the end of our time together, when we were left idle for a few moments at the top of the set, Fitzwilliam initiated a lengthier conversation.

"I have enjoyed our dance together immensely, Georgiana," he said.

"I too, Colonel, very much indeed."

"It is a pleasure I could well wish to have repeated, even tonight, but I must not be greedy; I must, unfortunately, be prepared to soon give you up to your many other admirers here present. You are sure to never be in want of a partner, which is exactly as it should be, especially on your birthday."

"Unless I am very much mistaken, you have been consistently occupied as well, sir. Who will be your next partner?"

"Ah, yes. I am to dance with our cousin Anne again. Thank you for welcoming her so warmly, by the way. I cannot tell you how much it means to her."

"It was no sacrifice. I spoke nothing but the truth when I said it is a pleasure to see her here. And looking so well, too! I cannot get over how much improved she is. I hardly recognized her."

"Very understandable. I have seen the transformation by degrees, but for you it has come all at once."

"Now, at last, she can begin living and taking her proper place in society. I suppose Lady Catherine has renewed hopes for her daughter as well – all those things Anne has been kept from by her indifferent state of health. Perhaps she will finally be presented at court."

"I know of no such particular plan, but you are quite correct about her ladyship's ambitions in general. With the primary obstacle removed, she has wasted no time in seeing that her wishes as regards to Anne's future are in a fair way to being accomplished."

He had a curious look on his face, which made me inquire what he had meant by so cryptic a remark. But then we were obliged to rejoin the dance before Colonel Fitzwilliam could answer properly.

"It is nothing I can speak of here," he said as we started down the dance. "All will be explained presently, however."

Much too soon, our time together was over. I was obliged to move on to other partners, none of whom could hold a candle to Colonel Fitzwilliam. His every look, action, and word filled my mind for the rest of the evening and then my dreams when I finally retired to my bed. The ball had been an unqualified success in every respect. I even dared to hope that, when I remembered the occasion in years to come, I would be able to mark it as the very moment of Fitzwilliam's change towards me, that his eyes had been opened that night, and that our one dance together was the beginning of a lifelong partnership to come. In this, however, I was sadly mistaken.

- 10 -

Aftermath

I slept well that night and entered the new day belatedly but in high spirits, still awash in the pleasant afterglow of all that had occurred at the ball, especially of Colonel Fitzwilliam's handsome attentions to me. I knew I would see him again soon, for he had stayed the night at Pemberley, as did Anne de Bourgh, the Heywood family, and all the Bingley party.

The Bingleys departed for Heatheridge shortly after our late breakfast. But their numbers were soon replaced by the Applewhites and Williamses who drove back out from Lambton where they had lodged.

I spent a good portion of the day with Andrea Heywood. She singled me out that afternoon with the request that I would take a turn with her. It was clearly too cold for outdoor exercise, so I suggested the long picture gallery instead.

"That will do perfectly well," she said. "I have not been to that part of the house in years, and I should very much like to see it again."

Accordingly, we excused ourselves from the others and made our way upstairs. Since we did not usually correspond between our meetings, we had all manner of things to catch up on as we walked. Then Andrea abruptly turned her attention to the pictures themselves.

"Who is that dour fellow with the great white beard?" she asked, pausing to inspect one of the dozens of portraits that lined the wall opposite the windows.

"That is my great-grandfather Horatio Darcy. He died long before I was born. And beside him is his son Reginald Darcy, my grandfather. I did not know him either."

"And this next one is your father, I think."

"It is."

"Yes, it looks very like how I remember him." We moved another pace or two forward, and she stopped again. "And here is your handsome brother. My goodness! I once fancied myself violently in love with him, you know. Did I ever tell you?"

"In love with William? No, you never did."

"It seems silly now – his being so much older and all – but that did not signify to me at the time. I daresay you will think I had been very foolish even to imagine it."

"I would think no such thing! One is everyday hearing of far greater age disparities in marriage."

"But can such marriages really be happy? I cannot countenance the idea for myself, and surely you would never consider such an union either. Now, if you were to fall in love with *my* brother, that would be different. He is fond of you, you know. And it would be a far more eligible thing, for he is only four years older, not eleven or twelve."

I felt my face growing hot. I was uncomfortable both that she should think such a match as I secretly aspired to an unhappy thing and at her suggesting her brother to me instead. "You must not tease me so, Andrea. Your brother is my friend; that is all. I have never considered him in any other light, and I feel quite certain that I never shall. If necessary, I would be much obliged if you would tell him so."

"Oh, dear Georgiana, it is just that I cannot help but imagine what fun we should have if we were to become sisters! Now, say you will not be vexed with me for that."

"I shall not be vexed as long as you promise never to suggest such an idea to me again, Andrea."

"Very well, if it must be so. I only wished to get you thinking."

So she said no more on that subject. But she had already accomplished her goal by making me think of something I never did before. I now had to consider that Henry Heywood might have discovered some romantic feelings for me, feelings I could never return. I hoped not; I hoped the notion of a match between us was all in Andrea's head.

With a dozen extra people in the house, I had little opportunity for conversation with Colonel Fitzwilliam that afternoon and none of it in private. Still, I did not despair of making some further little progress in that direction – perhaps the next day, after the others had all gone away, I thought. Maybe then I could resume the conversation we had left unfinished in our dance. Or he might take the initiative himself, seeking me out by his own desire. Nothing could be known until then.

With the tenor of the day more informal and our numbers greatly diminished from the night before, I did not object when I was later asked to play for the company. I knew Fitzwilliam always liked to hear me, and Henry Heywood had secured my promise to do so in any case. With the whole party's moving to the music room, and after his sister had finished her excellent performance, he came to escort me to the instrument. There he stayed under the excuse of turning my pages, and then, after leading a polite round of applause, returned me safely to my seat. Joining me there, he said, "That was capital, Miss Darcy, simply capital! I hardly know when I have heard anything better. It was not only skillfully done but with such wonderful expression. Andrea's playing was nothing to yours."

"I am gratified that you enjoyed it, Mr. Heywood" I said in response. "But there is no need to draw comparisons to your sister's performance."

"Quite right, for there truly is no comparison at all between the two."

I could not reply to this. I would have been uncomfortable with such extravagant praise in any case, but now I had the added worry for what Andrea had told me earlier. Could Henry's enthusiasm really be a symptom of love? My suspicions were further aroused by his manner of taking leave of me the following morning. The Heywoods' carriage awaited them, and we were all making our farewells when Henry drew me to one side for a few parting words.

"I hope I shall see you in town before long, Miss Darcy," he began.

"As I said before, our plans are not yet fixed. I think it unlikely, though, that we shall come before April or May."

"That seems an age from now. Will you not write to my sister so that I may have some news of you before then?" he asked.

"If she wishes me to."

"I am certain she does wish it. The two of you are just the same age, and I should be pleased for you to become even better acquainted. There can be no objection to it on either side, surely."

"I shall wait to hear from her then. Goodbye, Mr. Heywood," said I, offering him my hand.

He took it, pressed it tenderly, and gave me an earnest look. "Goodbye, Miss Darcy."

~~*~~

It was a relief when the Heywoods were gone, for I was now convinced that, however shallow they might prove to be in the end, Henry did harbor some romantic designs on me. Although I had noticed nothing unusual at the time, I supposed the inception of those feelings must be traced to when I had seen Henry last in London. How they had grown from so mild a beginning to a fevered pitch entirely in my absence, I could not begin to fathom. But so it must have happened. I could only expect that such exaggerated sensations would be suffered to die away just as swiftly when once again deprived of an object and, hopefully, without any lasting damage to our friendship.

Regardless, it was not Henry Heywood who dominated my thoughts that morning. Once he had gone, my mind quickly turned in the direction of my heart, to the question of what, if anything, would now arise between Colonel Fitzwilliam and myself. Only he, Cousin Anne, and Kitty Bennet remained with us – all family – and so surely we would have an opportunity for a private conversation ere the day was over. Before anything of the sort could occur, however, Colonel Fitzwilliam announced that he had some news to share and begged we would all be seated to hear it.

Looking back, I suppose the signs were all there for me to see – Fitzwilliam's hint at the ball that Lady Catherine had wasted no time securing her daughter's future; Anne's not only taking the seat beside him now, but having arrived to Pemberley under his protection in the first place. Yet I was too blind to see any of it, so I had no warning of what would come next, no chance to prepare myself for the fatal blow. It struck me completely unawares.

"Dear friends," the colonel began when we were settled.

He smiled, so I smiled benignly in return. At that moment, I was noticing how fine he looked, admiring the masterful way he had taken command of the room and counting myself lucky to be among his intimate friends.

"I am glad you are all here, for I have something very important to say. Some of you may have already guessed what it is. For the rest, it will probably come as quite a surprise..."

These words barely registered with me at the time. I was only thinking that whatever Colonel Fitzwilliam had to say, I should be more than happy to hear it.

"...Regardless, I hope you will share my joy at my good fortune, which is this. Anne and I are engaged to be married."

All the air seemed to escape the room in an instant.

I was too stunned to speak, and no one else did either. I could not at first believe I had heard correctly. And yet the undeniable evidence was there before me – Fitzwilliam tenderly holding my cousin's hand, his words still echoing in the silence. "Anne and I are engaged to be married," he had said. Nothing could be more unambiguous. Nothing could be more devastatingly clear.

I could not breathe. I felt as if I might swoon at any moment. Although I doubted my legs would support me, I knew my only hope was to get away before I completely came apart at the seams.

Somehow I managed to mumble a few words of congratulation as I fled the room. Then, when assured I was out of sight, I flew up the stairs, running as if my life depended on it. I had to reach the privacy of my apartments as soon as possible. The tears had already begun to flow; I knew worse was coming. I could feel a cry of agony rising up in my throat, one which no one else must hear. It must be forestalled a minute longer, just a minute longer.

In my own rooms at last, the door closed behind me, I ran to my bed – not to throw myself onto it but to gather all the pillows together in my arms. Then I buried my face in them and screamed with all my might.

~~*~~

My violent throes of anguish eventually subsided into shaking sobs of grief and finally an exhausted, tearful sleep. I woke perhaps an hour later, feeling only half alive. As my eyes slowly came into focus, I was further disheartened to see I was not alone. My personal maid waited near me, looking very worried indeed.

"Can I do anything for you, Miss?" she asked fretfully.

"Be not alarmed, Lilly," I said, trying to gather myself together. "It was only a sudden headache. Sleep is the best thing for it. Please help me out of my gown and then tell the master and mistress that I am indisposed and wish to be left alone."

It had been all I could do to say this much without breaking down again. I have no idea if Lilly believed me or not, but she mercifully held her tongue and did as she was told.

Under this pretense, I kept to my room for the rest of the day and all of the next, not wanting to see anybody. Whenever I heard someone approaching – the resounding footfalls of my brother or Elizabeth's lighter tread – I feigned sleep. The door would open, there would be a pensive pause, and then they would go away again, not wishing to disturb me. It was easier that way. I wanted no inquiries, no well-meaning solicitude on my behalf. I could not bear it.

Trays of food also came and went at regular intervals. On some basic level, I knew I should take nourishment, for myself and for the sake of my family. But I could not convince myself to eat one bite, even to spare the feelings of the people I loved.

By the next morning, all the fight and most of the flame had gone out of me, leaving only a hollow, insipid shell behind. At least that is the way it seemed to me. I could not imagine going on, and I was too weak to disguise my true situation any longer. Consequently, when I heard a light knock at the door, I did not even bother to close my eyes in pretend sleep.

It was Elizabeth, of course. Seeing my pitiful state, she hurried to my side. "Oh, my darling girl, what on earth is the matter?" she asked as she sat down on the bed beside me.

She was ever so gentle, ever so patient. She bore with my sobs and my tears, which had started again, triggered by her question. She held me, petted me, and rocked me much as I remember my own mother doing when I was a very small child. At last, when I was calm again, she gently coaxed, "Does this have something to do with Fitzwilliam's engagement to Anne?"

"Oh, Lizzy!" I wailed, and then my confession came tumbling out all in a rush. "The truth is, I have been in love with Fitzwilliam for a long time. It is not mere friendship or admiration I feel for him, not anymore. I love him as a woman loves a man, so deeply, so sincerely. Since he never married, I dared to hope he might learn to return my affection in time. Now that I am finally old enough, though, he has engaged himself to someone else! I can never tell him that I love him; I will never know if he could have loved me. How shall I bear it, Lizzy? How can I watch all my dreams turn to dust and see dear Fitzwilliam married to my cousin instead?"

- 11 -

Lady in Distress

Although I had thought anybody else's knowing all this would multiply my misery, instead my burden seemed a bit lighter the moment I shared it with Elizabeth. At least now I had a confidante, someone who could understand my disappointment and help me to bear it. That was clear at once. She would not pain me with useless platitudes or offer false hope. She understood, as I did, that the situation was impossible. Fitzwilliam would never break his promise to Anne, not that there was any reason to suppose he would wish to do so. All romantic interest between us had clearly been on my side alone.

Although I was not sorry to have confessed all to Elizabeth, I then quickly became alarmed to think that any other person alive should hear of the affair through her. She might tell my brother, I suddenly realized! If so, would Fitzwilliam himself learn of it as well? Feeling a wave of panic about to overtake me, I sat up abruptly and cried, "You must never tell a soul about this, Lizzy! I spoke in strictest confidence. Swear to me you will not say a single word."

Elizabeth, who remained at my bedside, looked puzzled. "Why should you worry?" she asked. "You have done nothing of which you need be ashamed. And besides, who would I tell but your own brother? Indeed, it is nobody else's business."

"No! Please, Lizzy, not even William!"

Elizabeth placed an arm about my shoulders, saying, "There, there. You must try to calm yourself, dearest, so that we may discuss this rationally. First, consider what an untenable position you place me in by this request. I am not in the habit of keeping secrets from my husband, I assure you, Georgiana. No wife should; it can only lead to mischief. Now you are asking me to withhold information from him that I know very well your brother would desire to be made aware of. And why should he not know it? He would only wish to help you through this difficulty as he has done in times past."

"Exactly! That is just the thing. I should be mortified for him to know I had got myself into another scrape over a man." I particularly had in mind the debacle with Mr. Wickham. From her look of consciousness and from her answer, I felt certain Elizabeth was thinking the same.

"There can be no reasonable comparison between this case and anything that has come before. All you have done is fall in love with a man whom your own brother admires exceedingly. If anything, that shows your judgment has improved – improved by a great measure, I should say. Your brother would be entirely sympathetic, I am sure."

"I'm sure he would be! He would be kind. He would pity me. But in the end, what would be accomplished by it? William would feel an awkwardness for knowing something so personal, and he would be frustrated that he could do nothing to help me. It would be upsetting him to no purpose. More harm than good will be accomplished by telling him. Cannot you see that? For my brother's sake as well as for my own, you must say nothing to him about this matter. Oh, Elizabeth, please!"

She was quiet for several minutes as she no doubt debated the merits of the question within her own mind. I held my tongue as well, although I did allow my countenance and the tears that had begun to flow again to continue pleading my case.

It was powerfully selfish for me to insist on having my way at the expense of my dear sister's conscience. I see that now. But I did not think of such things at the time. When one is drowning, one does not stop to consider if one has the right to survive at some cost to another. At that moment, one grasps at whatever help comes within reach. And so it was with me. I felt adrift at sea and Elizabeth was my only lifeline. I desperately needed her to be my trusted confessor. I depended upon her strength and her secrecy to sustain me until I could find my way back to solid ground again.

I could see her struggling, see her wavering between her original convictions and a giving in to my point of view. When she finally spoke, I knew I had won.

"If I am to do as you ask, Georgiana, you must do something for me in return."

"Anything, Lizzy! I will do anything you say."

"Very well, then. You claim it will be kindest to your brother not to worry him, but he *will* worry if he sees you in your present condition. So, for his peace of mind and for your own health, you *must* exert yourself. You must endeavor to assert some semblance of normal behavior as soon as possible. Understand? Otherwise, your brother will not need me or anybody else to tell him something is very wrong indeed."

I knew Elizabeth was correct. William was no fool, and I could not hide from him forever. So I promised I would return to my normal habits and cheerful appearance as rapidly as possible. It would be a ruse, of course (for I could see no chance of early recovery ahead), but hopefully a believable one.

~~*~~

Although I had been sincere in giving my promise, I am afraid I failed miserably at carrying it through. I had no appetite to speak of and no conversation either. In truth, I had no joy of any kind in those first weeks, not even in music. I got through each day as best I could; that was all.

I am certain William could not help but notice something amiss, but he mercifully let me be. For this and so many other things, I am forever indebted to Elizabeth. Apparently she was able to convince him that, as an adult, I was entitled to some privacy.

I was also for some time spared any sight or sound of Colonel Fitzwilliam – another saving grace. He did not visit. No letter came from him. And no one mentioned his name in my hearing – Elizabeth undoubtedly from knowing how much it would pain me, and the others by pure chance, I suppose.

That did not keep me from thinking of the colonel in private and periodically lapsing into a new fit of tears over the fact that he would soon be made another woman's husband. But it would have been far worse to be taken unawares, unexpectedly reminded of him while in company where I had no hope of preparing myself and less likelihood of hiding my true feelings.

As the weeks passed and as I deliberately turned my mind from Colonel Fitzwilliam to other things, I did grow stronger again. Kitty Bennet was still with us, having stayed on after the ball, and I felt a responsibility to do my part in contributing toward her entertainment.

Except for our like ages, however, we had little in common. Since she could not be interested in music or books, it was up to me to exert myself so much as to join in her pursuits. Here I discovered the benefit of frivolous distractions. Even *I* found it difficult to be melancholy when we were discussing the latest fashions for gowns or trimming out new bonnets.

Kitty was ultimately the one who first broached the subject of Colonel Fitzwilliam to me, however. It was February by then – a cold and damp month that had kept us too long confined indoors – and we were all looking for a way of relieving the tedium and gloom.

"I understand we are to have a dinner party," Kitty volunteered one morning while the two of us were sitting together at breakfast.

"Indeed? I have not yet heard of it, but it sounds a pleasant scheme. Is it to be a large affair?"

"I am unaware of any of the particulars. Elizabeth just mentioned it in passing an hour ago. It seems Mr. Darcy proposed the idea, and she has agreed to it. That is as far as I know. Do you think Colonel Fitzwilliam will be invited?"

I have no idea how I answered Kitty or even if I managed to do so at all, so completely was I overcome by her question. It was not simply the mention of Fitzwilliam's name, for this I might have successfully weathered. It was the sickening prospect she had suggested of his coming to Pemberley. Such a calamity must be prevented at all cost! Instantly resolving to question Elizabeth on the subject at my earliest opportunity, I excused myself from the table and went in search of her. As it happened, however, I met with my brother first.

"Ah, William," I said, drawing up short at unexpectedly confronting him in the passageway.

"Georgiana. You look as if you are on an important mission," he returned. "May I be of any assistance?"

Things had been rather strained between us for some time, which was entirely my fault. Since I would not tell him what ailed me, William had been reduced to walking on eggshells in my presence. Now here he was, making another effort to be on good terms with me again. I felt I owed it to him to try as well.

"Thank you," I said. "Yes, you are exactly the person who can. Kitty has just mentioned that we are to have a dinner party here at Pemberley, at your suggestion apparently. I wanted to know more."

"I thought perhaps you could… that we could *all* benefit from a little variety in this house. I hope the idea pleases you, Georgiana."

"A little addition to our society would be agreeable, certainly. It will not be a large party though, no London people or from beyond?"

"No, nothing on a grand scale like your ball. Just a few of our local friends. That seemed to me most comfortable and the very thing to relieve the monotony of this dismal weather. I have given Elizabeth my suggested guest list. I am sure she would welcome your help with the arrangements… if you are feeling up to it."

I ignored his implied question and instead answered, "An excellent suggestion. I will go to her at once."

For my brother's sake, I had evinced more cheer at the prospect of this dinner party than I truly felt. It might be very pleasant or it might not. Everything depended on the guest list.

Did William count his cousin, the colonel, as one of our 'local friends,' I wondered? I supposed it would depend on where Fitzwilliam was at the present moment, something of which I had no personal knowledge. He might be in London – certainly too far to come for a simple dinner party. The same was true if he were at Rosings in Kent. But what if he were in Derbyshire? That would be entirely different, for the Fitzwilliam family seat was no more than half a day's ride away, close enough to be manageable for someone motivated to come.

As I hurried to find Elizabeth, I prayed it would turn out to be one of the two former possibilities and not the latter.

Elizabeth was in her morning room, as I had expected, and I accosted her without preamble. "William has told me of the dinner party," I said. "May I see the guest list, please?"

I knew at once by my sister's expression that it would not be good news. "I did try to prevent it, Georgiana," she said apologetically. "I really did. But your brother was quite firm, and what could I say to dissuade him when I am expressly forbidden to speak of the only reasonable excuse for demanding a change?"

"The list, please, Elizabeth," I repeated with my shaking hand outstretched. She reluctantly complied and I glanced down the short column of familiar names: Ruth Sanditon, Charlotte Collins, Mr. Sanditon, Mr. Thornton, Charles and Jane Bingley, Caroline Bingley… *and Colonel Fitzwilliam.*

There was the dreaded name in indelible black ink at the bottom of the list. The document might as well have been a death warrant for how lethal a blow it felt to me. I sank into the nearest chair. "Fitzwilliam coming here?" I said when I had recovered enough to speak. "No, I cannot see him. It is impossible!" Tears, which were never far away these days, began to flow once more.

Elizabeth glanced about, hastily closed the door, and then came to kneel by my side. "I know it will be difficult," she said. "Still, you must try to bear his coming, dearest. This was bound to happen sooner or later. I wish for your sake it could have been postponed a few months more, but it cannot be prevented now."

"Then I shall simply say that I am unwell and keep to my room."

"That is precisely what you must *not* do if you wish to keep your brother in the dark about your feelings. He is unlikely to consider it a coincidence if every time the colonel turns up you take to your bed."

She was right, of course. I knew it even as I battled on in the hope of escaping my fate. I had many arguments at the ready, yet none of them could be supported under close examination. It amounted to this: I must either tell my brother the truth or be prepared to see Colonel Fitzwilliam very soon. I could likely choose between the two evils, but I could not avoid them both.

Elizabeth allowed me to grapple with my unhappy alternatives for a minute before saying, "So, Georgiana, there is still time; I have not sent the invitations yet. You can make a clean breast of the thing, telling your brother why you wish to have Fitzwilliam excluded. Or allow me to do it. It might be the least painful solution in the end." I could hear in her tone that she hoped I would choose to do so.

"No!" I cried. "Anything but that."

Elizabeth sighed. "Very well. That being the case, I suppose we should begin to consider how it might best be managed."

Elizabeth promised to help all she could – by contriving the least objectionable seating arrangement at table and by running interference for me any other time it might be needed. "You must be prepared to say a few words to him when he first arrives," she advised, "but otherwise you should be able to give him a wide berth."

We talked on these topics for another twenty minutes and on several other occasions when opportunity presented for a private word. With my sister's advice and steadfast encouragement, I did begin to feel less pessimistic; I started to believe it at least possible I might come through the trial in one piece. And, as the event transpired, I did survive it, but not without considerable embarrassment and distress.

Fitzwilliam was the same as ever, and yet, for the first time, I could not enjoy his presence. I could not laugh at his jokes. I could not revel in his charming ways and genial nature. Now these were only painful reminders of what I had lost.

I know I spoke to him when he came in the door. I hardly remember what I said, however, so discomposed was I. Probably it was something quite foolish – some nonsense about my shoes, I think – and then I believe I excused myself rather abruptly. In any case, I am sure it was a performance that did me no credit.

I was happy, therefore, when it was time to go in to dinner, where I knew I would be seated as far away from Fitzwilliam as possible. I hoped to neither see nor hear anything of him throughout the meal. To help ensure this, I devoted my full attention to the cordial conversation going forward between my brother and Mr. Sanditon, my two closest companions at table. Perhaps their topics – the progress of a drainage works at Reddclift, managing difficult tenants, planned agricultural improvements – did not always interest me so much as I pretended. But I liked listening to their friendly exchange of ideas and making an occasional contribution myself.

I took a momentary pause in their talk as a chance to introduce a subject of my own, saying, "I wish you would tell me something about your children, Mr. Sanditon."

"Certainly, Miss Darcy, if you wish it," he answered. "No subject could be more pleasing for me to speak of than my two daughters. Abigail is four, and little Amelia, just two."

"Abigail and Amelia? What lovely names."

"Yes," he agreed. "And I would venture to say that the names suit them. Although the girls are still very young, it is already plain that they, happily, take their looks after their mother, God rest her soul."

I wished to say that taking after their father's looks could have been no great misfortune either, but it would have been far too forward. Instead, I offered, "Then perhaps it is their character that they will learn from you, Mr. Sanditon."

"Perhaps. It is a heavy responsibility to think so, but one I daily pray to prove worthy of."

"Children are a great gift as well as a great responsibility, I believe."

"Quite. It is just as you say, Miss Darcy. My daughters are a gift to me indeed... and a great comfort. I hope you will one day soon have the opportunity to meet them yourself. Would you like that?"

"I would, very much indeed, for I am dearly fond of children."

A brief silence developed, followed by a noisy outburst from the other end of the table.

"Engaged to Miss de Bourgh?" Caroline Bingley exclaimed, looking straight at Colonel Fitzwilliam.

"Yes, just recently, in fact," he replied more civilly.

I can only imagine that Miss Bingley, who appeared to find this news most distasteful, had begun to form some early designs on the colonel herself. I was simply relieved that the dramatic announcement had drawn everybody's attention away from me, for I am certain that my countenance in that first moment could not have successfully born any scrutiny. Thankfully, though, I had a minute to steady my nerves, to harden my resolve of remaining composed and standing my ground. I did not flee the room as I had done before; that in itself I counted a victory. Instead, I took a deep breath and waited patiently for the sudden but by now familiar tightness in my chest to fade away. Then I calmly resumed my conversation with Mr. Sanditon.

That had been my strategy all along, to bear Fitzwilliam's presence by fully occupying myself with whoever else was at hand. Although I would have been perfectly content with somebody far less interesting, I was glad it had turned out to be Mr. Sanditon.

- 12 -

New Beginnings

I had a letter from Andrea Heywood shortly after these things had occurred, which did serve as another brief diversion from my troubles.

Berkley Square, London
My dearest Georgiana,

First and foremost, I must again offer my sincere thanks – on behalf of myself and all my family – for your including us in the delightful celebration of your birthday last month. I do not know when, if ever, I have enjoyed a ball more! And I must congratulate you (and your brother and sister) on the excellence of all the arrangements. Pemberley itself, the music, the food, the rooms: all these were as fine as I have ever seen in the best houses of London. Mama did make one remark about the country manners of some of the guests, but I could see nothing much in it myself. I thought everybody was extremely pleasant.

I hope you will be in town soon (and so particularly does one other member of my family). To own the truth, however, you have not missed much of consequence so far. Lady Bedford's soiree was well worth attending, if only to observe her husband behaving very badly, but otherwise London society has been dull indeed. I have not even a single new engagement or scandal to report. Things are sure to improve soon, though.

I continue at my music and French lessons to please Mama. But, oh, how tedious I find them! Sometimes I wish I had been born a boy, for men always have interesting business of one kind or another to take them out into the world.

My father has the bank, of course, and my brother is scarcely any less occupied there these days. Papa says Henry knows the workings of the place nearly as well as he does himself. I would wager it is true too. Henry is so clever and ambitious that he is sure to turn out a big success and an excellent catch for some lucky young lady. (You see how carefully I have kept my promise to you by not suggesting who that lucky girl should be!)

Write to me soon, my dearest friend, that I may know how you are getting on and how things are going forward at Pemberley. And do try to convince your brother to bring you to town as soon as possible. We are languishing here without you.

Yours ever,
Andrea Heywood

It was an amusing letter, although I hardly knew how to reply to it. So, having nothing fit to report at that moment, I set the missive aside. At the end of March, however, the situation was entirely altered, for there was by then news indeed, news of a most wonderful and joyous kind.

Pemberley, Derbyshire
My dear Andrea,

Thank you for your letter. I beg you will forgive my tardiness in answering it. I would have written sooner had I anything of an entertaining nature to report. But we have fared no better here than you have in London, I assure you. We have been very dull all winter as well, with nothing more than one small dinner party since January to provide some liveliness. And I cannot claim even to have taken much enjoyment in that, except it forwarded our acquaintance with some very agreeable friends who live not far from here at an estate called Reddclift – a widowed gentleman with two young daughters, his sister-in-law, and a friend who lives with her at the cottage. Perhaps you will remember them from the ball – Mr. Sanditon, Mrs. Sanditon, and Charlotte Collins.

But now, at last, I have something about which it is truly worth writing. Can you guess what it is? I did not. I probably should have, but in fact I had no suspicion that anything of the kind was coming until the information burst in upon me all at once. It seems I am to have a niece or nephew by the autumn! Is not this the most excellent news? Naturally, I could not be more pleased – for William and Elizabeth, of course, but also for myself. Next to having children of my own someday, I can think of nothing better to wish for.

As for our coming into London, I do not know when that might be reasonably looked for. Elizabeth's sister, Mrs. Bingley, is also expecting her first child, probably in May. Elizabeth has promised to stay with her through the event. So you see, since she will not wish to be so far away from Staffordshire as London until everything is safely concluded, and as we would by no means leave her behind, I think there is very little chance of our being in town before another six or eight weeks has elapsed. I trust, as you say, matters there will soon improve, and you will not much miss our company until then.

Please greet all your kind family from me and from my brother and Elizabeth as well. It is by their permission that I have told you of their happy expectations, which you now have leave to share with your family but not beyond. Best regards.

Your friend,
Georgiana Darcy

Perhaps if I had not been so fully occupied with my own situation, I might have noticed the change in my sister's state of health sooner. I might have marked the alteration in her appetite. I might have likewise detected her especial glow of spirits and the more tender care my brother suddenly took of her. But all these clues were lost on me. As I wrote to Andrea, the news took me completely by surprise. When Elizabeth told me, I reacted just as I reacted to nearly everything else at the time; I promptly burst into tears.

"My dear, my dear," cried Elizabeth. "Why so sad? This is happy news! Indeed, I thought you would be as pleased about it as your brother and I are."

I blotted my tears and schooled my countenance into a more appropriate expression as quickly as I could. "I *am* pleased," I managed to say in a shaky voice. "Very much so! I don't know what is the matter with me. I do beg your pardon, Lizzy."

"Never mind about that. I was only worried that I had somehow distressed you, which is the last thing I would have wanted."

"It was the shock; that is all."

"Yes, the shock," she repeated, although I felt sure we were both thinking that some part must be attributed to my fragile emotional state in general. "I should have prepared you for it and not just blurted the thing out to you so precipitously. I have known about it for weeks, and your brother nearly as long. But, once we decided it was time to tell you, I'm afraid I was too excited for patience. I had hoped it would cheer you. This is something we may all look forward to with pleasure."

"I agree. And it really does cheer me, I promise you." I then embraced her to carry home my point.

"Good," she said decisively upon drawing back again. "Then go say as much to your brother. He wanted me to break the news, but he is waiting in the library to hear how you bear it. Perhaps you will not think it necessary to bother him with how much of a start I gave you just now. I must have a flair for the dramatic. Someday ask me to tell you the clever way I found to deliver the news to *him*. Then, I think, you will be more satisfied with the manner in which I told you."

Elizabeth laughed with delight at her private joke, but I did not wait to demand her explanation then. Instead, I hurried to the library to congratulate William.

Their excellent news really did go a long way towards breaking through my perpetual state of gloom. I could feel the clouds that had long shrouded my spirit lifting a little more each day after that. Some credit for my improvement must also go to the season itself, for I could not help but feel more optimistic with the days growing longer, the flowers blooming, and my power to take regular airings restored. Resuming my charity calls proved likewise beneficial. No matter how determined I might have been before to imagine myself the most unfortunate creature in the world, it was no longer possible once confronted with irrefutable evidence to the contrary. Although I will not discount the genuine pain that stems from matters of the heart, others had the same and so much more to deal with. At least I had no worry, as many in the parish did, for my health or for how I was to keep my family clothed and fed. When I compared my privileged circumstances to what some suffered, I was truly ashamed for every minute I had ever wasted on self pity.

No, I would not have the idyllic life I had imagined with Colonel Fitzwilliam. That had been pure fantasy. It was now time to take a more realistic view of things, to assess the actual state of affairs honestly and without undue emotion. I was young, after all. I had excellent prospects, and every other cause to hope for a bright future. It was not sensible to suppose that Colonel Fitzwilliam was the only man on earth with whom I could ever be reasonably content. That would be far too perverse to be true. Romantic love was all very well, but it was not the only determiner of happiness in marriage. Many highly successful unions were founded on more practical considerations, I reminded myself. Friendship came first; love might follow. It oftentimes did, I understood. It would probably be the same for me.

In the most logical portion of my mind, I believed these things. My heart, however, remained less convinced. It lagged far behind in its willingness to give assent to a different standard of happiness, especially when I considered the model of a good marriage closest to me. Every day I observed William and Elizabeth's example. Every day I saw how they loved and doted on one another, so much so that I occasionally had to avert my eyes from it. To do otherwise would have been to feel myself the voyeur.

They did not mean to embarrass me or make a show. Indeed, I daresay they had no idea their mutual ardor was blazing bright enough for anybody else to see. It was just that, in the privacy of their own home, they were less guarded in their behavior than with strangers. I think they sometimes forgot I was even present. Then there would be a brief, caressing touch between them, a significant look, a knowing remark…

I do not pretend to understand all the mysteries of what passes between a husband and his wife. I only know that my own heart yearns to discover these same marvels for itself.

But I digress. What I mean to say is that my brother and his wife did not settle for less than the ideal, and I hoped not to either. And yet, one does not always immediately recognize who is (or is not) one's ideal partner. Consider how wrong I had been about Wickham's character. Now, in Colonel Fitzwilliam, I had imagined a lover where there was only a friend. And Elizabeth herself had proved the truth of this idea by misjudging my brother at first. It was from her own experience that she had recently recommended to me that I should keep open to other possibilities. "Your future happiness may not lie where you think," she had said.

Perhaps she was right. In fact, I earnestly hoped she was. With Colonel Fitzwilliam lost to me now, I had no choice but to look elsewhere for the companion of my future life.

~~*~~

Intercourse between Reddclift and Pemberley increased as the weather improved, a warm friendship between the two houses flourishing. Whatever reserves originally existed were quickly on their way to being overcome simply by the desire on the part of all concerned that they should be. Still, although my brother had called at the Great Hall early on in the acquaintance, Elizabeth and I had been no farther than Reddclift Cottage to visit the ladies. So I was particularly interested to hear the contents of a letter which arrived from Mr. Sanditon one day early in April.

"We are all invited on Thursday next to dine at Reddclift Hall," William said upon first perusing it. We three were taking some outdoor exercise together, walking along the path by the lake. The post had arrived just prior to our setting forth, and so, rather than waiting until our return to read his letter, my brother had brought it with him. "Mrs. Sanditon and Mrs. Collins will be there as well, of course. What do you say to that, Mrs. Darcy? A rare treat, I should think."

"An invitation to Reddclift? I am quite delighted! And we should take it as a high compliment. I daresay it is a long while since Mr. Sanditon has given a dinner party of any kind, considering his reclusive ways. Yes, it is an honor indeed."

"But do not you think," I suggested to Elizabeth, "that Mr. Sanditon is a great deal improved since we have known him?"

"How do you mean?" she asked.

"Well, consider the pains he takes to be kind to Ruth and Charlotte, how frequently he calls here, and that he made the effort to attend my ball. This invitation is another sign that he is willing to enter society again, at least in a small way. Perhaps it was only his wife's death that caused him to withdraw from it in the first place.

His true nature may not be nearly so reticent as it is generally thought to be."

My brother looked at me in some surprise. "That is a very astute observation, Georgiana, and I believe you may have hit pretty near the truth of the thing."

With Kitty Bennet having recently left us for Heatheridge, Mr. Sanditon's invitation was accepted for three. I felt my anticipation rising as the day of the event approached. I had a great curiosity to make the acquaintance of the little girls and to obtain a closer look at the house, of which I had already formed some mental picture through what had been told me and by having once glimpsed it myself from some distance the day Elizabeth and I called at the cottage. But now, as we drew nearer to it that evening, the place appeared to even more advantage, aglow as it was in the golden light of a late afternoon sun.

Reddclift Hall was indeed a very handsome house. It could not compare to Pemberley as to the scale of the place, but I liked its situation equally well. Whereas our house sat on gradually rising ground with fine prospects of lake, meadow, and deep shades, Mr. Sanditon's home perched atop a somewhat steeper eminence – lawns and a gracefully arching gravel sweep on the uphill side of the house, where the main entrance was, the ground falling away sharply on the other. I could only imagine there must be a spectacular view from the many windows on that aspect.

Our host greeted us immediately upon our arrival, helping me from the carriage after William and Elizabeth had alighted and offering me his arm, saying, "I'm so glad you have come, Miss Darcy."

"It was kind of you to invite us to Reddclift, Mr. Sanditon. I am very pleased to see it for myself at last."

"Would you like to have a look round the place before dinner?"

"I would, very much indeed, sir."

He smiled. "Then we must start with the prospect from the drawing room, before we lose the daylight."

We four walked straight through the hall into the drawing room at the back of the house, where Ruth and Charlotte were sitting. I greeted them, but I barely took notice of anything else; I was drawn at once to the tall bank of windows which spanned the full breadth of the room.

The whole valley was spread at my feet, with its meandering river and patchwork quilt of hedgerows and fields. Beyond, were more hills as far as I could see. I stood in rapt admiration of the sight for some minutes, not even aware that Mr. Sanditon had come up on my right side. "I never tire of looking at it," he said, giving me a bit of a start.

"I can see why, Mr. Sanditon. The view is stunning from this high elevation."

"Yes, I bless my grandfather every day for having the boldness to defy standard practice and build on top of a hill instead. There are some drawbacks, to be sure. The road in winter can be atrocious, for one thing. But when I see the sun rise from this spot or from the terrace, I cannot help thinking it is well worth a little inconvenience."

"I quite agree."

"Beautiful," I heard Elizabeth say with feeling from behind me. "…the view and the room itself. I must compliment your taste in the way you have furnished it, Mr. Sanditon."

He turned to her. "Thank you, Mrs. Darcy, but I deserve none of the credit for it, I assure you. That belongs entirely to my late wife."

When I could at last be persuaded to tear myself from the windows, our tour proceeded. There were plenty of handsomely appointed rooms, to be sure, but the other main highlight came upon our stopping in the nursery to visit Mr. Sanditon's daughters.

"Papa!" they cried in unison when he entered. They ran to their father and then, catching sight of three strangers, hid themselves partly behind him.

"Girls, I have brought you some new friends," he told them as he attempted to draw them forward. To us he said, "This is Abigail," indicating the taller of the two, "and this little one is Amelia."

They were enchanting creatures, just as I had been led to believe but, oh, so shy! I did not wish to frighten them, so I knelt down to their level. "I'm very pleased to meet you, Miss Abigail," I said softly, extending my hand. "My name is Miss Darcy."

She looked up at her father, who nodded his reassurance. Then, after another moment's hesitation, the girl took a half step forward to briefly shake my hand. "Hello," she said.

"My, you are already quite grown up," I continued, encouraged by my progress. "How many years old are you?"

Another hesitation, and then she said, "Four," holding up the correct number of digits. "But Amelia is only two."

Amelia, who had been carefully observing all this, was prepared to follow her sister's example as best she could. So I was on friendly terms with them both by the time we quitted the nursery a few minutes later.

"Thank you for your kind attentions to my daughters, Miss Darcy," said Mr. Sanditon as we moved on.

"Not at all, sir. I am grateful for the pleasure of seeing them. They are dear little creatures."

"Of course I would never disagree with you about that. I am glad you like them. The girls appear to have taken a fancy to you as well. They are often shy of strangers, but you won them over easily enough. You must have a natural talent with children."

"Thank you. But really, Mr. Sanditon, you are too excessive in your praise. I am very fond of children, yet I cannot claim any special capabilities."

"I am sure you are too modest, Miss Darcy."

We presently rejoined Ruth and Charlotte in the drawing room, where the collecting darkness outside had already begun to steal away the magnificent views. But it mattered very little, for it was soon time to go in to dinner, which proved to be a most agreeable meal, the food itself being excellent and the conversation flowing freely between the six of us friends. In such company, I felt completely at ease and able to forget my troublesome shyness, which was a genuine pleasure. In truth, the whole evening was a great success, at least it seemed so to me. It had been a long time since I could remember enjoying myself half so much.

- 13 -

A Different View

So full of our visit to Reddclift was my mind afterward that for a long time sleep escaped me. I lay abed that night thinking of all I had seen there and all that had transpired. It was not simply that I had been uncommonly pleased with everything the evening had entailed. What kept me awake was the dawning realization that Mr. Sanditon admired me, perhaps very much. In fact, looking back, I could not help but feel that there had been more to his invitation than the prospect of an enjoyable evening. Could it be that he had very particularly wanted me to see Reddclift? Was it possible that he had been imagining me as its next mistress and desiring that I should begin doing the same? By introducing me to his daughters, had he, without my knowledge, been auditioning me for the role of their new mother?

Oh, my! It was a shocking idea, but one which I could not entirely dismiss as pure fancy, especially when I recalled our conversation after dinner.

Our companions were busy at their game of Whist at one end of the drawing room – an exercise from which both Mr. Sanditon and I had asked to be excused – and he was leading me to the other. "Do come and have a seat by the fire, Miss Darcy," he invited. "Although it is spring, there is still a sharp chill in the air." I nodded and complied. He took the chair opposite me, drawing it a bit closer.

"This is a very comfortable room, Mr. Sanditon," I said after taking a minute to get settled and look about myself. "How clever your grandfather was to not obstruct the view with one massive fireplace, but instead building two smaller ones at either end of the room."

"I am glad you like it. And you are correct in your interpretation of his motive, although the arrangement does also provide the practical benefit of maintaining a more even temperature throughout the room. You will find it is the same with every aspect of the house, from the arrangement of the kitchen furniture to the placement of every door and window – beauty and utility combine to the best possible advantage." He suddenly looked conscious and dropped his eyes. "Forgive me, Miss Darcy. How I do carry on."

"You have no need to apologize, sir. It is perfectly natural that you are proud of what your grandfather accomplished here. Indeed, it speaks well of you that you esteem your heritage as you should."

"That is kind of you to say. I know Reddclift is nothing to Pemberley, and the Sanditon line is not so long and distinguished as some men can boast of. But it is a solid, respectable family, one with which no one need be ashamed to associate themselves."

"Certainly no one ought to, Mr. Sanditon."

"Some have in the past, Miss Darcy. My own father-in-law did not think it a connection that did him any honor. But he was a very proud man. I question if he would have thought anybody good enough to marry his daughter."

"He was extremely fond of her, then?"

"No, not at all. To him, she was only an object, something meant to add to his prestige by her making a brilliant alliance. When she failed to do that, he had no more use for her."

"Abominable, and how sad for your wife."

"Yes, exactly. His slights to me were nothing, but Maryanne was crushed when he cast her off like so much refuse. For what she suffered at her father's hand, I find it difficult to forgive him."

We were silent for a few moments, and then presently I said, "Her father's cruelty notwithstanding, surely the mistress of Reddclift can have had no cause to repine."

He brightened a little at this. "I trust she did not. We were happy here, although far too briefly."

"And you will rally again, Mr. Sanditon. You must, sir, for the sake of your daughters as well as yourself."

"Fear not, Miss Darcy. I am well. If you had seen from what a low point I started, I daresay you would now be congratulating me on my remarkable recovery. Much of the credit must go to the kindness of others, people such as your family. You cannot imagine what it has meant to me."

"Perhaps I can, Mr. Sanditon, more than you realize. I too have lost people who were dear to me."

"Yes, of course you have. Then you know how important it is to have friends about you at such a time. Did you, Miss Darcy? I would hate to think of your bearing the loss of your parents alone. But you need not answer. I should probably not speak to you about such personal matters, and yet it seems every time I see you, your sympathetic nature draws more from me than I ever meant to tell."

"I will take that as a compliment."

"As indeed you should."

From there we had moved on to less serious subjects, primarily music. He asked what piece I was chiefly working on and expressed his desire to hear me play again soon.

"I would invite you to do so now," he said, "but the pianoforte has been shut up too long with no one to play it. Perhaps you will do me the honor next time you come. It is quite a good instrument, I think – a Broadwood Grand."

"Yes, of course. I should be happy to."

"Very good. I shall have someone out to see that it is properly cleaned and tuned at once. I ought to have done so before, but there seemed little point. Knowing there will finally be an accomplished lady to play it again… Well, that is the only encouragement I have been wanting."

I was gratified at the time to have been of some service to Mr. Sanditon, a small help in restoring his life to what it had been before it was shattered by grief. Now, however, I wondered if I had been *too* encouraging. Had he placed too much store by my approbation of his house and his heritage? Had he seen more in my sympathy than I meant it to imply? When he kissed my hand at our parting, had he been thinking that it would be only a matter of time before we would see our guests off together?

One thing was certain; I would have to be more careful in the future, at least until I understood my own mind better. The idea of being courted by Mr. Sanditon was still so surprising and new that I could hardly tell whether to be pleased about it or not. When I had determined to be more open minded, to consider other possibilities, I had no notion of anything coming of it so soon. Now it seemed that one potential suitor had already been waiting in the wings.

No, come to think of it, there were two, as I was reminded by Andrea Heywood's next letter. Although she kept her word, strictly speaking, not openly urging a match between her brother and myself, she was nevertheless sure to mention Henry at every possible turn and in the very best light – what a genius he was at mathematics, how he had been universally admired at a ball they recently attended, and with what gallantry he had come to her aid when she had nearly been accosted by some drunken lout that same evening. Andrea also dutifully passed along her brother's particular greeting to me, repeating his wish, which exactly coincided with her own, that we should soon be in town.

I am sure it is a genuine compliment to Mr. Heywood's character that he has a sister who is so loyally enthusiastic for his claims. I myself have always thought well of him too. But, just as with Mr. Sanditon, I felt somewhat ambivalent about Henry's attentions. I suppose that meant I was indeed being open minded, just as I had planned, not forming any judgments too hastily. Time is what I needed most – time to recover from my attachment to Colonel Fitzwilliam, if that were possible, and time to discern what might constitute my happiness instead. I was in no rush (and in no condition) to make any decisions about my future at present. I hoped no one else would attempt to hurry me either.

~~*~~

"Georgiana," William called out as I passed the open library door. "Would you be so good as to step in here for a moment? There is something I would speak to you about."

"Of course," I said, entering the room where so many serious discussions had taken place over the years. If there were things of import to be decided or anything disagreeable to be related, more often than not it took place in the library. It seemed a good sign, however, that on this occasion my brother did not instruct me to close the door. "What is it?" I asked, taking the chair understood to be mine in these situations.

"Two things, really, both minor. First, I thought you should know that I have sent a letter to Lady Catherine."

"Indeed? I thought you had sworn never to speak to her again."

"Yes, I had. And it may all come to nothing in the end, but Elizabeth convinced me it was our duty to see what could be done toward a reconciliation."

"But she was so abdominally rude, especially to Elizabeth."

"I have not forgotten, believe me. However, if my wife can forgive the woman, I suppose I can as well. It is all for the sake of family unity, especially as it effects our ability to remain in close fellowship with Fitzwilliam once he is married to Anne. It all depends on our aunt now. She must show some sign of remorse, some willingness to meet us half way, or there can never be any true restoration. I hope you do not object to the idea."

"On the contrary. It seems a sensible and charitable way to proceed."

"Good. The other matter is that I was wondering if you would be willing to accompany Elizabeth to Heatheridge for a few days. I cannot break away just now, but she is longing to see her sister. Jane is in no condition to travel, of course, so it is up to Lizzy. Should you mind going as well, to keep her company?"

"Not in the least. I could do with a change of scene."

Travel always made me a little nervous, what with the ever-present chance of accident and the threat of highwaymen. Even when every possible precaution is taken, things can still go wrong. And yet, one cannot dwell on such ideas. If one is to go and do and see and live, rather than hiding at home forever, one must accept certain risks.

I hardly know why I mention this now, for nothing adverse occurred on our way to Heatheridge. We traveled thence without incident. We had an excellent visit of three days with Jane, Mr. Bingley, and Kitty Bennet. And then we returned to Pemberley in complete safely.

I was glad we had gone, however. I could see how much it had meant to Elizabeth, for one thing. And as for myself, being away had spared me from what would have been a very unwelcome encounter.

"By the way," my brother told us upon our return. "I had an unexpected visitor while you were gone. Fitzwilliam stopped here briefly yesterday morning."

I could say nothing.

With a furtive glance in my direction, undoubtedly to see how I bore the mention of the colonel's name, Elizabeth took up the conversation. "I am sorry to have missed him," said she.

"Fitzwilliam was likewise disappointed to not find you both at home. He was on his way to Kent and stopped to offer his congratulations to us. I am afraid we shan't see him again until we go to town. He tells me he will be needed at Rosings from now until the wedding, which is set for the second week of June."

With another sympathetic look at me, Elizabeth deftly changed the subject to our planned trip into town. I could not properly attend, however, nor could I very satisfactorily answer the questions put to me. *Was I looking forward to my London season? Would I not be happy to see all my town friends again? Had Andrea Heywood related any news in her recent letter?*

What did any of it matter? I could focus my mind on nothing but my brother's announcement of Fitzwilliam's upcoming wedding. Now that there was a date set, one not very distant at that, it all seemed suddenly more real. The hypothetical calamity had become the genuine article. It occurred to me then that I had unconsciously been thinking of the thing in terms of "if." *If Colonel Fitzwilliam actually marries Anne... If he is truly lost to me...* This had been my way of fending off the full weight of the blow, I suppose, and of allowing my required response to be likewise equivocating.

Although highly unpleasant, giving him up had appeared a reasonable concept when it was only a theory. Considering other options had been an interesting diversion when it was by my own choice. But now the harsh light of day had emerged and I could not refuse to see it. Softening the blow was no longer possible. The truth had to be faced, squarely this time. Colonel Fitzwilliam would indeed marry Anne, and I must find a way to get on with my life.

- 14 -

Regarding Mr. Sanditon

On the morning of the first day of May, Mr. Sanditon, who had come as far as Kympton on business, took the opportunity afforded by his close proximity to call on us at Pemberley. We were by then on such familiar terms with the gentleman that his visits were taken as a matter of course. It was only my new suspicion of his romantic intentions towards me that lent his coming this time a shade of awkward significance.

I could barely meet Mr. Sanditon's eye at first, let alone think of anything to say to him. When he spoke, my senses were on alert for not only what he said, but whether there might be any deeper meaning buried in his words, any hidden agenda. My brother I also observed, for it occurred to me that Mr. Sanditon might have already spoken to him to receive permission to court me. But no, if anything had changed, it was only in my perception. The others were behaving no different from before, I decided, which was a great relief, for I wanted us to go on just as we had been – all ease and friendliness between the four of us, Mr. Sanditon a comfortable addition to our domestic commonwealth.

No sooner had I finally convinced myself that this visit would be like any other when things took a dramatic turn.

Mr. Sanditon had stayed to tea, after which Elizabeth proposed a walk out into the gardens since it was such a fine day. That is where we were, strolling amongst the early roses, when the peace was disturbed by the delivery of a message from Heatheridge with the news that Mrs. Bingley's accouchement had begun. Elizabeth had promised to see her sister through the ordeal, so this was a call to action. With apologies to Mr. Sanditon, William ordered a chaise and four readied at once. He and Elizabeth then hurried back to the house to prepare for their immediate departure, leaving our guest to my care.

"You are not going with them?" Mr. Sanditon asked me.

"No, sir. Jane will want none but her closest family about her now. I should only be in the way."

"I cannot image that is true. But it is a delicate matter, and I am sure you know best."

We resumed our walk, the quiet only periodically interrupted by one or the other of us remarking on something of particular interest – the scent of an especially fine yellow bloom, a hare abruptly breaking from the cover of the knot garden upon our approach, the arrangement of clouds in the eastern sky beyond.

"Do not they altogether remind you of a child?" he said, pointing to one particular cloud formation. "A very cubby little sort of cherub? That is what I see."

"I was going to say a turtle, which is hardly the same thing, is it?" We both laughed. "Perhaps it is all in the way you look at them," I said, tipping my head first this way and then that.

"I think the difference is more to do with the eye of the beholder. I see a small child because I am the father of two. You see a turtle because… ah…"

He trailed off, and I looked at him with amusement. "Yes, Mr. Sanditon? This is highly instructive. I see a turtle because…"

"Well, to be perfectly frank, Miss Darcy, I have no idea why you see a turtle! So much for my theories."

Again we laughed. Then suddenly we were not laughing any more; we were only left looking at each other. Mr. Sanditon dropped his eyes first, and his countenance sobered.

"Miss Darcy, there is something… That is to say, I had not meant to speak of it so soon. But perhaps fate has left us alone for a reason."

My mind immediately detected the danger and sounded an alarm. *No, please do not say it!* I silently begged him. *Not now. Not so soon! I am nowhere near ready to hear it.*

"Miss Darcy," he began earnestly, despite the strength of my unspoken protestations. "Although we have only known each other for five or six months, I cannot help feeling it has been more than long enough to make us fairly well acquainted. And I must say that in that time I have formed the very highest opinion of you, dear lady.

It is not merely my mind that you have won over, however. My heart has been profoundly touched as well."

"Mr. Sanditon," I said, holding up my hand in hopes of stopping him before he could say more.

"Please, Miss Darcy, do allow me to finish what I have begun."

So I held my tongue and waited with dread.

"Thank you," he said. "You needn't look so alarmed, you know; I will make no demands on you, since I can see that I may have spoken prematurely. I do not flatter myself so much as to think you have necessarily become as attached to me as I have to you. But I thought, or at least I hoped, that you had begun to feel *some* degree of friendship towards me."

"Certainly, I have. I mean, I do."

"That is a good beginning, then, a very good beginning. All I ask beyond is to know whether or not you think there might eventually be a chance for more than friendship between us. It is my heartfelt desire that we should one day marry, Miss Darcy. Is it possible that you could in time learn to love me, even as I love you?"

That was the real question, was it not? Could I learn to love Mr. Sanditon? If love were a decision of the will, I would not have hesitated; I would have made over my affection to him at once, for that would mean the aching emptiness I suffered by my one-sided passion for Fitzwilliam would be gone forever. In its place would dwell the warm glow of *mutual* regard.

Unfortunately, it was a choice out of my power. The heart is a perverse organ, not likely to do as it is bid or even as would be in its own best interest. Perhaps in time, though, it might be brought to reason…

"Miss Darcy?"

"Oh, pardon me, Mr. Sanditon. I was thinking about your question. You have given me much to consider."

"True enough. I hope my sentiments have not come as too much of a shock to you. But I had the notion that, as perceptive as you seem to be, you could not have failed to have noticed my particular admiration for you."

My face grew hot, and I considered denying it. Yet I felt I owed it to the man to answer honesty with honesty. "You have not shocked me, sir, for I did suspect something of the kind, just as you say. I was only surprised at your directness and your coming to the point so soon. It caught me unprepared."

"In that case, I apologize. I daresay a truly sophisticated man would have handled the thing with more subtlety and tact. But I am a plainspoken fellow, Miss Darcy, and you might as well know it. I have always operated on the principle that one cannot go far wrong if one speaks the truth in sincerity."

"I certainly cannot fault you for that, Mr. Sanditon."

"Then please be equally plain with me."

"I shall do my best, sir, but I am afraid I have no simple, straightforward answers to give you. Would that I had! I will only tell you that I am very sensible of the honor of your proposals, and I *am* very fond of you. As to whether I might feel more than that in time… Well, how can I know? And I would not wish to encourage you falsely."

"Allow me to worry about that, Miss Georgiana. If you think there is a chance, even a small one, that will be enough for me. You do not find the idea necessarily disagreeable, then?"

"No, sir. I certainly would not characterize my feelings in that way."

"And you promise to think about my offer?"

"Yes, of course. After such revelations as you have made to me, it would be impossible that I should *not* think about them."

"Then I am satisfied. Take as much time as you need to get used to the idea. Consider how earnestly I love you. Consider what your life would be as mistress of Reddclift. I am sensible of the fact that, with your connections and rank, you could have every reason to aspire to something higher. With all your attractions, you might marry anybody – a man of title or great wealth. My own claims are modest by comparison. I can only promise I will do everything within my power to see that you are happy at Reddclift. Alterations to suit your taste, exertions for your comfort, allowances for your freedom of activity: nothing shall be left unattended to.

"That is what I offer you, Miss Darcy. If you can like it well enough, then I hope you will say yes. It is not for myself alone that I wish it; it is for Abigail and Amelia as well. They would be fortunate indeed to gain such a mother as you would be to them. Had I not been thoroughly convinced on that point, I would never have asked you. My own feelings must always be secondary to what is best for my children, as I am sure you can appreciate. Luckily, what is good for them in this case happens to be the very thing most particularly desired by their father as well.

"There. I think I have gone on quite long enough. Do you have anything you want to ask me, Miss Darcy?"

I swallowed hard, trying to take in all that he had said. I felt the weight of his regard quite keenly. That he was willing to entrust his precious daughters to me… Well, there could be no higher compliment than that, nothing that could gratify me more. I did have one question for him, though. "Have you spoken to my brother about any of this, Mr. Sanditon?"

"Spoken to Darcy? No."

"May I ask why not?"

"Because I had an idea that you would not like it, that you would wish to make up your own mind without anybody else being the wiser. Am I correct in thinking so?"

"You are indeed, Mr. Sanditon, but what led you to that conclusion? Because of my age, most men would probably have consulted my brother first, for permission and in the hope of enlisting his influence with me on their behalf."

"I would not want you to marry me only because your brother had already sanctioned the match. Nor do I expect that you would easily yield to anybody's persuasion in such a matter. As I have said before, I have a very high opinion of you, Miss Darcy – your character, certainly, but also your abilities. Despite your youth, I trust that you are entirely capable of making your own decision. I also trust that your good brother will not stand in the way of your happiness once you have."

Mr. Sanditon did not stay much longer. I think we were both satisfied that we understood each other and that there was nothing to be gained by belaboring the question at that time. It was left in my hands to judge what was best. He trusted me to do so, and I did not take the charge lightly.

Although I had dreaded being confronted with a formal proposal from Mr. Sanditon so soon, afterward I was almost glad he had asked me. Had he not, I would have been considering his suit anyway, convinced as I already was of his ultimate intentions. Now at least, I was in possession of all the pertinent facts. I also felt I understood the gentleman much better than before. His kind regard, his humility, his patience, his profound concern for his daughters, his confidence in me – all these spoke well of him. Not that I had been in any doubt of his good character before. This was a deeper glimpse, however, a look below the surface, and it had conveyed a most favorable impression to my mind.

I was left feeling a new tenderness for Mr. Sanditon and a new appreciation for his regard. I could now more clearly picture myself by his side at Reddclift. I could imagine our life together there, raising his two children and any others we might be blessed with, working in partnership to make Reddclift something we could both be proud of, something which would endure for generations to come. What made the situation all the more ideal was its proximity to Pemberley. My marriage would not divide me from all the things and people I held dear; they would always be only a short drive away. It would be a comfortable life, and one not devoid of meaning and satisfaction. That I could well believe. But was it enough on which to found my future? Were fondness and respect a suitable substitute for love – or preferably, the dependable precursors to it?

I thought and walked, walked and thought some more, all without reaching any conclusions. Mr. Sanditon might have expressed confidence in my ability to decide rightly, but I doubted it myself. The saving grace was that I did not need to make up my mind immediately. "Take as much time as you need," he had graciously said. Very well, then; I would do just that. Nothing in haste; nothing under duress. Those would be my watchwords in the weeks to come.

- 15 -

Making for London

I had five full days alone to reflect on what had passed between Mr. Sanditon and myself, five full days to agonize over the choice I had before me. That was the length of the interval my brother and Elizabeth were away at Heatheridge. I was not quite so self-absorbed as to never consider them, most especially the reason for their going. Thoughts of Jane and prayers for her safe delivery claimed their fair share as well. It was a relief, therefore, when a letter from my sister-in-law arrived to assure me that all was well in that quarter. In fact, the Bingleys were doubly blessed, being made the parents of not one but two healthy infants.

"A boy and a girl, according to your message," I said when William and Elizabeth alighted from the carriage upon their return. "How exciting! Now, do tell me the rest."

We exchanged embraces, and then Elizabeth held on to my shoulders, studying me closely. "Are you quite well, Georgiana? You look tired."

I was, for I had slept poorly the last several nights. "Oh, yes, I am very well," I lied, trying to arrange my countenance into a more convincing mask.

"No, Elizabeth is correct," said my brother. "Your color is off. You have been ill; I can always tell."

"It is nothing, really – only a headache this morning, which has gone. Now, tell me about the Bingleys' twins. I must know all."

Although I doubt that either of them was fully convinced by my explanation, to my relief, they pursued their enquiries into my health no further. Instead, Elizabeth answered my request for information with, "Well, I am no expert on babies, but to me they seem quite perfect in every way. The nurse pronounced them healthy, and I declare that they will grow up to look just like their parents. Little

Charles is the image of his father, and Frances favors Jane. Do not you think so, Darcy?"

"I can give you no account of it," he said dismissively. "How one can remark a resemblance between a newly born infant and any adult is beyond my comprehension. Apparently, it requires a livelier imagination than I possess."

"Your brother, Georgiana, pretends to have little interest in infants of any description. However, you would not have thought so had you seen the charming picture he made holding his niece and nephew." This brought a chastening glare from her husband, I noticed. "Nevertheless, I do not know when I have ever seen two people more thrilled to be parents and more suited to the role than Jane and Mr. Bingley."

"Is Jane recovering well?" I inquired.

"Amazingly well," Elizabeth answered. "After what she went through, I was surprised to see so little lasting effect. The nurse says if no fever develops within the week, there is nothing more to fear."

"And then we can set off for London," William said in conclusion of the former topic and introduction of the succeeding one. "Have you managed to work up any enthusiasm for our trip into town yet, Georgiana?"

"I hardly know. One day I am quite convinced that I never wish to leave Pemberley, and the next I am desperate to be off." I stopped with a little gasp, dropping my eyes and feeling myself coloring. "How silly of me," I added with a nervous laugh. "I really cannot imagine why I said such a thing. Please forgive my nonsense."

It was not silly of me to reveal so much of the way I was feeling; it was careless and stupid, since I had already decided to say nothing about Mr. Sanditon's offer at present. Every time I considered his proposal – and in truth I had thought of little else for days – I was torn between its merits and its compromises, between my long-standing wish to be treated as an adult and my desperate desire to avoid the responsibility of making a decision of such magnitude.

I had always been happy at Pemberley, where I prized the quiet atmosphere of its seclusion. When in my life any kind of trouble had threatened, my home had been my safe retreat. Why would I ever wish to leave it? Only recently, the peace of the place had been interrupted. Pemberley was no longer a perfect haven from trouble; my troubles had barged right through the front door. Bad news had found me there. Importunate questions had trespassed. Decisions were demanded.

Perhaps, then, it was time for a dose of new perspective. Perhaps an escape to a larger, noisier world would be just the thing. I could test my wings in a more cosmopolitan setting, be entertained and distracted nearly round the clock. In the frenetic pace of London society, I would have little time to contemplate my own troubles. Surely the perpetual racket of the place would drown out all else. I knew it would be only a temporary reprieve, but there was a certain attraction in it nonetheless. So I cheerfully promised my brother and sister I would go and make the best of it.

Elizabeth ventured one more attempt, in private, to solicit some further explanation for my odd comments and seeming distress.

"Is it Fitzwilliam?" she asked. "Perfect composure is not to be expected after only a few months, I suppose. Still, I thought you had got past the worst of it."

I felt like laughing and crying all at once, for poor Elizabeth did not know the half of it. Nor did I wish her to. "Nothing is amiss," I told her. "Nothing of any consequence, at least. Cannot a girl have her little mysteries and whims – and an occasional silly remark – without being called to account for every detail? Really, Lizzy, you make far too much of this nonsense. I know you mean well, but I would be very much obliged if you would say no more about it."

Perhaps I was a little harsh with her, but I needed to put an end to that line of questioning at once. I cannot even say why, or why I was unwilling to reveal to my sister the business concerning Mr. Sanditon. She had already proved herself a trustworthy confidante, yet still I held back.

I think it was my way of putting off having to deal with the situation. So long as I was the only one who knew of the question that had been asked, nobody else would be looking at me, speculating about what I would answer and when. Mr. Sanditon knew, of course, but he had promised not to press me for an early answer; I was to take all the time I needed. It turned out, however, that he was less capable of patience than he had professed to be.

~~*~~

When another week passed and we heard from Jane that all was well at Heatheridge, there was no more reason to delay our starting off for London. I had not seen Mr. Sanditon since the day of his proposal, but now I knew I would, at least briefly, for he was bringing Charlotte Collins to us the morning of our departure.

It had been my brother's idea. "Do you suppose Mrs. Collins would care to join us on our journey south?" he had asked Elizabeth when we three were gathered at breakfast the day after their return from Heatheridge. "We will have plenty of room for her, and she might visit her friends in Hertfordshire while we are in London."

"How kind you are, Mr. Darcy! I daresay Charlotte would jump at the chance. Perhaps it would even allow her to attend your cousin Anne's wedding, which would have been out of the question for her otherwise. I know she still feels an attachment to that family. You shouldn't mind, should you, Georgiana?"

"Not at all. Mrs. Collins is excellent company. I think it is an inspired idea."

A note had therefore been dispatched to Reddclift cottage, outlining the plan. Mrs. Collins shortly accepted the offer of transportation, with gratitude and with the information that Mr. Sanditon had volunteered to drive her over to Pemberley himself. Accordingly, they came. Upon entering the house, Charlotte immediately commenced to again thank her benefactors for the extraordinary kindness of conveying her into Hertfordshire.

While this exchange was going forward, Mr. Sanditon held my attention by means of a long, earnest look. Although it made me a little uneasy, especially for the worry that the others might notice, I could not turn away. It was an opportunity not to be wasted. His feelings I knew; it was my own I needed more chance to weigh. Did my heart leap at seeing him again? Did his presence kindle in me renewed ideas of domestic felicity? Was it pleasurable to imagine myself in his embrace? I waited for clear answers to come. I looked into my soul and Mr. Sanditon's eyes, but I could discern nothing definitive in either place.

Breaking the spell at last, the gentleman turned to my brother, asking, "How long do you anticipate being in town, sir?"

"At least a month, I expect."

"I know many people hold the London season as something not to be missed," continued Mr. Sanditon, "but I confess, I cannot fathom the attraction. I much prefer the quiet of a country life. Do not you agree, Miss Darcy?"

I could only blush and stammer.

William responded to the question in my place. "I believe all three of us prefer the country for the most part. Still, an occasional trip to town provides welcome variety. Business requires me to go in any event, and I shall be very glad for such agreeable company."

"Then all that is left for me to do is wish you a safe journey and an enjoyable stay. Meanwhile, I shall dearly miss your society here. Now that I have become accustomed to it, I shall not gladly return to my old reclusive ways. London's gain is my loss."

When it was time to go, Mr. Sanditon escorted me outside to the awaiting carriage, maneuvering so well as to have a few private words with me along the way. "I will miss you more than the others, Miss Darcy," he began in a low voice, audible only to myself thanks to the noise of departure preparations. "Have you been thinking about my offer?"

"Yes; I promised that I should."

"And have you come to any… conclusions?"

"No, sir. It has been less than two weeks, and you said I might have all the time I wanted."

"So I did. So I did. You are quite right to remind me, Miss Georgiana. It is just that when one has determined the companion of one's future happiness, one wishes to begin that future as soon as possible. Please forgive my impatience. I will not press you again; you have my word as a gentleman."

"Thank you. And you have *my* word that I will keep you in suspense no longer than absolutely necessary. You shall have my answer when I return, if not before."

"That is very fine of you. I will pray for your safe travels as well as for clarity in reaching your decision. I cannot help hoping it will turn out a mutually satisfying one. Until we meet again, then, Miss Darcy."

Since we had nearly reached the carriage door, I had no opportunity to respond, not that I had much of any use to convey. I merely said a civil goodbye and allowed Mr. Sanditon to hand me in to sit alongside Mrs. Collins. When my brother, who was already settled in the other seat with Elizabeth, gave the order that set the coach into motion, I took one last look out the window at Mr. Sanditon's receding figure. He waved and I smiled in return. Next time I saw him, he would expect to hear if I would marry him or not. At the time, I could only speculate as to when that scene would take place, and I could never have guessed all that would occur in the interim.

~~*~~

Due to my continuing preoccupation with Mr. Sanditon and his offer, I am afraid I made a very poor companion to my carriage mates, especially on the first day of our journey when I spent the greater share of my time staring out the window at the rain. My brother was just as unsociable, I noticed, although I could not begin to consider why; I had my own tangled problems to unravel.

Consequently, Charlotte and Elizabeth were left to entertain each other as well as they might over the miles of dirty roads and hours of travel. I suppose I did not hear above half of what they said between themselves – much of it talk about their shared past or people I barely knew. At other times, though, when they spoke of things within my scope of interest, passively listening to their commonplace chatter was a pleasant diversion from more serious contemplations.

"How long does your mother remain at Heatheridge?" I heard Charlotte inquire.

"She has promised for a month, but my own prediction has her hurrying for home somewhat earlier, Kitty in tow. Her nerves will simply not stand it for long. Two infants crying at once? As I told Jane, I think Mama will soon decide the greater felicity is to be found in boasting to her friends and neighbors about her grand-children from a safe distance."

"You could very well be right, Lizzy. And will Jane be sorry to lose her help?"

"I think not. I believe Mama's sole contribution to Jane's comfort came by her insistence beforehand that a nurse be hired for the baby, or babies as it has turned out. *That* is the only person whose help would be missed now." After a minute or two, Elizabeth struck off in a new line. "Your family will all be very pleased to see you Charlotte. I am so glad you were able to accept the offer of trans-portation, although I suppose Ruth was sorry to see you go."

"Perhaps so, but she would never hinder me. As for my family, I believe they *shall* be happy to have me home again, as long as they are guaranteed it is to be only a temporary arrangement. Considering that they long dreaded the idea that I might never leave for an establishment of my own, and then that I might return again when Mr. Collins died, a visit of a month cannot seem like much of a burden by comparison."

"Oh, Charlotte, you do make me laugh! How could a person as clever and useful as yourself ever be a considered a burden? I should think your mother ought to be glad for your assistance, especially with all your younger siblings."

"That is the problem, you see: too many mouths to feed already without mine adding to their number. No, they will be pleased to see me come but even more pleased to see me go away again."

We broke our journey that night at an inn where we had stayed many times before, and by the next morning, things were looking brighter in all respects. The dismal weather of the day before had dramatically improved, and with it my spirits. With so much country now between us, I was able to distance myself somewhat from my quandary over Mr. Sanditon. Anything could happen in a month, I reasoned, especially in London. The world might look an entirely different place by the time I left it again. Everything that currently seemed so ambiguous might well have settled into a clearly defined order by then. I would not need to speculate and conjecture any more; I would know where I stood and what to do. At least it did not seem unreasonable that I might.

But it was not only my outlook that had improved by the second day; my brother's had as well. In fact, the entire tone of our collective conversation had perceptibly shifted to something much more cheerful. No longer were any of us focused on what had been left behind. Now we talked of the anticipated pleasures awaiting each of us at our destinations.

Upon reaching Hertfordshire, we first drove to Lucas Lodge to deliver Charlotte to her family, and, after accepting an hour's hospitality there, we proceeded on to Longbourn. With Mrs. Bennet and Kitty still at Heatheridge, we anticipated finding only Mr. Bennet and Mary at home. The visit had not been prearranged, Elizabeth deciding that it would be great fun to arrive unannounced instead.

Mr. Bennet was indeed taken by surprise and delighted to be so, considering it a compliment to his own style of coming in on people unexpectedly. He quickly claimed my brother and sister for himself, ultimately convincing them that we should stay the night rather than continuing on to London.

"You must take pity on an old man who is sadly starved for good conversation," he said in pleading his case. "Fresh company and original ideas are what I require. Sir William Lucas and I have long since grown weary of each other's threadbare stories, and I must confess, Lizzy, that I often find your sister Mary's discourse unpalatable. It contains too much of the didactic for regular consumption, especially since I have quite given up any hope of self-reform."

Mary wisely pretended not to hear. Instead she engaged me to sit with her, taking turns at the spinet with her leading off. This arrangement was perfectly agreeable to me. While it is true that Miss Mary Bennet is not a great natural talent – something I had heard by report long before I first made my own observations – to my mind, what she lacked in ability she made up in sincerity of effort. In truth, I had much rather spend an evening with a person who shares my pure enjoyment of music than one who has achieved a mechanical proficiency without any investiture of the heart.

"You played that so beautifully, Miss Darcy," she said with a touch of longing when I finished performing a little something from memory.

"I thank you for your kind words, Miss Bennet. It gratifies me to hear that you found it pleasing. A compliment means more when it comes from one who has an educated ear. Your playing has improved as well, I think."

"I do hope so. Still, no matter how much I practice a piece, it seems I never can get it just right. If I aim for playing correctly, it comes out sounding so pedantic. If I set my mind on playing with expression, then accuracy suffers instead. You seem to have mastered both. How do you do it?"

"I have simply put to use the gift I have been given; that is how I look at the question. And I suppose I have been very well taught."

"The finest music masters from London, I presume?"

"Well, yes. In this, I have been very fortunate also. My brother has seen to it that I have had everything I needed by way of the best instruction. He is so good."

"I had very little guidance myself, and there is nothing I regret more in the way of my upbringing. My sisters all begged for a London season; all I wanted was a London music master."

"You must be proud of what you have been able to achieve on your own, Miss Bennet."

"I once was very vain of my abilities, it is true. But I have since then been suitably humbled. Now, especially when I hear a true proficient such as yourself, I hope I know better than to flatter myself that my playing is anything special."

"You must not despair, however. I daresay you are one of the most accomplished musicians in your local society."

"I do not despair, Miss Darcy. I play well enough for my own amusement and to be of some use to others. And I still dream of affording some proper instruction one day. I hardly know when that might be, though."

I wondered the same thing. Surely, if Mr. and Mrs. Bennet were inclined to help in this regard, they would have done so long ago. And Mary could have very few resources of her own. Yet I hoped she would find a way. Such a passionate desire for learning must not be forever thwarted.

- 16 -

The Season Begins

We said our farewells to Longbourn's inmates early the next day, and then an easy morning's drive took us to our house in town. The servants – the group made up of the permanent staff supplemented by those sent ahead of us from Pemberley – assembled to welcome us before we could exit the carriage. No doubt the look-out had been on in earnest, our arrival having been expected since the previous afternoon.

"Good morning, Watkins," said my brother to the butler upon entering. "I trust everything is in order."

"Yes, sir. You will find that all your instructions have been carefully attended to. The trunks arrived yesterday, and there are a few cards and letters waiting when you are ready."

"Very good. Mrs. Paddington, I hope you are well."

The housekeeper curtsied and replied, "I am, sir. I thank you. Welcome home, Mr. Darcy, Mrs. Darcy, Miss Georgiana."

Elizabeth greeted the senior servants, and I took my turn as well. It was a homecoming of sorts, for I had spent a good portion of my life in this house, and some of the faces before me I had known since infancy. I did not linger long, however; I was impatient to retreat to my own apartments in order that I might change from my traveling clothes and freshen up a bit. Lilly, my maid, followed me up. She had been with us since she was twelve and I, the same age. So it felt much as if we had grown up together. By rights, I should have called her by her surname, now that she was a lady's maid, but I could never get used to 'Perkins.'

"I am glad to see you arrived safely, Lilly," I told her.

"Yes, Miss, and I already unpacked your trunk and put away all your things. Your first true London season, Miss! Meeting fine beaux at all them fancy balls and parties! You must be very excited."

"Yes, of course," I said. Although I counted Lilly as a friend, not just a servant, I would not begin to try to explain my state of ambivalence to her. Would I be excited to meet new beaux, as Lilly termed them? If I were to meet a man who would make all the other problematic characters in my life fade to insignificance, that would be a wonderful blessing indeed. Otherwise, the last thing I needed was to add to my list of complications.

"A letter come for you, Miss," she said when we had reached my rooms. "Here it is. Maybe it be from one of your handsome beaux."

I took the missive and scanned the direction. "I am sorry to disappoint you, Lilly, but it is from my friend Andrea Heywood."

"But Miss Heywood, now, she has a fine-looking brother. Does she not?"

"As a matter of fact, she does. But that is neither here nor there, for I am certainly not going to marry him."

Over dinner, I informed my brother and sister, "I had a letter from Andrea Heywood waiting for me. She asks that we give her family the earliest possible notice of our arrival in town. It seems they have a whole host of social engagements in which they wish to include us."

"You and I can begin making calls and leaving cards tomorrow," Elizabeth told me, "while your brother attends to some business in the city. That should be prompt enough notice even for Miss Heywood. However, we need not feel obligated to her or to anybody else to set such a frantic pace for ourselves as some people deem necessary during the season, or to accept every invitation either."

"Certainly not," William agreed. "We shall be very selective. I know the goal is for you to meet new people, Georgiana – eligible potential suitors, if we are to speak plainly about it – but we owe our first duty to our confirmed friends, not to strangers."

"Of course. I would take no pleasure in always being surrounded by strangers."

We were silent for a few minutes while we continued our meal. When I glanced up at my brother, though, I could see he had something else on his mind, apparently undecided as to what to do about it.

Finally he said in a solemn tone, "One more thing, Georgiana."

"Yes, what is it?"

"While we are in London, you will oblige me by never going out alone. You are to always take your sister with you and at least one footman as escort. Is that clear?"

I hesitated, not because his instructions were imprecise, but because it seemed such an odd request, especially as to his manner in making it. Something about the business had given my brother obvious discomfort.

"As you wish, William," I said, choosing not to challenge his authority. Although I might have bristled a little at once more feeling myself ordered about like a child – no discussion, no explanations – in truth, following his instructions would be no hardship; they exactly reflected what would make me most comfortable in any case. Still, I could not help wondering what I was not being told. When I looked to Elizabeth for some clue, her carefully impassive countenance told me nothing.

~~*~~

Once we announced our presence to all our acquaintance in town, it did not take long before invitations began arriving. Elizabeth and I probably would have both engaged for attending more of these affairs than my brother could possibly bear. He really was very generous, however, and in the end I had no complaints. We attended quite as many balls and parties as I could have enjoyed without exhaustion.

I threw myself into the gaiety without reservation, and I think on the whole it did me good. Being kept so occupied every day left me little time to dwell on other matters, such as the difficulties with the two gentlemen who would have otherwise dominated my thoughts – Mr. Sanditon and his devotion to me, Colonel Fitzwilliam and his devotion to someone else.

"I think you are wise to enter into the spirit of things as much as possible," Elizabeth said to me one day after we had been in town a little more than two weeks. "Who can say what may come of it? You may yet meet someone, even tonight perhaps, who will make you forget your cares more permanently. Anything can happen at a ball, you know."

Even though Elizabeth knew my troubles only in part, I could not help hoping she was entirely correct. As for that particular night and that particular ball, however, nothing so revolutionary occurred. Instead of some new gentleman entering my life, I had someone very familiar to deal with.

Since Henry had been out when Elizabeth and I called at the Heywoods' townhouse the morning after our arrival, a few more days elapsed before I saw him at an evening party. The encounter did not take me by surprise. Since the soiree to which I refer was given by mutual friends, I had fully expected Henry would be there as well. I was even looking forward to it as my opportunity to evaluate his intentions in person, to see how much his feelings for me might have warmed or cooled since I saw him four months earlier. Then I could prepare my response accordingly. My dearest wish was that *no* response would be necessary, that his regard for me had been nothing more than a passing fancy encouraged by his sister. If it had fortuitously died an early, natural death, we might all go on happily as we had before.

Although nothing overt occurred at this first meeting or any of those that followed, I could clearly see that Henry still held me as the object of his special admiration. He was far more attentive than mere friendship required. Something needed to be done about it, I decided, and soon.

I liked the Heywoods very much and desired that nothing would occur to mar the friendship that had long persisted between our two families. For that reason – to spare Henry as much as possible and to avoid an unpleasant scene – I knew I must put him on his guard without delay. He must not be allowed to nurture the notion of a match between us. Even if I could have felt for him what I should to make our marrying eligible, there would always be another obstacle, one just as insurmountable. Henry's life was in London – his home, his family, his future with the bank. If I were to become his wife, I would be expected to make my home there as well, which would never do. Although I had no objection to visiting the metropolis from time to time, I could not have resigned myself to being a permanent resident.

No, it was quite impossible, and the sooner Mr. Heywood understood that, the better.

This was my firm resolve, to speak to Henry at my earliest opportunity. In the meantime, we kept ourselves very busy with dinners, concerts, and the opera, seeing the Heywoods here and there. It was not until the ball that I finally had the chance for private conversation with Henry. He wasted no time presenting himself when we arrived, promptly soliciting me for the first two dances. Andrea also hurried over when she saw me.

"Have you asked her yet?" she inquired of her brother.

"Yes, of course I have," he answered, irritably.

Turning to me, Andrea went on. "And I trust you have said yes, dear Georgiana. Surely there can be no one here with whom you would rather dance than my handsome brother!"

"If you will allow me opportunity, dear friend, I will give your brother my answer now," I said. "Yes, Mr. Heywood, I should be very pleased to dance the first two with you"

This much was true. It would be an evil to postpone what must be done, and the necessary communication might as well be delivered against the agreeable backdrop of a dance as any other place, I decided.

Satisfied of my acquiescence, Andrea gave my hand an affectionate squeeze and then drifted off to find her own partner. Mr. Heywood offered me his arm, which I accepted, and we strolled to where the set was forming up.

"You do me great honor, Miss Darcy," he said. "I hope to repay your kindness by being of service to you, seeing to your every comfort by staying close by your side throughout the evening."

Hearing this, I knew I could not delay; I must correct his ideas about me and about his position at once. "That is very generous, I am sure, Mr. Heywood," said I, "but not at all what I wish for."

We were set in motion as the music began.

"You cannot mean that," Henry responded at his first opening.

"Oh, but I assure you that I do," I said as we passed by one another again. "I would not lie to an old friend."

"Be that as it may," he continued, fitting bits of conversation in as well as the movements of the dance allowed. "I feel it my duty… indeed, it is my responsibility… to give you benefit of my protection."

I was glad for the time to think what to say which our being momentarily carried apart afforded me. When we came back together, I explained, "This is a private ball, Mr. Heywood. What possible danger could I be exposed to in this environment? And I have my brother watching over me." I nodded in William's direction. "He stands right over there. Do you see?"

Henry looked, and then, at the next opportunity, he continued. "Very well. Perhaps you do not require my protection, Miss Darcy. Still, I hoped you might be glad for my attentions; they are kindly meant."

We had reached the bottom of the set and were idle for a minute or two. Here was the chance to get my point across directly. "I do truly appreciate your kind attentions as a testimony to our friendship, Mr. Heywood, which is doubtless how you mean them. Nevertheless, it would be unfair to ourselves and uncivil to the company at large to keep too long to one partner. I know you must be of the same mind, for I remember quite distinctly that, when we last met in Derbyshire, you yourself expressed concern that I should spend so much time in the confined society of the country. Now that I am finally come to town, I feel certain you would not wish to restrict the variety of my social intercourse at the very outset of my season. Am I wrong?"

"Well, not when you put it like that, I suppose."

"Good. I knew we should be in agreement when once we properly understood each other. As your friend, I will always be happy to see you, Henry. And I will be equally happy when it is my turn to dance with you. But you and I are only friends, after all, which is not an exclusive arrangement. In such a case, the two parties must both be free to dance with others as well. You must allow it to be so."

Henry made no further remonstration, and although he labored through the rest of the first dance in a pensive silence, he recovered enough by the second as to behave much like his usual charming self again. For all this, I was profoundly relieved. I had clearly (and repeatedly) classified my feelings for him as 'friendship' – to the point where he could not have failed to understand me – and he had accepted it graciously, like a gentleman, without creating an ugly scene. Or so I thought.

~~*~~

My satisfaction over so adroitly managing the Henry Heywood situation was short lived, for as it happened, he came to the house the very next afternoon with serious business on his mind. Mr. Heywood was shown up to the drawing room where Elizabeth and I received him. My brother was out at the time.

Henry's visit was certainly unexpected, but I did not at first suspect anything unpleasant in it. I thought he must have come on some errand for his sister or his mother. But the earnest expression of his countenance and the formality with which he greeted us seemed out of place between friends of so longstanding an acquaintance.

"Please, sir, do sit down," invited Elizabeth, "and tell us to what we owe the honor of your visit. Do you bring a message from your mother?"

Keeping to his feet, he answered with a noticeable tremor in his voice. "No, ma'am. I come on my own account. I wonder if you would be so kind, Mrs. Darcy, as to grant me the honor of a private audience with your fair sister?"

At this, my composure began to crumble in bewilderment and dread. Although Henry's words and manner seemed to clearly indicate his amorous intentions, I simply could not believe that to be his true mission, not after the trouble I had taken to warn him off only the day before. Surely he could not have failed to understand me, I thought, even as Elizabeth agreed to his request.

"Of course, Mr. Heywood," she said. "Georgiana, you may stay and hear what the gentleman has to say."

Before I could recover enough to object, Elizabeth had exited the room, closing the doors behind her. I was alone with Mr. Heywood, and there was nothing to do but stand and face whatever would happen next.

Henry came closer, stopping less than three feet in front of me. "Miss Darcy," he began very tenderly, "you must know why I am here."

I *did* know then, but I said, "I cannot imagine, unless…" Breaking off in the middle, I circled away to reposition myself behind the sofa I had been in front of before. "I certainly hope your sister has not talked you into doing something… something silly."

"Andrea has nothing to do with this," he said with what I took for a mixture of pain and indignation in his expression. "And as for my intentions, I hardly think it silly for a man to apply for the hand of the woman he loves. It cannot be silly to desire an union so suitable and what must be to the mutual satisfaction of both families.

I should hope such honorable and sincere sentiments will never be laughed at by anybody, especially by you, Miss Darcy!"

"Forgive me, sir; I am not laughing. I do not find this situation at all amusing, I assure you."

"Then what *do* you think about what I have said?"

"I am truly at a loss, Mr. Heywood. Did you not understand my meaning last night, how I was attempting to caution you against this sort of thing by my talk of friendship?"

"If that was your intention, you should have spoken more plainly, madam. I would have you know that I heard something quite different from your lips, something far more encouraging. By speaking of the limitations of our being only friends, I believed you were giving me a hint that we should take this next step, that if we were engaged we might spend as much time together as we liked from now on."

"Sir, either your ears or your mind has deceived you if you think I meant to say any such thing. As much as I value you as a friend, Henry, it is my conviction that we can never be more to each other. Please pardon me, but I cannot accept your proposal."

He stood there a minute longer, turning his hat in his hands and not saying a word, before he finally was decided to some definite course of action.

"In that case, you must excuse me, Miss Darcy. I shall not trouble you any longer with my presence," he said, turning sharply and beating a hasty retreat.

As soon as he had gone, my tears began to flow – tears born more out of consternation than for sorrow. I still could not believe it had come to this after the pains I had been at to avoid such a scene! Too perturbed to sit still, I began pacing the room, giving vent to my frustrations as I went along. Even Elizabeth's entry did nothing to sidetrack me from my rambling rant.

"We were having a perfectly delightful time, were we not? Why must he spoil everything by asking me to marry him when he knew perfectly well that I must reject him? I was always extremely careful; he could not have misunderstood me. Yet it seems he prefers to deceive himself. He forces me to say things that will hurt him, and then he resents me for it. Is that fair? I like him very much, to be sure. I like his whole family! We have been such good friends, but now all that is ruined forever! Now, there will be nothing but awkwardness and irritation between us. Oh, why must men always make such a muddle of things? Why cannot they leave well enough alone?"

I then turned to address the remainder of my diatribe directly to my sister. "What a disaster this is, Elizabeth. I did try to stop him, to prevent the embarrassment of a declaration and refusal, but he *would* do it anyway. Can men never be satisfied with friendship? Why must they demand more than it is in my power to give?"

"Do try to calm yourself, dear," urged Elizabeth. "I know you are upset, and I understand your frustration, believe me. But pray, have a little compassion for poor Mr. Heywood. I am quite certain he did not fall in love merely for the purpose of vexing you. In any case, you must not condemn all men for the actions of one."

"But it is not just one man; now there are *two*!"

- 17 -

Secrets and Mysteries

"Now there are *two*!"

My impassioned words echoed in the room.

Immediately, my hands flew to cover my mouth, lest anything else incriminating escape. Elizabeth and I stood staring at each other, our eyes wide in astonishment. What a sight we must have made for my brother, who happened upon us just then.

Elizabeth regained her self command first. "My dear," she said to her husband, "I did not know that you were returned already."

"What on earth is going on here, Elizabeth?" he demanded. "Georgiana?"

Elizabeth waited for me to answer him, although I could not immediately say a word. I needed a moment to compose myself and blot away my tears. I then shot my sister a desperate look, hoping she understood my plea for her discretion, before turning to my brother.

"You have missed all the excitement, William. As you see, Elizabeth and I are still not recovered from the shock," I said, trying to still my quavering voice. "We have had an unexpected visitor this afternoon."

He looked startled. "Good heavens! Not Wi… I say, is everything all right?"

"Be not alarmed. It was only Henry Heywood," I said, attempting a bright tone. "And what do you think? He has made me an offer of marriage. Of course I have had to refuse him. I do not love him, and I could never resign myself to live all the rest of my life in London in any case. Still, I am sorry to have hurt him. And I would have kept the incident completely to myself, out of respect for Mr. Heywood's honor, except that Elizabeth was here when it happened, and so you must know it as well, Brother."

The effort of this speech took my last ounce of emotional strength. So when I felt more tears coming, I could not stop them. They slipped from my eyes and down my cheeks unchallenged. Nor had I the will to object to my brother's gathering me into his comforting embrace, as he had done countless times before. It was still a familiar refuge – although I visited it but rarely now compared to former years – and I rested there some minutes. At length, however, I was recovered enough to remove from it to the solitude of my own room.

I was vastly relieved that Elizabeth made no attempt to follow me upstairs, for this meant I would be spared, at least temporarily, her interrogation into my careless disclosure that 'now there are two.' I was thinking of Mr. Sanditon, of course, but I did not wish her to know. Yet I feared she would not easily be put off the scent. I'd had a look at her eyes before William came in, where I could almost see her mind at work, following the implication of what I had said to its natural conclusion. She was sure to ask me about it eventually. For the moment, however, I was safe.

I suppose William and Elizabeth decided between themselves what to say over dinner on the subject of Henry's proposal. The united front they presented was entirely calm, reasonable, and considerate.

"I trust you will not take this business with Henry Heywood too much to heart, Georgiana," said my brother. "I daresay it will all blow over in time with no permanent harm done."

"Poor Henry. He did look quite upset." Now that I had got over the worst of my exasperation, I could truly feel some compassion for him.

"He is young," said Elizabeth. "He will recover. And I am sure you did all you could to spare his feelings, so there is nothing at all to blame yourself for."

"I hope his family will see it that way as well."

My brother, sitting next to me at table, reached over to pat my hand. "You mustn't worry about that, Georgiana. I should think our friendship with the Heywoods is stout enough to withstand much worse than this. Now..." An abrupt change in his tone signaled a new topic. Turning to Elizabeth, he asked, "...is it all settled that Mrs. Collins will allow us to drive her down to Hunsford for the wedding?"

Ah, Colonel Fitzwilliam's wedding to Anne de Bourgh: not a subject I could enter into with any enthusiasm either, but one I had by this time learnt to hear mentioned with tolerable composure.

"Oh, yes," answered Elizabeth. "Sir William is to send her here in his carriage a day or two ahead. It did occur to me, Georgiana, that we might ask Charlotte to stay on with you afterward, as chaperone, if your brother and I have had our fill of London by then and you have not. She would make you a pleasant and suitable companion, and she might benefit as well by exposure to better society than is ordinarily within her reach. What do you think of the idea?"

Although this was the first I had heard of the scheme, I liked it at once. I was in no hurry to return to Derbyshire, especially since I was just as unprepared to give Mr. Sanditon an answer as I had been when I came away a few weeks before. So I said, "I am sure I should find Mrs. Collins's company very agreeable."

"Of course there is no need to decide anything now," said my brother. "We will all stay until the wedding, and after that we can make our arrangements. Although if business does not detain me, I am certain *I* shall be ready by then to be gone."

"As you speak of business, Darcy, it puts me in mind to ask why you returned so soon this afternoon," said Elizabeth. "You did say that you had something pressing that demanded your immediate attention, and yet you could not have been gone much above an hour, I am sure."

He frowned. "Yes, I had an appointment with someone, but the gentleman failed to keep it. I waited half an hour, and he never came. So it was a wasted trip."

"How provoking! I hope you will not consent to meet that unreliable fellow again. What good can come of doing business with someone who cannot be trusted to keep his commitments?"

"Unfortunately, Elizabeth, I may have to in defense of my own interests. We cannot always choose with whom we must associate." He sounded weary of the subject and did not elaborate further.

When I saw him weighed down by cares, as he looked at that moment, I did long to be of more use to my brother. Yet he had never allowed me anywhere near the business of managing Pemberley Estates. Here again, I was to be sheltered and shielded as a child, and a female one at that. Perhaps he would let Elizabeth help him, though. I did hope so. No man, no matter how strong, can go on carrying a great burden alone forever. And I feared that was exactly what my brother was attempting to do.

~~*~~

The next morning, I returned to my room after breakfast. Half an hour later, there came a knock at the door.

Entering, Elizabeth said, "Do you mind? I was feeling a little lonely downstairs."

"Of course not, but where is William?"

"Gone out on business again, I'm afraid," Elizabeth said with a sigh. "He would tell me no more than that, but at least it does give us some time for a private talk."

So here it was – the inquiries I had expected and dreaded. I turned and walked to the window, looking down at the street where carts and carriages rattled their way across the gray cobbles. "I was not aware that we had anything in particular to discuss, Lizzy."

"My dear Georgiana," Elizabeth responded gently, "I hope you are aware that your brother and I have tried to respect your privacy, even though it has often been difficult. It has distressed us both to see you suffering under such an obvious strain these several weeks past without knowing how to help you. Now that I finally have a clue to the cause of your distress, I cannot in good conscience turn a blind eye to it any longer. I must speak to you, dearest, about what you said yesterday, that *now there are two*."

I objected at once, claiming there was nothing to tell. I'm afraid I babbled on at length with nonsensical arguments that sounded weak, even to myself. Although I had rolled the question over and over in my mind, I had not been able to invent a single credible explanation for what I had said… except the truth.

"There is no use denying it," Elizabeth concluded. "The truth is that Mr. Heywood is not the only one, or even the first, to propose to you. Is that not so, Georgiana? There can be no other interpretation. I know you did not mean to say it, but since you *did* say it, you must tell me the rest. Have I not proved myself a trustworthy confidant?"

"Yes, but… Oh, Lizzy, it is so embarrassing and perplexing."

"I have some experience in these matters. Let me help you along a bit. I believe I can guess the identity of your other admirer. It is Mr. Sanditon, is it not?"

It was almost a relief to hear his name spoken aloud; my need for evasion was evidently over. "How did you know?"

"When I understood your meaning, there clearly was no one else it could be, although I was too blind to see it before."

I took a deep breath and let it out again. I felt the floodgates open and my secrets came pouring out. "I was blind to it myself for a time. In fact, I cannot even tell you when it started. I think perhaps he admired me almost from the beginning of our acquaintance. Mr. Sanditon has always been extremely kind and gentlemanly to me. Then, the night we dined at Reddclift, when I first suspected his intentions, I began to consider the idea myself, that I could make a life there as his wife if he asked me. It seemed at least possible we could be happy together. He certainly believes it, and so he has tried to persuade me."

"And to all this I was completely insensible!" confessed Elizabeth. "The two of you were rarely alone together. When did he find the opportunity to actually propose?"

"The day Jane delivered. Do you remember? Mr. Sanditon remained a while after you and my brother left for Heatheridge. That is when he formally declared his love, and I have been in turmoil ever since."

"What answer did you give him?"

"I said that I was very fond of him – which is quite true – but that I needed time to think. The day we left Pemberley, he pressed for my answer, and I told him I would give it when I returned. What shall I do, Lizzie?"

"Dear me! I cannot be the judge, at least not without being made more acquainted with the facts. You have had more time to consider. What is your own opinion?"

"Well, there are certainly strong points in favor of the match," I began, collectedly. I had so many times recited these very arguments to myself that it was no great difficulty for me to enumerate them likewise for my sister. "Surely even my brother would admit its aptness and desirability. Mr. Sanditon is a respectable gentleman and very nearly part of the family already. As for myself, I would dearly love to be settled so close to Pemberley, and I adore the little girls. I could never hope to find a better man as to character. And there is no one else that interests me in the slightest."

"Except Colonel Fitzwilliam," said Elizabeth gravely.

My heart stopped with a thud, and I inhaled sharply. I had not been prepared for *his* name to intrude into this conversation.

"Forgive me, Georgiana, but I must ask. How do your feelings for Mr. Sanditon compare with what you felt, or possibly still feel, for the colonel?"

"That is not fair, Lizzy!"

"I know it is a difficult question, but I think your answer would be quite germane. If you are still in love with Fitzwilliam, or if your feelings for Mr. Sanditon are feeble by comparison to what you once felt for the colonel, that *must* guide your decision. My dear Georgiana, please remember that you lack neither position nor financial security, and you will have a home at Pemberley as long as you wish. In your situation, there is absolutely nothing that should tempt you into matrimony – early, or indeed, ever – except love. Would it not be preferable to remain unmarried all your life rather than compromise on that principle of singular importance?"

What could I say to this? My conversation, so freely flowing a moment before, had a hit a dam that refused to be breached. I could not answer Elizabeth's questions. No matter which way I turned, no matter how diligently I looked for an alternative path to happiness, it seemed there was no way round Colonel Fitzwilliam. He had pledged himself to another woman, and still he would not let me go. Would I never be able to move forward without his specter haunting me every step of the way?

- 18 -

A State Visit

"I require your discretion in this matter too, Lizzy," I told her before our *tête-à-tête* concluded. Promise me not to tell William."

"More intrigue? Really, Georgiana, I think there are entirely too many secrets and mysteries in this household already! We would all do much better, I believe, if we were entirely open with each other – no more whispering behind closed doors, no more unexplained errands."

Although I had the distinct impression she was referring to a larger issue, I could only address my own situation. "I believe one must be allowed some privacy, even within one's own family. And I am not asking you to lie, simply not to mention this for the time being. William will know soon enough, should I decide to accept Mr. Sanditon; nothing can go forward without his knowledge and consent. Unless or until then, however, there is no need to tell him. If you are to be my confidential advisor, Elizabeth, I must know that I can trust you in this."

"You *can* trust me, and I *will* keep your confidence. In for a penny; in for a pound, I suppose. If I am to be reproved for dishonesty, it might just as well be for concealing two secrets as one."

A fresh pang of conscience assailed me. "Do not speak so, Lizzy, I beg you! You shall make me loathe myself for ever asking such a thing."

"Not at all," she said, rising to her feet. "I am sure that in your position, I should do exactly the same. In any case, who is there to judge? Only your brother, and I trust he would be the first to commend me for assisting you. I would by no means leave you friendless at this critical time, Georgiana. That would be the real crime." She held my shoulders and gave me a kiss on the cheek. "Now, remember what we discussed, my dear. You are not to allow anybody, not even the good, kind Mr. Sanditon, to talk you into matrimony until you are absolutely certain. Understood?"

I nodded solemnly.

"Very well. Then my work here is done, at least for the present. I think I had better see if your brother has returned from today's mysterious errand. I have a great curiosity to know what he has been up to all this time."

"Stay a minute, Lizzy, if you will. It seems we spend all our time talking about my concerns and problems. Tell me how *you* are feeling. Are you doing well, you and the child, I mean?"

"Very well indeed. I am vastly glad to have got over the early unpleasantness, and now nothing ails me at all. Oh, Georgiana, I know I said you should consider remaining single as preferable to marrying without affection – and I retract not a word of it – but I cannot help hoping you will someday know for yourself what I am feeling. The wonder of another life growing inside you – there is nothing else like it. Wait..." Her eyes lit with anticipation. She then took my hand and placed it flat against her rounded belly. "There!" she said moments later.

"Is that...?"

"Yes. That is your niece or nephew making its presence felt. All knees and elbows I think from the way it feels sometimes, but I trust the other parts are there as well."

"Incredible," I said in complete awe, withdrawing my hand after the movements had stilled.

"Yes, and I think I should simply burst from excitement if I did not share it with those closest to me – first your brother and now you."

"So, William has...?"

"Yes he has! Just yesterday, in fact." Elizabeth's smile was radiant. "Do not you think he has some right?" she added mischievously as she turned to go.

I felt my cheeks growing warm. Of course he had every right; he was the father. Still I did not always like to be reminded what that piece of information entailed.

After Elizabeth left me, I remained in my own apartment an hour longer, thinking over all that I had heard and experienced, thanks to her. Suddenly my sensible calculation of the points in favor and against marrying Mr. Sanditon, which I had dutifully debated back and forth with myself for weeks, seemed rather petty by comparison with the more profound issues at stake. Surely the miracle of life was not something to be explained by numbers on a tally sheet, nor could love be measured there.

As for whether or not I was still in love with Fitzwilliam, perhaps I would better be able to judge that when next I saw him. I hoped such an encounter would prove my ardor had significantly cooled – as I had assiduously schooled myself that it ought… that it *must* – and the perturbation I still felt on his account was merely a false remnant, a compliment to past devotion annoyingly slow to die away.

Regardless, it still made me wonder. Should I really allow my feelings for Fitzwilliam – past or present – to dictate what answer I gave to another man? That hardly seemed fair to Mr. Sanditon, to judge him up against someone who was not even a viable alternative. My choice was not between Mr. Sanditon and the colonel. My choice was between what Mr. Sanditon had offered me and… In truth, I did not know the rest of the equation. Only the future could fill in that blank.

~~*~~

One more equally sublime miracle was in store for me that day: the miracle of music, as performed by a very fine orchestra which happened to be in town. The entertainment had been my preference, and I could not have chosen better. It was a truly delightful concert that left me in raptures. As for my brother and sister, although they were not so effusive in their praise, their spirits seemed to have been elevated by the music as well. I believe we all three came home in a more contented state of mind than when we had gone out.

The lingering effect sent me to the pianoforte the next morning for a good two hours of dedicated practice. When at last I emerged from the spell the music had cast over me, I went to join the conversation I heard emanating from the next room.

"You have treated us to a very fine concert this morning," said William when I entered. "Just as pleasing as the one we heard last night, which I gather has renewed your enthusiasm to play."

"You are correct, as usual, Brother. I am rededicating myself to practice more diligently. I have been far too lax since we came into town."

"I can hardly agree with you there," said Elizabeth. "But by all means, play as much as you like. You will hear no complaint from either of us."

"Indeed," her husband agreed, "since we are the beneficiaries. Whilst you were playing, Georgiana, the morning post came and we read our two letters. They will both be of interest to you as well, I am sure. There is one from Jane and another from Fitzwilliam, in which he says some very pretty things about you, my dear."

I tried to remain calm as I received the letters from his hand and carried them across to the window, where I curled up in an oversized chair with my back to the others.

I forced myself to peruse the one from Jane first. It was laced with family news all through, and especially with colorful descriptions of the twins' rapid growth and developing personalities. It was a well-written, even entertaining missive, but in my impatience to get to the other, I barely did it justice. I could not wait to see what "pretty things" Fitzwilliam had said about me. Yet I knew it could not all be good, for I had seen the uneasiness in Elizabeth's countenance. I had to prepare myself for something unsettling as well. The letter read as follows:

My Dear Friends,

I trust you are all three in good health and enjoying your stay in town. You, Georgiana, must be especially admired wherever you are seen this season. I picture you now as I saw you at your birthday ball, dancing each dance with a new and eager partner. Regrettably, this time I am not so fortunate as to be one of them, although I am quite certain you are too merry to miss your old cousin in any case...

Here, then, was the "pretty" business to which my brother had referred. I took a moment to savor the words before I read on.

...Though nothing compared to London, Rosings is also playing host to an uncharacteristically busy season of activity of a different sort. There are parties, luncheons, fittings, and I

know not what. It is a great mystery to me. The prospective groom, I find, is required to be always present but never to interfere. There seems to be nothing of consequence for me to do. The ladies – in this case, primarily Lady Catherine, of course – command the attention and make every decision.

I fear that it has been a little too much for poor Anne, whose strength seems to be flagging under the strain. Her physician, Dr. Essex, appears to harbor some measure of concern for her as well, but he assures me there is no real danger. He is a fine fellow, by the way, and so solicitous of Anne. With his care, I trust she will rebound quickly once all the fuss is over. Still, it is a pity that she cannot enter more into the spirit of things, since I believe all these events are meant to please and honor the bride above anyone else. As it is, I think her mother takes the most enjoyment from them...

Poor Fitzwilliam. Knowing him as I did, I could well imagine his discomfort at being forced to endure such frivolous pageantry and especially Lady Catherine's heavy handed orchestration of the whole affair. Poor Anne, as well, for being so beaten down by it all.

...Lady Catherine, Anne, and I are coming into town on Friday. There is some shopping for wedding-related paraphernalia yet to be accomplished. I believe Anne and I are to be trusted with that. Meanwhile, her ladyship intends to call upon you, Elizabeth. She has resigned herself to do it, but seems none too happy at the prospect. Although she would never admit it, Darcy, I gather that the honor is being paid to your worthy wife on your command. I would dearly love to know what you did to humble the great lady so. At any rate, I am selfishly glad for the apparent reconciliation since it will clear the way for our continued close fellowship.

I must get this to the post now so that you may have sufficient notice to prepare yourselves for your esteemed visitor. I only wish I could be there. One day you must tell me all about it as I cannot depend on receiving an accurate account from our aunt.

Yours, etc.
J. Fitzwilliam

This was news indeed. Not only was my aunt to call on Elizabeth, but Anne and Fitzwilliam would be in town as well. He did not say they would stop; in fact he said they would be on a different errand. Still, I decided I had better prepare myself for the possibility. If it should come to pass, I would have my chance to judge the current state of my feelings for Fitzwilliam. I only hoped I would not be overwhelmed.

I gave myself a few extra minutes to school my visage into complacency before rejoining my brother and sister. "So we are to be visited by Lady Catherine on Friday," I said with some of the surprise I had felt upon first reading of it. "It must be nearly two years since I last had *that* pleasure. Shall you be nervous when she comes, Elizabeth?"

"I hardly know."

"She needn't be intimidated," said my brother. "Elizabeth was more than a match for our aunt last time they met." I understood him to mean when our aunt had called at Longbourn in order to extort a promise from Elizabeth that she would not think of marrying my brother. "And this encounter should be much less contentious."

"Let us hope so. For my part, I plan to be perfectly well behaved," said Elizabeth. Then, with an impish grin, she added, "And, should conversation lag, I can always flatter her. I might start by praising her usefulness at bringing us together. Shall I, Darcy? Oh, how distressed she would be to know that we owe our happiness, at least in part, to her!"

"Do you think we shall see anything of Anne and Fitzwilliam when they are in town," I asked. "The letter does not say."

"I think it is implied, however," said William. "They will no doubt all be driving up in one carriage, so I assume the two of them will at least step in to say hello."

The two of them. Yes, Anne and Fitzwilliam were a couple and I had better get used to thinking of them that way. The event that would forever make it so was fast approaching.

- 19 -

Lady Catherine

By Friday, I had prepared myself as well as may be for meeting Fitzwilliam and his intended bride face to face. Months had worn away the initial shock, and resignation had replaced despair. What had not changed in that time was the genuine affection I felt for them both. Fitzwilliam had no idea his engagement would injure me in any way. And despite the fact that Anne had unwittingly come between me and my wishes, I could not dislike her either. If she was to be Fitzwilliam's wife, I hoped that they would make each other happy.

I watched from behind the curtain when the carriage approached. After stopping in front of the house, Lady Catherine alone emerged from it, but I caught a glimpse of Fitzwilliam inside before the coach pulled away again.

My brother had decided it was important to allow our aunt to properly pay her respects to Elizabeth without distraction or witnesses, so I continued out of sight when she was shown in. Elizabeth later told us much of what had passed, but how I would have loved to witness that first meeting for myself – two strong-minded ladies, each sizing up the other to see if that one's will could be bent to her own. Elizabeth carried the day; she had a distinct advantage in that, as I understand it, my brother had very firmly defined in advance the required conditions for a reconciliation. Only if Lady Catherine met them was Elizabeth to invite us to join them.

Ten minutes accomplished it.

When William and I entered the drawing room, Lady Catherine, who had herself changed little in the two years since I last saw her, almost immediately settled her concentrated attention on me, as if she could not look away.

"Georgiana, come here," she commanded, continuing her inspection at closer range. "My heavens. Yes, you have the true look of her now, your mother that is. Of course, you were too young when she died to remember much about her, but you will have seen her portrait in the gallery at Pemberley. That likeness was taken when she was just your age, the year she married your father. The resemblance is quite distinct. Have you not remarked it yourself?"

"Oh, but my mother was so beautiful! I cannot see that I look a thing like her, Lady Catherine."

"You are too humble, child; you underestimate yourself. Nevertheless, I am very happy to see you again, my dear." She inclined her cheek towards me, and I dutifully kissed it. Then at last, she turned to my bother. "I am pleased to see you also, nephew. Are you well?"

"I am, and let me say how gratified we all are by the extraordinary improvement in Anne's health. I hardly knew her when she came to Pemberley in January."

"Yes. Dr. Essex is a clever physician, and he has done wonders for Anne. I have very high hopes for her now that her health no longer holds her back. She has such natural talent and taste; they have only wanted proper opportunity to develop."

"Is Anne enjoying all the wedding preparations?" It was a question I had purposely planned in advance to ask – one more step toward accustoming myself to the real state of affairs.

"To a degree," said my aunt. "Although, since Anne is modest by nature, it is an adjustment for her to be the focus of so much activity and attention. She has not the strength of spirit to carry it off, you see, so I have had to step in and manage the arrangements myself."

I daresay this disclosure came as a shock to no one. Lady Catherine had always acted as if she presumed that being in charge was her natural right. So hearing that she had taken control of the wedding arrangements was just as anyone who knew her would have expected. The wonder was that she would ever choose to set that prerogative aside, even temporarily, as she apparently had on this occasion in order to comply with my brother's stipulations. I could only conclude that she desired this reconciliation a great deal, probably a great deal more than she would have been willing to admit.

Lady Catherine went on, informing us, "I have assigned Anne and Fitzwilliam an errand on Bond Street today. They are to return here to join us when finished. I do hope they are not too long about it..."

My mind wandered from my aunt's continuing monologue at the disclosure of this new information. Although merely a confirmation of what we had expected, it still required a moment to properly digest the idea. I returned my attention to the room in time to hear Lady Catherine direct her next remark to Elizabeth.

"Mrs. Darcy, I hope you will do us the honor of calling at Rosings Park before you return to Pemberley. Perhaps the three of you could drive down one day soon. There is still time before the wedding."

The words took me by surprise, not only that Lady Catherine would issue such an invitation, but also the possibility that it might be accepted. Would I be able to endure such an ordeal – not minutes, but hours in Anne and Fitzwilliam's presence? Hopefully, I would be better able to answer that question by the end of the day.

"Possibly it could be arranged," Elizabeth said hesitatingly. "Will we meet the clever Dr. Essex if we are able to come?"

"He has been here in town these three weeks, so I should imagine not. Still, there are other inducements. The woods and groves of Rosings are incomparably beautiful in late spring, and I remember how fond you were of rambling about them when you visited two years ago. Darcy, you will want to see Fitzwilliam. And Georgiana, I must hear you play again; we have no time for that today, and *my* instrument is undoubtedly superior in any case."

William took the opening to interject, "Georgiana and Elizabeth collaborate for some first-rate duets, Lady Catherine; Georgiana plays while Mrs. Darcy sings. I do not believe you have ever heard my wife's fine singing voice, Aunt, which is a great pity considering your taste and appreciation for music..."

Once again, I could not properly attend. I thought I heard the sounds of a carriage slowing in front of the house. Then came a knock, approaching footsteps, the door opening, and the visitors being announced. At the last moment, I braced myself for seeing him, for seeing *them* together.

There was a jolt of sorts in it for me when Anne and Fitzwilliam entered, but no more than what I had prepared myself for. I was pleased to find I was equal to it and confident my countenance betrayed nothing of what I was feeling. No one in that room, except Elizabeth, had any reason to suspect me of suffering any inner turmoil on the occasion.

Anne looked fatigued, I noticed, just as Fitzwilliam's letter had given us to expect. He seemed well, though, and I could not help but be impressed by his attentiveness to her. During the short while they were with us, he stayed close by Anne's side, doing all he could for her comfort, including fielding his future mother-in-law's questions about the success of their errand. I was proud of him for his gallantry, but it was yet another reminder of what I had lost.

I know it was probably wrong to have been thinking in those terms – what I had lost in losing Colonel Fitzwilliam – since he had never belonged to me, except in my dreams. Still, that is the way it felt.

Over refreshments, the conversation continued to be dominated by her ladyship. As usual, she had firm opinions about everything, which she hesitated not to share. But it was clear she was making a concerted effort to be on best behavior, especially where Elizabeth was concerned – trying to earn her way back into my brother's good graces, I presumed.

In one of her brief pauses, Colonel Fitzwilliam addressed me very particularly, asking, "How are you enjoying your London season, Georgiana? Is it everything you had hoped it would be?"

"Yes, sir, it has been highly enjoyable," I returned. It was a bit of an exaggeration and yet exactly what was required of me. It hardly seemed the sort of question to which the asker actually desired an honest, detailed answer.

"And what has been your favorite part so far?"

This more specific question from him demanded a more unambiguous response. I said what immediately jumped to the forefront of my mind. "We attended a concert the other night that was simply superb. I cannot remember when I have ever enjoyed anything more."

"Ah, a concert. I should have known. Here I was imagining you dancing every night with a series of gentlemen admirers, and yet, when it comes right down to it, I suppose not one of them can compete with the master of the orchestra for your heart's true devotion. Poor young fellows," he said, shaking his head. "They do not stand a chance."

Although I desired to make some clever retort, all I could think is that he was right. None of the young men I had met since I arrived in town interested me in the least, but not because of the orchestra's conductor.

"You mustn't tease your cousin so, Fitzwilliam," Anne said quietly, laying a gentle hand on his arm. "You will embarrass her."

"You are quite right, my dear," he acknowledged. "It is a terrible habit, and I must vow to give it up."

"Well, now that is settled," said Lady Catherine, closing the subject. "Regrettably, we must take our leave. Mrs. Darcy, I thank you for your hospitality, and I trust you will forgive us our somewhat early departure. As I said before, I will not risk being caught on the road after dark. You will inform me if you find yourselves able to come to Rosings?"

"Yes, of course, your ladyship," said Elizabeth, rising, as did we all.

I watched our guests out the door, escorted by my brother, and then turned to Elizabeth, who was eager to speak to me.

"I was afraid this visit might disturb you, my dear – seeing Anne and Fitzwilliam together. I am relieved to find that you bear it with so much serenity."

"I wish I could say that perfect peace is what I feel, but it is all a guise, Elizabeth. I have told myself I must get accustomed to seeing them together and thinking of them as a married couple, which they very shortly will be. The sooner I accept that fact, the sooner I can seriously consider other possibilities for myself."

"I admire your courage and your determination. As time passes, it will become more comfortable. I hope that someday you shall once again find only pleasure in seeing both your cousins." Elizabeth gave my hand an affectionate squeeze just as William reentered.

I then excused myself to return to my one true consolation: my music. It was such a relief to resume my preferred place at the pianoforte, to allow my emotions, which I had carefully held in check while our guests were present, to pour out through its keys. In this, my private language, I could express all the things I could never say to a single person living, I could speak my feelings eloquently without fear of discovery. I often wondered how people who had no similar form of release ever managed. I could not imagine it.

- 20 -

Rosings Park

William and Elizabeth expeditiously settled between themselves that they would travel to Hunsford on Monday. Elizabeth then came to consult with me about my wishes, going so far as offering to contrive an excuse for me if I felt I could not endure the ordeal of so much time in Anne and Fitzwilliam's presence.

I had already decided what I should do, however. So I thanked her for her concern but said no excuse would be necessary. Encouraged by my success in their short visit, I began to think myself strong enough to face a longer one. Besides, I really did have a powerful desire to see Rosings again.

Meanwhile, there was another ball to attend. I had been dreading this particular one, not because I was suddenly disinclined to dance but because I should almost certainly see Henry Heywood and his sister there. Henry, I assumed, would simply avoid me altogether. I had no idea how Andrea would behave.

Since Henry's most unfortunate proposal, I had not heard one word from her, nothing even in response to a note I had sent. This was exactly what I had feared, that I would not only lose Henry's friendship through this regrettable affair, but Andrea's as well. And I had precious few close friends in London as it was.

It did not take long after our arrival to confirm that the Heywoods were present – Mr. and Mrs. as well as their two offspring. I prepared myself for what I knew would come next. William and Elizabeth, who had also seen them, made their way in the Heywood's direction, and I could not but follow.

Mr. and Mrs. Heywood's manner of greeting us was no less friendly than it had ever been, so either they did not know I had refused their son or they had very civilly decided to pretend that was the case. Not surprisingly, Henry, although he nodded to acknowledge my presence, neither spoke to me nor met my eye. Andrea did look at me, and I thought I saw in her countenance a longing to come to my side in the old way. But then, seeming to remember herself, she lifted her chin and directed her attention elsewhere.

I did manage to corner her later that evening, however, during the supper break. I sat down beside her where she could not very well avoid me, although even then she tried.

"Come, now, Andrea," I said to the back of her head. "May we not be friends again? I know you are disappointed by what has happened, but I did warn you, as I tried to your brother, that it must be so."

Finally she turned to me with a challenging look in her eye. "Why must it be so? Could you not at least have *tried* to like my brother?"

"I *do* like Henry, just not in a romantic way, as I told you before. I cannot help it. I wish that I could, for it would certainly save a lot of pain if people only fell in love with those who returned their affection instead of…"

"What? What is it? What were you going to say?"

"Just that; nothing more."

"Aha! I think I understand you now. You cannot give your heart to my brother because it already belongs to another man! Is not that so? A man who perhaps does not return your regard?"

I could see that I would be forgiven if only I would own that her theory was correct, which of course it was. Reluctantly, I nodded. "You will think there is a certain justice in it, that I can appreciate what Henry is feeling because I know what it is to have one's love unrequited. That is all I will say on the subject, however."

"Oh, my poor, dear, Georgiana!" Andrea gushed all at once as she leant in for an embrace. "How is it possible that anybody could help loving you? Who is this unfeeling cad? You must tell me!"

"He is not a cad, and I cannot tell you his name. It would be indiscreet since he is not a free man."

"Married?" she exclaimed, her eyes alight with very lively curiosity.

I hastened to correct her. "No, not married, but unavailable nonetheless, so I must learn to think of him no more. Dear Andrea, do not press me for information. It is too hard. Just say that you no longer despise me."

"Very well, we are friends again, although I suppose I really ought to have held out against you a little longer for Henry's sake. He may think it terribly disloyal of me to forgive you so soon."

~~*~~

We dined with the Applewhites on Saturday. Sunday, after church, we spent the afternoon in the agreeable company of the Gardiners in Gracechurch Street. Then Monday was upon us, and it was time for our visit to Rosings.

Despite my earlier confidence, I did not face the journey in perfect equanimity. Neither had I wavered in my decision to go, however. It felt as if this was the next necessary step to getting past the obstacle of Colonel Fitzwilliam, to putting him once and for all in his proper place. Whatever it would take to free myself, I was determined to do. I could not spend the rest of my life pining for him and being thrown into a panic each time he was expected.

My resolve was tested to the utmost and immediately since it was Colonel Fitzwilliam himself who met us upon our arrival at Rosings, helping Elizabeth and me from the carriage and then greeting us with a particularly charming speech.

"I am so delighted that you are come," he said merrily. "Rosings Park may be admired for its manicured lawns and generous glazing, but I believe it is only *truly* exceptional when graced by beautiful women. Darcy, I thank you for bringing them."

My brother rolled his eyes heavenward. "Shameless flatterer," he muttered, shaking his cousin's hand. "Still, I am glad to find you in good spirits today, Fitzwilliam. I suppose we owe it to the fact that your wedding is now only a few days off."

"What? Oh, yes, of course, the wedding," he agreed, nodding and smiling. "How fortuitous that you have come today, for I think I can promise that Rosings will prove far and away more entertaining than you ordinarily find it. Come in! Come in! Anne and her ladyship will be very glad to see you."

Competing with Fitzwilliam's charms for my attention was Rosings Park itself. The approaching drive had begun summoning up memories from the past, which became stronger as the illustrious lawns and topiaries came into view. The imposing structure of the house, with its grand front staircase, added the final element.

Although my aunt had always been rather severe, I remembered liking my uncle better. By both of them, we were always treated as favorites when we came – given the best hospitality the house could offer and encouraged to spend as much time there as possible. I know now that my brother's good opinion was being carefully curried as a match for Anne. I suppose that accounts for much of Lady Catherine's past deference to him. I think *I* was liked for the sake of my mother and as a sort of pet for Anne, who was a few years my senior. So although our regular visits to Rosings – first with our parents and later without – were hardly occasions of carefree gaiety, I did feel a certain tenderness upon their recollection.

Going inside, I continued to look about myself and renew acquaintance with familiar objects and rooms – the entrance hall with its polished marble floors, lofty ceiling and extravagantly large chandelier, and then the oversized drawing room, where we found Lady Catherine, Anne, and Mrs. Jenkinson, a woman long employed as Anne's companion. Everything was just as I remembered; the expensive furnishings were arranged exactly as before, and the three women had even seated themselves in the same places they used to do.

After the customary greetings and formalities had been accomplished, we joined the semicircle before Lady Catherine in her high-backed chair, from which she proceeded to hold court.

"How was your drive from town, Darcy?" she asked.

"Quite tolerable. The roads were dry."

"I understand that you brought Mrs. Collins with you from Derbyshire."

"Yes, your ladyship," said Elizabeth. "She was good enough to accompany us as far as Hertfordshire. She is visiting her family there and will come into London on Thursday, so that she may drive down with us for the wedding on Friday."

"It was very charitable of you to convey her so far," continued her ladyship. "I doubt that she could have afforded such a journey otherwise, with her modest resources. I shall be glad to see her again. She and Mr. Collins always suited me so much better than the *new* rector and his wife…"

While I listened to the subsequent enumeration of Mr. and Mrs. Chesterfield's deficiencies, I was at the same time observing my cousin Anne. The change in her was quite remarkable. Whereas only a few days before she had looked pale and listless, now she was entirely restored. Her color was high and there was a uncharacteristic spark in her eye. But when I saw her smile as she exchanged a meaningful glance with Fitzwilliam, I could look on no more. I turned away and attempted to give my full attention to what Lady Catherine was saying.

"...I have no complaint against his sermons," she conceded begrudgingly. "They always seem correct and well-considered."

"He also spends a great deal of time visiting the poor and infirmed," contributed Anne. "I have heard good reports of that sort from many people in the parish, and Dr. Essex says that he often encounters Mr. Chesterfield as he makes his rounds among the sick."

"From what you say, Anne, I am inclined to think well of the man," my brother declared, "despite his shortcomings," he added dryly.

"He sounds a lot like our good Mr. Thornton," I offered.

Lady Catherine then directed a change in subject. "Mrs. Darcy, when I saw you lately in London, you expressed an interest in making the acquaintance of Dr. Essex. I am pleased to say that he will be returning from town this very day. He sent word that we should expect him by dinner if not before. So, you may have the pleasure of meeting him after all... *if* you would care to stay."

"Yes, do stay," encouraged Fitzwilliam, with a grin. "It will certainly be worth your while."

As we had no pressing engagements in town, the plan was agreed to. Lady Catherine seemed pleased, and she soon called for some music. Elizabeth and I had come fully prepared for such a request. It was all decided; I would play and she would sing. So we passed without protest through the wide archway into the adjoining room to comply. In truth, I was very eager to do so; my fingers had already been itching to reacquaint themselves with Lady Catherine's pianoforte, which, as I remembered, was capital indeed.

We began with *Voi Che Sapete* from *The Marriage of Figaro*. Since it was one of my brother's favorites, his full interest was assured. Colonel Fitzwilliam was likewise very attentive. The same could not be said for Lady Catherine, however. Although she professed herself a very great appreciator of music, I noticed she was soon talking with Mrs. Jenkinson instead, going so far as to raise her voice to be better heard above the song. Mrs. Jenkinson had no choice but to listen to her ladyship as she talked on. The others, one by one, made their way out of the conversation circle and into the music room, forming a smaller but more genuinely appreciative audience. Elizabeth and I performed three more songs at their insistence.

What vexed me most about Lady Catherine's continued inattentiveness was that she apparently found it no bar to her afterwards passing judgment on the quality of the music. It was not on my own account that I took umbrage, for my aunt had only words of praise for me. It was on my sister's behalf that I principally felt offense. While Lady Catherine allowed Elizabeth to have a fine, natural voice, one not altogether lacking value, she pronounced the instrument unschooled and underdeveloped.

"Your parents should have engaged a master for you," she declared. "Then, with faithful practice, you might have been a true proficient instead of merely adequate."

After hearing this, William rose immediately, saying he was in desperate need of fresh air. This I could readily believe, since I felt much the same myself. At his invitation, Elizabeth, Fitzwilliam, Anne, and I all consented to join him for a turn through the gardens before dinner. Lady Catherine stayed behind, and Mrs. Jenkinson, who would not be joining us for dinner, took courteous leave of us and retired to her own apartment.

The cool air out of doors was a heavenly contrast to the overheated drawing room, where Lady Catherine's decree was that a large fire be kept always burning. By this time, my nostalgic feelings for visiting Rosings were already on the wane, and I began to regret that we had committed ourselves to staying through dinner. But then things began to look up with the arrival of the celebrated Dr. Essex.

We were strolling through the formal gardens near the house – Anne on Fitzwilliam's arm, and my brother escorting both me and his wife – when a gig, which Anne readily identified as belonging to the expected physician, arrived. A tall fellow climbed down from it and came in our direction to be introduced. A man of roughly thirty, Dr. Essex carried himself well and spoke with the intelligence and manners of a gentleman. I liked him at once.

"You are a miracle worker, sir," said William after the first flush of civilities. "I have long wished to make the acquaintance of the man responsible for my cousin's transformation."

"I was only too glad to help. I am sure my predecessor did his best, but it is high time medicine advanced beyond the dark ages. Patients like your cousin, Mr. Darcy, deserve all the benefits modern science has to offer." Dr. Essex then turned his attention to Anne. "I hope you are feeling especially well and strong on this *particular* day, Miss de Bourgh."

"I am well," she said with a nervous smile. "Whether I am strong enough or not, we shall soon discover, shan't we? But, now *you* are come, I feel up to any challenge."

"You have a surprising number of companions here to lend you their support," Dr. Essex pointed out, with a sweeping gesture to the rest of us.

"Aye. They are loyal friends, and I am grateful to have them with me, especially today."

I waited for someone to shed light on this enigmatic exchange. But Fitzwilliam, the most appropriate person to have done so, only said cheerfully, "Well, now that Dr. Essex has come, shall we all go inside? I'm ravenously hungry, and I can hardly wait to see what is in store for us at Lady Catherine's dinner table."

He then generously released Anne to the care of her physician and, to my amazement, offered me his now-vacant arm. I had no choice but to take it, and in this manner we six returned to the house.

- 21 -

Showdown

The dinner was very fine, of course; I would have expected nothing less at Rosings. It was difficult to properly appreciate the food, however, when I had the distinct impression that some mischief was in the offing. First, I had noticed Fitzwilliam's particularly playful air and that odd conversation between Anne and Dr. Essex in the garden. Then just before we sat down, I saw the colonel whisper something to Elizabeth and my brother, who now also seemed to be on alert. And Anne was not eating.

In truth, the only one behaving exactly like herself was Lady Catherine. She seemed to be savoring the food in a self-congratulatory fashion, but far more than that the opportunity of display and the larger-than-usual audience for whatever she chose to talk about. She carried on as if nothing were amiss. And indeed, when we had got safely past the soup and the fish without incident, I began to think I might have been mistaken about there being something unusual afoot.

Then, when Lady Catherine paused in her discourse long enough to sample the roasted pheasant, the wonder began to unfold.

I saw Dr. Essex give Anne an encouraging nod across the table. She then spoke up in a surprisingly bold manner, saying, "Mama, I have something important to tell you."

Her ladyship, who I suspect was unaccustomed to anybody speaking so firmly to her, least of all her daughter, stared back at her. "What did you say, Anne?" she asked. From my aunt's daunting tone, I believe the question was intended more to silence my cousin than to solicit information.

Anne seemed to cringe at this, but only slightly. Then, to my astonishment, she set her jaw, stood, faced her mother, and repeated her declaration. "I said I have something important to tell you."

"Anne, where are your manners? Sit down at once and hold your peace!" her ladyship commanded. "We have guests, and I will not have our dinner disrupted."

"If I have your full attention now, Mama, I *will* sit down. But I am quite determined to have my say; I will not be put off. As for our guests, there is no reason they may not hear; it will be common knowledge soon enough anyway."

The tension in the room was grown as thick as London fog. Although the conflict subsisted mainly between mother and daughter, there were no boundaries to hold it there, no dike to prevent it overflowing to the rest of us.

After a momentary pause to collect herself, Lady Catherine began shooing the servants from the room with a wave of her hand, saying to Anne, "Good heavens, child! What *are* you about?"

I wanted to know as well. I had no idea what was coming next, although it clearly would involve some unpleasantness. A quick look at my brother and sister showed them to be likewise mystified. We sat in hushed anticipation, all eyes focused on Miss de Bourgh, as if she were the diva on a stage. Never before had she betrayed the slightest resemblance to Lady Catherine in her person or style. Yet now, as she took full command of the room, it was clear that Anne had learnt more under her mother's tutelage than any of us had ever suspected.

Her head held high, she slowly sat down. Then, with quiet assurance, she announced, "There has been a change of plans, Mama. I have broken off my engagement to Colonel Fitzwilliam and consented to marry Dr. Essex instead." With this she smiled, reached across the table, and took the good physician's offered hand.

I gasped, but I was not the only one. It was so shocking a development that I think I should have fainted had I not been safely sitting down. This announcement of Anne's hit me with nearly the same force as Fitzwilliam's opposite one in January, the difference being that then grief had followed immediately after the shock. Now, although Lady Catherine looked positively horrified, *I* could find no cause for dismay, especially once I had ascertained Fitzwilliam's sentiments. A glance at his perfectly sanguine countenance reassured me. Rather than showing any signs of distress, he appeared to be enjoying the proceedings immensely.

My attention returned to my aunt, who looked as staggered as if somebody had stuck her. Staring at her daughter in disbelief, it seemed a full minute passed before her ladyship recovered enough to mount a retaliatory strike – a formidable one at that. "What utter nonsense!" the great lady barked out. "Why, the very idea is scandalous; every feeling revolts. Dr. Essex, unhand my daughter this instant! Anne, apologize to Colonel Fitzwilliam and our guests, and never speak another word about this madness again. Do you hear me?"

Anne remained remarkably calm under this onslaught. "I hear you clearly enough, Mama, but I have not the smallest intention of yielding. I am of age, so there is nothing you can do to prevent me from marrying whomsoever I choose…"

I could hardly believe it – the once weak and much put-upon Anne declaring her independence from her overbearing mother, whom she had never dared to oppose in anything before, so far as I knew. I felt it a rare privilege to have been allowed to witness such an impressive spectacle.

"…I *shall* marry the man I love, Mama. Anything else, I now realize, would be impossibly perverse," Anne concluded.

It took every fiber of my self-control to keep quiet and keep to my seat, for I felt a powerful impulse to stand and applaud, just as I had at the end of that inspiring concert we had recently heard. Anne's had been a similarly moving performance. What courage! What determination in the face of a fearsome foe! I had never been more impressed with anybody than I was with Anne that day, although I freely admit that my admiration was helped on in some measure by the fact that what she had done could not have been more exactly designed to match my own wishes. He was free again! Colonel Fitzwilliam was free! For the moment, I could think of nothing else.

"Fitzwilliam, do something!" I heard Lady Catherine say, her voice rising to nearly a shriek. "You are the injured party here. Can you not make my daughter see reason?"

"I fear it is a hopeless business, your ladyship," said the colonel. "She is determined to have her own way, and I am quite convinced that neither you nor I will be able to change her mind. You are correct about one thing, however. I am indeed the injured party, and, as such, I am entitled by law to compensation for my loss."

My aunt seemed to sink still further. "Heaven and earth, Fitzwilliam! You would not bring a legal action against us, surely."

Fitzwilliam's manner took on a more serious tone as he delivered his most important line with a very pointed look for added emphasis. "Lady Catherine, let us *both* carefully consider how we are to react to this surprising development. For my part, I am convinced that if you can find the charity to accept Anne's choice, I will be persuaded by your good example to likewise forgive the offense without prejudice."

"I see," said her ladyship through tight lips. Then she was silent. No doubt it was becoming clear to her, as it was to me, that the colonel's part in this family drama had not sprung to his mind spontaneously; it was premeditated. He was in league with Anne, and his veiled threat, although genuine, was intended to throw more weight on her side, to assure the proper outcome.

We all waited, but no further remonstration issued forth from Lady Catherine. Finally, Fitzwilliam rose, saying, "Very well. I think we understand each other, Aunt." He then turned to us. "Darcy, Elizabeth, Georgiana, let us withdraw and leave the three principal parties to work out the details. Our help can no longer be needed here."

We three followed Fitzwilliam's recommendation without a word, making our way out of the dining parlor and closing the doors behind. Elizabeth slipped her arm through mine, giving it a light squeeze – her silent way of letting me know that she was aware of and sympathetic to the way this news must be affecting me, the flutter of spirits it could not help but excite in my breast.

"This is quite a turn of events, Fitzwilliam!" My brother began when we were beyond the hearing of those sequestered in the dining room.

"I did promise that the evening would entertain," said the colonel with a swagger in his step. "I trust it did not disappoint."

"You bear your loss exceedingly well, Colonel," Elizabeth remarked. "Are you truly so serene, or do you play a part for Anne's sake?"

"I am no player, I assure you. I must even admit to being a trifle relieved that things turned out as they have. I thank you for your concern, Elizabeth, but you must have no more apprehension on my account."

"But how did all this come about?" William enquired as we took seats close together in the drawing room. "Some clarification is in order."

"And I shall be only too delighted to supply it," said Fitzwilliam. "The situation has been building for some time, it seems, although I was in the dark about it myself until very recently. I only knew that Anne was unhappy, and, as the wedding drew closer, she became more so. I pleaded with her to tell me her troubles, and finally the truth came out Friday night after we returned from seeing you in London.

"I suppose it was only natural that she should become terribly fond of Dr. Essex after all his kindness to her. She had no idea he returned her affection, however, and considered it an impossible match in any event. So Anne accepted her fate and consented to our engagement for much the same reasons that I did – a sense of family obligation, a desire to have things settled, and so forth. It had been easier to go along with the plans made for us by our respective parents than to fight them.

"Then, about a month ago, Dr. Essex declared himself. Improper, I know – to speak thus to a woman already engaged to another – yet I have not the heart to pass judgment upon him. With his encouragement, Anne began considering taking a stand for her own interests. Then, when she finally confessed the whole business to me, I gladly released her from our engagement, which cleared the way for what transpired tonight, my friends."

"And I trust it is all for the best," said my brother.

Oh, yes, I thought, for the best indeed! But my heart was too full to speak. Had I attempted a single word on the subject, I expect I should have broken down completely. Whether it would have been with tears or with uncontrolled laughter, I cannot say. Fortunately, though, nothing was demanded of me at the time. I was allowed to sit quietly by, trying to absorb the startling new information coming my way.

Elizabeth shook her head in wonder. "I can scarce believe it, though I have seen it with my own eyes – Anne standing up to her mother, daring her wrath, and her ladyship looking so completely devastated. I never thought to see the day when I might feel sorry for Lady Catherine, but I almost pity her now. She cannot have seen this coming. Still, do you really think she will give in to Anne's demands, Fitzwilliam?"

At that moment, our notice was drawn by the sound of heated but unintelligible voices coming from the dining room.

Fitzwilliam soon returned his attention to Elizabeth's question. "She has no very appealing alternative, as I believe she will discover. Perhaps even now she is playing her trump card – threatening Anne with disinheritance – but that would avail her very little. She would be risking public scandal and legal action, which would only be adding to her misery. And for what? She has no one else but her daughter to leave her money to."

"So you think it an empty threat, then," my brother asked.

"Anne and Essex are betting on it. After talking it through and looking at it from every angle, we all agreed it most probable that Lady Catherine will back down in the end to save her own face. Not that the couple couldn't manage without her money. He makes a respectable living and she has a tidy little fortune in her own name, which her mother cannot touch. But I hope, for all their sakes, they can come to some more amicable settlement, that Lady Catherine will be brought to reason, that she will rightly conclude the least damage will be done by managing the situation discreetly."

"I agree. The less fuss made over the change, the better," said Elizabeth. With a grin of amusement, she added, "Perhaps the wedding might even go on as originally planned. It is possible no one will notice or care that one groom has merely been substituted for the other."

When the dining room summit concluded, Lady Catherine went straight up to bed with a headache. We then learned what had been decided.

"Mama has agreed to everything," Anne announced with a sigh of relief.

"Yes," said Dr. Essex. "It was touch and go there for a while, but she eventually came round. We are to be married as quickly and quietly as possible in London, using the license I have already acquired."

"Mama says we may return here to live if we wish, although I believe we will want a place of our own before long. Hiram has great ambitions as to his career," she said proudly, taking her future husband's arm. "It would be far too limiting for his prospects to be confined to Rosings Park."

With everything so felicitously settled, it seemed a very natural time for us to depart the scene. Having now made himself a *persona non grata* to his aunt, Fitzwilliam announce his intention to go as well, requesting that his already-packed trunk be brought down. The carriages were ordered, and when they were ready, Anne and Dr. Essex saw the four of us out.

"Our sincere congratulations," said William on the steps.

I had recovered my composure enough by this time to open my mouth without fear. "Yes, I wish you both every happiness," I added.

"That means a great deal to me – to us," said Anne, smiling up at Dr. Essex.

"And you will all come to the wedding?" he asked.

"We would not miss it for the world," Elizabeth assured him.

Anne then turned to the colonel, laying a gentle hand on his arm. "Fitzwilliam, what can I say? I am forever in your debt."

"Nonsense! Glad to be of service, my dear. My reward is seeing you made so happy. And I suppose I must confess some small satisfaction in beholding my aunt's rather remarkable countenance this day as well. Should I live to be a hundred, I doubt I will ever forget that extraordinary sight." He then quickly took leave of us and drove off in his carriage. We followed directly behind him on the London road.

How different from what they had been only that morning were my sentiments on this return trip! For one thing, my conscience was newly clear. I could once more think of Fitzwilliam without the accuser charging me with coveting another woman's property. The colonel was a free man again, and I had just as much right to set my heart on him as any other. Of course, I was not so foolish as to believe that, with Anne out of the picture, he would instantly turn to me. But at least now there was a chance. At least now I was at liberty to do my best in finding out if he could learn to love me. For the moment, that was enough.

- 22 -

Staying or Going

I kept to myself most of the following day, meditating at length on what had happened at Rosings and the likely ramifications for those involved. In truth, though, I had no worry for Anne's happiness, and I could spare no more than a few minute's concern for my aunt's disappointment. I am a very selfish creature, and the lion's share of my solicitude I spent on myself. What did it all mean for me… and for Fitzwilliam? Did I have a realistic chance with him, or would thinking I might only spoil every possibility of my being happy with someone else? Until I knew the answers, it seemed I must perform a constant balancing act between hope and caution, trying to avoid falling irretrievably off either to one side or the other.

I suspect Elizabeth knew I needed time alone to reconcile myself to the new state of affairs, for she did not intrude that first day. Still, I knew she must eventually seek me out for a private chat, and so she did the next.

"I have sent a message to Charlotte Collins," she began when she found me alone in the sitting room, "relating to her the gist of what has taken place."

"What will she do now, do you think?"

"I encouraged her to come to us just as originally planned. She will still wish to attend Anne's wedding, despite the alteration in the particulars. And she had so looked forward to spending a week with us here in London. As for me, I shall be pleased to be gone from here immediately thereafter. This heat!" she exclaimed, working the fan she had taken to carrying with her at all times. "I cannot seem to abide it this year. I expect it is something to do with the extra weight I am carrying."

"No doubt," I said, although I really knew nothing about it. While it was true that the weather had grown uncommonly warm for

June, which did nothing to improve the close conditions in town, it did not yet seem all that objectionable to me.

"In any case," Elizabeth continued, "the sooner I am back in the cool of the north country, the happier I shall be. And what about you, my dear. What have you decided? Are you ready to return to Pemberley with your brother and myself, or do you wish to stay longer in town? I imagine that the recent incident may have caused some uncertainty."

I glanced at the door to be sure we were still alone before letting my sentiments be known to my sister. "Oh, Elizabeth, is this not the most incredible turn of events? I have thought of little else since. I know I should not let my feelings run away with me, but I cannot seem to help it."

"You *are* still in love with Fitzwilliam then."

It was not a question but a statement of fact, one with which I found I could not argue. So instead, I nodded. "Until the other day, I had nearly convinced myself that those feelings were dead, or at least dying. Now they have sprung back to life, and I wonder if there might still be a chance for us. I cannot abandon that dream so long as there is hope; I could never marry somebody else until I know for certain there is not. So, you see, it is impossible for me to return to Derbyshire and face Mr. Sanditon at present."

"Of course. Take as much time as you like, by all means. Yet you needn't be afraid to come home whenever you wish, even if you have no answer for Mr. Sanditon." She reminded me again of the gravity of such a decision, and then the conversation turned to less serious subjects.

Shortly thereafter, my brother joined us, saying, "What do the two of you have your heads together about this morning?"

"Your sister was just telling me that she wishes to stay on here for a while longer instead of returning to Pemberley with us," said Elizabeth. "You have no objection, do you, my dear?"

"Not if proper arrangements can be made. I will not consent to any compromise of safety or decorum, Georgiana, but I think prudent precautions are within our reach. Fitzwilliam is remaining in town for some time, I believe, and I know he would willingly serve as your guardian. Then, if Mrs. Collins can be persuaded to act as chaperone, I will be satisfied."

"She was quite enthusiastic when I mentioned the possibility to her," Elizabeth explained. "I believe she is not only disposed to agree to the office, but very much looking forward to the prospect."

"Very well, then, Georgiana, you may do as you please, although I must admit I will not be entirely easy until you are safely back at Pemberley with us."

"You worry too much, Brother," I said lightly. "Mrs. Collins and Fitzwilliam will look after me very ably."

So it was decided. William and Elizabeth would return to the country immediately after Anne's wedding to Dr. Essex, which was to take place approximately a week hence. I would remain in the townhouse to take in more of what the season had to offer, with Charlotte Collins and the colonel to watch over me. Although my brother saw Fitzwilliam's role as nothing beyond what it had always been – my guardian and protector – I soon pictured it growing into something far more satisfactory over the weeks ahead, its being transformed into something utterly new and wonderful.

Balance hope with caution, I reminded myself, as I had to again and again that summer.

I was next to see Fitzwilliam at the dinner party my brother and sister had decided to give as a way of taking leave of their friends. Attending would be the colonel, the Applewhites, the Hursts and Miss Bingley, Andrea and her parents. One person I would *not* see there was Henry Heywood, who declined the invitation with a vague sort of excuse. No further explanation was needed, however; surely both families could see the advantage in avoiding that unpleasant awkwardness which must otherwise have resulted.

Charlotte Collins would also be present for the party, as she was soon delivered to us by means of her father's carriage. After we all greeted her, Elizabeth took her up to show her the bedchamber that had been prepared for her use.

"I hear you and I are to become much better acquainted, Miss Darcy," Charlotte said when she returned. "Elizabeth tells me you wish to stay on here in London, with me as your companion."

"Yes, I hope you will not mind," I said.

"Mind? I am delighted! As I told your sister just now, it will be a great novelty for me to spend time in London accompanying you to your excellent affairs. I could never afford such luxuries on my own. And I trust you and I will deal very well together."

"I am sure that we shall, Mrs. Collins."

"Do you suppose that we could dispense with some of the formalities, my dear, at least when we are at home? I should be pleased if you would call me Charlotte."

"As you wish, and Georgiana will do very well for me."

It was the start of a new chapter in our friendship, although not one without its challenges. Just as I must learn to balance hope with caution in my thinking of Fitzwilliam, Charlotte and I would be required to establish rather a difficult balance of our own. On one hand, Charlotte had been given the responsibility of safeguarding my person and reputation from harm – a position of implied authority, further augmented by her widowhood and her considerable seniority of age. On the other, I was no longer a dependent child, and we must both have been sensible that my superiority of rank and financial status swung the pendulum back in my favor. Not that it should be a contest or that I had any intention of taxing my chaperone's patience. Yet it seemed a fine sort of line we would be walking together. I hoped our ideas might always coincide, but what if they did not? Whose will would then prevail? It was a question that would be tested in the weeks to come.

- 23 -

Farewell Dinner

Our dinner party was held three days after Charlotte's arrival. And, unlike the dinner at Rosings, the hostess made no attempt at pomp and ceremony, no exertion to overly impress her guests. We were all friends already, so there was no need for formality. As a result, the evening took on a relaxed tone, allowing the conversation to flow freely in the drawing room before dinner. I believe this was to everybody's taste, with the possible exception of Miss Bingley and the Hursts, who were always more occupied with establishing rank and displaying consequence than was either necessary or becoming.

I knew they had been included on the guest list only as a courtesy, and now we must put up with them as best we could. My brother had the misfortune of having them at his end of the table at dinner, and he did not appear to be especially enjoying the conversation. Although I could not hear everything that was being said, I gathered there was much discussion of the inhabitants of Heatheridge House and when a visit there might be arranged for Miss Bingley and the Hursts.

Conversation with those seated nearer to me claimed most of my interest. Andrea was close by and, with my approval, Elizabeth had placed Colonel Fitzwilliam directly across from me. What a contrast to that dinner party at Pemberley only a few months before, where every effort had been made to prevent my having to see or hear him!

Of course, there was still my ever-present shyness to overcome, along with my consciousness of the recent change. I had planned that I should make no reference to those events myself, but Colonel Fitzwilliam, who obviously suffered no such reticence, dove directly into those waters.

During the fish course, he leant forward and asked with a wink, "Do you suppose Elizabeth has any lively entertainment planned for us tonight, Georgiana, such as what we enjoyed at Rosings Park?"

"I should imagine not, Colonel," I said, a little unsure of myself. "It would take something quite extraordinary to equal what we observed over *that* dinner. Although you were not merely an observer, as I was. You had an important part to play."

"True. Perhaps I should have given the stage a try. Do not you think I performed my small role with distinction?"

"It was very well done indeed," I answered, warming to the subject. "One would naturally conclude that it was the work of considerable study."

"Oh, some trifling bit of rehearsal was required, it is true, but I find that when one is speaking from the heart, the words flow off the tongue with little difficulty." He changed his joking tone for something more serious as he said this. "Truth and right were on our side. There are no better weapons to have at one's disposal."

"In any case, you did Anne a good turn. I hope she will be very happy."

"By releasing her, I have done what I can to prevent her being otherwise… and myself too, perhaps."

And perhaps one other, I silently added. "As my brother said that night, I trust it is all for the best." We were silent a moment and then I asked, "What are your plans now, Colonel?"

"I have hardly had time to consider. My only definite idea is to stay well clear of my father until he has had time to recover from this latest setback. He can be no more pleased with the change of plans than Lady Catherine was. Thinking he finally had me well settled, he will not take kindly to his excellent scheme being overthrown at the last minute. Fortunately, I was able to write in time to prevent his coming to London, and now I intend to keep my distance as long as possible – take in what's left of the season and so forth."

"That is my plan as well," said I.

"Really? Who are *you* desperate to avoid?"

I started at this, thinking that he had somehow divined my situation with Mr. Sanditon. But he was only teasing, I realized. So I said, "Oh, no, not that part. I only meant that I intend to take in what remains of the season."

He looked surprised. "You do not return to Pemberley with your brother, then?"

"No, I do not. William has given me leave to stay on a while longer, and Mrs. Collins has agreed to serve as my companion and chaperone."

"Then we shall undoubtedly see much of each other in the days to come," he said, beaming warmly across at me.

"Undoubtedly," I agreed, returning his smile. That was precisely what I had in mind, after all.

Then the colonel went on. "You must call on me for anything you need, my dear. I am more than happy to stand in for your brother. You know I have always seen you as something of a younger sister in any case."

This last drew me up short, causing me to wake from the pleasant delusions I had been entertaining until that point, and reminding me that to Fitzwilliam I was a sister, not a potential mate. I hope I managed not to sound as deflated as I felt. "Thank you, Colonel. You are too kind."

My dreams were very far from coming true.

~~*~~

I had no more conversation with Fitzwilliam that evening.

When we ladies withdrew to the drawing room after dinner, I gravitated to Andrea's side. There I would be safe, I thought, and I would have something different to distract me. Unfortunately, Andrea had the same person on her mind, as I soon found out.

Elizabeth, who had been detained by some conversation with my brother, presently joined us. "I understand we are to expect a visit from you at Pemberley, Miss Bingley, Mrs. Hurst," she said as she sat down across from me in the circle of women. "How delightful!"

Although Elizabeth put on a good show of being pleased, I knew her true sentiments could not have measured up to that artificial mark.

"Yes," said Caroline, her manner all ease and friendliness. "Mr. Darcy insisted we come, and from there we can drive over to Heatheridge as often as we like. It is the perfect solution."

"We are so desirous of seeing our new niece and nephew," Mrs. Hurst explained to the others. "Twins, you know."

Approving female noises arose and a brief discussion of the infants in question followed. When a silence ensued at the close of this topic, Andrea proposed a new one.

"What is Colonel Fitzwilliam's story?" she asked out of the blue. "He seems a very interesting gentleman."

"He is soon to be married," Caroline answered brusquely by way of contradicting the prior remark, for no man could be truly interesting if he were not also truly available.

Elizabeth looked at me and then explained, "Actually, there has been a change of plans. The couple has since amicably parted ways."

"Now that *is* interesting. Do tell us more," Caroline insisted.

"There is nothing more to tell, Miss Bingley," said Elizabeth. "They both decided that it would be better to give up their engagement, so that is what they have done. The details are nobody's business but their own."

Someone asked Mrs. Applewhite for a description of her recent travels on the continent, and thus the subject of Colonel Fitzwilliam was abandoned by the larger group. It did not prevent Andrea from canvassing it further with me, however. After the men rejoined us, she drew me aside to a corner of the room where we could speak privately.

"So this explains the snatch of your conversation with the colonel that I heard over dinner – that he had released a lady so she might be happy, and himself as well. I admit I am as curious as Miss Bingley. So I ask again, what is Colonel Fitzwilliam's story? I believe you once told me he was some sort of relation, but I cannot recall anything else."

"He is my cousin. More than that, however, he is a very dear friend to my brother and to myself. My father held him in such high regard that he designated Fitzwilliam to have a share of the guardianship for me."

"So, he is like a second elder brother to you. How reassuring."

"Yes, exactly," I said, a sigh escaping my lips before I could prevent it.

"You sound none too pleased about this second brother of yours."

"Oh, no, the colonel is an excellent man, and he is to be commended for the conscientious way he executes his duty to me. Sometimes, though, I could wish that…"

"What?"

"Nothing. One should not repine over things that cannot be changed."

"So there is an aspect of the situation you would change if you could. I see."

Something in Andrea's tone made me turn sharply to look at her. "For heaven's sake, Andrea," I exclaimed when I saw her nodding at me with a sad smile. "Kindly direct your sympathy elsewhere. You can know nothing of the business."

"I can guess, and then you shall tell me how near the truth I have come. Colonel Fitzwilliam is the man to whom you have lost your heart. Now deny it if you dare."

It seemed I was pathetically inept at keeping secrets, this one in particular. "There would be no point in denying it, would there? You would never believe me, in any case. But how did you know?"

"Evidence, my dear Georgiana. It is everywhere for the keen observer to collect. But what settled it is the way you speak of him now and how you looked at him over dinner. I am not blind to these things."

My hands flew up to cover my burning cheeks.

Apparently reading my mind, Andrea said, "Do not be afraid. I daresay no one else will have noticed – not the gentleman himself, at least. Men have no penetration when it comes to matters of the heart. You observed how clueless my own brother was, though I know you spoke plainly enough to him. So Colonel Fitzwilliam is your man. Intriguing choice."

"Impossible choice!"

"Really? It may have been while he was engaged, but not so now. Why do you still despair?"

"He perpetually thinks of me quite as a younger sister. He said it again tonight! I suppose it is only natural that he should, considering the gap in our ages. You yourself have acknowledged that to be an obstacle. When you talked of your one-time attachment to my brother, you said it would be foolishness to consider such an union."

"Pish posh. Why should you listen to me? Do not you suppose I would have changed my tune quickly enough had your brother ever shown the remotest interest in me? Now, tell me the truth; is this a passing fancy you feel or an enduring love?"

"I wish it *would* pass. I have tried to let it go, believe me."

"Well then, if it is real love, we shall have to do something about it."

"Do something? What can you mean? Oh, Andrea, take care!"

"You needn't look so panicked, my dear. I have no intention of shouting it from the housetops. I hope I know how to be more discreet than that! No, I only mean that some thought should be given to the matter, some strategy for a successful campaign enacted."

"You make it sound as if we were going to war."

"It is war of a kind, and to the victor go the spoils. I only mean that the victor should be you... not Miss Bingley."

I had to laugh at this. "Oh, Andrea, you are a true friend. But I should not want Fitzwilliam if I had to win him by combat or trickery."

"Of course not; we shall never stoop so low. Our task is to make him see once and for all that you are definitely *not* his sister; you are an eligible young woman whom he would be very lucky to get. After that, he must choose what to do about it – fall in love with you as he should or walk away."

"And if he walks away?"

"Well, then he will have shown himself unworthy of you, and we had best start looking about for somebody better. Make that two somebodies, for I must have my share in the fun."

- 24 -

A Joining and a Parting

My brother and sister began their departure preparations the following day. The plan was that the four of us would attend Anne's wedding together the next morning. Then, since the church was across town and along their way, William and Elizabeth would continue on directly from there, Charlotte and I being conveyed back to the townhouse by another means.

Accordingly, we set off for the wedding quite early, the carriage already loaded with trunks and cases to support the travelers' long journey ahead.

"It is not too late to change your mind," my brother had suggested the night before. "I cannot quite understand your wanting to stay on, and you know that my personal preference would be to have you return to the country with us."

"If I did that, especially at this late hour, it would be a cruel disappointment to more than one person. Mrs. Collins would miss her chance at a London season. And what would become of Kitty? The carriage would be full and you would have to renege on your offer to transport her for another visit to Pemberley."

"That is beside the point. I am happy to do a good turn for Mrs. Collins and for my sister-in-law whenever I can, but you are my first consideration."

"Well, then, be assured that I am sincere in my desire to remain here in town. Although you have apparently had your fill of parties and dancing, William, I have not. Is that so hard to conceive? I still have high hopes for what remains of the season. Perhaps I will have a surprise for you when it is over."

"I do not much care for surprises."

"This would be a very agreeable surprise. Even you should be pleased."

I later wondered if that were true, however. If, by some miracle, all my hopes for Colonel Fitzwilliam actually came to pass, would my brother be pleased or would he not? Shock might be a more likely reaction, at least at first. I doubt the idea of a match between the two of us had ever occurred to my brother. And no doubt it was just as far from Fitzwilliam's mind at the moment. It would be my job to change that. It would be my job to help him see me in a different light. Then, as Andrea had said, it would be up to him what, if anything, to do about it.

I could start my campaign at once, I decided, for I would see Fitzwilliam at the wedding and afterward.

The church was far from crowded when we arrived, which was exactly as we had been led to expect. The communication we received from Rosings, acquainting us with the particulars of the wedding arrangements, had stated that the guest list would be very limited. The same letter also requested my services as bridesmaid to Anne, which I considered an honor, and my brother to give the bride away. I cannot imagine that Lady Catherine was very enthusiastic about this choice. But with Anne having no father alive or any closer male relative available, it obviously had to be either my brother or Fitzwilliam. And Fitzwilliam would not do at all under the circumstances.

All was accomplished without incident. Anne looked truly beautiful in her dove gray gown; no one could deny it, least of all her admiring groom. Dr. Essex cut a rather dashing figure in his wedding clothes as well, but I could not quite forget that a different man had originally been meant to stand in that place. How relieved I was for the change! Instead of taking his place beside the bride, Fitzwilliam looked on serenely from the pews, along with the others in the small congregation.

Only my aunt appeared ill at ease with the proceedings – sour-faced with disapproval one minute and rigidly resigned the next – yet she did nothing to interfere with the brief ceremony. I was truly worried for her by the end, however. She had grown so pale that I was afraid she might swoon when she attempted to rise and exit the church. I was not the only one to have noticed either. I saw Fitzwilliam first and then my brother offer their arms to her in turn, only to be soundly rebuffed in favor of a gentleman whom I did not know.

It must have been a trying day for Lady Catherine, one far from over too. On we all went to the wedding breakfast – a veritable feast laid out for us at a respectable establishment nearby. Here the mother of the bride was more in her element, however. Having made all the arrangements herself according to her ostentatious tastes, she regally presided over the meal, smiling benevolently at her guests and ordering about the servants hired to wait on us.

As for my making any inroads with Fitzwilliam, I was able to accomplish no more than seeing to it that our eyes met on more than one occasion. He seemed to be very occupied with other people – first in earnest conversation with my brother and then with the bride and groom. I knew my turn would come, however, for the colonel was to drive Charlotte and myself back to our townhouse later on.

Meanwhile, Elizabeth drew me aside for some heartfelt communication.

"You will be leaving directly, I suppose," I began.

"Yes, very soon. We cannot afford to delay if we are to cover the necessary ground, considering we must stop in Hertfordshire to collect Kitty as well. My dearest wish is that we should make Pemberley tomorrow, even if we must drive into the night to do it. Fortunately we have the extra daylight hours of June to light our way."

"Are you certain it is wise to attempt so much, Elizabeth, especially for one in your condition? Perhaps Longbourn is a more realistic destination for today, with your late start and all."

"Now you sound like your brother, Georgiana! Mr. Darcy likewise worries it will be too trying for me. But I intend to be very firm. Stopping overnight at Longbourn would do me more harm than good, I assure you – adding full a day more to our journey and also subjecting me to many additional hours in my mother's company. I cannot think of anything that would try my strength more excessively than that just now."

"I suppose you know best what you can bear." I was then struck by a sudden pang at the thought of losing my sister's company. Impulsively embracing her, I said, "Oh, Elizabeth, I shall miss you so!"

"And I you," she said holding me tight for a moment. "But we shall both write frequently, agreed?" I nodded. "Good. And we will see each other again before long. Remember that whatever happens here or fails to happen, whatever you decide about Mr. Sanditon or even should you fail to decide, you may come home any time you like. You shall always be welcomed with open arms to Pemberley."

"I know, and I thank you. It is perhaps the only solid rock upon which I can stand at the moment. Everything else seems to be constantly shifting beneath my feet – first one way and then the other. One minute my dependence is all on Colonel Fitzwilliam, and the next I think of dear Mr. Sanditon and I wonder."

"You would do better to begin by depending on neither one of them, Georgiana. No man can make you happy if you are not content within yourself first. No man will thank you for expecting it of him either. Find your own peace here," she said, patting a spot over her heart, and the rest will soon settle into some order too, I trust. I shall pray daily that it does, that your feelings will sort themselves out properly and that wisdom will guide your actions and decisions at every turn. God is the very best counselor, after all, if one will but listen to Him."

"Doubtless what you say is true, Lizzy, but I often find it difficult to distinguish if the counsel I hear in my head is truly from Him or only a product of my own faulty way of thinking."

"Then that will be one more cause for prayer – that you may know the difference! Well, my darling, I must fly. You see, here comes your brother to collect me."

"Are you ready to go?" he asked Elizabeth, tenderly laying hold of her hand. "It is time we were on our way if we are to make good progress before nightfall."

"Yes, my love, as I was just explaining to your sister."

I followed along when they took their leave of the newlyweds and of Lady Catherine. Then came our own tearful goodbyes in the doorway before they entered their carriage and were driven away.

As I waved at the retreating equipage, I was filled with a mixture of sadness and exhilaration. I would miss William and Elizabeth excessively, it was true, but there was also a certain thrill for what lay ahead, for knowing I was on my own now, relatively speaking. It would be up to me how I conducted myself, and the results would be my responsibility as well.

I did take Elizabeth's parting advice to heart, however, and it moderated my ambitions as to Colonel Fitzwilliam. I would still endeavor to let him see me in a new way, but it must not be the way of a dependent and desperate female. I would not throw myself at his feet. No, I should appear to more advantage if I presented myself as a mature and competent young woman, one who was ready for the responsibilities entailed of being a gentleman's wife and mistress of a manor house, Colonel Fitzwilliam's or otherwise.

It occurred to me that I was very ill prepared for either. I suppose I had some notion of how a wife should behave, thanks to Elizabeth's example. And I knew that the lady of the house was expected to create a gracious home for her family and guests alike. I could contribute music, but I would need to further overcome my shyness to be more comfortable as a hostess. And as to running a household, I was almost completely at a loss. The current Mrs. Darcy managed everything at home now. And before she came, Mrs. Reynolds had carried on mostly alone (probably with some direction from first my father and then my brother) since my mother, the former mistress, had died. I had been the presiding mistress of Pemberley in name only during that interval, and I still would not know where to begin if ever I were left on my own.

That must change, I decided.

Whether it be at Reddclift Hall, a townhouse in London, or as a help to Elizabeth at Pemberley, I wanted to be of some practical use. Everybody seemed to consider that my pursuit of excellence in music was achievement enough, that and my efforts on behalf of the parish poor – something which I had always been allowed to assist with. But surely I was capable of more. A truly accomplished woman must have something to offer beyond the purely ornamental; she must know how to manage servants, how to keep accounts, to exercise economy where appropriate, and to see to it everything necessary for keeping a household running smoothly is done. I had very little idea about any of these things at present, but I could learn. I *would* learn, and I would begin at once.

Maturity, competency, and self-reliance: these goals would guide my behavior henceforth, I vowed. No hysterics; no more emotional outbursts; and certainly no throwing all caution to the wind, as I had once done to my discredit and near ruination. Instead, I would be true to myself and to the temperate statutes of my upbringing. Come what may, I would then at least have nothing for which to reproach myself in the end. It seemed a fine and reasonable resolution at the time, but it would prove one very difficult to keep.

~~*~~

"A capital wedding!" exclaimed Fitzwilliam in high spirits as he, Charlotte, and I drove away from the scene in his carriage. "Do not you think so, ladies? The brevity of the ceremony was just what I would wish everybody to emulate, and no fault can be found with the breakfast. Lady Catherine, despite her frustration at the event, was not miserly there. I hardly know when I have partaken of such fine fare at a wedding."

"As you say, Colonel," Charlotte answered, "one can find no fault there. Her ladyship certainly knows how to do these things with style."

"Very true," he agreed. "And what say you about the affair, Miss Georgiana? Certainly you must have some opinion."

"It was well done indeed, but what truly matters is that the couple should be happy together. And I think they will be. That is my greatest cause for celebration."

"Of course," he agreed. "Leave it to the true romantic in our midst to remind us of what is most important. While I was thinking only of filling my belly, you were wishing for our friends joy eternal."

"The two are not mutually exclusive, you know," I rejoined.

"What do you mean?"

"You spoke as if one's mind could only care for one or the other – either happiness or more tangible considerations. I should hope that we are all capable of doing both. One is not exclusively either a romantic or a pragmatist."

"Naturally, my dear. I stand corrected. I simply find it hard to spare a single thought for the ethereal plane when overcome by the need for food!" he said, laughing. "And I was deuced hungry, I can tell you."

A little further on the colonel raised a new subject, saying to me, "Your brother has this morning asked that I accompany you ladies on your return into Derbyshire, a request with which I shall of course be more than happy to comply. I put myself and my carriage entirely at your disposal – while you remain in town and then ultimately for your journey home. I hope the arrangement will also be agreeable to both of you."

"That is very generous, Colonel," said Charlotte.

"Yes," I quickly agreed, "very generous, and nothing could be more agreeable, provided we are all desiring to leave London at the same time. Otherwise, I would not wish to impose on you. Mrs. Collins and I are both grown women, and we are quite capable of making our own arrangements, I believe." Charlotte looked askance at me but held her tongue. In truth, I had never been allowed or required to do any such thing. I simply had not wished to appear an overly dependent female – my first attempt at putting my new resolutions into practice.

Fitzwilliam appeared uncertain, but he said, "No doubt it is so. Nevertheless, I hope you will not deny me the pleasure of being of service to you."

"No, indeed!" I insisted, suddenly fearing that instead of sounding independent I had only sounded ungrateful. So I added, "I thank you most sincerely for your kindness, Colonel."

Yes, this was going to be another fine line to walk.

- 25 -
Dreams Past

I had no idea why, but I felt a great uneasiness for the travelers that evening. Perhaps it was Elizabeth's suggestion that they might drive late into the night that had alarmed me. And then there were the standard risks of travel. People died on the roads every day, although it is something that does not bear thinking of. One cannot stay perpetually at home for fear of some unlikely mishap. One might just as easily die at one's own house, I reasoned, by tumbling down a flight of stairs, being struck by lightening in the garden, or as the result of falling from a horse. I should have known better, but that is what I was thinking of as I lay awake in bed. And so that is what I dreamt of when I finally slept. Lethal hazards filled my path wherever I turned, indoors and out. One calamity or another seemed determined to take me victim.

I awoke perfectly unharmed, however, except for a few frayed nerves. As for my brother and Elizabeth, I knew I would not feel completely comfortable until I received a letter saying they had traveled safely. Such a missive did indeed arrive five days later – not much more than a few lines, really, in my thoughtful brother's fine hand. He knew I would be waiting to hear from him.

Dear Georgiana,

This will be just a brief note to assure you that we reached our destination without incident, or nearly so. As I feared, the long hours of travel seem to have been too much of a strain on Elizabeth, resulting in a very upsetting nightmare for her while we were on the road – some alarming business about a carriage accident. This was so uncharacteristic an event that at first she attached undue significance to it. But I believe that, now we are safe at home again, the effects have faded away and have been attributed to the proper cause. Kitty will keep Elizabeth occupied, but her companionship is a poor substitute for yours. Return to us soon and, in the meantime, do allow Fitzwilliam to keep watch over you, for my sake as well as for your own.

Love,
William

So it seemed my worries were in sympathy with Elizabeth's own unrest. And although my brother claimed nightmares were uncharacteristic of his wife, he could not have said the same for me. He knew better, for there was a time, mostly in the distant past now, when my sleep had rarely been peaceful, when fearsome apparitions regularly visited me. I always attributed the malady to the early loss of my mother, for that is when the terrors of the night began in earnest.

My nurse when I was very young was Mrs. McFadden, and she would often tell me fairy stories to put me to sleep at night – harmless tales of a clever goose outsmarting a fox or a gentle lamb and his friends gone adventuring to escape the stew pot. The one I liked best, though, was the tale about Robin Redbreast, who flew far and avoided many perils to achieve his goal of singing for the king. I can still hear Nurse adeptly performing all the different voices of the story in her heavy accent of the north.

"'What'll we give to wee Robin for singing us this bonny song?' asked the king," she would say at the end. "And the queen answers, 'I think we'll give him the wee wren to be his wife.' So wee Robin and the wee wren were married that very day. And soon they flew away home to Robin's own waterside, where they were happy together all their lives long."

I begged for the story every night, I remember, and good Mrs. McFadden nearly always obliged. But sometimes, when she was cross over some piece of my mischief or other, she would talk to me of fairy beasts instead.

"Fairy beasts!" I exclaimed in wonder the first time I heard her speak the mysterious name. "What are they?"

"Oh, my!" said she. "Have I never told you of them before? Why, they are unpleasant creatures with very sharp teeth who live in the forest. You'll never see them for they only come out at night.

That's when they begin lookin' for naughty children in need of punishing."

I imagine my eyes were wide as saucers by this point, which was no doubt the effect Nurse intended.

"You don't want to hear what fairy beasts do with naughty children when they find them, do you?"

I had to know, so I nodded.

"Well," she said, "you needn't worry overly. Most times it's not so very bad – usually only a finger or a couple of toes they nibble off while you are asleep, occasionally a nose. 'Tis only the really *wicked* children who are carried away completely and never seen again." She let that sink into my brain for a moment. "But I trust *you* will never misbehave so contemptibly, Miss Georgie."

"No, ma'am," I whispered, "never!"

It was an effective means of discipline, for after hearing this story, the mere mention of fairy beasts was enough to bring me sharply back into line. And that was all I thought about it until my mother came to bed with the child who would have been my younger sister. The little creature, whom I was allowed to see only once, died in the night just two days after her birth. My father said the infant had been taken to heaven by the angels to be with God, but I was too young to understand.

I now know there had been others – babies either miscarried, born dead, or too sickly to survive long in the world – during the decade following William's birth and before my own. Each one apparently took a toll on my mother's constitution and on her peace of mind as well. I can see how it would have been difficult for her to become attached to any child after so many heartaches. William she clearly loved, but I believe that Mama could never entirely trust that I would not leave her as the others had.

Instead, she was the one to leave me.

When I was only six, she was again brought to bed of a dead child, and the struggle to deliver it, knowing there would be no happy outcome, was too much for her.

Nurse told me matter-of-factly that my mother had been taken away to heaven. Papa was too distraught to spare any comfort for me. It was William, by then nearly a man, who stepped in to save me. He became my champion and stronghold that day, and so he has remained at every point of crisis since. He was also the one – not

Nurse nor Father – who did the most to see me through the nightmares that followed.

In my immature mind, fairy beasts had somehow replaced angels. When my younger sibling and then my mother were carried off in the night, I was certain it was the work of those woodland beings with the sharp teeth who liked to punish the wicked. But it seemed one did not have to be so very wicked after all, for I could not conceive of what horrible crimes these two could have been guilty. That being the case, no one was safe from the fairy beasts. Would I be their next victim, I wondered? Or William? Or my father? I could keep these fears somewhat at bay during the daylight hours, but not after dark. And so the nightmares began, persisting in some form and with considerable frequency for months until at last they exhausted themselves.

Exhaust themselves they finally did, however. Yet, ever since, I have been particularly susceptible to threatening dreams. So I have learnt to be careful not to knowingly expose myself to the stuff of nightmares, to be particularly circumspect when choosing the kinds of stories I will and will not read, for example. My brother, I believe, who unfortunately has ample experience with this frailty of mine, tries to shield me from everything potentially alarming. After the business with Mr. Wickham, he became more determined than ever to cosset me from all unpleasantness, even from life in general. It is an impossible task, and I think Elizabeth has helped him to see this.

As for my views about my departed mother, they grew more rational in time. I learnt to accept the fact that she had not abandoned me by choice (the equally defective idea that succeeded my childish blaming of the fairy beasts), and if she had cared less for me than I had for her, that was not her fault either. In the end, sorrow had stolen away her ability to give her whole heart. Yet I cannot think of her short existence as devoid of joy or meaning. She was fortunate enough to live in comfortable means from the day of her birth to the moment of her death. She was the object of deep adoration for her husband and two surviving children. And she had known what it was to appreciate beauty in its many forms.

Years after her passing, Pemberley House continues to stand in testimony to her singular style – every picture hung according to her careful instructions, all the furnishings selected and arranged to suit her exquisite taste. I am told that even the gardens bear Mama's mark here and there.

Although given a free hand, Elizabeth has chosen to change very little since her arrival. "How could I hope to improve on anything?" she once said on the subject. "After all, I fell in love with Pemberley just as it is."

So, there we live surrounded by reminders of my mother. Yet it is at the pianoforte where her memory is most unmistakably revived for me. Lady Anne Darcy, unlike her sister who never learned, was ever celebrated as a superior musician, during her lifetime and beyond. And she was my first music teacher. It pleases me more than I can say that I have inherited a measure of her talent; in me, that portion of her is kept alive. She may be gone, but the connection I feel to her is unbreakable – timeless, reaching even across the great divide between this world and the next. Although I love music for its own sake, because of my mother, I could no more give it up than I could cut off my arm or my leg. It is the one blow I should never survive.

- 26 -

On the Town

Although my brother and sister had gone away, invitations continued to arrive for me, so many that I need not have stayed at home a single night if I did not like to. I would often discuss the options with Andrea, who had clearly taken my courtship on as her personal project, and then also with Charlotte. Andrea was always in favor of bypassing any event that did not offer dancing, but Charlotte recommended a broader range of experiences. As fond as I was of dancing, I could not countenance doing it every night, especially to the exclusion of all other forms of entertainment. I must hear a concert on occasion and attend the opera as well while these things were within my reach.

Nevertheless, dancing was the staple of my leisure diet and, according to Andrea, the most natural path to falling in love. "If you attend enough balls," she told me, "something is bound to happen. You have the sort of grace and figure that attracts attention on the dance floor, Georgiana. Use it to proper advantage and either Colonel Fitzwilliam will fall in love with you or someone else will. It is just a matter of time. Mark my words. And as to your figure, you would do well to show it off a little more, or I suppose I should say show off a little more of it. We must go shopping, my dear, for gowns with less lace and more *décolletage*!"

I was not at all certain she was right. Nevertheless, I could not help feeling anticipation rising within my breast on the threshold of every evening out. Would this be the night, I wondered each time, when magic would occur?

Where was Colonel Fitzwilliam in all of this? Usually right by my side, and I could not have been more delighted. He came by the townhouse daily to inquire about the plans Charlotte and I had made. His carriage was cheerfully offered, as was his escort – offered and accepted. I wished to seem mature and independent, yes, but I was not so foolish as to reject the chance of spending night after night with the man whose love I hoped to eventually inspire.

Although he was careful not to monopolize my time, Fitzwilliam always claimed his share – asking me for the standard two dances at a ball, sitting with me at a concert, and keeping close during an evening party. I basked in his assiduous attentions when I had them to myself. And I could be happy even when I did not, seeing him in high spirits and knowing he would return to me in the end to escort me home. In the meantime, I was confident he had not forgotten me. He would often make a point of catching my eye across the room, when he was dancing or talking with someone else, smiling at me and occasionally giving me a playful wink.

Much of this I knew that I could (and should) attribute to ordinary familial fondness. At times, however, it did truly seem to me that something had altered between us, that we were dealing more on an equal footing with each other instead of the past child-and-guardian model.

During the supper break at a ball that first week after William and Elizabeth had gone, he looked at me very thoughtfully and said, "You have changed."

"Have I?" I responded, surprised but exceedingly pleased that he had finally noticed. "Well, I suppose it must be that I have grown up."

"Yes, so it would seem."

"One cannot remain a baby forever, even if one should wish to. As for me, I like being an adult, and I appreciate being treated as such."

He looked a little chagrined. "I suppose that is more easily done without your parental figures hovering too close by. "

"How perceptive you are, Colonel. Yes, it is difficult to assert oneself in a new way when one's relations are reluctant to see things change."

"Your brother may well want to keep you a child forever; I suppose he cannot help it. But I no longer think of you in that way."

"Thank you, Colonel. That means a great deal to me."

"You are a grown woman, and I will not be the one to hold you back. After all, one cannot prevent the caterpillar from becoming the beautiful butterfly she was meant to be." He suddenly looked self-conscious, as if he had startled himself by saying so much.

I was just as amazed, and too overcome by the sentiment to make any reply. It was one of the pinnacle moments of my life to that point. I had never been happier – or more hopeful for things turning out well with Colonel Fitzwilliam – than I was during those first several days on my own in London.

Even Andrea, who had carefully promoted and observed all these developments, was duly impressed. "You have the good colonel eating out of your hand, my dear," she told me. "I do not know when I have ever seen a man so devoted. I should not be surprised if you were to hear something serious from him soon, and I hope you will not mind if I take at least a bit of the credit when you do. He may have done very well on his own, it is true, but I like to think a hint by me here and there might have helped him along a little."

This was the favorable state of affairs. I am completely at a loss, therefore, to account for what happened afterward. I can recall no event that might have altered his feelings so unmistakably – no argument, no unpleasant incident between us or others – but it seemed the colonel rapidly lost interest in the busy slate of activities we had been enjoying together until that time. The various entertainments held no more charm for him, or perhaps it was only his perpetual companion that could no longer fix his attention.

That next week, he bravely suffered through an opera with me, which I knew in advance he would detest. He seemed to like the Puttnam musicale better, though, at least until the singing turned to Italian. But I thought a ball would be more to his taste, considering how merrily he had danced and carried on at my birthday ball and others. So off we all went to the Hunt Club the following evening. This night would tell the tale, I theorized. Either Fitzwilliam would be his old convivial self, or I would know that something had gone terribly wrong between us.

Fitzwilliam danced the first two with me, which I enjoyed immensely. He seemed to as well, but then he spent the rest of the night in a most spiritless fashion. While I danced with partner after partner – some of them very charming but none who could hold a candle to the colonel in my eyes – he retired to a corner, making little effort to engage in conversation or any other kind of social intercourse. Every time I looked for him, there he was: alone, arms crossed, staring out at the company or back at me, and leaning against the wall as if it were his assigned duty for the night to act as buttress to that spot.

Finally, I could abide it no longer.

I thanked Mr. Frank Osborn, my most recent partner, and then went to find Charlotte. She had taken a chair where she had a clear view to the dancing, and she was talking animatedly with some other ladies of a similar age (no doubt chaperones, like herself). Although I hated to interrupt, it could not be helped.

"Excuse me, Mrs. Collins," I said, leaning close to her ear, "but I'm afraid we must go."

"Go?" she returned in obvious surprise. "The night is still young. Are you unwell?"

I took the offered excuse. "Yes. It is only one of my headaches. That is enough, however. I cannot bear to dance any more, and the noise and press of the crowd are becoming uncomfortable as well."

"Then we should go, by all means," Charlotte agreed, rising to her feet. "Where is the colonel? I've not seen him these two hours."

"I believe I know where to find him," I said.

I led the way and we collected the colonel from his corner. As I had anticipated, he made no difficulty about departing early. On our way to the exit, I saw Miss Bingley and the Hursts, apparently just arriving. In my peevish state, I would much rather have escaped another encounter with Caroline, who had made a pest of herself only the night before at the musicale, maneuvering to join our party and plying her charms on the colonel. Now she waved to get our attention, making herself unavoidable.

"Yoo-hoo." She called as she approached. "Fancy running in to all of you two nights in a row," she said, smiling. Then, turning to the colonel, she added, "You are not leaving so soon, I hope."

"I'm afraid we must, Miss Bingley," said Fitzwilliam. "Miss Darcy has a headache."

"Oh, no! Dear Georgiana, how dreadful!"

"'Tis nothing serious," I disclaimed. "Just enough to spoil any enjoyment I might have in staying."

"What a shame," Caroline lamented. "And it looks like such a lovely ball, too."

"There will be other nights and other balls," I observed "Now, if you will excuse us."

"Yes, of course. I would not detain you for the world!"

I hurried on before she could say anything more.

In the carriage, we three rode along is silence for some time. I tried to keep my countenance composed, my emotions outwardly under control. Inside, however, I was simmering with embarrassment and indignation that I should find myself in this position. I was thinking of what I could say to Colonel Fitzwilliam to release him from the obligation of accompanying me everywhere I went, when it was so clearly become for him a trial of monumental proportions. He had never complained, and yet I felt unaccountably angry with him, perhaps for his failing so miserably at hiding his boredom that night in particular. We had started so well, but now even the dances we had shared were tainted with the suspicion that he had only performed them as a duty, a job to be got over with as soon as possible.

"You needn't bother to call on me tomorrow," I finally said to him when I had sufficiently hardened myself against the threat of tears. "I plan to spend the entire day quietly at home."

This seemed to take him aback. "Perhaps it is for the best," he said uncertainly, "considering your illness tonight."

"And besides, I have been taking up entirely too much of your time. It is not fair. You must have plans of your own, things that interest you more."

"Not at all," he claimed. "There is nothing I would rather be doing than accompanying you and Mrs. Collins wherever you care to go."

I required a moment to consider what my rejoinder to such a obvious falsehood should be. "That is a noble sentiment, Colonel, but you must forgive me if I do not take it at face value. No one who observed you at the opera the other night could be convinced you were enjoying yourself. And tonight, you gave every appearance of being bored to tears."

"I sincerely apologize if I gave that impression. It did not occur to me anybody could be watching. In the case of the opera, it was the company, not the entertainment itself, that I enjoyed. As for tonight…"

"Yes?"

"Well, my only excuse is that, after you, I saw no one there with whom I was the least bit interested in dancing."

"…or even conversing, apparently. No, I cannot allow you to make such a sacrifice again, Fitzwilliam. You must go your own way, and I must go mine. We will see less of one another, but we will spend our time each doing what we like best. That is only right."

His expression was difficult to read. Was he offended or only relieved? I could not tell. However, he very calmly said, "If that is what you truly want, I will not oppose you. Mrs. Collins, what is your opinion of this new plan?"

"I think perhaps Miss Georgiana goes too far. While I agree that it is only right we should impose on your kindness as little as possible, it is also true that Mr. Darcy's express wish was that you should safeguard his sister's comings and goings where prudence requires. Some compromise may be in order."

I made no reply to this nor to any of their conversation that followed. I turned a deaf ear to my two companions and my eye to the darkness outside the window all the way back to our house. There Colonel Fitzwilliam saw me safely inside the front door and then promptly left us.

- 27 -

Housekeeping

I kept my word about staying quietly at home the next day, turning my attention with some eagerness to my project of discovering more about managing a household. I first cornered Mrs. Collins on the subject.

"It occurs to me, Charlotte," I said at the breakfast table, "that I have much to learn when it comes to what is entailed in being the lady of a manor house. Everybody seemed to think I was too young to worry about such things before, but now it is clearly time that I should. Can you tell me what you know from your own experience? I would be very much obliged."

"You want *me* to teach you?"

"Yes, why not?"

"Because my experience is so limited. Hunsford parsonage can hardly be called a proper manor house, and it cannot be compared to the kind of home you are likely to be mistress of one day. Nor can Lucas Lodge for that matter. You want Elizabeth's help."

"I most certainly do, and I will consult her as soon as I return to Pemberley. But I am eager to begin learning immediately. Surely you can teach me something. Is the management of a small house so very different from that of a large one?"

"Perhaps not in generalities. However, the complexity of the task multiplies as the size of the household grows."

"Then understanding the workings of a small house first sounds like the perfect place for me to begin. One must learn to walk before one can run. Is that not so?"

In this way, I coaxed Charlotte into giving up some of her secrets – how she had learnt to make do on a modest income and with a very limited number of servants, the practical chores that had to be accomplished daily to keep on top of every situation.

"Economy was my watchword from first to last," she said in conclusion. "There was no money for extravagances, but Mr. Collins seemed satisfied so long as he could be sure his style of living was becoming to the station he occupied. He did not wish to be seen as living either too high for a clergyman or too low for one so fortunate as to enjoy the patronage of Lady Catherine de Bourgh. The other thing he cared about was that I should not be miserly when it came to how our table was supplied. So I cut corners in other places but not on the food I set before him. Of course, much of what we ate came straight from the garden or the hen house. Occasionally Lady Catherine would make us a gift of some joint of meat that we otherwise could not have afforded."

Here Charlotte stopped abruptly and looked down at her plate without further comment. I was mystified until I realized what had happened. No doubt what she said at the last had reminded her of the circumstances of her husband's death, for, as I understood it, it had been a joint of mutton from her ladyship's stores that had proved Mr. Collins's undoing.

"I am sorry for how it ended, Mrs. Collins," I said. "And yet, from the way you speak of it, I am inclined to think you enjoyed your time at the parsonage."

"Oh, yes. After growing up in a large, somewhat unruly family, it was a pleasure to establish some order in a home of my own. I did not even much mind our financial constraints. They challenged my ingenuity, and it became a matter of considerable satisfaction when I succeeded in overcoming them. But I daresay you will never need to worry about such mundane matters, Miss Georgiana. You will not be collecting your own eggs or mending stockings to put off buying new."

"Perhaps not, although what you have told me gives me more appreciation for those who do."

Having finished our breakfast as we talked, we both stood to leave.

"I do not know what else *I* can teach you," said Mrs. Collins. "Have you thought of speaking with Mrs. Paddington while you are here? She has the management of this grand house, which is more on a level with the sort of establishment you can expect to be mistress of in the future."

I thanked Charlotte for her kind help, and then I wasted no time following her suggestion. I immediately went in search of Mrs. Paddington. I knew her less well than I did dear Mrs. Reynolds, the housekeeper at Pemberley, but I felt certain she would be willing to assist me if I asked her.

When I explained my intentions, at first Mrs. Paddington, like Charlotte, resisted. "Why, Miss Georgiana," she exclaimed, "there can be no call for you troubling your head over tedious business like ordering supplies, linen rotations, and planning menus. Mrs. Darcy has left all that in my charge. She says you are here to enjoy yourself, and that if you want or need anything, it is to be taken care of at once."

"That is very good of her, I am sure, and of you, Mrs. Paddington. But I am tired of always being taken care of. I am not a child anymore, and it is high time I found out how to do certain things for myself, beginning with running a household. You must see that I will need to know these things when I marry. How am I to manage the job if I have never learnt?"

Although she still looked dubious, she said, "Very well, Miss. It shall be according to your wishes. How can I help you?"

It was another measure of progress, and I was excited for what lay ahead. "Might I simply follow along with you a while as you go about your normal duties?" I asked. "You could explain to me in a general way what you are doing and why, and more particularly, what decisions you are free to make on your own and which ones come from the master or mistress. That way I will begin to understand where one person's responsibility leaves off and the other's begins. Do you see? I hope that will not be too cumbersome. You must tell me if I begin to make a nuisance of myself. I would not wish to cause disorder in this very orderly house by my interference."

"I am here to serve you however you see fit, Miss, and I'm sure you will be no bother at all." Then a worried look creased her face. "You do not mean to follow me about all day every day, do you?" she asked.

I could not help laughing a little. "No, of course not, Mrs. Paddington. You should never get your work done if I did that, and I still have my other engagements. Perhaps you could make a few notes when I am absent, though, things you come across that you think I should know. Then you can catch me up later."

"Very good, Miss. That I will. Now, if you are ready to begin, I suppose the first thing you should know is that this house functions very differently when the family is here from when you are all away..."

From then on, I tried to spend some portion of each day conferring with the housekeeper, following her and her jingling ring full of keys up stairways and down passages, watching her work and asking all manner of ignorant questions until I was not quite so ignorant anymore. I learnt that Mrs. Paddington not only supervised but, in most cases, hired the female servants who worked under her. She kept the accounts and was in charge of ordering all the household supplies – from coal for the fires to new linens for the beds and tea for the table – adjusting allowances for when the townhouse was occupied only by the permanent staff to when it swelled with the Darcy family members, the additional servants we brought with us, and all our invited guests.

"Mrs. Darcy gives me a pretty free hand when she is not in residence," Mrs. Paddington told me, "especially for what needs to be decided right away. However, she does take an active interest. The lady of the house needn't be bothered with all the day-to-day details, but she ought to set the tone and let the housekeeper know what is expected of her. And naturally I would not presume to make any major purchases or decisions without consulting with her first."

"It seems you carry a heavy weight of responsibility here, Mrs. Paddington," I remarked, being more and more impressed all the time with her knowledge and efficiency. "And you bear it well."

"Thank you, Miss," she said, obviously pleased with the compliment. "I should hope that I do. It is my life's work, having come up to this position from my early days as a housemaid. I know this townhouse inside and out, and I hope to still be at my post for many years to come."

I could see her pride in her upright, almost regal posture; I could hear it in the tone of her voice. Just like Charlotte, Mrs. Paddington took great satisfaction in a difficult job well done. I shall never again think of truly *accomplished* women without including her on my list.

"I hope you will be too, Mrs. Paddington," I said and meant it. "We are very lucky to have you."

- 28 -

Correspondence

I had quickly answered my brother's brief note with an equally brief missive of my own, doing nothing more than assuring my relations of my continued health and safety. So little time had passed since we had parted that there was nothing else to tell on either side. Two full weeks were now gone, however, and the thick packet that arrived in the post from Elizabeth promised well for more news.

Dear Georgiana,

I trust the second half of your London season is turning out to be all you had hoped. Your brother and I carry on very well here.

I understand that, in his earlier letter to you, he mentioned my harrowing nightmare on our return trip. I wish he had not, for I begin to feel quite foolish that I made so much of it at the time. Contrary to the implications of that dream, no accident awaited us on our travels, and nothing more has come of it since – no repeat of the nightmare itself nor have any events transpired relating to it. So much for my early predictions that the dream must be prophetic. I am very glad to be wrong in this case.

Shortly after our return to Pemberley, we had a pleasant visit from Ruth and Mr. Sanditon, who were naturally both disappointed that you and Charlotte had not traveled with us and both wondering when we expected you home again. We could shed very little light on that subject, of course, not knowing the answer ourselves. Mr. Sanditon then charged me most strictly that I should deliver his cordial greetings and best wishes to you (and to Charlotte) in my next letter. I do so now, not knowing whether there will be more of comfort or torment in it for you.

Jane and Mr. Bingley also came calling and, oh, what a delight it was to see them! They are two of my most favorite people in the whole world, as you well know, but now they have the added advantage of bringing their children as well. The little darlings had grown and changed so much in the short weeks since I saw them before that I should not have recognized them again. But within the space of a few minutes, we were all on the most familiar terms again. Mrs. Grayling, the nurse, rules where the infants' care is concerned, and I am afraid I was forced to give them up to her before I had quite finished fussing over them. Nap times are apparently to be strictly observed!

I assuaged my disappointment by remembering that it will not be long before I have a child of my own, one I can hold and coddle as much as I like.

I have put it off as long as I could, but I must address you on a far less pleasant topic, dearest. Your brother and I had both hoped there would be no need, that the situation would be cheerfully resolved before your return, but there seems little chance of that now. And we agree it would be better for you to be forewarned than taken unawares. I must speak to you, dear Georgiana, about the problem of the Wickhams.

As you were already aware from my sister Lydia's uninvited appearance at Pemberley in January, Mr. and Mrs. Wickham were briefly stopping with the Bingleys at that time. Now Mr. Wickham has been discharged from his position in the regulars, and to Heatheridge they have both returned with seemingly little intention of ever leaving again. This must not continue indefinitely, but neither will Mr. Bingley's conscience allow him to throw his unwelcome guests out with no place to go. Mr. Wickham, you see, has limited resources and no good prospects of employment on the horizon.

Your brother has proposed what he believes is the most viable solution to the current dilemma, although I cannot say it is one with which I am entirely comfortable, especially for your sake, my dear. Although if he can bear it, perhaps you can as well.

William means to give a cottage and farm on the outskirts of Pemberley over to the Wickhams for their use, in the hopes that they will make an honest go of things there. The plan is to move them to the cottage soon, against their wills if necessary. Reasonable people would be grateful for being provided a respectable place to live at no expense and the opportunity to derive a good income from it. But I fear my sister and her husband have seldom shown themselves to be reasonable or responsible. Still, I suppose we must hope for the best.

The cottage where they will be living is miles away from Pemberley House itself, your brother assures me. And Mr. Wickham will be warned in the strictest terms never to set foot anywhere near the grounds. Therefore, there can be no reason you should ever cross paths with the man anymore than when he was in Newcastle. I trust that sets your mind at ease.

As you may remember, Miss Bingley and the Hursts will presently be arriving here for a stay of undetermined length. All I know is that they will not remove from here to Heatheridge until the Bingleys' other houseguests are gone. What a tangle! I pray it is all peacefully settled soon – before the baby comes and before my patience runs too thin.

Do write soon to let us know how you, Charlotte, and Colonel Fitzwilliam have been getting on since we left you. Not a day passes that we do not miss you all. Your brother sends his love, as do I.

Elizabeth

Wickham living so near to Pemberley? I did not like it. No, I did not like it one bit. If anybody had asked me, which of course they had not, I would have been glad to advise against such an idea. I supposed it was true that there was no reason my path should ever cross with his, and yet I felt a great uneasiness at the prospect all the same. I could hardly have said what it was I feared – not really for my safety, since I did not believe Mr. Wickham had any reason to despise or harm me. He had always resented my brother, however. This forced removal from the comforts of Heatheridge could be one more excuse, and then what mischief might he be capable of?

Such were my thoughts, but I kept them to myself when I sat down an hour later to write my response. There would be no point of my raising an alarm when the decision had already been made. For all I knew, the plan might very well be enacted, for better or for worse, before my letter even arrived.

So I tried to be sensible and mature. I thanked my sister for her letter and for the cautionary information about the Wickhams' situation specifically. I gave a general account of my activities during the two weeks past, praising both Charlotte's comfortable chaperonage and Colonel Fitzwilliam's kindly escorting us to our evening affairs. I did not mention that I had asked him to be less conscientious in that regard from now on. Nor did I feel it necessary to disclose my recent interest in household management. I could anticipate that Elizabeth would be curious for news on the romantic front. But since I had nothing to report, I scrupled not in addressing my letter to both my brother and sister.

"Ah, Charlotte," I said seeing her when I came down to send my finished letter off to the post. "I have just been answering a letter from Lizzy, in which she said I am to greet you cordially from Mr. Sanditon."

She held up a letter of her own. "And here is another greeting from him. Ruth has written, and she has given me permission to share this with you. Would you care to read it?" she asked, passing the folded paper over to me.

I could see that it was not long, so I read the letter where I stood.

Dear Charlotte,

Although I miss your company, I am pleased for your sake that you are able, by Miss Darcy's sponsorship, to stay and taste the many delights of a London season. What balls and parties you must be attending! I picture you in very grand surroundings with all the best of food, company, and entertainment at your ready disposal. You (and Miss Darcy, of course) deserve nothing less.

Things go along much quieter here, although no less enjoyably I think. My brother-in-law asks to be remembered to yourself and to Miss Darcy, by the by. He has invited me four times to dine at the great house since you went away, and to see the little girls. He continues to show me kindness at every turn, thinking of things large and small that might add to my comfort here at the cottage and beyond. His carriage always comes to take me to church, of course, but now, more often than not, he is in it. Mr. Thornton (who also sends his warm regards to you both) is so pleased. He has suggested to Mr. Sanditon that next time he should bring his daughters with him.

Speaking of Mr. Thornton, he insisted we take tea with him at the parsonage last Sunday after church. I have long had a great curiosity to see inside the place, so I was eager to accept the invitation. What a snug little house it is too! And what a shame it has no mistress, only a housekeeper and a maid to provide the woman's touch a bachelor's residence would otherwise lack entirely. It surprises me that Mr. Thornton is not yet married, as charming as he seems to be. But then, he is still young.

My goodness, how I do carry on! I doubt you will be the least bit amused by what I think of Mr. Thornton's house! It is just that there is so little news to tell that my mind began to wander. This must be my excuse.

I will close for now, since I have nothing left to say worth reading. You may share this letter with Miss Darcy if you think she would be interested in my ramblings. My best to you both,

Ruth

"It sounds as if Ruth is getting along very well," I remarked when I had finished. "I am glad she has Mr. Sanditon to look after her, and Mr. Thornton takes an interest as well. That is good of him."

Charlotte paused a minute before commenting, and I could see she had something of import on her mind. "So you allow it to be a good thing for Ruth to have her protectors, and yet you will not accept the same kind service from Colonel Fitzwilliam. The more I have thought about it, Georgiana, the more firmly I believe you were unwise in dismissing him the other night. I am certain that your brother, to whom we are both answerable, would not like it if he knew you planned to go out tonight without an escort."

I considered my next words carefully, lest this difference of opinion should grow into something more serious. Here was that fine line to be walked again, balancing between Charlotte's authority and my superiority of situation.

"As I understand it," I said, "William only meant that the colonel should make himself available to us for those occasions where his protection was necessary. Surely, in a good part of town, we might travel safely half a mile to a private ball with no more than three men to guard us. We shall have the coachman, groom, and footman as it is. Really, Charlotte, I think you are over scrupulous in this case. There is absolutely no need for us to drag Fitzwilliam along to an affair he would undoubtedly find just as tedious at the last ball."

"That was only *your* interpretation of the situation, Georgiana."

"Ha! Can there be any other?"

"I believe so. People are often too quick to jump to conclusions of that sort. Things are rarely as simple as they appear, and I think you may have injured the colonel by making him feel he was no longer welcome to accompany you."

"If that be the case, which I doubt, he will soon recover and come to thank me for sparing him sitting through another opera or the chore of bracing up a wall all night at a ball. No, I am quite sure this will be better for us all in the end. I found it impossible to enjoy myself when I knew he was miserable. Would I be any kind of friend to him if I allowed that sort of torture to continue?"

Although Charlotte still held to her view that I had misjudged the situation, she did concede that we had no need of Fitzwilliam's escort that night. In return, I consented to graciously accept his help when it really was required for prudence's sake. Thus Charlotte's and my first disagreement was satisfactorily resolved with us remaining friends – fine line successfully walked, for the moment at least.

- 29 -

Just Another Ball

I continued to think of the news from Derbyshire as I went about my business that afternoon – spending an hour with Mrs. Paddington, another at the pianoforte, and finally preparing to go out. Hearing glowing reports of the Bingleys, Ruth, Mr. Thornton, and Mr. Sanditon made me feel like dashing home at once to see them all again. The next moment, however, I remembered it was not – could never again be – as blissfully simple as that. Now there would be a Mr. Wickham in the neighborhood to cast a ominous shadow over my world. And Mr. Sanditon would be expecting my answer.

Ruth's letter had served to remind me once again of what an excellent man he was, and yet I knew no more what to tell him than I had the day I left Pemberley. This time in London, which I had so counted on to make all things clear, had only served so far to muddy the waters still more. Henry Heywood made a brief disruption, but the effects of his misguided offer had thankfully not lingered. It was Colonel Fitzwilliam who had done the real damage; he was the one who refused to go away.

I had been so happy when I first heard he was free again, but now I wondered if it had only been to open old wounds to fresh pain. If he could not return my regard (and there was still no real evidence that he could), it should have been better that he continued to recede from view, as he had been well on his way to doing before his engagement was broken off. Instead, his renewed presence made it more difficult for me to see my way ahead. At this point, I did not know which way to turn. Should I continue to hope for him, or would that only increase the depth and duration of my suffering when that hope had eventually to be put to death?

"Oh, dear!" exclaimed Lilly, breaking in upon my reverie. "You cannot go to the ball looking like that, Miss." She had just finished arranging my hair and stepped back to appraise her work.

"Why? Is there something wrong with my gown?" I asked, taking a critical look in the glass.

"Not your gown, Miss, your face. It was completely spoilt by that frown you was wearing a minute ago. You looked like you had taken on the weight of the world."

"Ah, yes. Well, it shall not occur again. Thank you for the reminder, Lilly." I schooled my features into a more pleasant arrangement.

"There, now," she said, appreciating the result. "That is much more the thing. I daresay no gentleman could resist you now. Will that fine Colonel Fitzwilliam be escorting you again tonight, Miss?"

"No, he will not. Mrs. Collins agrees that I do not require an escort on this occasion, and the colonel has other plans, I should imagine."

"Too bad, although I suppose there will be lots of other first-rate gentlemen for you to dance with."

"I certainly hope so, Lilly. It would be a very poor excuse for a ball if there were not."

Andrea, who spotted me almost as soon as I arrived that evening, flitted over to my side at once with her hands outstretched to take mine. Her smile quickly faded, though, and she asked, "Where is Colonel Fitzwilliam, my dear?"

"I told him his services were not required."

"You did not!"

"More or less. Those may not have been my exact words, but that was the general idea."

"Why on earth would you do that? My dear friend, how can you expect to secure him if you are so uncivil?"

"It was not my intent to be uncivil; quite the opposite. I meant to be kind. Oh, Andrea! Have you not seen his pained expression these last several days, his growing boredom at being dragged to one affair after another? The whole thing has gone off, and so I had no choice. I have released Fitzwilliam from waiting on me hand and foot, and I mean to call on him only when absolutely necessary from now on."

"This makes no sense! How could he have been so keen, showing some very promising signs one minute, and completely reverse himself the next? Are you certain he has made up his mind against you?"

"If he ever thought of me at all! I begin to be convinced he never did. Perhaps he suddenly became aware of my feelings for him, though, and that is why he shied off. As careful as I tried to be, I may still have given myself away. In any case, I know no other way to account for Fitzwilliam's change in behavior. Do you?"

"Hmm. 'Tis perplexing indeed. Well, then, I suppose we shall just have to start all over again with somebody else. There is still time. What about that handsome Mr. Osborn? He is exceedingly eligible in every way I know of, and he always pays you particular attention."

I heaved a great sigh; I could not help it. I was suddenly weary right down to my bones, and the thought of beginning a new campaign, of setting my sights on somebody else at this late date, was more than I could cheerfully entertain. I was too tired to go on, and surrender sounded like a much more attractive solution. "Perhaps I would do better to admit defeat," I said, "and gracefully retire from the field for now. I would just as soon go home to Pemberley and try again next season… if nothing else comes along in the meantime."

"Nonsense! I will not listen to such talk, not from you, Georgiana! No opportunity to discover your true happiness should be wasted. You cannot expect the man of your dreams to come riding up to your front door, especially hidden away in the countryside as you are in Derbyshire. Now, what about this Mr. Frank Osborn?"

So I danced with Mr. Osborn again when he asked me, and I tried to keep an open mind. In truth, I was not quite ready to give up on some measure of success. While there was any life left to my London season, there was still hope.

I had to admit that Mr. Frank Osborn, whose acquaintance I had first made at my birthday ball, would be a good choice for me, according to society's standard criteria – a very suitable prospect. He was certainly younger than Colonel Fitzwilliam, and handsomer too, if I were being completely objective. Undoubtedly wealthier besides. He was the eldest son, not the second, and so he would inherit his father's country estate (which was, charmingly enough, in Derbyshire) as well as considerable other property. So I had been told. And as I had noted before, he danced and conversed well too. It was difficult to find any fault with him – other than that he was not Colonel Fitzwilliam... or Mr. Sanditon either, for that matter.

Nevertheless, we carried on together for two dances complete. And then I had the supper break with him as well, for which Andrea managed to join us. With her support and encouragement, our conversation flowed smoothly along.

As it turned out, Mr. Osborn had a flare for humor and storytelling, which I found genuinely appealing. So did Andrea it seemed, and I noticed that the gentleman directed his efforts at least equally to that quarter, where he found a still more eager and appreciative audience.

I did not mind. Nor did I mind that, when supper was finished and we had returned to the ballroom, he invited Andrea to dance the next two with him. With a apologetic shrug in my direction, Andrea followed the handsome Mr. Osborn out onto the floor. At that moment, I could see she had given up her campaign to get me married off and turned her attention to pursuing possibilities of her own, which was just as it should be.

I had no real interest in Mr. Osborn, and it was a relief to have some time to myself. In order to avoid acquiring another partner too soon, I quietly eased myself away from the dance floor, slyly slipping through the crowd of interested onlookers to the back of the room where I expected to be safe from any unwanted attention. To further ensure my seclusion, I found a dimly lit corner with a potted palm to provide additional privacy. I needed space to breathe, if only for a little while. I intended to ignore everybody, and I hoped they would have the courtesy to do the same for me.

But that is when I saw a masculine figure standing on the other side of the palm and looking in my direction. "Hello, Georgiana," he said in the rich baritone I knew so well.

- 30 -

Friendly Advice

"Colonel Fitzwilliam! What do *you* do here?" I asked in an accusatory tone.

"Delightful to see you too, my dear," he said lightly, coming round to join me on my side of the palm.

"Sorry. I only meant that I am surprised to find you here since I said you were not needed tonight." Now I had only made things worse, but thankfully the colonel seemed determined to ignore all insults and keep the mood jovial.

"Yes, I recall you were very clear about that. However, I had an invitation of my own, and I suppose I may go where I have been asked, with or without your permission."

"Of course you may. And are you enjoying the ball so far?"

"Very much so, although I have only recently arrived. I am still getting the lay of the land before plunging in. Despite what you may think, my friend, I do intend to participate in the exercise."

We both turned back to watch the dancers.

"I am glad to hear it," I said presently, "For a minute, I thought you might have come only to spy on me." Though I kept my eyes straight ahead, I made sure I was smiling when he looked round sharply at me. Consequently, he was reassured that I was teasing, and he followed suit.

"Spy on you, eh? Well, I find it interesting that you should think so – revealing even. It makes me wonder if there might not be something you are hiding. Is that why you preferred me not to come tonight?"

"Really, Colonel! You almost make me wish I *did* have something scandalous for you to discover. What sort of thing did you have in mind?"

"Oh, I don't know. Perhaps you wished me absent so that you could carry on more freely. Some young ladies have been known to flirt outrageously – first with one man and then another – as soon as their guardian's head is turned. I have even heard that it can become quite a serious entertainment, with bets laid down on the outcome as to who can collect the most marriage proposals in one season."

"Shocking! I had never heard that such a sport existed."

At that moment, I made a risky decision to up the ante of the game we were playing. Where it would lead, I had no idea, but I felt I had little to lose.

"And besides," I continued, "I am afraid I would hardly be considered competitive with only two proposals so far… although there is always a chance at more. The season is not over yet." A sideways glance told me I had got his full attention.

"Two proposals! *So far*?"

"Why, yes, that is correct. But as I say, I think there is a reasonable chance of at least one more, if I am patient. Mr. Frank Osborn has taken an interest."

"Good god! You cannot be serious!"

Turning to him with a challenge in my voice, I said, "Why? Do you think it so incredible that any man should want to marry me, let alone more than one?"

"No, no, of course not. You are a very… a very desirable young lady, and I am sure there are many… No, I was only just taken off my guard; that is all." His discomposure then seemed to change to alarm. "You have not actually accepted one of these gentlemen, have you, Georgiana?"

"Not yet. I prefer to keep my options open for the time being. One does not like to rush into such an important decision, especially when one may not yet have considered every possibility."

He put his hand to his forehead. "And your brother, does he know and approve of all this?"

"Surely what I do and do not tell my brother is my own affair. As to his approval, I fail to see where that enters in. According to my limited experience, young men will rarely be kept from proposing just because somebody would rather they did not, whether that be the lady herself or her father or her brother… or even her guardian. They get carried away by love, I suppose, and no one can stop them."

"This is your experience, is it? Young men forever getting carried away by love? I wonder, then, that you have been able to hold these ardent suitors at bay."

"They may be ardent, sir, but they are also *gentlemen*," I said very pointedly.

"Of course. Forgive me. That was uncalled for. You must understand that this comes as quite a revelation to me, quite a lot for me to absorb in such a short time. I may not yet be thinking clearly."

"That is the most sensible thing you have said on the subject."

"No doubt. No doubt. So there are two suitors so far. Am I allowed to know who the gentlemen are?"

I thought of Mr. Heywood and Mr. Sanditon then, and I felt a strong pang of guilt for bandying their earnest suits about so flippantly. The least I could do for them was to protect their identities. "It would hardly be honorable for me to mention them by name," said I.

"Naturally, but you do expect Mr. Osborn to soon add his name to your list?"

"Why not? He likes me; I like him; and you must admit it would be a very eligible match."

"I admit nothing of the kind. I hardly know the man. What mystifies me most, however, is how you can speak of this in so detached a manner, as if you were only deciding what gown to wear of an evening. Were not you the one who spoke out for the singular importance of happiness when it came to Anne's marriage. Where has that romantic gone?"

"If you recall, I came out in favor of balancing the romantic side with the practical. I may speak to you about the one, Colonel, but hardly the other. On the subject of love, I keep my own counsel."

"All the same, as your friend and guardian, I feel bound to caution you to bear in mind the seriousness of the question. This is not some harmless game you are playing at."

"More advice? Everybody seems very free with their advice to me, as if I had no sense of my own."

"None of us acts wisely all of the time. If you will not take advice from me, however, I must hope you will be less reserved with others – your brother, his good wife, or even Mrs. Collins if you need someone close at hand. I'm sure they would all tell you the same thing, that is to think very carefully before committing yourself in a way you may later regret. I know something of what I speak. As your brother was quick to point out to me, I made a fortunate escape from what would probably have been an very unsatisfying marriage when Anne did me the favor of changing her mind. She is an excellent lady in many respects, but I did not love her. By her example, I trust I am now also made wiser. Do you remember what she told her mother?"

"That she would marry the man she loved, meaning Dr. Essex, and that to do otherwise would be impossibly perverse."

"Exactly!"

"So, you intend to follow her example, Colonel, to marry for love?"

"Would not you agree that is the only acceptable course?"

"I would agree that it is the *best* arrangement, all other considerations being equal. But you will admit it is not always possible. Most people must give some consideration to money when they marry, even the younger sons of earls, I believe. And then there is the possibility that one's affection may not be returned. What then?"

"Perhaps it would be in time, though. I would be willing to wait a long while for that chance."

"Would you?"

"Yes, I would indeed, Georgiana. And I hope you will not cheat yourself by settling for less than what you deserve either."

"And what, in your opinion, is that?"

"A man who will love you with all of himself, and forever."

The music of the dance had ended, and it was as if the colonel's final statement echoed in the relative silence that followed. We stared at one another a few seconds more until I could bear the suspense no longer. I tore my eyes from his and gave my attention to my gloves. With an entirely unnecessary tug on each, I said, "It seems you have managed to give your advice after all, Colonel."

"Yes, well, I hope you will not resent me too much for it, not so much at least that you disregard what is most worthwhile in it."

"You may sleep well tonight, sir, knowing you have done your duty by me. You have stood in the place of my brother once again and given me appropriate counsel."

"Georgiana, I do not wish to be your…" He broke off without finishing.

"Pray, do go on," I encouraged him, suddenly hopeful of some clear declaration of his intent.

He dropped his eyes from mine. "I meant to say that I do not wish to be treating you as a child. I promised I should not do that anymore and I aim to keep my word. We are both adults, and more than that, we are the best of friends. At least I have always judged it to be so. Consider my advice, then, as from one good friend to another. Please."

"One friend to another," I repeated, a disappointed sigh inadvertently escaping my lips. "Very well."

"And you will remember what I said?"

"Of course, although I can make no promises as to abiding by it. The ideal you speak of is not always achievable."

"I pray it will be for you, though, my dear. Now, would you care to dance?"

As he led me out to find a place in the forming set, I could not help thinking how different I would have felt at that moment if he had just professed himself my lover instead of my "good friend." He had been given the perfect opportunity to do so, and yet he had very definitely chosen not to. The truth was he cared about me, he wanted the best for me, but that was as far as he could go. He meant – very kindly but very firmly this time – to put me on my guard.

It was all somehow familiar. My face grew warm with embarrassment as I realized why that was so, and I hoped that the flush I felt would be attributed to the exertions of the dance.

Nevertheless, I could no longer look my partner in the eye. I had just remembered how I had, at another ball some weeks earlier, participated in a conversation of a similar character, the difference being that this time I found myself on the opposite side. Before, I had been the one who had gone out of my way to be sure Henry Heywood understood that, his romantic optimism aside, we could never be more than good friends. He had refused to understand me, and an ugly scene has resulted with hurt feelings still not fully healed.

Now it was my turn, and I decided right there on the dance floor that I would not be so stubbornly dense as Henry had been. I would take the hint kindly given me rather than inviting further mortification for myself (and for Colonel Fitzwilliam) by pressing ahead any longer. I had had my chance. I had taken my best shot. There was nothing more to be done except to bow out of his life as quickly and as completely as possible.

- 31 -

Urgent Business

I hardly know how I got through the balance of the evening, but the next morning I told Mrs. Collins I wanted to leave for home as soon as it could be arranged. The first step, as she quickly pointed out, would be to speak to Colonel Fitzwilliam about it, to be certain he could make himself available to accompany us. Before we could even convey the information to him, however, he stopped by the house of his own accord.

"I came to tell you that I must go out of town for a few days," he announced when we three were assembled in the drawing room. "A bit of business that will not wait. I hope it will not create any inconvenience for you ladies." Looking at me specifically, he added. "I thought you could probably spare me easily enough. You may miss the use of my carriage more."

"Where are you headed?" I asked.

He hesitated and then answered as vaguely as possible, simply saying, "North."

At this, Charlotte became quite animated. "Ah, to the north, you say, Colonel. Well, the timing could not be more ideal, for Miss Darcy was just telling me she is determined to quit London for Pemberley immediately. Could not we all go together in that case? I daresay we could be ready to depart sometime tomorrow or by the next day at the latest."

Colonel Fitzwilliam seemed taken aback. "I am surprised to hear this, Miss Georgiana," he said, avoiding Charlotte's question by returning his attention to me. "I thought you intended to carry on until the end. Why, only last night you spoke of being patient and waiting to see what might yet develop before the close of the social season. I am sure you did. Has something occurred to change your mind?"

I could not say the truth – that I was heartbroken to have failed to attract the only man in London for whom I cared, and that I was now desperate to get away from the scene of my disappointment, that I could no longer bear to breathe the marriage-market atmosphere of the place, to endure the false flattery of fortune hunters or even the sincere attentions of well-meaning gentlemen who had no chance with me. Least of all could I bear continuing to do so in *his* presence, the kind, patient, self-sacrificing, *brotherly* Colonel Fitzwilliam. I nearly choked at the thought of it.

Since I made no reply, Charlotte comfortably filled in the resulting silence.

"I believe it is a very sensible decision, Colonel. When one has had enough of something, it is wise to say so and move on. I myself have been thinking the same, how refreshing it will be to return to beautiful Derbyshire after the noise and soot of London… which brings me back to my earlier question. Could we not all travel north together?"

"Would that it could be so, Mrs. Collins, but my business is of such an urgent nature that it requires my earliest possible attention. A delay of even a day or two is not to be contemplated. In fact, I must depart almost this minute. I only stopped to explain."

I finally found my voice. "And how long will you be away, sir?"

"Five or six days perhaps. No more than a week, in any case. You and Mrs. Collins might use the time to pack up your things and say your farewells. After I return, we can set out again just as soon as you please."

My alternate plan was conceived before he finished speaking.

"You shall not much mind a small delay, shall you?" Charlotte asked me. "A few days can make no difference."

"Not at all," I agreed. "The colonel must do as he judges best, and we shall get on very well on our own." I rose and the others did likewise. Holding out my hand to Colonel Fitzwilliam, I said, "I would not detain you from your urgent business another minute. Goodbye."

He took my hand, pressed it, and I could have sworn he was on the point of carrying it to his lips when he let it go instead.

"Safe journey," Mrs. Collins told him in farewell.

"Thank you, madam. I will return as soon as possible. You may be assured of that. Until then, goodbye, Georgiana," he said with a look of some significance, as if he meant to convey more to me than his words had expressed.

I just nodded and watched him stride purposefully from the room. Out on the street, he gave one final salute up to me at the window before climbing in his carriage and being driven away. In one respect I was happy to see him go. Nevertheless, my eyes followed his departing equipage to the end, not willing to break that last thread of connection to him a moment sooner than necessary. After all, I did not know when I would ever see him again.

~~*~~

That was the point of leaving London after all: to avoid spending any more time in Colonel Fitzwilliam's company when it had become so painfully obvious that he could never return my affection. And yet the travel home, the primary means by which I could sever myself from his continual presence, would require days more of the same. Or so I had thought. Now, by absenting himself, Fitzwilliam had given me the opening I needed to avoid that final trial.

"We are leaving the day after tomorrow," I announced to Charlotte as soon as Fitzwilliam's carriage was out of sight.

"What? No, you heard the colonel. We must wait for his return. I thought you agreed."

"I only agreed to the arrangement so that the colonel's conscience would be clear when he left us, but I intend to depart the day after tomorrow as originally planned. We can hire a carriage. We have servants to accompany us. What is there to stop us?"

Charlotte looked truly alarmed, and she walked up and down the room before answering, coming in very close to my face when she did so. "I am happy to give you your way in most things, Georgiana, since I am very sensible of the fact that I have only enjoyed this London holiday by your good pleasure. Still, I have a duty to perform, a responsibility to Mr. Darcy and to Elizabeth as well as to yourself. I must not allow you to do anything that may place you in jeopardy. This plan of yours is unsafe, and it is not on my authority alone that I say so. You know perfectly well that your brother directed most particularly that Colonel Fitzwilliam should accompany you home, so I cannot approve of your doing otherwise. We must by all means wait for your cousin's return."

"Dear Charlotte," I said, trying to sound patient and reasonable, when in truth I was probably neither. "You and I have become good friends, and I know you only want what is best for me. Your scruples on my behalf do you great credit, but I truly believe they lead you astray here. Although I know that my traveling with the colonel's escort was my brother's preference, he could not possibly have foreseen what complications might arise to make such a plan impractical. Circumstances have changed and we must adjust."

"What circumstances have changed except the colonel's brief absence? I do not understand your impatience, Georgiana."

"No, of course not." Indeed, why should she? I hardly understood it myself. "I'm sorry to be so unclear, but I simply cannot countenance the idea of remaining here another week waiting for Colonel Fitzwilliam's return; my nerves could not abide it. Trust me when I tell you that what is best for my health and my peace of mind is that I should be got home to Pemberley as soon as possible. I am depending on you to support me in this."

After ten minutes' more discussion of the subject, Mrs. Collins remained unconvinced. I did move her so far as to promise she would think about what I had said and if my request could be accommodated without significant compromise to safety. In the meantime, she agreed there would be no harm in undertaking the preparations for our departure – things that would have to be done whether that event took place in a week or in two days.

I busily wrote notes to closer friends, announcing my imminent departure and delivering my regrets that I would not be able to attend a ball or a party I had previously planned to. A note would not do for Andrea, though; I would take leave of her in person.

Henry was on his way out when I arrived at the Heywoods' house. "We meet again, Miss Darcy," he said upon running into me in the entry hall.

It grieved me to notice how it still pained him to be in my presence, and yet I had more sympathy for him than ever in light of my own recent disappointment. "Yes, sir," I said, "I hope that you are well."

"I cannot complain. Now, if you will excuse me, I am needed at the bank."

"Please stay a moment, Henry," I said, placing one hand on his arm to detain him. "I am leaving town soon, and before I go I just wanted to say once more how sorry I am for the unpleasantness that occurred between us. I hope someday we will be good friends again."

His expression softened. "Someday, perhaps. Not yet, but someday. Goodbye, Georgiana."

I smiled at him and he was gone, replaced instantly by his sister, saying. "What is this you have told Henry? Did you say you are leaving? Come sit down. Drink some tea with me, and I will talk you out of it."

She had taken my hand and was leading me up the stairs to the drawing room before I could argue. "I will drink tea with you, Andrea, but you should know that I have quite made up my mind. Now there is much to be done, so I may not stay long. I would not leave without seeing you, though. What a good friend you have been to me these past weeks! I will not forget it."

"You mustn't speak as if we were never to see each other again. Now sit down and explain yourself. I had such high hopes when I saw you dancing with Colonel Fitzwilliam last night, and yet today you are determined to run away? What has happened?"

"Oh, nothing so very tragic. I simply had the mortification of hearing my own words spoken back to me; that is all. I am glad Henry is gone for he was another reminder. Just as I talked very pointedly to him weeks ago about our being only friends, trying to warn him off, these were the very things I heard from the colonel last night. I did not wish to believe it anymore than your brother did at the time, but I have seen sense and taken the hint. Now I cannot wait to be off. Colonel Fitzwilliam has gone out of town for a few days on business, so this is my chance to make good my escape without him following dutifully along, something I could not bear."

"Oh, my dear! Then I suppose it must be so. But promise me you will write. And do not despair; the most surprising things can occur. One minute you may think all is lost, and the next…"

I then perceived in her countenance a mixture of contrasting emotions. I saw true pity and regret for me, yes, but something else as well. "Do you have anything you want to tell me, Andrea?" I asked.

"Oh, Georgiana, you are so wise. I cannot hide my feelings from you. I had the most enchanting time last night!"

"Thanks to Mr. Frank Osborn?"

"You have guessed it! I hope you will not mind. After all, I did first suggest him as a match for you."

"Not at all, my dear. I am delighted for you both."

It was true; I was happy for my friend. And yet, I felt all the lonelier somehow when I left Andrea for knowing that she might have so effortlessly found what continued to evade my grasp. And I would miss Andrea for herself too. She was the only one with whom I had shared my whole heart as to Colonel Fitzwilliam; she was the only one except Elizabeth who knew even half of what my heart had been through these past weeks.

The solution for such self-indulgent thoughts was hard work, I knew, and I set to it with even more vigor when I returned to the house after seeing Andrea. I had already told Mrs. Paddington of my plans for soon decamping to the north, setting things in motion. But there was packing still to be done as well as a myriad of other tasks and arrangements necessary before I could go. Although I was in a hurry, I did not wish to leave things in a state of disorder. That would not be the mature, responsible thing to do, and I had not forgot my resolutions. One other of my resolves was in more serious danger of collapse – the one that I would not behave rashly – for I felt that if I could not persuade Charlotte to my plan, I might very well go ahead without her approval. One way or another, I fully intended to quit London long before Fitzwilliam returned.

- 32 -

Trouble at Pemberley

If I had lacked sufficient incentive to return to Pemberley as soon as possible, more arrived for me the next afternoon. While I was continuing about packing my cases with Lilly's help and still wondering if Charlotte would agree to go when I wished, one of the maids brought up a letter for me.

"It come express, Miss," she said, "So Mr. Watkins thought you would want to see it directly."

I thanked the girl and took the letter, feeling an instant jolt of anxiety as I did so. Was someone ill? Had there been trouble with Mr. Wickham? A serious accident perhaps? I could think of no *good* news that would prompt the urgency implied by an express from Elizabeth, whose hand I recognized at once in the direction. I immediately dismissed Lilly and sat down to read.

Dearest Georgiana,

I do not mean to alarm you by writing in this manner. Be assured that everyone here is safe and in good health...

There, at least, was some relief.

...although, as you will see, I have my reasons for wasting no time in communicating with you.

We have had some drama here of late. The Wickhams' forced move to the cottage went as well as could be expected, and we all wait to see whether it turns out to be a success or not. Miss Bingley and the Hurst will be leaving us tomorrow, now that there is room for them at Heatheridge. And just this morning I had a fright while I was walking on the path by the stream...

A fright? What could she mean, I wondered? A dangerous animal perhaps, or an intruder? And waiting to see what will happen with the Wickhams? I did not like the sound of that either.

...It will probably turn out to have been nothing in itself, but the event led to a conversation between your brother and me that constitutes the real necessity for this letter.

I am afraid the conversation to which I refer became rather heated on both sides, something that has rarely happened between us in our married life and never this severely. I will not burden you with the details, nor would I have troubled you with even this much except it does concern you in one way.

I know not how it happened, but it seems your brother became aware that I have been keeping things from him. He was very displeased with me and even more so that I refused to give up my secrets when he asked...

Oh, no! *Her secrets*, she says, but Elizabeth was only being kind. It had been *my* secrets, not hers, that had caused this trouble. How could I have allowed this to happen?

...I cannot say that I much blame him, except that his irritation appeared to me to be beyond what I would have expected according to the circumstances. In any case, I trust all would soon be put right between us if I could set his mind at ease with the truth. Perhaps what he is imagining is something far worse.

So now you understand why I am appealing to you for help. I have not betrayed your confidence, my dear, but I must now earnestly ask your permission to do so. I am hoping that your sentiments have changed somewhat, that having your brother learn of your situation with the two other gentlemen will not grieve you so much as it once might have done. I truly believe he will think none the less of you for it, and I promise we will both be grateful for your helping us back to a good understanding. Write as soon as you are able.

Elizabeth

I was grief stricken when I read this – grief stricken and ashamed down to the depths of my soul – that through my selfishness I should have been the cause of such discord between the two people I treasured most in the world! Oh, how I wished I could have at that moment thrown myself at their feet and begged forgiveness!

I read the letter through once more, as a penance and to be sure I understood what Elizabeth meant to convey. I could see that she had taken care to spare my feelings by couching her description of events in moderate language. Imagine! To be showing *me*, the cause of all her trouble, such mercy while under duress herself! Here was the true definition of kindness.

Yet I was not fooled; I could decipher the truth well enough. William had been more than "displeased" and "irritated," or there would have been no urgent need for a remedy. No, there had been an argument unprecedented, with angry words hurled and probably hurtful accusations into the bargain. Who knew how much damage had been done? And it was all my fault. The only consolation was that Elizabeth believed it also in my power to mend the rift.

I did not hesitate; I went straight to my writing desk. My only thought was that I must set things right as quickly as possible. William and Elizabeth must not suffer one more moment of estrangement than absolutely necessary. I poured out all that was in my heart and prayed it would be enough.

Dear Elizabeth,

I was quite distressed by your letter, as you might well imagine. How selfish I have been to impose so long upon your good nature and sisterly friendship! If I have caused any irreparable harm to you or my brother by insisting on your secrecy, I shall never forgive myself. By all means, you must explain whatever you feel necessary to make my brother understand that you have not been false to him in any way. If he is angry, let it be with me, for it was I who refused to tell him about my situation or allow you to do so. You always urged me to be open with him; I will gladly testify to that at any time. I just pray it is not too late to undo what damage I may have done.

Tell my brother what you will. I am beyond caring. My hopes for Colonel Fitzwilliam have all been in vain. Make no mistake; he is kind and attentive as always, so I can find no fault in his behavior. He watches over me just as my own brother would do, which is precisely the problem. Even after all the time we have spent together, with ample opportunity for him to see me in a different light, Fitzwilliam continues to treat me as if I were his sister. There is nothing more I can do to encourage him, at least not within the bounds of propriety. I can only conclude that he is incapable of caring for me as I had hoped.

The fact that he cannot return my affection does not change what I now know with certainty; my attachment to him is just as strong as it ever was, perhaps stronger. I was only deceiving myself when I thought otherwise. Under the circumstances, it would be wrong of me to accept Mr. Sandi-ton's generous proposal, and I shall have to tell him so when I return. Perhaps in time I will be able to love someone else. Until then, I must be content to remain single. As you see, Elizabeth, I have taken to heart the wise counsel you gave me on that subject.

Now that everything is settled and my decisions are made, I am desperate to be home again. I miss Pemberley and both of you excessively, and there is no reason to linger here a moment longer. Consequently, Mrs. Collins and I are leaving almost at once and should be back with you the day after you receive this letter. Give my brother my love and my apologies. For the trouble I have caused you both, please forgive me.

Georgiana

The moment I finished, I sealed the letter and took it downstairs. "Could you see to it that this is sent at once, Watkins? And it must go by express." My hand was shaking when I gave the letter to the butler, and Charlotte was standing there to hear and see all.

"What on earth is the matter," she asked in a hushed tone, drawing me to one side.

Only then did I feel the dampness on my face, the tears that continued to flow. I must have looked a fright, but I cared not. "Trouble at Pemberley," said I, "and it is all my fault. Oh, Charlotte, there can no longer be any question about it. I must get home as soon as possible."

- 33 -

Desperate to be Gone

The only good in all of this was that Charlotte's sympathies were now thoroughly engaged on my behalf. She could see how genuinely distressed I was, and her inherent compassion compelled her to alleviate my suffering if she could. But, of course, I had also inadvertently aroused her curiosity.

"Trouble at Pemberley? What do you mean?" she asked in some alarm, leading me into the small sitting room to one side of the hall and closing the door. "Is Elizabeth unwell?"

"Not unwell in body, no. It is more an affliction of the mind and heart." I paused to control my emotions and to reflect on how much to reveal. Charlotte was a good and trustworthy friend to both Elizabeth and to myself. Still, I trembled at the thought of once again injuring others, this time by compromising privacy without permission. And yet some further explanation was clearly necessary. "Friction has arisen between Elizabeth and my brother, I am sorry to report, an argument of serious consequence apparently. And as I said, it is all my fault."

"That does not seem likely; you were not even there at the time."

"Nevertheless, it is true. Oh, Charlotte, I have been so stupid, so thoughtless! The truth is, I insisted on Elizabeth keeping some... some personal business of mine to herself – that she should not breathe a word of it even to my own brother. Now my horrid secrets have created this terrible rift between them, and I cannot help fearing the damage done may be irreparable."

"So that is it. Yes, distrust between a husband and wife is indeed a serious matter. And yet Elizabeth is too sensible to allow a misunderstanding to remain a permanent stumbling block. We must hope Mr. Darcy is as well, I suppose. Surely, when all is explained, things will soon be set right."

"That is what Elizabeth said in her letter, but I think she was only trying to spare my feelings. I have given her leave to speak to William freely now; I only hope it is not too late."

Here again, tears overtook me.

Charlotte silently ushered me to the sofa and sat down beside me. Presently, she said, "I have been thinking a lot about your request to depart London immediately, and this is what I propose."

At this ray of hope, Charlotte had my rapt attention.

"Suppose we were to hire a carriage for the short distance from here to Lucas Lodge, taking a male servant with us for protection. I daresay my father could see us the rest of the way from there."

I was totally amazed by this simple, elegant solution. "Do you really think your father would do it, Charlotte? I would pay all the expenses, naturally, but it is such a long way for him to go, there and back again."

"Oh, yes, I am quite sure he would. My father has long expressed a desire to see Derbyshire. He would like to meet my benefactor, Mr. Sanditon, of whom I have told him so much, and to finally set eyes on Pemberley. This will be just the excuse he has been looking for, and even Mr. Darcy should approve the arrangement. My father's escort can be no less satisfactory to him than Colonel Fitzwilliam's."

I, of course, agreed to the plan at once, and preparations for our departure swiftly moved forward. It was good to both be pulling together as a team now, especially since Charlotte had more experience with some of the practical tasks ahead. Only on one minor point did we briefly find ourselves at odds again.

"I shall send a message to my father," Charlotte told me as we were discussing the details of our plans, "telling him of our coming tomorrow. We can stay the night at Lucas Lodge, and then set out for Pemberley the next morning."

I held my tongue, conscious of how much I owed to Mrs. Collins – for her benevolent chaperonage these weeks in London and especially for her cooperation in the current undertaking. Though I averted my eyes, I could sense Charlotte studying me, and my inner conflict must have been apparent.

"You do not approve of this idea," said she at last. "I can see it in your countenance."

"I am sorry, Mrs. Collins. It is just that staying the night in Meryton feels like a full day wasted when we could have been half-way to Pemberley instead. It was undoubtedly premature of me, but I did write to Elizabeth that I would be home the day after tomorrow."

"The day after tomorrow! How did you suppose you were going to manage that, Georgiana, when we had not yet even come to an agreement between ourselves?"

I shook my head. "I had not quite worked that part out yet. I should have been glad to travel post day and night if that was required. But then, dear Charlotte, you came along with the perfect solution! Do you think that, if we sent an express to your father to forewarn him, he could have himself and his carriage ready to set off as soon as we arrive tomorrow?"

Charlotte laughed, and at first I did not know if her reaction boded well or not. "Anything is possible," she said presently. "When you have made up your mind to something, you are a force to be reckoned with, Miss Darcy. I shall write to my father at once."

This final obstacle cleared away, all was soon on pace for an early departure. The hired carriage was ordered for first thing in the morning, and the packing of trunks was shortly completed, except for those few items that must be added at the last moment. Watkins had assigned a footmen to accompany us as far as Lucas Lodge, and I knew the rest of the servants would be assembled in the morning for our departure. I felt I owed Mrs. Paddington more than a passing nod of farewell, however, so I went in search of her before I retired for the night.

"Mrs. Paddington, you are the one thing I shall be sorry to leave behind me tomorrow," I told the housekeeper when I found her, as expected, still at work in her offices.

She rose and took both my hands in hers. "You are a dear one, Miss," she said. "I shall be very sorry to lose your company. I've come to look forward to our little daily chats."

As had I. Mrs. Paddington had taught me so much, and yet our intercourse had not been all business. There had been mirth and warm regard developed in it as well.

"And now I suppose you must take the rest of your lessons at Pemberley," she continued.

"Yes, no doubt I still have much to learn. You are well rid of me, Mrs. Paddington, and of all my annoying questions. I will soon be bothering Mrs. Reynolds and Mrs. Darcy instead of you."

"Tush! You are no bother, child! Why, it has been a boon to my ego to have you hanging on my every word as if each one were gospel. You may be sure nobody else in this household does so!"

She laughed at her joke, and I joined her. Then I kissed her cheek and said goodnight.

I was weary when I finally crawled into bed, and yet I could not sleep for the feeling that I had forgotten something important. So I again examined the mental list I had compiled of things that must be done before our departure. Not an item had been neglected, though; not a detail unattended to. Everything had been done as it should be, so why did I still feel so unsettled?

I tried to dismiss my doubts and think of something else at random. My mind settled on Colonel Fitzwilliam at once – not with romantic regrets this time but rather concern for his welfare. I knew then what I had forgotten to do, so I got up, relit my candle, and went to the writing table again.

Although he had avoided saying so, my guess was that the colonel's business in "the north" was actually in Derbyshire, where his family resided. It seemed entirely possible, therefore, that I might encounter him on the road or that he should hear of my return through mutual acquaintances. But what if he should not? What if he should travel all the way to London again and find me gone? The least I could do was to leave him a note of explanation as to my change of plans – an explanation and an apology.

Writing this letter would not be easy, I realized after two failed attempts. It required a delicate balance – another occasion for walking a fine line – between honesty and discretion. I must say enough to make myself clear but not so much as to give my true sentiments away. He should know of my respect and gratitude but not be bothered by any useless allusions to a disappointed love. After much thought, much effort, and a few more tears, I was at least reasonably satisfied.

Dear Fitzwilliam,

I will endeavor to reach you with word of my change in plans. If you are reading this, however, I must suppose that such measures as were within my reach have utterly failed.

Just as urgent business called you suddenly away, the same occurred for me after you left. I can assure you that

Mrs. Collins and I have taken every prudent precaution. In fact, her father is to escort us to Pemberley in your place, so you need have no fear for our safety. Although unavoidable, I do regret inconveniencing you and beg leave to sincerely apologize for whatever measure of distress you may feel upon returning to London only to find me already gone.

Allow me to say how grateful I am for your unstinting kindness to me these past weeks and, indeed, for your faithful friendship these many years. No one could have asked for a more benign and dutiful guardian. Now that I am grown, however, I expect we will see much less of each other in future, which is only natural and right. You will marry and have a family of your own to fill your days. Perhaps, in time, I will do the same. May we both find happiness on our chosen paths.

Georgiana

It was brief and to the point; that was as it should be. No need for a long, drawn-out farewell. This was likely not a final parting, merely the close of the former chapter. Our relationship henceforth would be changed, diminished. He must know that, and I… I must learn to accept it.

I folded the letter, sealed it, and entrusted it to the butler's care the next morning, saying, "If Colonel Fitzwilliam should turn up looking for me, Watkins, please see that he gets this."

- 34 -

Homeward Bound

The hired carriage had once been elegant, I suppose, before it had weathered and worn into a hackneyed remnant of its former splendor. I cared not two straws for that. To me, it looked grand standing at the curb in the dewy morning air, for it represented the glorious means of my escape from London, the first step on a stair that would take me north to Pemberley, where I longed to be.

I could picture dear Mrs. Reynolds there, bustling the maids to prepare my rooms and perhaps arranging the menu for my first meal back. She always made such a special fuss over me when I had been away.

I was less confident of my brother's and my sister-in-law's reception. Would they have forgiven me yet? More importantly, had they forgiven each other?

With the distance dividing us, I felt completely at a loss, separated from the people I loved and cut off from any current information of how events might be going forward at home. Elizabeth's allusion to high drama at Pemberley had left me feeling unsettled. Obviously the most pressing problem by her report was the misunderstanding between William and herself. That overshadowed all else. But as we rolled along on the first leg of our journey, I could not help giving some thought to the other matters she had mentioned in passing.

I could well imagine that Miss Bingley and the Hursts had been unwelcome impositions at such a time. However, it was the presence of Mr. Wickham in the neighborhood that most concerned me. I worried he would find a way to make more trouble for my brother, especially if the removal from Heatheridge had stirred new resentment within him, which seemed likely. He would perceive the eviction as an insult, a humiliation, and he was not the sort to simply turn the other cheek.

It was an old fear come back again – the fear that we would never be entirely rid of the specter of Mr. Wickham. During our first week in London, before I knew anything about the current situation, I caught sight of a man who I thought might have been he, lurking in a dark corner across the street one evening. That may only have been my mind playing tricks on me, but having him actually living on the grounds of the Pemberley estates was no illusion. His presence there was very real, and I was sure he would make it felt, one way or another.

"Only another mile or two now," said Charlotte, calling me out of my reverie.

I smiled at her. "Your family will be happy to see you but probably not very happy with me for carrying you away again so quickly."

"You should have no worries on that head, Georgiana. I had a nice, long visit with them a few weeks ago. I should think they are well satisfied with that."

When we arrived at Lucas Lodge, I was relieved to see a carriage standing there at the ready and Sir William waiting for us.

"Capital! Capital!" he exclaimed as he handed me out. "How very good to see you again, Miss Darcy. I cannot tell you how delighted I was to hear I could be of service to you. Hello, Charlotte, my girl. Do come in, both of you. Refresh yourselves for a few minutes, and then we can be off on our travels."

We did as he suggested. A chance to stretch one's legs is always welcome on a long journey, and transferring the trunks from the hired carriage to Sir William's would take some minutes in any case. Twenty could easily have turned into forty minutes or an hour, however, had it not been for Sir William's own eagerness for the road. When the servant informed him that all stood in readiness, he immediately commenced shushing his wife and children and steering all of us out the door. The leave-taking ceremonies were hurried through, and we were soon on our way again, having lost very little time.

When we had waved out the windows to the Lucas clan and then achieved the main road, I began to thank Sir William most earnestly for his kindness, finishing with, "...I truly do not know what I would have done about getting home otherwise."

He looked pleased. "Nonsense, Miss Darcy. I am very gratified to be of service. And it gives me something useful to do with new places to see besides. I am a man of leisure now, as you may know, having given up my business some years ago and with my term as mayor long since finished. But when one has no set occupation, there is always the danger of becoming too sedate. So it was high time I had an adventure of some sort."

"It almost sounds as if you miss your former occupations, sir. Can that be the case?"

"Well, one must accept that one has an obligation to uphold one's place in society. A knight of the realm must be seen to be living as a gentleman, not sullying his hands with trade. Still, I am not too proud to admit to you, Miss Darcy, that I sometimes do miss aspects of my former life. Oh, those were glorious days when I was mayor! You must understand that His Majesty the King himself visited Meryton during my tenure – not the son who now sits on the throne in his stead, but the father, before he lost his senses – and as mayor I had the honor of addressing a speech of welcome to him."

I glanced at Charlotte, but she appeared entirely disinclined to join the conversation. No doubt she had heard all her father's stories before, probably more than once. I did not mind humoring the gentleman, though. His stories were new to me, and we had many hours to fill.

"Did you, indeed?" I asked. "A speech before the king; how thrilling. Were not you nervous to do it?"

"Well may you wonder, Miss Darcy. Well may you wonder. I daresay most would have been, and I did suffer great anxiety in anticipation of the event. Yet, once I began, it seemed as if I had been born to it. I do not think I flatter myself too excessively to say that my efforts were counted a resounding success. It was the highlight of my life… that and what followed."

I could see that he desperately wanted to be asked, and so I obliged him. "Why? What followed, sir?"

"I was invited to St. James's, Miss Darcy, and there I received my knighthood!" he finished in near ecstasy.

I tried to look properly impressed while I thought of something appropriate to say. In truth, I was amazed. Although I had heard that knighthoods were given away very cheaply these days, I had assumed it would take more than a pretty speech to earn one. I could hardly say what I was thinking, however. "I can imagine no clearer proof that your sovereign was exceedingly pleased with your service, Sir William. It must have been a proud moment, for you and for your family."

"None prouder, Miss Darcy. None prouder. Is not that so, Charlotte?"

"Oh, yes, Father – a proud moment for all of us, indeed."

After a pause, Sir William continued. "You are very good, Miss Darcy, to listen so patiently to an old man boasting about his small triumphs. To you, I daresay, these things are mere commonplace. No doubt you have been to St. James's many times."

"We go exceedingly rarely, Sir William, I assure you."

"But you have been presented, I am sure."

"Yes, sir, last summer."

I went on to give Sir William a brief account of how it had been. Then I continued to think of that event in the long silence that followed.

It had been a matter of some debate for weeks, I remembered. Personally, I was terrified at the idea of being presented at court. My brother was ambivalent at best and certainly would not have pressed for it had he been left to himself. It was Elizabeth who championed the cause.

"Georgiana simply must be presented," she told my brother in no uncertain terms over dinner on what was not the first occasion the topic had been broached. "You know as well as I do – no, better! – that is the proper thing to do. Would not your mother and father have wanted it so, Darcy?"

"My father would have judged as I do, that it is a thing of little importance. He never cared for pomp, and he never aspired to the life of a courtier."

"And yet, it must have been your father who saw to it that you attended a levee at an appropriate age and were yourself presented."

"That was only to fulfill a promise he had made to my mother before she died."

Elizabeth did not have to say anything more. My brother's own words had provided the conclusive evidence in the case, and his reasoning did the rest. If my mother had desired her son presented at court, clearly, as my guardian, he could do no less for me.

The matter was thus determined, and, once again, I had little to say about it. I am proud to have been responsible for one augmentation to the plan, however, when I suggested that I should prefer not to endure the ritual alone.

"I should feel so much easier if you were being presented at the same time, Elizabeth," I said.

"I? Be presented at court? Surely not!"

"No, wait," said William. "I think Georgiana has a point. You have married into a family of rank, Elizabeth, and so it is perfectly appropriate. More than appropriate, really. Just as in Georgiana's case, it is the proper thing to do. We cannot have you being the only one amongst us excluded from an acquaintance with the royal family. That would be unfair."

"But the expense! I will not hear of such wasteful extravagance on my account."

I rushed in to assist my brother. "You made no complaint about expense when you were speaking of me."

"*That* was completely different," she said, pretending not to see the feebleness of her own argument.

"A train for your gown and a few feathers added to your headdress – what is that, Elizabeth?" asked my brother. "A trifle, and it cannot be otherwise the least inconvenient, since we are going on Georgiana's account anyway."

Elizabeth's protests fell on deaf ears, as mine had done, and it was soon decided. We would all three go to London and accomplish the fearsome ordeal along with some other business my brother had to settle in town.

Sponsors were soon arranged for both of us, and Elizabeth and I began preparing our wardrobes and practicing our low curtseys at once.

"What I still cannot understand," I said to her one day after we had been reviewing the required protocol, "is how one can be expected to back away from the throne without tripping over the required three-yard-long train."

"I daresay we shall find out more details before the time arrives," replied Elizabeth. "If, as we have been told, there is an attendant to arrange the train in the first place and another to announce the lady's name, perhaps there will be someone to assist with carrying the train backwards out the door again as well."

For our rehearsals, we nominated my brother to preside as sovereign while Elizabeth and I took turns at the other roles. I would play the lady being presented while she scurried about performing the duties of all the attendant lords-in-waiting. Then we would reverse roles. This was great fun as long as we remained in the safety of a Derbyshire drawing room, but it became more dauntingly serious the nearer St. James's we came.

I was glad it was tolerably warm that day, since we would have been obliged to leave behind any wraps we had brought. And although I would have been terribly nervous in any case, it seemed that much worse for being so exposed. I wore yards and yards of fabric, and yet most of it was draped uselessly over my arm in the form of a train as I exited the carriage at St. James's. Meanwhile my neck and shoulders were completely bare. I was not alone, of course; Elizabeth and every other lady there to be presented also followed the same rules of attire.

How I got through it, I do not rightly know. At every moment – from when I quitted the carriage until I returned to it – I fully expected disaster. I was shaking so violently that I felt certain I would trip, fall, or forget what I was to do.

Although Elizabeth assured me afterward that I had done everything exactly as we had rehearsed so many times, I cannot verify it from memory. Those few minutes are mostly a blank to me. Thus my account to Sir William Lucas that day on the road to Pemberley was not short in length and detail by design, but rather by necessity.

- 35 -

Bump in the Road

If one has the need or desire to spend lengthy intervals in deep contemplation, then there is nothing like a long carriage journey for it. No matter how amiable one's companions may be, conversation eventually lags, leaving vast tracts of time with nothing to fill them but one's own thoughts.

We had made good progress on our first day, covering so much ground that on the second we expected to easily reach our destination. Unfortunately, by then we had also exhausted every topic for discussion we could conceive of. Even Sir William, with his garrulous ways, seemed to have run out of stories to tell.

My mind was therefore in want of occupation, and it easily slipped into a place of retrospection, reviewing the last couple of years and considering what had been their effect on me. On the surface, it might not look as if anything had altered. I knew different, however. I was no longer the naïve child who had been so mesmerized by Mr. Wickham's cunning charms. I was not even the same frightened girl I had been when I was presented at St. James's. Although I never expected to be completely free of my innate shyness, experience had changed me, matured me, given me more courage and confidence. That is what I carried home with me from London. My weeks there had not been wasted; my painful struggles were not entirely in vain. Whatever the future held, I felt as if I were better prepared to face it than I had been only a few months before.

Elizabeth's parting words of advice came back to me then. I heard her telling me once again that contentment comes not from discovering what one needs in another person – in the love of a man, more specifically in my case – but from finding peace within oneself. She had astutely diagnosed my problem. Had I learned the lesson, though? Was I cured of my unrealistically romantic notions? Not fully perhaps, but I thought I was well on my way.

The idea of remaining on my own no longer panicked me. Instead of thinking in terms of replacing Colonel Fitzwilliam in my affections with someone else, I now was able to consider replacing him with no one at all. I could conceive of the possibility of filling my life with different kinds of worthwhile pursuits – music, yes, but more than that. If I did not marry, I would have the leisure to dedicate myself to charitable works, or perhaps I would write or paint. The idea of studying landscape design or architecture was also intriguing. Many options were open to me, thanks to my financial independence, something for which I must always remember to be grateful. I also felt a solemn responsibility to use that gift wisely, to benefit more than myself.

How vain the London season seemed in hindsight – vain and self-indulgent. While it was true that for ordinary folk finding a viable match was often a matter of survival, the same could not be said of the *ton*. No, the extravagance and show were more about making profitable alliances, about marrying one vast fortune off to another, many times with little regard for the wishes of the young people involved. Another thing to be grateful for – that my family placed no pressure of that sort on me. No one had argued that I must accept Henry Heywood when he asked me because it would be advantageous to ally our two families and sources of wealth. And despite what Mr. Wickham had warned me of years before, my brother showed no sign of forcing me to marry someone I did not like simply because he was rich or titled.

Yes, there was much to be grateful for, and so I determined to put my petty disappointments behind me once and for all and think more of others.

I suppose most people experience such moments of spiritual clarity and selflessness from time to time, remembering that we were put on this earth to honor God and do good works. Perhaps I am particularly weak, however, for I find it difficult to live long on that lofty plane, to maintain in thought and deed the ideals to which I sincerely subscribe. The cares of this world begin to creep in from the right and from the left, and I am unable to hold them completely at bay.

That second day in the carriage would be no different. Although I basked in the warmth of pure contentment for a long while as we jostled along down the road, satisfied that I had reached a new level of peace within myself, such a state can never be sustained. A simple thought or distraction is often enough to break the spell. In this case, something of a more violent nature would occur to disrupted my tranquility.

~~*~~

We had left Lemley, the last coaching town, with a fresh set of horses that we expected to see us the rest of the way to our ultimate destinations.

"Not long now," I said, mostly for Sir William's benefit. "Another ten or twelve miles to the village of Lambton, I would guess, and then five more from there to Pemberley."

"That is good news, Miss Darcy," said he. "Despite my genuine enthusiasm for making this little expedition, I believe I shall be just as pleased when the journey is completed."

"As you say," agreed Charlotte. "It is quite remarkable how a comfortable carriage grows proportionally less so with the passing of each hour spent in it."

"Indeed, Daughter. Yes, indeed."

"You must both take something to eat with us before you continue on to Reddclift," I suggested. "Then, in a day or two, when you are fully rested, perhaps you can drive back over for a proper dinner and a tour of the place"

Sir William was in the process of thanking me for this invitation when I heard a strange creaking noise and felt the first shudder. Immediately, our forward momentum slowed.

"What was that?" I began to ask.

Before I could get the words out, however, there was a loud crack of timber and the coach lurched to a sudden halt, falling off to the right at an abnormal angle. In those few moments, all was chaos. We three tumbled from our seats, but it must have been far worse for the men riding outside. I heard them shout when the carriage buckled beneath them, and the horses whinnied their alarm as well.

Then the coachman appeared at the window, calling out, "Is anybody hurt in there?"

After we had struggled upright and taken stock of ourselves, Sir William answered. "No, Figgins, I believe there is nothing worse than a few bumps and bruises here."

"Broken axle, sir," the coachman continued by way of explanation as he opened the door to let us out. "I heard her startin' to give way, so I pulled up as sharp as I could. None of the lads is hurt either, but now we're in a fix. You and the young ladies might as well climb out and try to make yourselves comfortable. We ain't going anywhere for quite a spell, I'm afraid."

I noticed my hand shook when I held it out to accept Sir William's assistance from the tipping carriage. Although it was true that I had nothing worse than a bump on the knee, I felt quite shaken for the shock of the thing and for the dawning knowledge of what might have happened. If we had been traveling faster or along the edge of a precipice at the time… Well, that did not bear thinking of.

Instead, the only casualty seemed to be Charlotte's trunk, which had come loose from its fastenings in the accident, fallen to the ground, sprung open, and spilled some of its contents out onto the road. Charlotte and I set about tidying up that situation whilst the men – the coachman, groom, and footman in addition to Sir William – tended to the horses, examined the carriage, and discussed what was to be done. Presently Sir William returned to us with the results of their conference.

"The thing is beyond repair, apparently. Nothing will do but a new axle, and as you can imagine, we have not a spare with us."

"What is the solution, then, Papa?" asked Charlotte.

"There is no alternative but to send to Lemley for assistance. Though it is well behind us, I am told it is still the nearest town of the sort to employ a wheelwright. Let us just hope that an axle of the right size already exists and does not need to be manufactured from scratch. Figgins, excellent fellow that he is, will take one of the horses and go himself. If we are very lucky, he should be back in a few hours with the implement we need and help to install it. Still, it will be a long wait with a good chance darkness will fall before everything is set to rights again. Figgins suggests, and I quite agree, that we should seek shelter in the meantime. We passed a farm house less than half a mile back. Perhaps they would be willing to show us a little hospitality under the circumstances."

This was clearly the only sensible thing to do. The sky threatened rain, and the bleak local landscape provided nothing in the way of shelter or comfort – not a single tree nor even an accommodating rock to sit on. So we started back along the way we had come – Charlotte, her father, and myself – reaching the farm house Sir William had spoken of within fifteen minutes.

A man in his prime, who turned out to be the proprietor, saw us approaching and came to meet us. Sir William explained to him our predicament, finishing with, "...And so we were hoping you might be willing to assist us."

The farmer, who had introduced himself as Mr. Tinker, said with a humility typical of his breed, "You are welcome to anything I have, sir, if that will be of any use."

"Thank you. That is most kind. You haven't a carriage by any chance, I suppose."

"Not likely, sir. Not much call for carriages here. We make do with a cart and a mule, and the mule come up lame just yesterday."

"In that case, my good man, I ask only for a little food and shelter, especially for the ladies, until repairs are made and we can be on our way again. We will, of course, be more than happy to compensate you for your trouble."

Mr. Tinker insisted it was no trouble at all and quickly took us inside to his wife.

The cottage was as tidy inside as it was out, with only the inevitable clutter of children and daily living in evidence. Mrs. Tinker, who obviously had no forewarning of our entrance, hurried to wipe her hands on her apron and then removed it before coming to meet us.

"This here is Sir William Lucas, Annie," said her husband, "his daughter Mrs. Collins, and Miss Darcy. Their carriage broke down out on the road out in front of our place."

"Pleased to meet you all," she said with a self-conscious curtsey. "Dear me! A carriage accident! Is anybody hurt? Miss Darcy, I see your gown is torn at the knee."

"It is nothing, Mrs. Tinker," I replied. "We are all perfectly well, I do assure you."

Three children, no doubt intrigued by the presence of strangers, had crept forward one by one for a look at us. I saw a boy of around nine and two younger girls who instantly made me think of Abigail and Amelia, Mr. Sanditon's daughters.

"This is Fred," said Mrs. Tinker, "and Alice, and little Bess. The baby's sleeping, but I'm sure he'll be up to greet you 'afore long."

Sir William clasped his hands together and exclaimed, "Capital! Allow me to congratulate you on a fine family, Mr. and Mrs. Tinker. Yes, a very fine family indeed!"

We could not have hoped to find ourselves in better hands. Although Mr. Tinker soon had to return to his work out of doors, Mrs. Tinker made it her first priority to see that we were comfortable, apologizing all the while for the modest style of her arrangements. "We seldom get visitors here," she said, "as remote as we are. So this is a special occasion. I just wish I had something more suitable to put before you. It will only be stew tonight for supper, I'm sorry to say, but you're welcome to share what we've got. We can always fill up on bread and vegetables. With a big garden, we never want for vegetables."

Charlotte and I did our best to set Mrs. Tinker's mind at ease, assuring her that simple fare would be perfectly agreeable and much appreciated. I took my turn at apologizing too. Our unexpected presence would clearly tax the Tinkers' resources to their limits. And although I suspected they would prove too proud to accept any payment in return, I was determined to thank them in some appropriate way for their generosity. I considered that perhaps a fine, fat goose delivered just before Christmas would be the very thing.

After eating some supper, Sir William walked out late in the day, taking bread and cheese to the men and hoping to find Mr. Figgins back from Lemley with good news.

"I am told it will be sometime tomorrow before repairs can be made," he reported with a sigh when he returned. "The wheelwright has nothing exactly correct in his small stock, according to Figgins. Some modifications will have to be made to what he does have before it will suit our needs. He promises to bring the replacement axle to us first thing in the morning." Turning to Mrs. Tinker, he added, "I regret that we must impose on your kind hospitality a while longer, dear lady. I myself prefer to spend the night in my carriage, where I can keep watch. The night is warm and I shall be very snug inside, now that it has been propped upright again. But I would be much obliged if you could find a bed for the young ladies."

I was very much obliged to her as well, especially when I discovered she intended to give up her own room to us.

"Henry and I can bunk in with the children for one night," she insisted. "No trouble at all."

If I had needed an example of what it meant to think more of others, to put the needs of someone else before my own convenience, I could not have asked for a better demonstration.

- 36 -

Foreboding

That night, as Charlotte and I prepared for bed in our borrowed room, my growing disquietude prompted a question from her. "You are uneasy tonight, Georgiana. Are you unhappy with our situation? The room is not at all what you are used to, but the bed is clean and looks comfortable enough."

"No, it's not that; I certainly have no complaints for myself. And although I hate to put the Tinkers out of their way, I know it could not reasonably be helped."

"What then?"

"I am thinking of my brother and Elizabeth. Oh, Charlotte, they will be wondering what has become of us, perhaps worrying unnecessarily. I wish there were some way to get word through to them. Perhaps if I had stayed with the carriage, I could have found someone passing by who would have been willing to deliver a message. I did not think of it before, and now it is too late."

"Of course it would be preferable to keep your family from wondering, but there is no reason they should be overly anxious. Delays of this kind are so commonplace as to take no one by surprise; as often as not a horse will come up lame or a carriage needs repair. They will think nothing of your being a day behind what you had planned."

I hoped Charlotte was correct. And yet as I lay awake in bed that night, listening to the sounds of my companion's peaceful slumber, I could not dismiss the feeling that there was something terribly amiss at Pemberley, some severe distress befallen them. Perhaps it had begun with my failure to arrive as expected, but it did not end there. My fears grew, minute by minute, to encompass a far greater calamity than that, although what exactly it might be I could not rightly say.

Before I could be carried too far down this path, I had to check myself. I knew that if I fell asleep contemplating possible disasters, my dreams were sure to reflect that turmoil. So I deliberately redirected my thoughts to something more congenial, recalling a conversation that took place before our accident.

I had been looking out the window, enjoying a particularly fine prospect, which I had seen before, when Sir William broke the silence.

"You smile, Miss Darcy. Do you spy something that pleases you?"

"I do indeed, Sir William. Look at that charming little village across the way," I said, pointing.

He turned his head in the direction I indicated, and Charlotte also leant forward for a better view.

"I know not what it is named," I continued, "but I have always admired how pretty it looks tucked between those two hills with that arching bridge the only way in or out. I make a point of watching for the place whenever I pass this way."

"No doubt you have traveled this road dozens of times before, Miss Darcy, beginning with when you were but a young girl, I should imagine."

"Many times, yes – to visit our relations at Rosings or going to London and back. I was at school in town for some time as well. Otherwise, I have traveled very little."

"And why should you want to? From what Charlotte tells me, there can be no finer place in all of England than Pemberley. For one so lucky as to live there, coming home must always be the happiest part of any journey."

"Oh, yes," I had agreed wholeheartedly at the time. But now I felt my cheerfulness fade. Perhaps it was bringing that picturesque village to mind once again, or perhaps it had more to do with the understated affection I had noticed between the father and daughter with whom I had shared this journey. For whatever reason, I was powerfully reminded of one return to Pemberley that had not been at all joyful.

I was twelve at the time, and William and I had been away visiting our Aunt, Uncle, and Cousin de Bourgh when we received the urgent summons. My brother, to whom the message was addressed, told me only that Papa was ill and wanted us home.

As a child who had already lost one parent to illness, it took no more than those few words to mightily alarm me. My fears were further awakened by what I observed in my brother's demeanor. He had grown quite pale and there was a grim, hardened set to his mouth. Plus, his haste to be gone told me there was no time to lose.

Looking back, I can more fully appreciate what William must have been feeling. He cared deeply for our father and would miss him. But beyond the grief, he must have felt the inescapable weight of responsibility shifting even then onto his young shoulders.

We left immediately, and all the way home I fretted over what I would find when we arrived. I thought of Papa and pleaded with God that he would not be taken from me. Although my father had never been overly demonstrative of his affection nor indulgent with his time, I knew that I was loved. And I believed that I was safe so long as my stalwart parent was there to watch over my world. He seemed so strong, so confident, so immovable that it defied logic that he could be defeated by something as insubstantial as an illness one could not even see. And yet in my heart, I feared the worst.

After silently pondering these things for more than a day as we rode side by side in the carriage, I looked up at my brother. With tears already pooling in my eyes, I asked him, "Is Papa going to die?"

I could see the sadness in his own eyes as William stroked my hair, waiting as long as possible before delivering the blow. "I am sorry, Geegee. I wish I could spare you, but yes, I believe he is going to die. That is what the medical men who have been attending him predict. We will find out the truth soon enough. In the meantime, we must prepare ourselves but also continue to hope for the best. Understand?"

I nodded and blinked, which sent the unshed tears rolling down my cheeks at last. William put his arm about my shoulders and drew me closer. He spent the rest of our journey alternately trying to comfort and distract me. It was he who the same day first pointed out to me that charming village I have so admired ever since, suggesting it looked as if it might have come out of one of the fairy stories I still liked to read. Even this could not make me long forget what lay ahead however.

Upon our arrival to Pemberley, we were told that Papa was very weak but still alive, and so we went directly to his bedside. I can still remember how strangely diminished he looked lying there, almost shrunken into himself and at least ten years older than when I had last seen him. Gone, seemingly overnight, were his robust physique and his larger-than-life presence, both stolen away by some murdering sickness which the doctors could neither clearly diagnose nor cure.

"Come here and kiss me, my child," this man, whom I barely recognized as my father, said in an unfamiliar, raspy voice.

My courage faltered and, as I so often did, I looked to William for reassurance. He nodded and sent me forward with a gentle nudge. I dutifully kissed Papa on the forehead and then focused my attention on his eyes, where he seemed most like his former self.

"You are a good girl," he said, "and I have always been proud of you, Georgiana. You must learn to listen to your brother now, though. He will look after you when I am gone."

"Yes, Papa," I managed through my tears. Papa then turned to William and I gave way.

"I am glad you have come in time, son," he said, a note of relief sounding in his words. "It is a heavy mantle I must now pass on to you, but one I am confident you are able to bear."

"Father, I am grieved, grieved and afraid," said William, his voice faltering. He was on one knee at the bedside, holding my father's hand in both of his.

"You mustn't fear for me or for yourself either. I am going to join your mother, and you... Well, you are ready to come out from behind my shadow. I have taught you all that I know, so you are fully equipped to assume your place as master of Pemberley. Take as much care superintending it as I know you will with your sister. It is a living, breathing thing with many souls dependent on its continuing to prosper."

William waited silently while Papa gathered enough strength to speak again.

"I tell you nothing new, my son. These things you have understood from your youth. I am only pleased to have been given this last chance to encourage you... and to see my children's faces again."

These were Papa's final words. After looking once more with watery eyes from my brother to myself and back again, his lids closed, he presently fell into unconsciousness and, soon afterward, breathed his last.

I fled the room as soon as it was over to seek comfort in Mrs. Reynolds's arms, but William remained more than an hour longer. When he finally emerged, he looked haggard, as if he had been through a brutal battle and barely survived. I believe during that time he had fought against and finally come to terms with the new realities of his situation – not only Papa's death but also the end of his own life as he had known it before. Nothing would ever be the same for him again. Although William had never been frivolous, now any carefree feelings were gone. At three-and-twenty, he was suddenly responsible for not only the care of a younger sibling but also the management of a small empire.

My life had changed too, but not so severely. I had merely lost my father; William had lost his youth and his freedom as well that day. A less conscientious person might not have allowed his new responsibilities to bind him. In fact, I have heard of cases where the opposite was true – a young man, suddenly finding himself in charge of his father's riches, runs amok and ruins his family. My brother is cut of much sturdier cloth, fortunately. He took his new position seriously, so seriously that I rarely heard him laugh or saw him being playful after that – not until he married Elizabeth, at least. That finally revived him.

William fulfilled his responsibility to me very admirably. No one could have asked for a more caring and conscientious brother to watch over her growing up. And yet I still miss my father, even after all the years that have passed. Time has eased the pain, but I still grieve. I still remember, even when I do not wish to.

I did not wish to that night in the Tinkers' cottage, and yet despite my best efforts to the contrary, my thoughts had come full circle; after briefly taking a more cheerful turn, they had run back to contemplating calamity again – the dark despair of when I returned home to find my father dying. What would I find at Pemberley this time, I wondered? I prayed God I was wrong, but my every instinct told me it would be something equally harrowing.

- 37 -

Rescue Party

Although I was spared the nightmares I had worried would be mine, I awoke the next morning with no diminishment of my misgivings. I still had the powerful sense that fresh calamity hung in the air, that something more serious than the breakdown of a carriage or a misunderstanding between husband and wife was in the offing.

Charlotte was still asleep, so I remained quietly in bed for a time, my mind searching for answers. I had never known the gift of second sight in the past, nor had I ever received a particular premonition that had come true. I was not even certain I believed in such things. So I had no idea what to do with these new, uninvited sensations. I did not like their frightening effects, but neither could I seem to rid myself of them. Then my vague impressions of danger started to take a more specific turn. My worries began to coalesce about the person of Elizabeth. *She* was the one in peril; I was almost sure of it. And yet what good did knowing do when I was in no position to help or warn her?

All I could think was that I must get home as quickly as possible. Toward that end, I rolled over and jiggled Charlotte's shoulder. "Time to wake up," I said insistently, repeating the practice until it had the desired effect.

Charlotte left the coziness of her bed without much complaint. By then, we could both hear that the family was up and moving about downstairs, so it would have seemed rude to lie abed any longer. It was more difficult to persuade Charlotte to leave the relative comfort of the cottage, however.

"I am certain my father intended we should wait here," she said as we were dressing. "It will cost no more than twenty minutes to retrieve us once the carriage is repaired, and we should only be in the way in the meantime."

"Your father said the new axle would be here first thing this morning, and twenty minutes is more than I am willing to sacrifice for the sake of convenience. I cannot explain how I know it, Charlotte, but Elizabeth is in danger. For her sake, it is most vital that we waste no time in reaching Pemberley."

Charlotte's love for Elizabeth, and possibly for me as well, overcame any further objections she may have had to my seemingly irrational fears. She agreed to walk out to the carriage as soon as we could civilly take leave of the Tinkers.

Mrs. Tinker also did her best to dissuade me from leaving and, as expected, she refused any offer of payment for her trouble. In the end, she accepted only our thanks and a kiss on the cheek from me to express my sincere appreciation.

Unfortunately, when Charlotte and I reached the carriage, it had not yet been returned to operating condition. In fact, the promised help from Lemley did not arrive until half an hour later. The men then set to work immediately but, from what I could tell, difficulties plagued them at every turn. It looked as if it should be a long wait after all, which I would have cared little about were it not for my concern for Elizabeth's safety. I could only think how precious time – time which should have been spent helping my dear sister – was being lost as each idle minute ticked by.

Then I noticed a large party of horsemen approaching from the north, trailed at some distance by a carriage. It was quite an unusual sight, and all eyes turned from their work to watch the spectacle. I was wondering at the meaning of it, even growing a little fearful, when I began to suspect something familiar in the figure leading the group rapidly onward. As they drew nearer, I was certain.

"It is my brother," I said to Charlotte, who was at my side. "Sir William, it is my brother," I called out to him and to the others.

Then I took another look. "And Colonel Fitzwilliam," I added. Although I suppose I should not have been so surprised that William would come in search of me, I was entirely mystified as to why a party the size of a small army would accompany him. And what on earth was Fitzwilliam doing among them?

These questions were set aside for the moment, for William was upon us. He drew his horse to an abrupt halt, quickly slipped from the saddle, coming to my side and taking me into his fervent embrace. "Are you well, Georgiana?" he asked a moment later, holding me at arm's length and studying my person for any ill effects. "There has been trouble here. Have you come to any harm?"

"I am well," I quickly assured him, "as are the others. Only a few bumps and bruises. It was a minor accident caused by a broken axle, and Sir William has been taking very good care of us."

"Thank God," he exclaimed as he took a moment to shake Sir William's hand. "Elizabeth was so certain it had been something much more serious."

"Elizabeth!" I repeated, reminded of my former alarm. "How is she? If she has been worrying about me, I believe I have spent the same hours fearing something ill had befallen her. In fact, I had the most compelling premonition."

William laughed, more from relief than amusement, I expect. "What is it with the female mind?" he asked. "Always imagining the worst and perceiving mountains of trouble where there are only molehills. To answer your question, my dear sister, Elizabeth has suffered nothing more severe than another nightmare. That is what sent me out on this search, her conviction that it meant you were in distress. I do not mean to make light of such dreams; you know yourself how terrifying they can be. It is simply a profound comfort to find it was all for naught in this case. Doubtless she will be restored to perfect peace as soon as she sees you are safe and well. In light of that," he said turning to Sir William, "I propose to take the ladies ahead with me, in the carriage I have brought. Would you care to join them?"

"I thank you, Mr. Darcy, but I will remain behind for as long as it takes."

As these two continued to discuss the arrangements, I took a step back. My concern had eased considerably at hearing my brother's report that Elizabeth was well. And yet, like he had said of her, I would not recover completely until we were safely reunited. My sense of foreboding had been too pronounced to be forgotten so easily. In any case, although sorry for the anxiety that had prompted it, I was grateful help had come to return me to Pemberley without further delay.

All this time, Colonel Fitzwilliam had remained in the background, dismounted from his horse at a distance of several yards and not saying a word. Our eyes finally met then, and we exchanged nods of acknowledgement. From his perplexed expression, I guessed there were as many unanswered questions and feelings on his side as on mine.

Despite the trouble I recently took to avoid him, I had to admit it was good to see his face again. I could not touch the familiar lines of his brow, his cheek, his mouth. Indeed, I never had, although I had imagined it often enough. Instead, I traced them once more with my eyes. I allowed myself that small, bittersweet indulgence.

A pang of conscience shot through me next, and I wished I had a copy of the note I had left for the colonel in London, to hand to him now by way of explanation. No doubt he was wondering why I had not waited for him there. Perhaps he felt hurt, even betrayed. After all, I had agreed to his plan and then immediately done just the opposite. My guilt faded, however, when I remembered that Fitz-william was not where he said he would be either. What had become of his so-called urgent business, for the consideration of which he could not delay his departure even a single day? He had preferred to leave me behind instead. Now he had turned up exactly where he knew Charlotte and I wanted to go, at Pemberley, and as part of this ridiculously large search party. How could he possibly account for it?

I wanted answers, yet it hardly seemed the ideal time and place to pursue the matter, standing out in the middle of a public road with so many other people about. Still, I considered approaching him. We would surely both be easier when in command of all the facts. He looked as if he might be of the same mind. Before either of us could act on those impulses, however, the opportunity was lost. With a flurry of activity in response to my brother's orders, Charlotte's trunk and mine were quickly transferred to the other carriage, into which we ourselves were helped straightaway.

"Good news that Elizabeth is well," Charlotte said as we got underway.

"Yes," I agreed. "All the same, I will not feel quite easy until I see her for myself. I hope you will not mind awaiting your father at Pemberley."

"Not at all. He will likely be no more than a few hours behind us, and I can think of no more comfortable place to be stranded for a time than at Pemberley."

"Even so, you must be impatient to reach your home again, and to see Ruth. I have kept you away for weeks beyond what you originally intended."

"It was no sacrifice. Altogether, it has been a thoroughly enjoyable experience. Think of the balls I have attended, the fine houses I have seen, the ladies and gentlemen I have met. I know it was only as your chaperone, but it made no difference to me. I was proud to be known as such, and proud that you behaved yourself in a manner requiring very little correction from me. We have become good friends, I think."

I nodded. "I am happy you feel that way too. As to my behavior… Well, I did give you *some* difficulty."

"I suppose. I did find your whims and emotional eccentricities difficult to fathom at first. Once I understood how you felt about Colonel Fitzwilliam, though, it all made perfect sense."

I looked at her aghast, and yet I was by then well enough acquainted with her to recognize that she knew what she was talking about. There was no use in denying anything. And after all, we were friends, as she had said. "You knew?" I asked. "All this time and you never said a word?"

"Not at first, but then the evidence kept mounting, day by day. As for speaking of it or not, that was up to you. Other than this one conversation, I will never mention it again… to anyone."

"Thank you, Charlotte. I know I can trust you to keep your word. And I suppose I do not mind so very much that you have guessed my partiality, even though it has come to nothing. It is, however, quite distressing to find out I have been so easily seen through."

"Not so easily as all that, Georgiana. And for what it may be worth, I too believe Colonel Fitzwilliam is an excellent gentleman, well worthy of your admiration. I am glad to have had the chance to know him better."

My gaze shifted. Looking past Charlotte and out her window, I had a clear view of Colonel Fitzwilliam, comfortably erect in the saddle and riding alongside our carriage. Yes, he was worthy of my admiration. No matter what lies I told myself, what rationale I used in the future to talk myself out of being in love him any longer, I could never say I was better off without him and mean it.

~~*~~

We finally arrived at Pemberley about midday, and I was looking forward to retreating to my rooms for a rest as soon as I had seen Elizabeth. Instead, when William asked her whereabouts upon entering the house, the butler handed him a note.

"Madam is not at home, sir," Henderson said. "She was most insistent that I should give you this as soon as you returned."

A tone of alarm sounded in my brain at once, and I waited in awful suspense while my brother examined the brief missive.

"Lydia has been hurt in a fall, and Elizabeth has gone to her aid," he told me a moment later. Although he spoke calmly, I could see a dark cloud of concern already forming in his mind. Turning back to the butler, he began firing rapid questions at the elderly man. "How long ago was this?"

"It was ten o'clock this morning. I remember very particularly because I had just…" He was interrupted before he could finish.

"Never mind that now, Henderson. How did Mrs. Darcy travel? Did someone prepare a carriage for her?"

"No sir. It is my understanding that no one was available to do so. Mrs. Darcy went with the gentleman who brought the information of her sister's being ill. It appeared to be someone she knew."

William froze, his face a mask of dread as he asked, "What was the gentleman's name, Henderson?"

"He did not give it to me, sir, but I overheard Madam calling him Mr. Wickham."

My brother turned on his heel and bolted back out the front door, shouting orders to the men, who had begun to disperse. He called for fresh horses and an immediate departure on a new mission. Now it was Mrs. Darcy who had gone missing.

- 38 -

Lost and Found

I trailed my brother to the door in a state of shock. Colonel Fitzwilliam was standing there and took my hands. "Try not to worry, Georgiana," he said earnestly. "We will find her." Then he dashed away along with the rest of them.

I felt just as helpless as I had early that morning when the premonition of Elizabeth's danger first struck me. Although I had finally reached Pemberley, Elizabeth had already slipped somewhere beyond my reach. Whatever horrors she might be experiencing, I was powerless to do anything for her.

"Perhaps it is not at all what you dread," Charlotte tried to persuade me. "The whole thing could be perfectly innocent. It is possible Mr. Wickham meant only to fetch Elizabeth for Lydia's sake."

"I wish I could believe it," I said, rubbing my arms, suddenly feeling cold all over, though it had been a warm day. "If experience has taught us anything, it is that there is absolutely nothing innocent where Mr. Wickham is concerned. This is exactly as I had feared. Even had I no prior warning of danger, however, I would still have imagined the worst, as my brother so obviously has too, to hear Elizabeth was actually driven off by that man, regardless of the excuse he gave. What could she have been thinking, to go with him?"

"If he truly was up to no good, Wickham could not have hit upon a more effective strategy. Elizabeth is ordinarily very sensible, but I daresay she would risk almost anything if she believed one of her sisters was in trouble."

Charlotte and I waited and worried together the next two hours and more. Mrs. Reynolds came in periodically, wringing her hands and wanting to do something to help. She was as much in need of comfort as either of us, I believe. In fact, it felt as if the whole house held its breath for news of its beloved mistress.

At last we heard a carriage and horses on the drive, but it was a false alarm; it was only Sir William Lucas, who then had to be informed of the current crisis. Shortly thereafter, however, the other carriage came and we hastened to the door. What I saw did nothing to allay my fears. On the contrary, the picture of my brother's stricken face through the carriage window immediately confirmed the gravity of the situation. Then the door opened to reveal the motionless, bloody form of Elizabeth, cradled in his arms.

I felt faint at the sight and leant back against the doorframe for support.

"She is still alive," my brother said as he bore her up the steps, "Fitzwilliam has gone to Kympton for the surgeon… and for the vicar."

Charlotte took charge. "Carry her upstairs, Mr. Darcy," she instructed. Then she sent a maid to fetch warm water from the kitchen. Elizabeth was soon washed, dressed in clean night clothes, placed in her bed, and given a cold compress for the lump on her head. Everything that could be done for her was done. And then, while we waited for more help to come, my brother began to unburden himself to me.

"He had abducted her," he said flatly, sitting beside me on the sofa at the end of the bed with his elbows on his knees and his head in his hands. "God only knows why, but that was apparently his intention from the beginning. The business about Lydia being injured was a complete fabrication – a ruse to persuade Elizabeth to go with him it seems. I went to the cottage straightaway and saw Mrs. Wickham for myself." He looked up then. "She was unharmed, and she claimed to be completely ignorant of her husband's whereabouts or activities. I daresay it is true. In any case, I finally convinced her to consider where Wickham might go, assuming he wanted to carry on some business well concealed. She described a rough lane she and her husband had explored when they were recently out for a drive. That is where we ultimately found them."

"Elizabeth and Wickham?"

"Yes, it was exactly the kind of out-of-the way place that would have suited his nefarious purposes, even an old abandoned cabin at the end, which I had all but forgotten. They never made it that far, though. There was an accident of some sort, apparently." He shuddered, took a deep breath, and shook his head before continuing. "A horrific scene: the gig smashed to pieces, the horse with two broken legs, and Elizabeth nowhere in sight." William got up again and returned to Elizabeth's side, clasping one of her limp hands in his. "I at last found her in the brambles. You know the rest."

"Not quite. You have not said what became of Wickham," I gently pointed out.

I saw the muscles of his jaw clench at this, but soon he said, "Mr. Wickham has cleverly managed to save his family the embarrassment of a trial while at the same time depriving me the satisfaction of seeing him hanged for his crimes."

I gasped a little. "Is he dead, then? Is that what you mean?"

My bother nodded. "Killed in the accident. Broken neck it seems."

I was still trying to digest all this new information when the surgeon arrived in Elizabeth's room, sent up from below without delay. William went to him at once, shaking his hand and saying, "I appreciate your coming, Mr. Poole."

"When I heard what had happened, I came as quickly as I could, Mr. Darcy. Now, tell me the situation."

"She was thrown from a gig, sir. I found her unconscious, and so she has remained."

Charlotte here added, "The blood seems to have all come from shallow cuts and scratches, Mr. Poole. I could find no obvious injury except the bump on her head."

The surgeon nodded and then dismissed us from the room, retaining only Charlotte to assist him. My brother did not go willingly until I convinced him that it would be best for Elizabeth's sake to allow the surgeon to get on with his work uninterrupted. We retreated downstairs, which is where we were when the rector entered.

"Mr. Thornton," William said, reaching out to take his hand. "Thank you for coming. Your help and comfort are most grievously needed just now." He went on to fully apprise Mr. Thornton of what had transpired and what we knew of Elizabeth's condition, finishing by saying, "Please pray for her… and for the child."

"That I began as soon as I got the news," said Mr. Thornton, "and I will continue until the danger is past. Is there anything else I can do?"

William closed his eyes for a moment, rubbing his temples as if his head were pounding, which no doubt it was considering the strain he was under. "Yes, there is one more thing, Mr. Thornton," he said. "Someone really must tell Mrs. Wickham what has happened. I cannot possibly leave Mrs. Darcy, and presently there is no one else to go."

"I am honored to be of service," the rector responded. After giving his friend a few more words of encouragement, Mr. Thornton departed on his somber errand, leaving my brother and me to await Mr. Poole's report in much perturbation of spirit. Finally the surgeon came down.

William snapped to attention. "Tell me, sir," he begged. "How does my wife do? Will she recover?"

"These things are very difficult to predict," replied Mr. Poole directly. "In truth, it could go either way."

My brother was no doubt as stricken to hear this as I was. I stifled a sob; he turned his head aside and pressed a clenched fist to his lips, breathing heavily into it.

"Come now, Mr. Darcy, take heart," Mr. Poole advised more cheerfully. "There is good cause for optimism in your wife's case. She has not sustained any serious injuries that I can discover other than the blow to her head, which is responsible for her loss of consciousness. Yet even in that there are positive signs – some involuntary movement and normal reflex of the eyes. Furthermore, she is young and strong, which gives her the very best chance to come through this with all her faculties intact. By tomorrow, I expect we will have a much better idea."

"And the child?" William choked out.

"All I can verify for you now is that it lives. We cannot rule out the possibility that some harm has been done – by the accident itself or by your wife's unconscious state. We must hope Mrs. Darcy revives in time to deliver the child without further complication, and then we shall see."

According to the surgeon, it was simply a matter of waiting. There was very little more he or anybody else could do for Elizabeth, although, when pressed by my brother, he did suggest that talking to the patient might be of some use. William took this directive very seriously, beginning the work as soon as Mr. Poole had gone. He held and squeezed Elizabeth's hand, stroked her face and hair, and spoke to her gently, but with strength of purpose.

"If she can hear our voices, it stands to reason she will do everything in her power to follow them back to us," he told me. "She is lost and we must guide her home."

Charlotte and I were allowed to take our turns at Elizabeth's bedside, but even then my brother refused to leave the room for either food or rest.

Colonel Fitzwilliam returned with the Bingleys just before dark, Heatheridge having been the final stop on his mission for my brother. I was able to give the three of them the most recent report of Elizabeth's condition, after which Jane and Mr. Bingley went up to see her for themselves.

Alone with Fitzwilliam then, I said, "Thank you for all you have done for us today, Colonel. It was very good of you."

"Think nothing of it. You know I would do anything in the world for Elizabeth, for Darcy, or for you. How are you holding up under the strain, my dear? You look rather done in."

This was all the provocation I needed.

I had been trying my best to behave sensibly, to keep my unruly emotions under some control all day, even in the face of potential disaster. No, in truth I had been doing so under duress for over a week now as a part of my pledge to be more mature in thought and action. But I was weary of it, weary in my body, soul, and spirit. My remaining resources, at a very low ebb, were insufficient to keep the accumulated tears dammed up any longer. To my great mortification, they chose that very moment, as I stood before Fitzwilliam in the hall, to come flooding forth.

I lacked the strength or will to run away, and there was nowhere to hide. Instead, I did the most embarrassingly childish thing I could imagine. I covered my face with my hands and cried aloud.

Strong arms encircled me in a moment. This had been my brother's office many times before. It was not in *his* embrace I rested on this occasion, however, but Fitzwilliam's.

- 39 -

The Morning After

Fitzwilliam held me until my tears were all spent, and I allowed it. After all, I told myself, the action was consistent with his chosen role in my life. He was doing nothing more than once again standing in for my brother, comforting me just as William would have. It was a purely friendly and fraternal gesture… on his side. But *I* could not think of him as my surrogate brother. I could not feel the same as if he were. Despicable creature that I am, even with Elizabeth lying upstairs fighting for her life, I could not forget that this was the man I loved whose arms were so closely wrapped about me, upon whose shoulder I laid my cheek, whose scent and nearness I drank in greedily, thirsty as a man just come in from a desert.

Thinking of Elizabeth, however, did help me to pull myself away at last. My conscience told me I must set my mind on more important things – my sister's misfortune and my brother's grief – not on the fact that I would likely never know the bliss of Fitzwilliam's embrace again once I let him go. Such feelings demonstrated a sliding backwards from the progress I had fought so hard to win.

Extracting myself and taking a step away, I said, "Forgive me, Colonel. That was a very childish display. I'm sorry to have subjected you to it."

"Not at all, my dear," he kindly replied, giving me his handkerchief.

I thanked him and began blotting my face dry. "The events of the day… Well, it has been a little too much for me."

"Naturally. No explanations are necessary."

His words reminded me of the unfinished business between us – the explanations which definitely *were* needed on both sides to account for our recent behavior – but once again, it was not the proper time.

"It is late," he said, echoing my thoughts. "You should perhaps try to get some sleep."

"And you. You must be exhausted from all the miles you have ridden today. Will I see you tomorrow?"

"Undoubtedly. I am going nowhere until I know Elizabeth is out of danger."

"Goodnight," I said, offering him a weak smile. I then went upstairs to check on the patient again before attempting to get some rest. I doubted that anyone in the house would sleep soundly that night, not with Elizabeth's life still in jeopardy and the final outcome unknown.

I found Jane, who had refused to quit her sister's room, curled up awkwardly on the paisley sofa at the foot of the bed – as close to her sister as she could reasonably stay. My brother also remained faithfully at his post in the bedside chair.

"Do you intend to sit there all night?" I asked softly, coming to his side.

He looked up with tired eyes. "I do. I would not have her wake to find me absent, not for anything."

Giving his shoulder an encouraging squeeze, I left him, retiring at last to my own room. There I prayed as I had never prayed before. Elizabeth must live and recover. She had brought so much light and vitality into our world that I could not imagine going back to the way things were before, and I did not want to.

In truth, though, I knew it would not be going back; it would mean plunging into a new, deeper darkness if Elizabeth were to die. I supposed I could survive it, but I wondered what would become of my brother. Now that he had fully invested himself in their future together, he was especially vulnerable. Could he recover and go on alone? Was his heart strong enough to absorb such a blow? I prayed there would be no call to learn the answers to these questions.

~~*~~

Elizabeth may have been the only one at Pemberley who slept soundly that night. Then, just before dawn, she opened her eyes from her strange slumber to find her husband there, asleep with his head resting on the bed beside her and still holding her hand.

I am not privy to all the details of what passed between them in those first minutes when my brother woke to find his wife conscious. When I was summoned and came in, Elizabeth was asleep again – a normal sleep this time, without the attendant fear that it might be a permanent state – and Jane sat with her.

William and I embraced a few feet away, our exchanged smiles evincing a new optimism. "So she has actually spoken to you?" I asked him with hushed excitement. "And was she entirely in her right mind?"

"Very much so, except she remembers nothing of the accident. That was to be expected. And she has felt the baby move, but she dares not move a muscle herself for the pain it causes in her head. She quickly discovered as much upon waking."

We fell silent, both content to stare at Elizabeth's sweet face in repose, to watch the regular, reassuring rise and fall of her chest with each breath. Her color had improved as well, I noticed. Although there remained some blatant reminders of what she had recently come through – the lump on her head and the fresh abrasions to her skin – it was easy to overlook these, especially after Mr. Poole's pronouncement later that morning that Elizabeth was out of danger.

She was awake once more when he came, and after examining his much-improved patient, he delivered the joyous news we had all been waiting to hear. The surgeon did sound a note of caution as well, however, reminding us all that Elizabeth's recovery might be discouragingly slow and possibly never fully complete. He prescribed strict bed rest for the time being, and that she should avoid becoming overexcited.

"That is my advice," said he, "and I charge you, Mr. Darcy, with making sure it is carried out."

"It shall be done, sir. Depend on it."

Mr. Thornton, who had spent the night at Pemberley maintaining a vigil of prayer on our family's behalf, was allowed the next audience with Elizabeth that morning. Here again, I remained quietly in the background, not wanting to interfere yet unwilling to tear myself away either. We had lived with the terror and uncertainty for so many hours; it seemed as if equal doses of security and calm were required to counteract it. I stayed to gather more and more evidence that all would be well in the end.

Mr. Thornton bowed and smiled, and came alongside Elizabeth saying, "I must be getting back for Sunday services. Still, I could not be satisfied to leave without seeing you first, Mrs. Darcy."

Carefully, she opened her hand to receive his. "How good you are, Mr. Thornton," said Elizabeth in little more than a whisper.

"Sometimes the answers to our prayers are not what we expect, or they are very long in coming. On this occasion, however, God has graciously given us precisely what we asked for and as immediately as we could possibly hope. I am most gratified to see you looking so well again after the scare you gave us yesterday."

"It seems that I have had quite the easiest time of it. Everybody else apparently suffered a great deal of worry and distress on my account, and all the while I was sleeping peacefully, completely unaware of my own peril." She smiled feebly. "Even now, I am kept in comfortable ignorance of just exactly what has happened."

"It amazes me that you are able to joke about your present circumstances, Mrs. Darcy. But then, that is one of the things I have always admired about you – your ability to find humor in nearly every situation. I believe we would all be better off if we could take ourselves, and even our troubles, less seriously. Well, I really must be off to church now, or they will have to start without me."

"Thank you again, sir, for all you have done," said Elizabeth, warmly.

During these exchanges, I observed that Elizabeth had already mastered the art of lying perfectly still, of speaking without too much exertion or volume, of turning her eyes toward someone without turning her head, all in an effort to avoid any exacerbation of her ever-present headache, according to what William had said. It was for the rest of us to follow suit – to talk softly, to stand where she could see us without straining, and above all, to avoid disturbing the bed.

When Mr. Thornton had bowed and said his good-bye, Elizabeth noticed me and spoke my name. So I went to her.

"I must not stay long," I said when I had positioned myself in her line of sight and gently taken her hand. "You need your rest, Lizzy."

"True," she agreed. "My eyelids grow heavy even now. We will talk more later, but I could not rest until I had seen and touched you for myself. We have been parted too long, and I have suffered so much anxiety for your safety. I suppose your brother has told you this."

"Some, yet as you can see, I am home again, safe and sound."

"Yes, thank God. I am satisfied," she said sleepily as her eyes closed once more.

I did leave the room then, joining the Bingleys and Colonel Fitzwilliam in the drawing room downstairs. We spent a comfortable hour together in quiet conversation until we were told that Elizabeth was awake again. The Bingleys, who had been patiently waiting their turn, went up to her then, leaving me alone with the colonel. I felt uneasy at once. My emotions were still running too close to the surface. The memory of crying in his arms the night before was too fresh. Offering an imaginary excuse to leave the room, I was starting to rise when Fitzwilliam detained me.

"Wait, Georgiana," he said. "Now that your sister is well on the road to recovery, perhaps you would not mind taking a moment to clear up a point of confusion for me."

"Yes, of course, if I can."

"Then may I ask what caused the abrupt change in your travel plans? I admit I was more than a little surprised when I learnt that you and Mrs. Collins had set off from London on your own, without awaiting my return. I can only suppose you must have had some pressing reason for doing so."

I had anticipated this conversation taking place, of course, but at a time of *my* choosing. Being accosted by it unexpectedly threw me into a strange humor. To my discredit, I did not respond to the colonel's inquiry with the respectful, apologetic tone of the note I had written for him in London. Instead, I was sharp and flippant.

"I daresay you want a logical explanation, Colonel, but I have none to offer you, nothing that would hold up under scrutiny at least. Call it caprice if you like," I said lightly, "but I was suddenly desperate to be back at Pemberley."

"I am truly grateful that you arrived in safety. All the same, you should have waited. It was not prudent for you to travel unescorted, even as far a Lucas Lodge."

Spoken like a true elder brother, I thought with vexation. My annoyance showed in my answer. "Thank you for your kind solicitude, Colonel Fitzwilliam, but I beg you not to trouble yourself.

After all, the part of my overprotective elder brother is already being played perfectly adequately by my *real* elder brother!" I stood to go.

He stood likewise. "Forgive me, Georgiana. Have I done something to offend you?" asked a mystified Fitzwilliam. "I was only concerned for your well-being."

I stopped and turned on him. "If you were so concerned for my safety, I am surprised that you could in good conscience go off and leave us in London on the invented pretense of some urgent affair."

"It was no invention. I had important business here in Derbyshire."

"What business could have been so urgent or so secretive that we could not all have come together?"

No doubt my crossness and accusations had by this time begun to overcome the colonel's easy temper. He responded very much in kind.

"I regret that I cannot give you a satisfactory answer at present, Miss Darcy. However, since you feel entitled to excuse your own actions on the grounds of caprice, perhaps you will be so good as to allow me the same privilege."

At a loss for any worthy rejoinder, I quit the room with very little satisfaction. Later, upon further reflection, I felt even worse for what had passed between us, for my part in it especially. I could not condone my harsh words to Fitzwilliam. He had always shown me the utmost kindness, never more so than in the last few months. Was it his fault that I now found his brotherly manner – which had always been acceptable in the past – no longer palatable? No, it was not, and I had no right to blame him for what he could not help.

One more uncomfortable encounter awaited me that day. Early in the afternoon Mr. Sanditon and his sister-in-law arrived, having come directly from church where they had lately learnt of Elizabeth's accident from Mr. Thornton. When I received them, my composure faltered, and Mr. Sanditon did not seem to bear the sight of me with much tranquility either. He must have known I could be there, but perhaps he had been so preoccupied with Elizabeth's plight that he had failed to adequately prepare himself for that possibility.

"Good day, Miss Darcy," he said when he had gathered his thoughts. "How is Mrs. Darcy?"

I had begun to assure our guests that the patient was out of danger when my brother came in to take over the office. "Yes, I am happy to report that Elizabeth continues to improve, hour by hour," he said.

"Thank heaven," said Mr. Sanditon. "I am profoundly relieved to hear it."

Ruth asked, "Might I be allowed to see her, Mr. Darcy?"

"Of course. I will take you up myself. I only stepped a way for a few minutes and was about to return."

This left me alone with Mr. Sanditon. An awkward silence ensued, the unanswered question between us making its presence felt in the room like an unwelcome third person. Though neither of us had set out to have our long-postponed discussion on that particular day, the opportunity was obviously at hand.

Mr. Sanditon presently stood as if he had decided on a definite course of action. "Would you take a turn in the garden with me, Miss Darcy?" he asked. "It is a fine day for it."

I hesitated, not sure I was any more prepared for this conversation than I had been the last. And yet, there seemed little use in delay. "As you wish," I agreed. "We can talk more freely there."

Words did not come any easier for me for the change to less formal surroundings. Several minutes passed with only birdsong to interrupt the stillness between us.

Mr. Sanditon began at last. "I am delighted that your sister-in-law is so much better, Miss Darcy. We were quite shocked to hear of her accident, and we wanted to offer our best wishes as soon as possible."

"That was very kind of you, Mr. Sanditon." I could feel my suitor's gaze resting upon me while I kept my own eyes aimed squarely at the pathway in front of my feet.

"I am also pleased to find that you and Mrs. Collins have returned safely from London. Did you enjoy your stay there as much as you anticipated?"

"Yes, thank you. The society was very lively, yet I am glad to be home again. I have missed Pemberley and all my friends hereabout. How are Abigail and Amelia? I often think of them, and I wonder if they will remember me. I have been away so long."

"They are well, thank you, and I am certain they could not forget you so soon." After another pause, he continued. "As gratified as I am to know that you think fondly of my daughters, Miss Darcy, I cannot help wondering if you had any warm reflections about their father whilst you were away."

I turned to him with a mixture of anguish and apology. "Mr. Sanditon, I…"

"No, no; it is quite all right, Miss Darcy," he said when I could not go on. "No words are necessary. I can read my answer in your countenance. It is what I have been expecting all along, I think."

We walked on in silence whilst I tried to organize what more I should to say to him. He was a gentleman of the highest order, and he deserved an explanation. At length, I tried again. "Sir, please forgive me for keeping you in suspense so long. I did not take the honor of your proposal lightly, and I wished to give it every possible consideration. Although I have the deepest respect and warmest regard for you, sir…"

"Say no more, please. I understand perfectly."

- 40 -

Aftermath

When the Sanditons departed, they took Mrs. Collins along with them as the most convenient means of returning her to Reddclift cottage and guiding Sir William, who followed in his own carriage, thither as well.

I forced myself at my first opportunity afterward to speak to Fitzwilliam again in order to relieve my guilty conscience. When I approached him in the passageway, however, he ducked through the nearest door, shying off like a wounded animal afraid of being struck again. I could not blame him, but nor would I be deterred by it.

"Please, Colonel," I began, following him into the breakfast room. "I only wish to apologize for my rudeness earlier; then I will leave you in peace. I had no right to say the things I did to you. I beg you would forgive me."

He turned to look at me then, an unreadable blend of emotions playing across his countenance. "It is done, of course," he said. "Allow me to apologize for my part as well, Georgiana. Although I did not mean to, I obviously upset you somehow."

"No, the fault was entirely mine, sir; you must allow me to own it."

Remembering the sentiments I expressed in the London note he never received, I decided this would be my chance to convey the gist of them – things that needed to be said between us, not only by way of apology but to make clear it was time for a change between us. Matters could not go on as they had before; I could not bear it.

"No one could have asked for a better guardian all these years," I continued. "Your duty is effectively done, however, now that I am grown. And I expect we will see much less of each other in future, Colonel, which is only natural. Whatever occurs, know that I wish you well."

"I do not understand," he said, looking puzzled indeed. "Sometimes you speak in riddles, and this one sounds like a goodbye."

"Not goodbye, exactly. I just mean to thank you for your kind offices on my behalf in the past and to acknowledge that things are at a point of change between us."

"Are they?"

"Yes, of course they are. I am grown, as I said, and I no longer require a guardian. One or both of us will probably marry, and then our places will be with our spouses and families. You must see that change is inevitable."

"I suppose it is true, and yet change such as this can be a good thing, in fact an excellent thing. If I am no longer your guardian, then I am free to be something else. Would not you agree?"

"Exactly. That is what I have been trying to say. You should see yourself as free of that responsibility, and now we can both get on with our lives, whatever they may entail."

I was satisfied when we parted that we had left matters on a good footing, that we understood each other at last. But the more I thought about the conversation later, the less confident I became. I began to think it might have been the colonel, not I, who had spoken in riddles.

~~*~~

The remainder of the day passed uneventfully. Elizabeth had little trouble complying with Mr. Poole's prescription for plenty of sleep. It seemed she could barely stay awake above half an hour at a stretch in any case. A family member attended her at all times, and my brother, who still could not be comfortable with his wife long out of his sight, only left the room for brief periods.

Elizabeth reported feeling markedly improved by the next morning. Although still drowsy, her mind was less clouded, and the steady pounding in her head had somewhat diminished. She was even able to sit up in bed with help and the support of several pillows. The draperies were kept partially drawn since bright light had proved just as painful to her as did loud noise and abrupt movement.

I sat with Elizabeth that afternoon while my brother attended to some pressing business. I had been longing for a private audience with my sister-in-law to further the discussion in person that we had begun a week before through the post. I would have liked to ask her about her recent harrowing experience as well, but that was out of the question. Her doctor had strongly recommended against broaching that topic with her, and besides, she remembered very little.

"I am glad to finally have you to myself," I told her in opening our conversation. "How much has happened since we last had a real talk!"

"A great many things indeed," Elizabeth answered, still careful to speak softly and move as little as possible.

"Lizzy," I continued, dropping my eyes. "One matter has been weighing very heavily upon me. Ever since I received your letter in London, I have been miserable over the trouble I caused you. Now tell me, has everything been set right betwixt you and my brother?" I asked, feeling on the verge of tears again.

"Yes, yes," Elizabeth whispered. "Oh, my dear, you need have no more anxiety on that head, and I am sorry that you have been left so long to worry about it. The details are unimportant and are really best forgot as soon as possible. Suffice to say that the largest share of the problem turned out to be a nasty misunderstanding. Once that was laid bare, the rest of the difficulty was soon cleared away."

"I am so relieved to hear it! Was my letter of any use to you?"

"It helped us a great deal, Georgiana. Thank you. I appreciate what it must have cost your modesty to reveal so much."

"Does my brother know all, then?"

"He does, but you needn't be uneasy. He is not angry, and he has promised to be very discreet. You may open the subject with him if you choose; otherwise I doubt he will ever mention it."

I rose and went to the window, gazing through the gap in the curtains. "I have made such a wretched fool of myself, Lizzy. Romantic folly can perhaps be forgiven at fifteen, but three additional years should yield at least a little more sense."

"My dear girl, you must not be so severe upon yourself. Come here." Elizabeth stretched out her hand to me and I obediently came to her side and took it. "Now listen to me. No one could consider you foolish for falling in love with such a fine man as Colonel Fitzwilliam. And, in determining not to marry anyone else under those circumstances, you have demonstrated good judgment."

"The way you put it makes my behavior sound perfectly rational. I doubt that I deserve such a charitable interpretation, Elizabeth, but I thank you nonetheless." Then I remembered Mr. Sanditon and frowned. "I spoke to Mr. Sanditon when he was here yesterday and gave him my regrets."

"Poor soul. How did he take the news?"

"He was such a gentleman about it that it made me even sorrier for disappointing him."

"There was no help for it, though. It had to be done, and I am sure you were as kind as possible."

I had tried to be, it was true. Nevertheless, I continued to suffer some guilt on that score. I could not help thinking how he must have felt to know, once and for all, that I would not marry him. Because of my own recent disappointment, it was not difficult for me to imagine.

~~*~~

Next day, Elizabeth left her bed for the first time. She took her initial tentative steps across the room on the arm of her husband, slowly moving to a settee by the window for a change of attitude and scenery.

This I later learnt from my brother. He had come to sit beside me on the piano bench where, at Elizabeth's request, I had been playing for the first time since my return to Pemberley.

I slid over to make room for him. "Could she hear the music all the way up in her room?" I asked him. "I tried to choose songs that would carry."

"She could hear, and she said to tell you how much she enjoyed it. Although in truth I think she may have asked you to play simply to get you out of the room."

"Why would she do that?" I asked, tinkling a little tune from my childhood on the keys.

William copied me two octaves below. "So that she could corner me into answering her questions. I have had to tell her all I know of what happened that terrible day."

"I thought Mr. Poole advised against such a thing, believing it would be too upsetting for her."

"True enough, but she has been remembering bits and pieces – enough to frighten her. She convinced me she would be easier knowing rather than imagining the rest. Then she heard the Bingleys carriage leaving and some explanation had to be made for that."

The Bingleys, I knew, had gone to take Lydia to Kympton to see her husband buried.

"How did she take the news?"

"She is back in bed and asleep now, not too much the worse for hearing the truth, I hope. She grieves for Lydia, for all the damage done, and for the senseless nature of the crime. I think we are all feeling the same, especially knowing how much worse the outcome might have been."

"What do you suppose Wickham meant to accomplish by such a rash course of action? I cannot understand. He had to know he would never get away with it."

"If Elizabeth fully recovers her memory, she may be able to tell us more, although I hardly know whether to wish for that or not. Perhaps it would be better if she never recalls whatever that horrid man said and did. In any case, I can only conjecture that, out of his discontent and implacable resentment against me, Wickham had been watching for an opportunity to take some kind of advantage. I suspect he was behind Elizabeth's scare on the path some days before. And then, when he saw our party leave that morning, he apparently decided to make his move."

"I am in part responsible, then. If I had not been late arriving, you would never have gone in search of me and given Wickham an opening."

"We could all play that game, Georgiana – Sir William for not maintaining his carriage in better condition, you for the timing of your trip, I for bringing the danger so near our door in the first place, and even Elizabeth for allowing herself to be duped – each blaming ourselves when Wickham is the only one who deserves reproach. There is no profit in that kind of thinking. Let us just be grateful to have come through this thing relatively unscathed. At least we know that villain will never bother us again, or anybody else either."

I was told that Mrs. Wickham had accepted an invitation from the Bingleys to convalesce at Heatheridge. Accordingly, after the funeral, the whole party returned to the cottage to pack up her belongings, and thence to Pemberley House.

I had no desire to see Lydia Wickham. What could I possibly say to her? Could I say I was sorry for her loss? Not truthfully, and it would be unkind to say what I was actually thinking – that her husband had been a despicable character, and that I was glad it had been he rather than Elizabeth who died in the accident. No, far better to keep clear of her altogether for the short time she would be with us. Although I could not help wondering what Elizabeth was saying to her that afternoon when they met again.

Elizabeth must have many of my same feelings towards Mr. Wickham, and yet she loved her sister too or she would not have risked so much to try to help in her purported time of need.

"It was very enlightening," Elizabeth told me later of their meeting. "I will never agree with my sister on the subject of her late husband. She cannot see or will not admit that he is criminally responsible for what happened to me. Had he lived, she would have been forced to confront the truth when the facts came out at trial. As it is, she will be spared that discomfort. I suppose she is now free to remember Wickham as she wishes, and clearly the reflections she prefers cast him in a much more favorable light than he deserves."

"But you said that the interview with Lydia was enlightening. What did you mean by it?"

"Oh, someday I will tell you the whole story, Georgiana. It is too convoluted a tale for my muddled mind to properly convey at the moment. But it relates to that awful misunderstanding between your brother and myself. I very cleverly managed to coax Lydia into confirming my theory, which was that Wickham was at the heart of the matter with his wife as his unwitting accomplice."

"So much mischief wrapped up in one man," I said, shaking my head as I mentally reviewed his long list of misdeeds. "What will Lydia do now?"

"I suspect she will return to Longbourn to be comforted by our mother and await the birth of her child. Did you know she was expecting? No, of course you did not. It is a recent development and I have had no opportunity to tell you."

I am not precisely sure why I found this information unsettling, except that it meant we might not be entirely free of Wickham in the future after all. His blood would continue to flow through the veins of his son or daughter, and perhaps his discontented spirit too. I wondered if the sins of the father would live on through his offspring as well.

- 41 -

Unfinished Business

I was glad I had taken an interest in learning something of household management while I was in London, for that enabled me to be of practical help to Elizabeth during her incapacitation. I could spare her any thought to the routine chores she normally did every day and be more confident in handling specific tasks she assigned to me. By making myself useful, I felt as if I contributed in a small way to her recovery.

Mr. Poole continued monitoring his patient's improvement, and presently gave his blessing to Elizabeth's leaving not only her bed but her room as well. Although her headache was still with her and not all the gaps in her memory had yet filled in, she was making steady progress. She moved about slowly, but under her own power now. And except for a daily nap, she spent most of her time downstairs with the rest of us.

Five days had passed since the accident, and Jane was enough satisfied with her sister's recovery as to want to be at home with her children again. After the Bingleys departed with Lydia, our only remaining houseguest at Pemberley was Colonel Fitzwilliam, and I could not help wondering why he stayed on so long. Although I had made a point of speaking to him that one time, to apologize and set him straight, I had avoided him as much as possible ever since. However, as the size of the party round the dinner table diminished, we were necessarily drawn into closer company. No longer was there any chance of distancing myself from him, of avoiding the torment of hearing his voice and seeing his dear face. His perpetual presence had become a source of more pain than pleasure to me, and I knew the sooner he was gone the sooner I might be restored to some semblance of peace again.

One morning after Fitzwilliam had been at Pemberley well above a week, I found him sitting with my brother and sister-in-law in the library. Their conversation ceased when I paused at the doorway.

"Come in and join us," Elizabeth invited.

"Yes, do," my brother added.

"Oh, no, thank you," I said, declining for more than one reason. I had the distinct impression I had interrupted some business in which I had no part. Secondarily, I was still on a mission to avoid Fitzwilliam whenever I could. So I gave my excuse, saying, "I was just on my way to the music room. I have been far too neglectful of my practicing lately."

"Very well, dear," Elizabeth said, "if you had rather."

I moved on, and their conversation presently resumed. I could not hear what was being said, but I did distinguish the clap of the library doors sliding shut before I entered the music room and took my seat at the pianoforte.

I had spoken to Colonel Fitzwilliam about change, and yet perhaps nothing had changed after all. Matters were still being discussed behind closed doors without me, just as when Fitzwilliam came to Pemberley all those months ago. In this case as in that one, I would probably never know what was being debated in my absence, how decisions made in private might effect me.

I pretended not to care and threw myself into my music with perhaps a little more vigor than I would have otherwise. I was glad for the difference between my fine pianoforte and the harpsichord of yesteryear. Now when I pounded the keys, I had the satisfaction of a correspondingly loud response. The composer may have denoted mezzo-piano, but I made free to interpret the first piece I played in double-forte if I liked.

And I did like to. I found the exertion very remedial to my aggravated spirits, in fact. I was much calmer by the second piece and accordingly able to somewhat decrease the volume with which I played it. The music eventually had its way with me, as it always did. When each melodious phrase went forth and faded, so did a little more of my irritation until I was reasonably composed again.

While I was still wending my way through this second piece, I noticed I was no longer alone. Colonel Fitzwilliam eased into my view, coming to stand beside the instrument. I did not stop, however, for I had much rather play for than talk to him at that moment. That being the case, I felt most unlucky upon realizing I was very near the end of the piece. I did surreptitiously repeat the whole last section once, hoping he would get bored and go away again. I then had no choice but to end it.

"That was well done," the colonel said. "A very spirited rendition. When you play, you really bring the music to life, far more so than with most other performers I have heard, although I remember feeling the same when I was young, listening to your mother."

This poignant mention of my mother took me by surprise and made it difficult to stick to my purpose, which was to avoid becoming drawn into conversation with him if possible. I smiled to acknowledge his compliment, and then I immediately began paging through my music for something else to play. Before I could begin, however, Fitzwilliam came round to my side.

"Did you wish to turn the pages for me?" I asked, since it was the only explanation I could think of for his approach.

"No, I do not wish to turn your pages. I will do so as often as you like in the future, but not now."

"What, then?"

"Something far more important." He took both my hands in his and gently turned me toward himself. To my total astonishment, Fitzwilliam then dropped to one knee in front of me. "Dear Georgiana," he began in earnest, "I am now at liberty to tell you that which has long been in my heart. Will you hear me?"

Although too overcome to speak in any case, I found I had not the slightest objection to hearing whatever the colonel might wish to say to me on bended knee. I nodded my acquiescence, and he was sufficiently encouraged to go on.

"I have just come from your brother, who has given me permission to speak to you. I have known you all your life, dear Georgiana. And while it is true that for most of that time I felt merely a fraternal affection for you, which was as it should be, something revolutionary has since occurred.

"When I danced with you in January at your birthday ball. My eyes were opened to see you as you truly were – no longer the child I was dotingly fond of. You had become an entirely new creature. As I said of you in London, you were like a butterfly who had shed her cocoon, turning into a beautiful woman with intelligence and grace. And yet you retained all the youthful charm I adored. The picture was thus perfectly completed, and I thought how lucky some young man would be to make you his wife.

"Then this summer, when we were thrown so much together in town, I soon began to think differently. Without knowing when or how it had begun, I realized I had developed feelings of a most tender nature for you myself, and I could no longer countenance the idea of your marrying anybody else. I had fallen in love for the first time, you see, in love with that charming young woman I spoke of a moment ago. I had fallen in love with *you*, dear Georgiana."

I opened my mouth to say something – I hardly know what – but no words came out.

"Allow me to finish before you speak," he continued. "I know you have other offers, probably ones more eligible than mine as to status and fortune. You certainly have the right to hope for something better than a second son with very little money. But there can be no one who knows you better or loves you more. There can be no one who would defend your honor and the honor of your family more vigorously than I would. I will tell you what I told your brother. If I am so fortunate as to win your favor, my darling girl, I promise that your heart will be safe in my care."

Fitzwilliam looked to me with hope in his eyes, awaiting some kind of response. I was completely dumbfounded.

After all the months of pining and misery, after all the emotional ups and downs I had suffered through, it seemed my long-cherished wish of a future with Fitzwilliam was at last within my grasp. Yet to suddenly find myself the object of his love was so wholly unexpected that I hesitated to answer, not from any indecision but from disbelief. Whilst my heart told me to leap into his arms before I could awaken from the dream in which I found myself, my mind – at least that portion still capable of rational thought – insisted on some clarification.

"You say you have been in love with me for some time now, Fitzwilliam. If I am to believe you, you must explain something to me. Why have I never seen any sign of it, any change in your manner, any gesture or word of peculiar regard? You very particularly called me only your 'friend.' You continued to behave toward me just as you always have – much more like a brother than a suitor."

"Oh, my dear girl, if you only knew how difficult it has been for me to show so little when I felt so much. But I was honor-bound to speak to your brother before giving you any idea of my true affection. That is why I had to take a step back from you in London, and *that* is the urgent business which took me from London into Derbyshire. Nothing less important would ever have induced me to leave you, even for a few days."

"So that is why you were at Pemberley when the trouble broke out?" I asked shyly.

"Yes."

"Oh, I see."

"Do you have any more questions for me?"

"No, I do not believe so."

"Then tell me, dearest Georgiana, do you think in time you could learn to love me? We have agreed that our relationship must change. Now that I am released from being your guardian, is it possible you could learn to think of me as your husband instead? I am willing to wait as long as it may take, but please say that I have some chance of winning your heart."

Now that I had recovered my power of speech, now that my one reservation had been very satisfactorily overcome, it was time to give my answer. This was the most important moment of my life, and I wanted, for once, to be suitably eloquent. Although I cannot be sure I fully succeeded, Fitzwilliam was pleased with what I said and that is all that really matters.

"There is no need to wait, John," I began, "for my heart already belongs to you, and to you alone. It has for some time."

At this news, he jumped to his feet and pulled me upwards into his arms, all in one swift movement. For a second, I thought I might cry from the swell of emotion that rose within me. I laughed instead, and then I tasted my first kiss from my future husband. I had shed enough tears for a good long while.

~~*~~

That first kiss was all I could have hoped it would be – sweet, tender, and yet stirring something deep inside me that had long awaited release. It quickly led to several more as Fitzwilliam and I privately celebrated our new understanding there in the music room. I was surprised at my own eagerness, at my lack of shyness in this unfamiliar situation. The man himself was not unfamiliar, though;

that made all the difference. I had known and implicitly trusted him all my life. Now that we had declared our mutual love, there was no holding back.

Fitzwilliam had to make the first move to interrupt our passionate embrace. With a low chuckle, he said, "I am delighted by your enthusiasm, Georgiana, as it exactly matches my own. Unfortunately, we are not married yet. I think it would be wise to remember that fact before we are completely run away with by our feelings."

I laughed as well and eased my hold from about his neck. "I suppose you are right. Then shall we go share our good news with my brother and Elizabeth? They are no doubt waiting in some suspense."

"Of course. I only hope they will be pleased. I believe we can count Elizabeth on our side, but your brother seemed none too happy when I asked his permission to address you. To own the truth, he put up quite a strong resistance, going so far as to accuse me of being no better than a common fortune hunter. Can you believe it? I trust he will come round in time, though. I put his unfavorable reaction down to my taking him by surprise. I daresay the idea of a match between the two of us never entered his brain before."

I smiled, knowing this was not precisely the case, thanks to my letter. I thought it more likely that William had been testing his friend's resolve, not allowing him to get his way without proving he was willing to fight for it. How I wish I could have been hiding in a corner listening to *that* conversation.

- 42 -

Epilogue

There are no words to adequately express my elation at this surprising turn of events. My heart flew to new heights of rapture, carried aloft by love even beyond where the ecstasies of music had ever taken me. My joy at knowing I would soon be Fitzwilliam's wife felt all the more exquisite for my having been so thoroughly convinced that such an outcome was impossible. Before, it seemed I was always crying; now at last my turn to laugh had come – to laugh, to smile, to sing, to dance.

Colonel Fitzwilliam remained at Pemberley for most of the next two months, demonstrating daily the same faithful devotion to me as he had previously, only in a new role. Eager as he was to shed his reputation for "brotherly" behavior, I soon found there was yet another fine line to walk – balancing the exuberance of our affection with the need to maintain respectable boundaries before the wedding.

In this regard, we were materially assisted by the forbidding presence of my brother. Although he had proven his amiability by consenting to the marriage, he had also appointed himself our unofficial watchdog and magistrate, enforcing the laws of propriety from dawn until dusk with his dour, disapproving looks.

"He does not mean to be officious," Elizabeth explained when I complained to her. "It is just that he is having a little difficulty relinquishing his role as your protector after all these years." With a grin, she added, "I trust that once you and Fitzwilliam are actually married, he will leave off his interference."

I was obliged to Elizabeth for this clarification and for her further assurance that, despite appearances, my brother was pleased with the match. "He said that if he had to give you up to anybody, he could not have chosen a better man himself."

The match soon had the approbation of Fitzwilliam's family as well as my own. Although my fortune cannot compare to Anne de Bourgh's projected inheritance, apparently the earl had decided to be satisfied. Even Lady Catherine de Bourgh condescended to write a tolerably civil letter of congratulations. The news of our engagement was also well received at Heatheridge by Jane and Mr. Bingley, whose own generous natures predisposed them to wish every person of their acquaintance the same felicity in marriage they themselves continued to enjoy. I doubt if Miss Bingley was as genuinely pleased, however. At her age, to have yet another man who had piqued her interest and excited her ambition slip through her fingers and beyond reach was more than she could be expected to endure with serenity.

Whilst all the focus at Pemberley had been on Elizabeth's recovery and then on the excitement of my engagement, another member of the family had been waiting his turn to take center stage, which he did the first week of September. It seemed only just and reasonable that Elizabeth, now fully restored to health, should be granted an uncomplicated delivery of her first child after all the trauma and pain she had so recently endured. And so it was.

"I have a son," my brother announced with a dazed expression.

"That is excellent news!" I cried, rising to meet him.

Fitzwilliam, who had been waiting with me, shook his cousin's hand. "Congratulations, Darcy! And are mother and child both doing well?"

"Very well, it seems. The nurse has examined the child and verified that he is strong and perfectly healthy – no harm done by recent events. I was allowed to hold him, just for a few minutes, and I need no further proof that miracles happen every day. As for Elizabeth," he added with warmth and pride, "she has come through the ordeal like a champion."

These were things I was able to confirm for myself later that same day when I went in to see Elizabeth, who had my new nephew in her arms. The sleeping infant was swaddled from head to foot with only his red and wrinkled face showing, that and a few tufts of dark hair framing it.

"What do you think of him?" Elizabeth asked once I had my first look. "Is not your nephew the most beautiful creature you ever beheld? Here, you must see his hands," she said, eagerly unwrapping the tiny, but perfectly formed appendages for my inspection. The mother than placed her finger where the awakening child could grip it. "Like his father's, these hands must one day be strong enough to hold the reins of a powerful horse… and of all Pemberley, for that matter."

Elizabeth then passed the infant to me. I stared at him in wonderment for some minutes, examining the wispy lashes lining his nearly transparent lids, admiring the rosebud curve of his lips, and stroking his petal-soft cheek. "Remarkable," I pronounced him, but it did not seem anywhere near adequate.

"Your brother has consented to calling him Bennet – Bennet Fitzwilliam Darcy. In fact, it was his own idea. Since he himself was christened with his mother's maiden name, he wants the same for his son. I could not be more pleased, and so will my father be, especially as he has no sons of his own to carry on the family name."

"Bennet," I repeated, still looking at the child. "A fine-sounding name, and I think it suits him." Then I wondered which of his parents he would grow up to most resemble. Better than one or the other, I could hope that the finest attributes of both would be best expressed in this their offspring. Only time would tell.

A great host of visitors came and went that autumn – the Fitzwilliams, the Bennets, the Gardiners, as well as local friends – all eager to celebrate the happy developments at Pemberley with us. Although in the past I might have begrudged these repeated disruptions to peace and quiet, I found nothing could now touch my exultant mood.

The only awkwardness I anticipated was in my first meeting with Mr. Sanditon after the announcement of my engagement. However, even that passed off better than I could have expected. According to Elizabeth's information to me, upon the excuse of friendship, my brother had sent early notice of the development to Reddclift, his true motive being to discreetly forewarn Mr. Sanditon lest he should be taken unawares. Perhaps it was due to this advance knowledge or perhaps a lessening of his own attachment that the gentleman seemed relatively unaffected when I saw him.

In any case, I no longer worry he will languish in want of female companionship. Mr. Sanditon created quite a stir one Sunday by bringing his two young daughters with him to church for the first time. Few of those present had ever seen the little girls before. So they, and by association he, instantly became objects of fascination, especially amongst the unmarried women in attendance. I believe Mr. Sanditon, who had before been considered by some proud and unsociable, now appears in a more sympathetic light. With his daughters easing the way, I would not be surprised if he were soon to find a lady who will cause him to forget he ever thought of making *me* his wife.

I had a delightful congratulatory letter from Andrea in response to all our news.

"Dear me!" she wrote. *"What a time you have had at Pemberley! Carriage accidents, an abduction, a surprise declaration of love, and finally the birth of an heir! However, I admit that, all things considered, I am most partial to the news of your engagement to that charming Colonel Fitzwilliam, for in this I take some credit myself. Did I not always promote his attentions? Did I not always say it would be so in the end? I must by all means come for the wedding. When is it to be?"*

October. The wedding took place on a cool, crisp Tuesday morning in October. The sun was out for the occasion and the birds were singing, at least that is how I remember it. But perhaps all the brightness and song were in my heart instead, for I felt as if I were floating on air as we made our way to the church in Kympton.

I wore my mother's silk bridal gown, preserved for decades for just this eventuality. It seems that before she died, Mama left instructions with the housekeeper as to the care of the gown, saying, "Keep it safe, Mrs. Reynolds. I would like to think that one day it might be worn again by my dear little girl on her wedding day." How could I then do otherwise? I did not wish to. The gown itself was precisely the kind of thing I would have chosen in any case – simple and elegant – and it kept my mother with me that day. Knowing she had thought of my future happiness, all those years ago, banished any lingering suspicions that I had been unloved by her.

I like to think my father was present for the ceremony as well, represented in the person of my brother, for several people afterward remarked how much seeing us there, together and in our wedding clothes, reminded them of attending the marriage of our parents so long ago.

No doubt my brother was impressively handsome, but I only had eyes for Fitzwilliam. My heart nearly stopped beating at the sight of him in his red officer's dress coat, waiting for me at the head of the aisle. I still could hardly believe my wishes and dreams of so many months' duration were finally coming true, that out of all the women in the world Fitzwilliam loved me, that we would be well and truly married in a matter of minutes.

Mr. Thornton, who officiated at the ceremony (which was fairly brief and followed immediately by a hearty breakfast, according to the groom's particular request), offered words of guidance and inspiration. I hope I shall remember half of them. If not, I need look no further for an example of the marital ideal of which he spoke than my own brother and sister-in-law, who have had a two-year head start.

Though some months have now passed, my heart still flutters a little whenever I think of or refer to Fitzwilliam as "my husband." And yet, so he is indeed. The mysteries of the connubial union, upon which my earlier curiosity had shed so little light, continue to unfold before me. Day by day I discover something new about myself, my husband, or about the two of us together. For one thing, I have discovered that I have more love to give than I before imagined. The losses and disappointments of the past have not stolen that capacity from me; they only serve to emphasize its importance.

Love given away does not subtract anything from the giver, I find; it multiplies. And soon I will have another object on whom to lavish that inexhaustible store, as the growing roundness of my belly attests. Our goal now is to settle into our new home before the baby arrives, and it is a goal well on the way to being accomplished.

We began looking for a suitable property as soon as we returned from our wedding trip to Wales. Just as I remembered Jane predicting months before, I did not much mourn the idea of leaving Pemberley for an establishment of my own with my new husband, especially when I discovered that I would be close enough to visit my former home as often as I chose. For I also recalled what I had heard at that same time about the place named Northam Hall.

"I wonder if it is still available," I said to Fitzwilliam as we, arm in arm, strolled the grounds of Pemberley, to which we had temporarily returned. "The Bingleys certainly spoke well of it; my brother said it was sound from a business point of view; and I recall Elizabeth remarking on a delightful music room."

"Sounds perfect. And where is it located?" Fitzwilliam asked.

"Here in Derbyshire, only about twenty miles east, if I am not mistaken."

"That would put it within an easy distance of my family as well, possibly even within the same borough," Fitzwilliam remarked, seeming to catch my excitement. "I still have not given up the idea of standing for Parliament, you know."

I paused our walk, smiled up at him, and laid my free hand on the side of his cheek, once again glorying in the fact that it was well within my rights to do so. I could trace the familiar planes of his beloved face anytime I wished – now become familiar by touch, not only by sight and imagination as before.

"You may do anything you like, my dear," I said. "But, as I have told you, I love you just as you are, and I care nothing for fortune or prestige. You are equally desirable and distinguished in my eyes without the letters M.P. after your name as you ever would be with them. It is character that makes a man, not possessions or titles."

"You are too good to me, my love," said Fitzwilliam, bending to kiss me tenderly. After a pleasantly protracted interval, he added, "And wise far beyond your years. No one will ever be tempted to call you a child again."

Author's Afterword

I hope you enjoyed hearing Georgiana's side of the story. Now I would like to invite you to read (or reread, as the case may be) this book's companion, *The Darcys of Pemberley*. There you will discover all the intriguing things happening beyond Georgiana's view. What was said during those conferences behind the closed library doors at Pemberley? How did the break between Darcy and Elizabeth come about, and how was it mended? Was Wickham involved, and what actually occurred during his kidnapping of Elizabeth?

As I said in the beginning, these two books go hand in hand since one fills in the "off-camera" scenes of the other and the thoughts hidden from view. Although each is complete in itself, I trust that together they supply a richer reading experience than either one alone.

About the Author

Shannon Winslow specializes in writing fiction for the fans of Jane Austen. Her popular debut novel, *The Darcys of Pemberley* (2011), immediately established her place in the genre, being particularly praised for the author's authentic Austenesque style and faithfulness to the original characters. She has since followed it with two more *Pride and Prejudice* sequels (*Miss Georgiana Darcy of Pemberley* and *Return to Longbourn*), a stand-alone Austen-inspired story (*For Myself Alone*) and a "what-if" story starring Jane Austen herself (*The Persuasion of Miss Jane Austen*), in which the famous author tells her own story of lost love, second chances, and finding her happy ending.

Her two sons now grown, Ms. Winslow lives with her husband in the log home they built in the countryside south of Seattle, where she writes and paints in her studio facing Mt. Rainier.

Learn more about the author at her website/blog:
www.shannonwinslow.com

Made in the USA
Coppell, TX
03 September 2024